Crocodile Tears

Mark O'Sullivan

TRANSWORLD IRELAND

TRANSWORLD IRELAND
an imprint of The Random House Group Limited
20 Vauxhall Bridge Road, London SW1V 2SA
www.transworldbooks.co.uk

CROCODILE TEARS
A TRANSWORLD IRELAND BOOK: 9781848271562

First published in 2013 by Transworld Ireland,
a division of Transworld Publishers
Transworld Ireland paperback edition published 2014

Copyright © Mark O'Sullivan 2014

Mark O'Sullivan has asserted his right under the Copyright, Designs
and Patents Act 1988 to be identified as the author of this work.

A CIP catalogue record for this book
is available from the British Library.

Addresses for Random House Group Ltd companies outside the UK
can be found at: www.randomhouse.co.uk
The Random House Group Ltd Reg. No. 954009

The Random House Group Limited supports the Forest Stewardship
Council® (FSC®), the leading international forest-certification organisation.
Our books carrying the FSC label are printed on FSC®-certified paper. FSC is
the only forest-certification scheme supported by the leading environmental
organisations, including Greenpeace. Our paper procurement policy
can be found at www.randomhouse.co.uk/environment

Typeset in 11/14pt Minon by
Kestrel Data, Exeter, Devon.
Printed and bound by
CPI Group (UK) Ltd, Croydon, CR0 4YY.

2 4 6 8 10 9 7 5 3 1

For Joan, Jane and Ruth

Monday, 22 November

1

The girl who called herself Daina struggled along the steep incline of Abbey Street. She was late for work again. Her weight hampered her, as did the tightness of her stonewashed denim jeans and jacket. A cocktail of frosted mist, sea air and perspiration stung her eyes blind. Early-morning traffic, a slow line of it, descended the hill into Howth village. Drivers glanced her way but none registered her distress. The lives of others meant little or nothing to them now that the Monday-morning radio news had sent a double chill through their bones. An icy spell of epic proportions was forecast for later in the week. And the IMF were in town.

Daina allowed herself a brief reward when the turn-off for Attenboy House came distantly into view. She stopped to catch her breath by the large plate-glass window of the abandoned charity shop. Her reflection embarrassed her. She thought the dyed hair absurdly black for a natural redhead. And it was, cheapening her, but in a naive way. She swept the lank fringe back from her forehead, opened the zip of her jacket and ran on. A couple of passing schoolboys made no secret of their amusement at the thick-lipped folds of her bare midriff. The fact that she had to go to work as usual when her sister didn't was the least of life's injustices for Daina that Monday morning. Worse had already befallen her. Much worse lay in store.

Five minutes later, by the electronically controlled gates at Attenboy, she punched a code into the keypad and squeezed herself through the gap before it had grown wide enough to let her comfortably through. Stumbling inwards, the young Latvian girl began to run again when she saw Dermot Brennan's silver Mercedes on the tarmac drive below. The front passenger door hung open. He'd usually left for work before Daina arrived. Even when she arrived early. A panic of excuses broke out in her mind as she approached the house. None quite convinced her.

Attenboy House was a two-storey limestone pile, solid, undistinguished and lodged toad-like on the receding gradient. Its eight-window span suggested an ancient vigilance while the twin-columned portico announced its original owner's arrival at prosperity back in the 1890s. In the foggy beyonds lay a walled garden, a heather- and furze-clad cliff, and a cold sea.

As she turned in by the gable end of the house, Daina hesitated. The usual tidy symmetry of Attenboy and of its owners' lives had been further disrupted. Anna Brennan's retro Morris Minor station wagon wasn't in its usual place on the cobbled courtyard. Nor was it in the russet-bricked outhouse they used for a garage, the door of which had been slid back. The doors of the other outhouses stood slightly ajar. All four of them. The back door of the main house too. Daina approached it cautiously, listening. In her two months of working there, she'd never arrived to a silent house. Anna Brennan liked her music, liked it classical and liked it loud.

In the kitchen, no signs of a disturbance caught her eye. Everything was in its place apart from a brandy bottle on the counter by the sink that should have been in the library's drinks cabinet. Only later, as she spoke to the ugly detective, did it occur to Daina that she might have done something other than venture recklessly if nervously further into the house. She might, for example, have rung the house phone, waited for someone to pick up. Or rung Anna Brennan's mobile, or her sister Sonia's back at the flat on Mountjoy Square. She found nothing amiss inside the house apart from the silence. And her employers' absence.

Out in the courtyard again, Daina stood motionless. The mist had thickened, dampening the cobbles. Dimly aware of the cold, she rubbed her fleshy arms with her hands and couldn't remember having taken off her jacket. She was torn between two fears: a mounting apprehension over the Brennans' disappearance and a dread of coming to the attention of the police.

A breeze had started up. Trees whispered, ghostly. Shredded shavings of tree bark skittered noisily across the cobbles, unsettling her with their suddenness. Loose on their hinges, the doors of the outhouses flapped and creaked their warnings. Through the ragged boundary of recently thinned leylandii conifers she saw Kitty Newman next door stepping out of her steepled conservatory for a smoke.

It wasn't true what Daina was to tell the girl who looked too pretty to be a policewoman and too young to be a detective, that she'd called out at once to the Brennans' neighbour. In fact, she ducked briefly out of sight of Mrs Newman to debate the matter with herself. While she did, the outhouse door to the left of the garage swung open and she screamed. She couldn't take her eyes from the body, and yet would retain no precise image of it even twenty minutes later when the first squad car came.

Dermot Brennan lay face down on the packed-clay floor of the outhouse. He was dressed in weekend casuals. Denim jeans, a red Munster rugby shirt, unlaced work boots, no socks. His right arm extended along the ground as though reaching for something he'd lost under the old worktable. His left, twisted at a curious angle, lay beneath his body. The legs too seemed impossibly awry. At the back of his head, the large blood-burst had already dried to black.

Daina ran, making for the gap in the conifers that Anna Brennan had used when she was still on speaking terms with Kitty Newman. The narrow passage hadn't been made with Daina in mind. She emerged on the other side scratched and bloodied along the arms. Mrs Newman had retreated to her conservatory and locked herself in. She watched the dumb-show of Daina's slow collapse by the waist-high ovoid sandstone sculpture on the side lawn. First, the Latvian girl sank to her knees. Then she toppled sideways, decimating a cluster of yellow day lilies in the flower border.

Kitty Newman rang the Guards from her mobile, locking herself further and further into the house until she reached an attic shower room from which she had an overview of Attenboy House. Nothing moved down there. While she waited, she tried to assure herself that whatever had happened over there had nothing to do with her intervention in the affairs of the Brennans. Surely not.

2

Big and bug-eyed and hunched over the steering wheel, Garda Dempsey negotiated the gaps opening in the city traffic. There was something child-like about his concentration, his delight at being exempted from the rules governing ordinary mortals. Detective Sergeant Helen Troy wondered why the Guards attracted so many of these overgrown boys whose voices sounded like they'd just broken and whose social skills were of the schoolyard variety.

When they'd got through on to the clear run of Howth Road, she said, 'Lose the siren, will you?'

He threw her a churlish look and flicked the switch.

He didn't like her. Hardly surprising, Helen thought. It was her first case with the National Bureau of Criminal Investigation, her first outing as a detective sergeant too. One of the youngest in the country. Of the female variety. Another token woman was how Garda Dempsey and his pals saw her. Love to see her fail he would. Report back gleefully to the boys at the station. First scene-of-crime with CI, she imagined him relating, and she makes a pig's arse of it before Leo gets out there to sort things. Should've shunted her back into Juvenile Liaison or packed her off to the Central Vetting Unit in Tipperary keeping an eye out for paedos, he'd sneer. Some kind of women's work anyway.

Somewhere in his mid-twenties, Dempsey hadn't yet begun to tackle the complexities of adulthood, Helen decided. He looks at me and thinks I have it all, but all I have now is the bloody job.

One of her mobile phones rang. The state phone, her work phone. She snapped it up too urgently and Dempsey registered her nervousness with a smug side-glance. She checked the caller ID. Sergeant Martha Corrigan back at the NBCI desk in the Harcourt Street HQ. A Rose of Tralee winner back in the mid-nineties, Martha had no pretensions and never overplayed the hand Nature had given her.

'Detective Sergeant Troy speaking.'

'Leo's flight's delayed, Helen. You'll have to hold the fort for the best part of the morning, OK?'

'No problem, Martha.'

'Try not to, eh . . .'

'Try not to screw up?'

'Don't be silly,' Sergeant Corrigan said in her usual no-nonsense way. 'What I'm saying is, tread softly out there. This could be a minefield.'

'A minefield as in . . . ?'

'As in the dead man was some kind of builder cum property developer and he's politically connected.'

'Thanks for the warning, Martha.'

'Gerry Cooney's the local detective sergeant you'll liaise with out there. Take no notice of his old guff. Gerry's just a sex-starved prick.'

'Charming,' Helen said. 'Does he have a problem with our team moving in there?'

Some local units, Helen knew, didn't take kindly to the NBCI encroaching on their territories.

'Not at all. Less work and less responsibility for himself is how he sees it. Oh, and the Technical Bureau should be with you within the hour.'

'Thanks, Martha.'

Sergeant Martha Corrigan's had been the only welcoming voice since she'd arrived at her new posting on Thursday last. They hadn't been expecting her until December. A mix-up, she'd explained, the paperwork mislaid. There was no desk for Helen. The auburn-haired sergeant told her to use Leo's desk until he got back from holidays. He never used it much anyway, she joked, which explained why it was so tidy. Firmly but politely Helen had refused. She'd sort it with Superintendent Heaphy but had yet to meet him. He was away at some conference in Budapest. The top brass were always away at some conference.

She'd been left sitting on a plastic chair twiddling her thumbs for two days. Some kind of test, she supposed. She didn't know whether she'd passed or failed or who the examiner was. She wondered if it might be Leo.

Dempsey had slowed the squad car. He peered out beyond Helen to his left as though he might be lost – an expression not much different to his usual vacuous, open-mouthed stare.

'Do we know where we are?' she asked.

'Yeah, Howth.'

'Well that's a relief because we could be in Galway, it's taken you so bloody long to get us here.'

'What's the rush anyway?' the young Garda said. 'Leo won't be here for a while yet.'

She let the jibe pass. Detective Inspector Leo Woods

15

remained an enigma to Helen. Whatever she knew of him came from the unsolicited comments of Martha Corrigan and Dempsey. In Martha she detected a certain respect for and even awe of *our Leo*. From the young Garda there was respect too but tinged with an unpleasant, sneering undertone. *A regular babe-magnet he is.* Maybe the inspector's reputation reminded Dempsey of his own mediocrity.

According to Martha, Leo had done everything. Tackled the Provos through the late seventies and early eighties. In the mid-eighties he'd run a couple of IRA informers, while the nineties saw him go toe-to-toe with the new generation of crime gangs in the city. All of which seemed to Helen the unlikeliest preparation for his next incarnation: a peacekeeper with the UN. A living legend in Angola to this day, Martha claimed. Sarajevo and Kosovo followed. So what's he doing back here working on the ground floor again? Helen had asked. It's a miracle the man is working at all after everything he's been through, was Martha's answer. Then she'd ended the conversation, her pale face flushing to an unexpected ruddiness.

The road swept upwards so that Helen got a brief, hazy glimpse of the sea. Low clouds pushing in over the water, dark as the day of her father's funeral three years before. She'd stood between her brother Jamie and her ex, Ricky, even then only half believing they were all together in this. Till death do us part. And part us it did, Helen thought, all three of us.

Dempsey swung the squad car left into Napier Road. Her trepidation turned to nausea. She'd made it into CI and up to detective sergeant before her thirty-fourth birthday as she'd hoped she might. Just. At the weekend, she'd celebrated the big three-four in a rented apartment near the cemetery in

Glasnevin. Ideal location. Two people showed up, and the second one was her reflection in the mirror.

Up ahead to the right, a couple of squad cars were parked, one to each side of a pillared entrance. As Dempsey steered towards the gateway, Helen looked at the letters carved into the limestone nameplate. Attenboy House. The same hands, she thought, chisel out the names we put on our houses and the names we put on our gravestones.

Christ, Helen, she told herself, you need to lighten up.

Apart from the backpack, Detective Inspector Leo Woods carried no baggage. He went along the moving walkways towards the Arrivals Hall at Dublin Airport waiting for his mobiles to find a network. Made you feel young, these walkways did. Fooled you into thinking your small steps were great strides. But false momentum was better than no momentum, he supposed. In the intervals between walkways his legs felt heavy, and it wasn't down to age. Not altogether. He'd been up since five after three hours of drugged sleep and wild dreaming. The dogs again, tearing him to pieces. Even the good side of his face looked a mess after the dog dreams.

As he passed into the Baggage Hall, his mobiles found a network. The same three messages rang in on his work phone and his personal phone, all of them from the peerless Sergeant Martha Corrigan.

What time are you in? Martha.

Which flight is it? Martha.

Ring when you get in. Urgent. Martha.

Leo stepped aside from the wave of commuters. He watched his fellow Paris passengers filter through, rested a while on a bench near the baggage carousel and let the passengers from a few other flights through too. Prague, Málaga, Dubai.

Now that he'd stopped moving, the cold began to take a grip on him. Served him right, he thought, for wearing a summery fawn linen suit on the off-chance he'd meet anyone who knew him. They'd think he was coming back from the sun when, in reality, he was coming back from a place colder than the dark side of the moon. The mask-maker's room in Paris. But old habits of secrecy persist long after they need to.

He rang Harcourt Street while he waited for the next flock of passengers to come in.

'Leo. You're back?' Martha Corrigan sounded relieved.

'Yeah, just in. What's the big emergency?'

'We've a suspicious death in Howth. Looks like you're on it.'

'Christ, Martha, I'm in serious need of prolonged sleep. Can't you pass it on to someone else?'

'Superintendent Heaphy's orders, Leo.'

'Isn't he in Budapest?'

'Yeah.'

'He rang from Budapest?'

'From the airport. He's flying home this morning,' Martha said. 'Which means this is heavy-duty stuff, Leo. The dead man's Dermot Brennan. Builder/developer. There's talk of his being connected to one of our Junior Ministers but we don't have all the details yet.'

'To hell with that, Martha. This government's up shit creek anyway.'

'Precisely,' Martha Corrigan said. 'And what happens in the last days of empire, Leo?'

'Ah, pay-day for favours done,' Leo said, his stumblebum

brain slowly waking. 'Time to hand out the lollipops. And Heaphy's looking to be bumped up to chief superintendent, yeah?'

'You should be pushing for superintendent yourself, Leo. No one deserves it more.'

'Politicking is not my game, Martha. Never will be.'

Sensing he was being watched, Leo looked at the faces going by and those further off at the baggage carousels. Then he looked down. A small child stood gaping, pointing up at him. Leo stepped on the child's foot. The shrill cry pierced his brain. The child hobbled away at speed. Leo ducked into the Gents.

'What's all that racket, Leo?'

'One of my fans, Martha, looking for an autograph.'

'Good trip, was it? Get some sun?'

'I sat in the shade. So, what's the story in Howth?'

'We sent out the new girl to hold the fort for you and she's—'

'The new girl?'

'Helen Troy. Came earlier than we expected. Nice girl. Bright as a button,' Sergeant Corrigan explained. 'Anyway, the story is there's no sign of the dead man's wife out there and she's not answering her mobile.'

'Who found the body, then?'

'A young Latvian girl who works for them. She made her way to the next-door neighbour's garden and collapsed. Now she's clammed up. Besides which, she doesn't appear to have much English. We sent for an interpreter.'

'Anything useful from the neighbour?'

'Helen's talking to her at the minute. Seems she saw nothing much.'

Another troop of bleary-eyed passengers gathered at the

19

baggage carousel nearby. Leo looked up at the monitor over-head. A flight from Reus. Where the hell was Reus? Must be a Ryanair destination, he mused, aching for a cigarette. He strolled through the blue EU passage and headed on towards the sliding doors that led into the main body of the airport.

Strange that whenever you arrived at those doors, there was this sense of expectation, this brief, irrational conviction that someone might be waiting for you out there. Someone you knew or someone holding up a handwritten sign with your name on it. No matter that it had been years since anyone waited for Leo at Dublin Airport or anywhere else. He looked up anyway, scanned the faces out beyond the barrier. As usual, all he saw was the variety of reactions to his own damaged face. Curiosity, surprise and, sometimes, revulsion.

Welcome home, Leo, he told himself.

3

Attenboy House smelled of money subtly spent. Perfection without the frills of excess oozed from the industrial chic of the kitchen and the retro Scandinavian furnishing and decoration of the ground-floor rooms to the understated Parisian apartment feel of the bedrooms above. As Detective Sergeant Helen Troy went through the trophy house, she warned herself to keep a lid on her prejudices. She was in the negative equity trap. An apartment down in Tipperary that she didn't need any more and couldn't sell, and a mortgage that her ex-partner had stopped contributing towards. Contempt for the dead man's profession might easily skew her reasoning, she knew. She suspected that the next-door neighbour shared this contempt but more especially disliked Anna Brennan.

While the Brennans' home was at least giving a reasonable impression of warmth, Kitty Newman's house had felt cold and peculiarly empty. From the outside a modernist collection of stacked cubes, its rooms were too large, too high-ceilinged and too insistently white. A steely lack of comfort marked the furniture. The paintings adorning the walls, all originals, added little colour to the interiors. Mrs Newman herself was small and spare and had a preoccupied, edgy air about her. Botoxed liberally and not entirely expertly, her face looked scarily young and frantic. A divorcee, she lived alone.

It seemed to Helen that there'd been a falling out between the two women. 'No, we're not at all close,' Mrs Newman had said, 'never really were.' An offended tone to her declaration. She'd been let down by Anna Brennan in some way was Helen's guess. Still had her mobile number though and some suggestions as to where her neighbour might be, her eyes darting about nervously as she spoke. The holiday home down in County Waterford or the apartment in Nice. Always assuming, she'd added, that the banks hadn't moved in on them. Then, she'd taken Helen aback.

'Does Stephen know yet?'

'Stephen?'

'Her son. He lives at some kind of hippy-type animal shelter out in the Dublin Mountains. Poor boy. Very . . . troubled.'

Kitty Newman's eyes had widened just then, fixed themselves on Helen. Rowing back on her words but uncertainly.

'Not in the sense of . . . I mean, he and Dermot didn't get on but it could never come to, well, you know . . .'

'Do you have a phone number for Stephen, Mrs Newman?'

She didn't have; nor had Helen found one on the list of numbers posted above the kitchen phone in Attenboy House. Stephen Brennan's phone number was also among the many things that Daina didn't know. The girl was a mess. Her arms scratched and bruised, her clothes wet from the fall in Mrs Newman's garden, tears breaking out with every question of Helen's and making an absurd mask of her over-indulgent make-up. I go home, was all she had to say, I go home. Soon, Helen had told her.

As she moved into Dermot Brennan's bedroom, the young detective saw that the duvet on his bed had been thrown back and that his bedside lamp still shone. The lights on the landing and in the downstairs hallway were switched on too, suggesting that the attack had taken place close to or after nightfall, or perhaps in the early morning.

Helen eased out the top drawer of the bedside table with a latex-gloved hand. The drawer held some books – *The Wasp Factory* and *We Need to Talk About Kevin*, both of which surprised her, though she didn't quite know why – an iPod and an unopened packet of condoms. The lower drawer contained a laptop. Hoping against hope, she switched it on. Not just a blank screen but a black screen. On the top right-hand corner, a tiny name and logo: DOLMencrypt. The laptop was protected. One for the Technical Bureau, then, though she presumed a password was still required.

The ensuite bathroom and dressing room at first revealed nothing apart from the expensive cut of his few suits, a predilection for blue shirts and a stockpile of worn-out denims and red rugby jerseys. The jerseys put her in mind of Ricky, the boarding school rugger-bugger turned bass-guitar rebel. She caught a glimpse of herself in the long mirror to her left. She wasn't sure she liked her hair so short after all. Did it somehow make her look even smaller than she already was? Above her reflection she noticed a leather satchel on a high shelf behind her. She stood on a chair and opened the clasp of the bag. It was filled almost to the top with wads of €50 notes. Thousands, tens of thousands.

Her work phone rang.

'Detective Sergeant—'

'Helen, this is Leo, Leo Woods. How's it going out there?'

She felt her mouth go dry, told herself she was being ridiculous. His voice was pleasant, easy-going, nothing like what she'd expected, though she couldn't have said exactly what she'd expected.

'Sir. Still waiting for the Technical Bureau and I've asked the station in Passage East to check out the holiday home and—'

'The holiday home?'

'Sorry. The Brennans have a place down in County Waterford. The next-door neighbour thinks Mrs Brennan may have gone there for the weekend but she's not answering her mobile and Passage East Station haven't got back to me yet. And I'm waiting on a call from Martha on the son. Only son. Stephen. He lives in some animal welfare home in Wicklow. We don't have a name for it so Martha's checking to see if—'

'Are you doing anything else besides waiting, Helen?'

She didn't know whether or not he was joking. His relaxed tone hadn't changed but she found herself blushing madly, felt defensive, went on the offensive.

'As a matter of fact I am. I've just found a bagful of cash in Dermot Brennan's dressing room. Plus, he and his son don't get on. And he and his wife don't sleep together. Which, OK, isn't unusual except that he may have been playing the field. Also, I found a laptop in his room but it's encrypted so we'll have to—'

'Steady on, Helen. Do us a favour, would you?'

'Yeah?'

'See if you can find any Solpadeine there, will you? I'll be with you in about twenty minutes.'

Solpadeine? I'm a detective at a scene-of-crime, Helen

thought, and he wants me to go searching for headache tablets? But he'd already switched off and she was left cursing at her phone.

Down below, the white Technical Bureau van pulled into the cobbled yard followed by a squad car. She watched from the window of Dermot Brennan's bedroom as three men and a young woman emerged from the van. They were joined by three plain-clothes detectives. The Howth brigade, she supposed. She wondered which one was Detective Sergeant Cooney, the sex-starved prick. It wasn't always easy to tell. The sex-starved, yes. The pricks, no.

Leo pocketed his mobile phone and sighed. The youthful energy in his new detective sergeant's voice had him sinking back into seedy depression again. He wiped a couple of tears from the drooping lid of his left eye, the bloody irony of which was that he hadn't actually wept for almost thirty years. Not since Iseult.

His driver was the silent type, which suited Leo's mood. They were on the coast road out to Howth. Mudflats stretching over towards Bull Island to the right. The long, low wall and high trees of St Anne's Park to his left. Found bodies in both expanses in his time: two murders, a suicide and an abandoned blue baby dead before it had left the womb. If you hung around long enough, he mused, every landscape became a burial ground to you.

The flat breast of the Howth Head peninsula loomed in the distance. Bleak morning mist giving way to blustering, spitting breezes. Along the pathway by the water, joggers conspired to make him feel like a faltering wreck nearing his first heart attack. Occasional clusters of palm trees punctuated the long stretch of James Larkin Road – exotic refugee families abandoned and huddling on a northern shore. Aren't we all refugees? Leo thought. The Brennans too, perhaps.

Composing one after another imagined tirade against Detective Inspector Woods, Helen continued her search of Dermot Brennan's room until a second squad car rolled into the cobbled yard. From the passenger side, a tall man emerged. Pepper-and-salt hair that was strong but unruly in the breeze. She couldn't see his face. On this coldest of days, he wore a crumpled fawn-coloured linen suit, light blue shirt, brown and blue striped tie. Not your usual detective's gear. A touch of dowdy class about it. Inspector Leo Woods? With his tall man's slight stoop, he ambled across to the Technical Bureau van. He leaned against the rear door as the Bureau technicians and the plain-clothes men donned their white coveralls. He seemed in no hurry to see the body.

Helen pulled in a deep breath, picked up Dermot Brennan's laptop and left the bedroom.

4

'Heard you were away on a holiday, Leo.'
'You heard right.'

Leo waited for Detective Sergeant Gerry Cooney's inevitable slice of innuendo.

'Let me guess. Bangkok?' Cooney said with a lewd emphasis on the second syllable as he eyed Leo's linen suit.

The young woman in white hooded coveralls behind Cooney rolled her eyes. Not his first sophisticated quip of the morning, Leo supposed. Cooney shot a wicked glance in the technician's direction and then in Leo's. The detective sergeant's shaved bullet head and his knowing squint always put Leo in mind of some character in a Hieronymus Bosch vision of Hell's lower depths.

'Sex tourism. Could it be Ireland's way out of the recession, do you think, Leo? Only we'd have to import most of the women. Throw on those coveralls and we'll get it over with. This fellow's beginning to smell.'

Respect for the dead had never been Cooney's forte but Leo detected real contempt in his tone now. Property developers, bankers and their political friends ranked alongside pimps and paedophiles these days in the estimation of many. Leo wasn't their number-one fan either but he'd have to protect against this antipathy hampering the investigation.

As the others headed to the outhouse, Leo scrabbled with the plastic bag containing the new-issue blue NBCI coverall. He tried tearing the plastic with his teeth but that reminded him of the dog dreams and he ripped it apart with his hands instead. He bent down to get the leggings of his blues on. His brain swam like some pickled thing in a jar, a fork poking and prodding at it.

'Inspector?'

The woman's voice, too sudden and too close by, knocked him off balance. He keeled forward but she grabbed his shoulder and stopped his fall. He swung around too quickly. The full-on view of his face caught Helen off guard. His left cheek sagged crookedly, pulling down the lower eyelid and exposing the well of tears, pushing down the corner of his mouth so that it slavered wetly.

'Christ's sake, don't creep up on a man like that.'

'I'm sorry.'

People did this all the time. Apologized for what they saw. He'd grown used to it. As a rule there were few repercussions for him these days, beyond an occasional descent into bitterness. But every rule has its exception. Self-consciousness kicked in again when he found himself in the company of attractive women. No matter that Helen Troy was probably half his age and wouldn't have looked at him twice even if he'd grown old gracefully.

'Don't mind me, Helen. I'm tired, hung over and back from holidays.'

The young detective made a conscious effort to look at him directly without favouring his better side.

'Listen, Helen. Let's get the formalities out of the way. I

wasn't born this way and I haven't had a stroke so I'm not likely to fall dead at your feet any time soon. This is Bell's palsy and it's permanent and I've gotten used to it, more or less, so you'll have to get used to it too, OK?'

She nodded, silently cursed Martha Corrigan and Dempsey for not having warned her what to expect.

'Can I help you with the blues?'

He'd gotten his feet into the one-piece suit but couldn't find the sleeves.

'If you don't mind. I'm not up to puzzles this morning.'

Leo stood up and let her dress him. It felt oddly reassuring. He didn't quite know whether it made him feel very young or very old. The blue coveralls provided as little protection from the cold as his linen suit but he felt warmer anyway.

'Speaking of puzzles, what do you make of this bag of cash? How much do you reckon's in it?'

'Can't say exactly. Tens of thousands, I'd imagine, and all in fifty-euro notes. I'll let you find the zip yourself.'

Turning from her, he burrowed with thick, frozen fingers into the crotch area as she slipped quickly into her blues. She threw out some theories on the bag of cash by way of diversion as he fumbled.

'Blackmail, it occurred to me. Or maybe he was about to do a runner. Or just keeping it where the taxman or the banks can't get at it. That's how they work, isn't it? Payments off the radar, brown envelopes, all that. I found a laptop in his bedroom. We might get something on that. Then again, these people are hardly likely to incriminate themselves with emails and—'

'*These people?*'

'Builders, property developers. That lot.'

Leo pulled the elasticated fringe of the hood forward as

far as he could on the left side. He turned the undamaged side of his face towards Helen. She saw that he'd once been a handsome man.

'Mr Brennan's been judged pretty harshly already this weekend. Maybe we should reserve our own judgements until we find out why,' Leo said. 'You didn't find any Solpadeine, did you?'

'No, sir,' Helen said.

'You didn't look for any, did you?'

'No, sir.'

Leo laughed. He liked her. Still had the bloody headache though.

5

The interior of the stone outhouse hadn't seen so much light since the roof went on a hundred years before. Blackened cobwebs dusted the walls. Rat and mouse droppings littered the earthen floor. Dermot Brennan lay among them, seeming to stir with every flash of the crime-scene photographer's camera. The odd disarray of limbs suggested a drunken fall. Then again, a violent death didn't allow much time to compose one's corpse. Still, Leo thought, a big man like Brennan might have been taken down more easily if he'd been drinking. The musk of ancient hay did battle with the stench of death. Leo's brain couldn't decide on a winner.

Alongside the body lay an iron crowbar four feet long and bloodied at one end.

Disorder reigned among the rusted contents of the work-bench and shelving but wasn't recent. An antique flat-tyred bicycle and a cracked leather armchair retained the dust of years. On the floor beside the armchair lay an old coil of rope like a moulted, dried-out serpent skin.

'Nothing's been touched,' Detective Sergeant Gerry Cooney said as he stood over the corpse before one of the technicians tapped him on the leg, gesturing to him to move back. 'Apart from the crowbar. Seems like there was no struggle. Several blows to the back of the head. And a kick in the ribs for afters. Maybe. Show him, John.'

The technician raised the dead man's red rugby jersey and exposed a large bruise along the side above the waist. Leo peered at the purple and yellow blossom.

'Not the crowbar?' he asked of the technician, but Cooney cut in.

'No. Might've been the impact of the fall, of course. But my guess is a good-riddance kick.'

'He's, what, six one, six two, weighs maybe sixteen, seventeen stone?' Leo said. 'So the first blow had to be a hell of a shot to put him down and keep him down.'

'A lucky shot or one hell of a strong bastard swinging the crowbar,' Cooney speculated.

Leo surveyed the walls either side of the doorway. Not a lot of space to hide in to the left from which the door opened outwards and no hiding place to the right. Someone Brennan knew then, maybe, following him inside? Someone he had no reason to distrust. Or had no reason to fear, which might not be the same thing.

'Any sign of a mobile or car keys?' Helen asked.

'Patience, love, we haven't turned the bugger over yet,' Cooney said.

A pair of technicians raised the body a little by the shoulders. Helen caught a glimpse of Dermot Brennan's twisted face and recoiled, covering her distress with an exaggerated search through her jacket pockets for a notebook and pen. She wondered what Leo must be thinking.

'No mobile there,' Cooney reported, and the white-suited technician began to fish in the dead man's pockets.

The side of Dermot Brennan's face that had lain against the earthen floor was distorted in rigor mortis. Leo turned briefly away from the ghastly mirror image then, steeling himself, looked closer. The victim's upper lip had been split, one of his front teeth chipped.

'D'you think he might have taken a punch, John?' Leo asked.

'Possibly, but then again it may have been the fall.'

Cooney, stooping down over the body, checked the livid bruise again.

'No car keys here either, Leo,' John said.

'How long do you reckon he's been lying here?'

'Forty-eight hours, give or take. Pathologist won't be here for a while but that's my guess.'

'Early Saturday morning then,' Leo said, and turned to Detective Sergeant Cooney. 'So, what do we know about Mr Brennan, apart from what he did for a living?'

'Not an awful lot, to be honest,' Cooney said. 'Bought this place five, six years ago. A dodgy deal it was too, according to rumour. The last owner was an old lady, a Miss Duffy. She'd been in a nursing home for a couple of years and sold the house dirt cheap. Had no idea of its real value and—'

'Is any of this actually relevant, Gerry?' Leo interrupted, and all eyes were fleetingly on the bullet-headed detective.

Cooney's gnarled and puckish face darkened.

'Sure it's relevant,' he said. 'I'm painting a picture here for you, Leo. A picture of a crook. One of that small band of crooks who've screwed us all and left us in the clutches of a little Indian man from the IMF.' He turned to Helen. 'Are you writing this down?'

'I don't need to, your every word is etched in my mind.'

Detective Sergeant Cooney looked her up and down and

33

thought he might be in love again. Or what passed for love in his scatological brain.

'Ah, a fighter,' Cooney said. 'Don't you just love it when they put up a fight, Leo?'

He'd deepened his voice a semi-tone and then another. It wasn't enough, Helen thought. He still sounded like someone was squeezing his balls.

'Dermot Brennan,' Leo said. He felt tired, exasperated. 'What else do we know about him, Gerry?'

'Kept to himself,' Cooney said sulkily. 'Wasn't a mixer and wasn't involved in any local activities that I know of. Wasn't a member of the golf club, didn't have a boat. Only place I ever saw him was at Mass on Sundays.' He ignored Leo's feigned look of surprise. 'His wife had a charity shop in Abbey Street but it closed up recently. She's no joiner either. Some looker though, I can tell you, she's—'

'OK, Gerry,' Leo said. 'Get back to me when you've dug up some real info on him, will you?'

On all fours, the technicians were sifting through some patches of loosened clay on the floor. The glaring arc light pierced Leo's temple and left him momentarily snow-blind. His head took a dizzy spin. He held himself up with the aid of the work bench, which offered Cooney an opportunity for a modicum of revenge.

'Hands off the furniture, Leo.'

'Never occurred to me before, Gerry, but your bald head in that white hoodie? It's like a baby's arse in Pampers.'

'Piss off, you ugly—'

From the courtyard outside, a shrill cry reached them. A woman's voice keening but abruptly cut short. Leo and Helen stepped outside. Over by the back door of the house, Garda Dempsey knelt by the prone body of a woman. He cradled her head on his lap but his hands were heavy and useless about her.

'The wife. Who the bloody hell let her in? Bring her into the house, Helen,' Leo said. 'And don't let her over here, OK?'

Leo went back into the outhouse. He hated these first moments of distress in a case – the wife, husband, child or whoever reacting to the news. The hysteria of others always set off a vague panic in him, a sense of his own mental fragility.

As Helen hurried across the cobblestones, she saw a green retro Morris Minor station wagon abandoned by the front gate. Just the thing for the wannabe lady of the manor was her first cruel thought. She reached Dempsey and gestured at him to hand the woman over. The young Garda seemed reluctant to surrender the lush waves of red hair that now filled his hands. She leaned in closer to the woman, who hadn't yet opened her eyes.

'Mrs Brennan?'

The answering sounds that came were neither words nor cries. Grief made most people ugly, Helen thought, herself included. Not Anna Brennan. Even in anguish her lightly freckled face retained a sculpted perfection, and Helen could tell it was a natural perfection. Her eyes showed themselves, a stunning lapis lazuli.

'I have to see him,' Anna Brennan said as she raised herself with their help.

'Not just yet, Mrs Brennan,' Helen said. 'Let's get you inside.'

The woman broke free of Dempsey and tried to get beyond him, her gaze fixed on the outhouse. He spread his arms like a farmer herding cattle. Helen took her by the waist and steered her to the back door of the house.

'But my son's lying there . . . Oh, God . . .'

A bewildered Dempsey shrugged in answer to the detective sergeant's unspoken question as they went inside. Helen sat the woman down at the long kitchen table. She wondered if Anna Brennan had misheard the young Garda as he'd tried to explain what had happened. Or assumed that her son was the more likely victim? She stood before the woman, took her hand.

'Mrs Brennan, it's your husband who's been assaulted. And, I'm afraid, he's dead. I'm so sorry.'

Anna Brennan tilted her head a little to the side and struck a beautiful, frozen pose of immense sadness. At first, Helen didn't believe in it. Then, because no crocodile tears came, she felt persuaded.

'We need to contact your son, Mrs Brennan.'

'But he didn't do this.'

'Of course not. But we have to let him know, don't we?'

Her brilliant blue eyes lowered, Anna Brennan drew in a long, laboured breath. Her inward gaze seemed, at once, angelic and forlorn. She surveyed her glossy-magazine kitchen, all burnished steel and dark hardwoods. She began to tremble violently, her pallor suddenly green, the freckles on her face like spatters of mud.

Helen looked around the kitchen to see if there was anything she might use to keep the woman from fainting. On the kitchen counter by the sink and alongside a block of carving knives was a half-filled brandy bottle. She thought better of it.

'Get a doctor,' Helen told Dempsey.

The mist had lifted and the cold deepened. A hint of yellow-gold washed the red-brick of the walled garden Detective

Inspector Leo Woods strolled through. He wondered if the Brennans employed a gardener, the place was so picture perfect. Apple and pear trees had been trained up the side walls, berry and currant bushes decorated the end wall. Box-hedged rectangles, eight in all, filled the inner spaces between pebble paths. Not a weed to be seen. Apart from the rapidly incinerating contents of Leo's cigarette.

He plucked, squeezed and sniffed at blades of rosemary, leaves of mint, withered tendrils of dill. He tested a cane superstructure laced with runner bean plants, tugged the stem of a radish from among its brethren. Two radishes grew from the same stem. Only now, as he scraped the clay from the aberrant pair, did he feel his mind rejoining his body. He yawned. The day began to seem real to him. Then he began to seem real to himself.

At the centre of the walled garden stood a polished sand-stone sculpture. Egg-shaped, about three feet high, a faint cleft along its front. To each side of this divide were two further deep indentations suggesting closed, death-mask eyelids. He tried to find some hidden meaning in it but only briefly. He didn't believe in hidden meanings. The only thing he liked about the dinosaur egg was the almost velvety texture of its surface. He checked that the thing was securely cemented to its plinth and sat on it.

A long arched upper window at the back of Attenboy House overlooked the walled garden. Red and blue stained-glass panels along the outer edges made something bejewelled of the weak reflected sunlight. Leo looked along the eaves above the window. He wondered what kind of man Dermot Brennan was. Had been. Hadn't especially feared for his own safety, for sure, what with no CCTV cameras, a pretty basic alarm system that in any event had been switched off and a lightly bolted door on the end wall of the garden. All of which rendered the electronically controlled front gates next to useless.

So. Early Saturday morning. Very early. Still dark or dawn maybe. Dermot Brennan is woken by a noise? Or some perceived but silent presence? Inside the house or out? Half expected or altogether unexpected? The victim switches on his bedside lamp and dresses quickly. Or vice versa. Anyway, he moves down through the house, each light he switches on a warning to any potential intruder. Does he call out? Is there a name on his lips or just an unspecified challenge? Mobile phone in his hand, his pocket, somewhere about him. Does he use it? And if he does, who does he call? And why? And what were the chances they'd ever find the bloody phone anyway? Slim to zero. It had obviously been stolen so that it could be dumped or destroyed, right?

This was how Leo always began. Imagining alternative realities. What other kinds of realities were there? he mused.

He buried his cigarette butt among the radishes. He took out another menthol-tipped cigarette from the box, snapped off the tip and lit up again. He spat the loose tobacco flakes and dumped the tip in his jacket pocket along with all the other tips and the balled tissues dampened by the waters of his leaky eye and his saliva.

So. Brennan swings the back door open. And no one's there? Or someone's there and he says, Who the hell are you and what are you doing here? Or he says, *You*? What do *you* want? But if no one's there, he looks across the cobbled yard to the outhouses. The slide-locks are on the outside of the doors. So. Are all the doors already open? And, if so, why? Someone's been looking for something. Does Brennan know what they're looking for? They? More than one intruder?

And is any or all or none of this connected to the bag of cash in—

'Inspector Woods? Sir?'

At the wrought-iron gate of the walled garden, Detective Sergeant Helen Troy waited for a response. Already a little afraid of him, Leo knew. Or wary, in any case. He hadn't noticed until now quite how young she looked. Maybe it was the way she stood. A kind of tentative leaning forward suggesting a willingness to please. He dismounted the work of art.

'Oh,' Helen said, looking beyond him as he approached. 'That sculpture. There's another one just like it next door, sir.'

'Looks to me like a second-rate Barbara Hepworth rip-off,' Leo said. 'And, for Christ's sake, call me Leo.' He stubbed out his cigarette on the pebbled path. 'And when you do call me, try to notify me first of your presence, will you? A little wave, a delicate yoo-hoo or something, OK?'

'I've got a number for the son,' she said flatly. 'But he's not answering his mobile. Seems he lives at the Argos Sanctuary, some sort of animal shelter run by a middle-aged German woman. Gudrun Remer. Not Anna Brennan's favourite person, I gather.'

'Have you rung this sanctuary?'

'Not yet.'

'Why not?'

'Maybe I'm jumping the gun. Maybe she misheard Garda Dempsey when he told her, but Mrs Brennan assumed it was her son who'd been murdered,' Helen explained. 'I think we need to be there when Stephen gets the news. See how he reacts, see if he lets anything slip.'

'Good,' Leo said. 'Good stuff.'

'And another thing,' Helen said, still the little girl desperate to please, or at least not to disappoint. 'When she heard it was her husband, I got the sense that she was, well, less than surprised. Shocked, yes, but not surprised. The doctor's with her now. I don't imagine she'll be up to questioning for a few hours yet.'

More to this young one, Leo thought, than most of those who'd come under his wing this past while. Apart from Detective Garda Ben Murphy, of course. The Boy Wonder in Superintendent Aonghus Heaphy's eyes but not in Leo's. Like the young man, Helen had a mind of her own, the balls to speak it. So to speak. Unlike him, she didn't leave Leo feeling irritated and mistrustful.

The breeze, trapped between the garden walls, swirled and caught his weak eye, drawing a tear. He wiped it away annoyedly with his fist.

'What about the Latvian girl? Has the interpreter shown up yet?' he asked.

'He's on his way,' Helen told him. 'Daina – the girl's name is Daina – she's been sedated now but she was pretty hysterical. Wanted to leave, then wanted to ring her cousin, Sonia. Lives with her on Mountjoy Square apparently. I had to take the phone from her.'

'Right then. You head over to the Argos Sanctuary and talk to the young lad. I'll talk to Mrs Brennan. That OK with you?'

'Yeah, no problem,' Helen said, grateful to have been entrusted with the task. 'Can I get you a padded jacket, sir?'

'Leo,' he insisted. 'Why? Do I look cold?'

He looked down at his cigarette hand, which was shaking like a junkie's. He felt another tear on his cheek and fished around among the debris in his pockets for a dry tissue but couldn't find one. Helen passed him one without comment. Never went anywhere without a packet of tissues these days.

6

Beneath an overcast sky, the Dublin Mountains were jagged, stony outcrops tufted in sparse growth. The distance from one house to the next lengthened as they drove so that minutes went by between each one. Silence seemed the appropriate response to the grim landscape. Silence was what Detective Sergeant Helen Troy and Garda Dempsey, in agreement for once, offered each other. So long did it last that Helen felt almost disappointed when she saw the makeshift sign. White-painted lettering on a rough board announced The Argos Sanctuary. Dempsey got out and opened the rust-flaked front gate.

Renovations on the low cottage, thirty yards back from the road, had evidently been started and left uncompleted many years before. A long open sore in the plasterwork marked the junction with a flat-roofed extension that had never been painted. A straggle of galvanized sheds and wired pens radiated from the rear of the cottage whose damp-stained walls, rusting iron window frames and threadbare curtains gave an impression of lost ideals. Or maybe just lazy ones.

'Shower of wasters,' Dempsey said. 'Probably still in bed.'

The front yard they drove into was a mudbath. Yelping cross-breeds vied with one another to scare off the white, yellow and blue-striped beast. Among them an ancient Alsatian lumbered, his hair gone to woolly disarray, exuding that melancholy peculiar to old dogs.

'No car or van that I can see,' Helen thought aloud.

'And if there was, you can be sure those crusties won't have tax or insurance.'

The young Garda had had enough of the kamikaze terriers throwing themselves against the squad car. The driver's door he swept open caught one of the smaller dogs in mid-air, tossing it like a leaf in the wind. The old Alsatian barked once, as though reminded of long-ago battles, and sloped stoically away. The others followed him, sneaking backward glances, miming defiance. Helen planted her Doc Martens in the mud and headed for the cottage. Dempsey made to follow her, one foot emerging but not quite touching the ground. He changed his mind, waited to be asked. Or told to. He wasn't. He sneaked out his Smartphone for a quick game of iShoot.

The glass panel on the cottage door had been replaced with a loose strip of plywood. Helen knocked on the outer frame. Then she tried knocking on the plywood, which gave way and fell from sight. She saw into the hallway, a floor covered in newspapers and peppered with dried mud. The walls were green and not clean. A stewy stench of stale sleep and yesterday's meat reached her. Helen stepped back just as the door was opened with an angry flourish.

'You break down my door! Why do you do this?'

The woman holding the rectangle of plywood was middle-aged. Her hair untidily shaped by sleep, she wore green gum boots and a long red gypsy dress patterned with small orange flowers. Smudged eye shadow lent her a theatrical air. Gudrun Remer, Helen presumed.

'Sorry about that,' Helen said. 'But it was in pretty bad shape anyway.'

'I will make a complaint. You police, you think you—'

'Is Stephen Brennan here?'

Gudrun Remer looked from Helen to the squad car, now more wary than combative. She brushed a hand through her hennaed hair, a few greys showing at the centre parting. The accumulation of hard years had lined her face but not altogether ruined it. Her gestures were overdone, breasts thrust forward from a shivering, arms-folded huddle.

'If this is about the court case, I have told my solicitor that Stephen is not well,' she said. 'I have delivered the doctor's certificate this morning.'

'Court case?'

'A peaceful protest until you people charged with your batons and tear gas,' Gudrun said. 'Doesn't it ever bother you that you serve the system not the people? I suppose not. That would require some independent thought.'

'There's been an incident at his parents' home,' Helen said, ignoring the barb she'd heard once too often before from her good-for-nothing brother. 'I need to talk to him. Where is he?'

'He is sick in his bed for two weeks. I cannot disturb him.'

Petulance in a middle-aged woman bordered on the ridiculous, Helen decided, a bubble to be burst. She burst it.

'Stephen's father is dead. We believe he may have been murdered.'

Gudrun Remer took a backward step and a second one to steady herself. Then she fell into a nervous, girlish

43

preoccupation with fingering strands of her hair. She didn't speak. Didn't, Helen sensed, allow herself to.

'So? Is Stephen here?'

The woman turned and headed down the filthy hallway. Helen followed. One of the bedrooms they went by didn't have a door. Another didn't have a bed. Both were occupied though there was neither time nor sufficient light to count the numbers nor determine the genders. Five, six bodies in all, she thought. Gudrun paused at the last door along the hallway. She spoke in a dramatically urgent whisper.

'Stephen is a kind boy in his heart, gentle. This will be another great trauma for him.'

'Another?' Helen said.

Ms Remer's petulance was showing again, ageing her. Helen noted the wrinkles around the German woman's pouted, embittered lips, the tobacco-stained teeth, her deeply furrowed forehead, the refusal to answer.

'Where was Stephen on Friday night, Ms Remer?' Helen asked. 'Early Saturday morning?'

'In this house. Sick. In his bed. I have told you this.'

'Does he sleep alone?'

'*Bitte?*'

'If he sleeps alone,' Helen said, 'then how do we confirm he didn't leave during the night at some point?'

The German woman considered the question. A deep chesty cough from inside the bedroom upset her calculations. Her concern for Stephen was real, Helen thought. Whether or not this concern was solely maternal, she couldn't yet tell.

'He does not sleep alone,' Gudrun Remer said.

'So he slept with these people in the other rooms?' Helen said, indicating the hallway behind her.

44

'No. On Friday night there was only Stephen and me,' the woman said, and opened the bedroom door hoping, it seemed to Helen, to cut off this line of inquiry.

Inside was an oasis of warmth and tidiness. The clearly expensive mahogany sleigh bed in which Stephen slept seemed oddly out of place in the run-down cottage. Under the heavy patchwork duvet, he wore a multi-coloured hand-knit cardigan. Strands of fair hair clung wetly to his face. He had his mother's pellucid flesh tone, her high cheekbones. A turf fire glowed in the tiled hearth. Alongside, a period chair upholstered in red velvet added a further incongruous touch to the room. Above the fireplace was pinned a large poster, a checkerboard gallery of police mugshots under the headline Baader-Meinhof Bande.

Scarcely masked by the smell of turf smoke hung the un-mistakable musk of cannabis. The aroma of her early days with Ricky.

She wasn't sure if she could trust the thin-limbed chair but she sat down anyway. Over by the bed, Gudrun leaned in over the young man. She pinned her unruly hair back with a free hand as she shook him softly awake. Her deep violet nail polish was lurid and carelessly applied.

'Stephen? Poor Stephen. You must wake.'

The period chair creaked under Helen's shifting weight. On the wall opposite the end of the bed was a revoltingly graphic animal rights poster. A young dog, its head encaged in a metal frame whose struts pierced the skull, a flap of skin peeled back revealing raw and bloodied bone. The eyes dully perceived the banality of hell.

Stephen Brennan woke and caught sight of Helen. She felt as though she was a creature from someone else's dream, such was the distance, the lack of surprise in his gaze.

'Stephen,' Gudrun said, 'it is bad news . . .'

He raised himself, found a dizzier height on the stacked pillows. Illness became Stephen, lent gravity to his boyish face. His voice too, a little hoarse, added to the impression of world-weariness.

'What?' he asked of Gudrun. 'Who are you?' he asked of Helen.

'Detective Sergeant Helen Troy,' she answered. 'I'm afraid there's been an—'

'It's Dad, isn't it? He's dead,' Stephen said.

That same sense of inevitability she'd seen in his mother. His pale blue eyes, bloodshot and bleary, gave a passing impression of grief. He might have said more if Gudrun Remer hadn't immediately smothered him in an unwelcome embrace. When she moved away and he sat up, the woollen cardigan he wore fell open revealing a T-shirt front. On it was an image of Jim Morrison's grave at Père Lachaise cemetery in Paris. Above and below, a line from Morrison's signature tune: This Is The End. He swung his legs out from under the bedsheet.

'Have you picked up Sean Doran yet?' he asked as he wiped the sleep and a careless forelock of hair out of his eyes.

7

Leo's face unmasked people. Something of their true natures, he always imagined, was revealed with their first glimpse of it. In some cases, much of their true natures. He paid forensic attention to this initial, unguarded reaction. Nothing was gained that he could precisely measure or, sometimes, even articulate. An instinct, a feel for character, for what an individual might or might not be capable of. Sometimes he got it wrong. Sometimes he didn't even catch that first impression.

The problem with Anna Brennan was that the stunning effect of her distinctive eye colour constituted a mask in itself. Leo found that he couldn't see through that blue he struggled to find a name for. Ultramarine? Cobalt? He knew the blues but he didn't know the shades.

He and Mrs Brennan sat at opposite sides of a long oval table in the library of Attenboy House. Apart from the PC, the expensive sound system and the glass-fronted drinks cabinet, the high-ceilinged room retained its Victorian feel. Walls of book-lined, dark-timbered shelving; a roll-top writing desk; a pair of bath chairs by the black marble fireplace; footstools.

Yet, Leo observed, many of the books were of recent or relatively recent vintage. Anna, he guessed, was the reader, the books being of the kind aimed at the intelligent middle-aged woman. The paintings were hers too, no doubt. Mainie Jellett abstracts, Estella Solomons landscapes.

'Well,' she began in answer to the question that had been hanging in the air for what seemed like an eternity, 'I spent the weekend at our cottage in Passage East. Alone. I left the house here late Friday afternoon. About four o'clock. Daina can confirm this. I dropped her at the railway station on my way.'

No sense of privilege or pretension in the accent. A Midlands flatness to it, a kind of matter-of-factness. No silver spoon there, he thought. Or if there had been a silver spoon, it was a teaspoon rather than a soup ladle. A shopkeeper's daughter maybe, but a small shop. She played with a light pink paper tissue. She hadn't had to use it yet.

'I see,' Leo said.

He didn't tell her that he'd already spoken to the Latvian girl through an interpreter. A trying half hour it had proved too. Daina's reaction to his face had been a rather innocent kind of horror that Leo found himself able to forgive. Unfortunately, the horror soon morphed into fear-filled obstinacy. Added to which, the delay in translation gave her too much time to think between questions.

All the same, he didn't see Daina as a player in some domestic dispute at Attenboy. Questions about her own circumstances bothered her more than those concerning the Brennans. She lived in an apartment in the city with her cousin Sonia and some Latvian friends, had no boyfriend, had a second job in a small food store along the city quays on Bachelor's Walk. She was nineteen, she'd insisted once too often, nineteen. She had something to hide but he doubted it had anything to do with the murder.

'How did you come to hire Daina?' he asked Anna Brennan now.

'Kitty Newman's girl, Sonia – she's Daina's cousin,' Anna said. 'I really don't see that this has anything to do with Daina.'

'Just dotting the ts and all that, Mrs Brennan. And she's been with you how long? Three months?'

'Something like that, yes,' she said. 'I took her on because she needed the work. I never had a, whatever, a housekeeper before this.'

Anna looked out of the long bay window at the silver Mercedes. One of the Technical Bureau team was dusting the steering wheel for prints in the dim light. Another circled the car on all fours, sifting through the pebbles. Beyond the drive, Leo noted, the lawn had been cut, and too tightly. Brown stains spotted the green velvet like cigarette burns on the baize of a snooker table. Whoever cuts grass in November anyway? Someone who knows nothing about gardening. Or someone who wants a carpet for a lawn; someone who still believes you can have a perfect life if the things around you seem perfect.

'We haven't always lived like this, you know,' Anna said. She was still staring out of the window but more distractedly now. 'This house, the car, the help . . .' She faltered. She took up the tissue again, picked at it. 'Twenty years ago we had nothing. Less than nothing. You remember Black Monday in nineteen eighty-seven?'

'Yeah,' Leo said.

'We lived in London back then. Dermot was renovating houses and selling them on. Then the market collapsed and we lost everything. Took us ten years to get back on our feet again. We came back to Ireland in ninety-nine and got lucky. Thought we got lucky. Dermot had plenty of work. We found a nice house in Rathmines and I took over a second-hand bookshop there. Stephen seemed so settled in his school. Everything was so new. But it didn't stay new for long.'

'I'm told your husband and son didn't get on?'

'A simple personality clash, Inspector,' Anna said, plucking the tissue apart. 'Dermot was outgoing, physical, practical. Stephen couldn't be more different. More like me, I suppose.'

'Did you and your husband get on?' Leo asked.

'Not of late.'

Her frankness was disarming. Maybe, Leo thought, too consciously disarming.

'Why is that?'

Tiny shreds of the pink tissue paper had gathered on the polished oak beneath her hands. Fallen cherry blossoms came to mind. Leo looked at her face. Followed its slow passage as she lowered it. A Noh mask, he thought, a Magojiro. The illusion of a changing facial expression depending on your angle of view and all created by the subtle sculpting of the mouth and brow. And by the actor's craft. Anna Brennan would not be an easy woman to fathom. She swept the bits of paper away, gave Leo the full-on azure dazzle.

'Are you married, Inspector?' she asked.

'Was,' he said, unsettled, the long morning weighing upon him. 'Many moons ago.'

'Well, you'll understand then,' she said. 'Our marriage had its ups and downs like everyone else's. And the downs, they can start with some misunderstanding and grow into months of bloody misery. But you always imagine that things will sort themselves out. Assume there'll be enough time to . . .'

She dropped the remnants of the tissue paper, held out her empty hands. Leo had been waiting for her to weaken. Now he felt like a bloodhound, a dirty old dog, but what else was a policeman to do? No wonder he had dog dreams.

'And this misunderstanding,' he said. 'What was it about?'

'Oh, the usual silly stuff.'

'Not a serious marital problem then?' Leo asked more directly still.

The indignation she tried to hide bested her. She punished Leo with a look of contempt.

'We've never gone in for . . . whatever you want to call them . . . *serial affairs* and all that nonsense. We're not that kind of people. We don't entertain, don't move around in these ridiculous glossy-magazine circles. We don't collect friends in high places. None of that.'

'What about enemies? Is there anyone who might have wanted—'

Her sudden laughter startled Leo. His heart began to race unpleasantly. A text rang into his work mobile and sent his pulse further into overdrive. He pressed his fingers into his eyes. He wished he could get the hell home and go to bed. She was still there when he opened his eyes again. Beauty always was. Always waiting around the corner to remind you of what you can never have.

'You're asking me if Dermot had any enemies? He was a builder and a developer, for Christ's sake,' she told Leo. 'A scapegoat for what's happened to this green banana republic.'

'So you believe his death is connected to his business dealings?'

'That's not what I'm saying,' she insisted. 'I don't understand why you're assuming it's some kind of deliberate murder. Couldn't it have been a break-in? Mightn't he have caught someone snooping around the outhouses?'

'I'm not assuming anything, Mrs Brennan,' Leo said. 'When did you last speak to your husband?'

'The last time I saw Dermot was on Thursday evening. Seven o'clock or so,' she said. 'He generally left for work around eight in the morning. I don't get up until nine, half nine.'

'And on Thursday, did he mention anything that might be relevant? Any sense that something was bothering him, anything out of the ordinary at all?'

'We didn't speak, Inspector. That's the terrible thing.' Her head bowed, she cried quietly. 'I can barely remember when we last talked.' She looked up at Leo. Her eyes were still pools reflecting a perfect sky. 'Dermot was a good man. Honourable. Loyal, absolutely loyal. He didn't deserve this.'

Leo knew he couldn't push her too much further. Just a little further. Just a little hunch.

'Did Dermot try to ring you in Passage East, to make up, maybe?' he asked.

The question collapsed her. She lowered her head to her folded arms on the table. Her crying turned to punched sobs, growing in rapidity and depth. A few words escaped now and then, staccato and self-punishing.

'Yes . . . yes . . . but I'd switched off . . . I'd switched off . . . the bloody mobile.'

'Did he text? Leave any messages on your phone?'

She shook her head. Leo waited. Nothing more emerged, nor did she come up for air. He placed a hand tentatively on her shoulder.

'I'm sorry, Mrs Brennan,' he said. 'There's no easy way to go about this.'

No answer came. As he stood up to leave, Leo took note of the PC. Have to have the Technical Bureau take a look at that, see what it might reveal. He wondered if, like the laptop, it too would prove inaccessible.

A crunch of pebbles from outside alerted him to the squad car that had brought him to Howth. It was reversing down the drive and he'd left his overnight bag on the back seat. He didn't want anyone looking through his stuff, the new masks especially. He got up and walked quickly to the library door, closed it and then ran to the open front door. In the glassed-in porch, Helen stood with a tall young man. The son, he supposed. He bore the greenish pallor of sickness but his eyes brightened with prurient fascination when he saw Leo.

'Be back in a minute,' Leo said and shouted at the car. 'My bag! My bloody bag's in the car!'

Down at the entrance to Attenboy, a couple of TV cameras were trained on the house and he ducked back into the porch. Helen tapped him on the shoulder. He turned. She proffered his backpack and a quizzical look.

'My toothbrush,' he explained. 'And . . . you know . . . stuff.'

A loud outbreak of recorded brass and strings from inside the house startled them. They looked at each other; the same question crossed their minds. She's playing music at full blast while her husband's body still lies in the outhouse?

'Mahler,' Stephen Brennan said. 'The Resurrection Symphony.'

The volume suddenly decreased but the music was still loud. Because Leo was tone-deaf it was little more than noise to him. But he followed the words sung by the chorus, hushed as they were.

Aufersteh'n, ja aufersteh'n wirst du,
Mein Staub, nach kurzer Ruhe!

Rise again, yes, you will rise again, my dust, after a brief repose. Tell that to Dermot Brennan, Leo thought.

8

The hall-stand stood directly opposite the open library door. An elaborate darkwood construction, its mirror was almost entirely covered by the coats and jackets hanging there. A long, narrow and unobscured sliver remained. In it, Leo observed Anna Brennan and her son. All the while Helen, her voice as close to a whisper as the interminably crashing finale of the music allowed, filled him in on the brief interview with Stephen Brennan. In the library the whispering was more urgent. Leo studied the reflection of their mime show. The mother questioning, pleading. Her son wary, uncertain. Both of them staring into each other's eyes as though searching for signs of culpability.

'But he refused to tell me who this Sean Doran guy is,' Helen said in conclusion.

'And you reckon Gudrun Remer's lying about his alibi?'

'Just a gut feeling,' Helen said. 'She's implying he slept with her but I'm not so sure.'

'OK,' Leo said. 'By the way, there's a PC in there. Better have it checked out later. Emails, files, whatever.'

'No problem,' Helen said. 'That music, it's a bit weird, isn't it? In the circumstances, I mean.'

'There's no accounting for grief,' Leo said, but didn't add that he spoke from personal experience. With grief. And music.

Helen followed him into the library, notebook ready to hand. Leo turned off the Mahler and the silence seemed as vast as the music had been loud. Over by the oval table, Anna and Stephen held each other, he more loosely than she. They weren't quite in this together, Helen reckoned. They watched Leo as he pretended an interest in the Bang and Olufsen sound system.

'Great set-up this,' he said, leaning in close to the player. 'Does it play those MP3 things too?'

'What kind of ridiculous question is that?' Stephen blurted out. 'My dad . . . my dad's out there . . .'

'Well then, let's try another question instead, son,' Leo said. 'Who's Sean Doran?'

Mother and son looked at each other, then away at the paintings, the bookshelves, and down at the parquet floor, the rectangles of Moroccan carpet. Anna pulled out a chair from the table and sat.

'I shouldn't have mentioned his name, I know,' Stephen told his mother. 'But it had to be him, didn't it?'

The obstinate tone in Stephen's voice felt like the legacy of a spoilt only child. Anna shook her head, less in disagreement than in quiet despair. She steeled herself to speak. Now that she needed a paper hankie, she failed to find one in the sleeves of her cardigan. Stephen appeared to blame himself for her distress but only briefly. He had to be, what? Twenty-two, twenty-three, Leo thought, and he hadn't yet solved the adolescent conundrum as to whether he loved or hated his mother.

'Five years ago,' Anna said, 'Dermot built a housing

scheme in Hearnstown for a group of investors. I'm sure you've heard of the place. One of those new urban centres at the edge of the city. Every amenity, et cetera, et cetera. The future of town planning and all that.'

As Anna Brennan spoke, her son found himself a seat below a Mainie Jellett painting on the other side of the room. They seemed deliberately to avoid eye contact.

'Dermot warned them that the site was on a floodplain. But they persuaded him that a new drainage project was about to get approval and would solve the problem. They came up with reports, test results and whatever else. So he went ahead and did the job. Honeyvale Heights it's called and—'

'You believe all that crap he fed you?' Stephen interjected.

'It's all true, Stephen,' Anna insisted. 'They tricked him into—'

'They?' Leo asked.

'The others . . . the consortium. Anyway, that's not the point. What I'm trying to explain is why Sean Doran was so angry with Dermot, why he made those threats. Not that I believe for one moment that the man had anything to do with this. Don't drag him into it. He's suffered enough already.'

Her voice had cracked. This, Leo thought, was the meat on the bone then.

'So, Sean Doran bought one of these houses,' Leo said. 'And?'

'Late last year the estate was flooded and the houses were badly damaged,' she said. 'And his wife . . . well, his wife had a miscarriage. Stress, they said. And a few months back, a breakdown. She tried to kill herself. She's been hospitalized ever since.'

'It isn't a hospital, Mum,' Stephen said, 'it's a mental institution.'

'And what form did these threats take?' Leo asked, ignoring the young fellow.

'Phone calls mostly,' Anna said. 'He came here once. Five, six weeks ago. Dermot tried to explain his side of the story but all he got was "you'll be sorry you ever built those houses". That kind of thing. Which was understandable, and Dermot understood. Believe me, Inspector, he really did.'

Stephen stood up abruptly, went along by the bookcases as though deciding what to borrow. His mother continued, taking no notice of him.

'Dermot was trying to work something out. Some kind of compensation.'

'Like what?' Stephen put in. 'A new wife maybe? Or some free electro-shock therapy?' He'd ambled across close to Helen and his next question was for her. 'What happened to Dad? How did he die?'

'A blow to the head,' she told Stephen. 'We found a crowbar beside him.'

His mirthless chuckle sent a chill down Helen's spine.

'Did you hear that, Mum?' he said. 'The crowbar. How bloody ironic is that?'

'Stop it, Stephen, please,' his mother said disconsolately.

'Pulling the Bar, he called it,' Stephen told Helen. 'The game was the Brennans' speciality for generations. A tug of war with the crowbar. And Dad never lost. Never lost.'

He pressed his forehead against the books. Their spines bent and crackled under the pressure. He couldn't hurt himself enough so he gave up.

9

Leo often wondered about this obsession with keeping his work desk at the Harcourt Street HQ and, more especially, his house in Ballsbridge so neat and clean. He was inclined to think that because his life in every other sense was such a mess, he needed the comforts of orderliness. House-wise. Work-wise. Already he sensed that the Brennan case might not lend itself to a swift tidy-up.

Most cases were, in reality, quite straightforward, a logic and order easily put on motives and events. Instinct told you when you had a mess on your hands. A mild perturbation unsettled you. Sleep proved elusive. And, deep down, the conviction grew that something had already been missed. Some glaringly obvious detail. Some subtle but instructive nuance.

Tired as he'd been, Leo had done his usual tour of the house in Serpentine Crescent on his return. Checked the alignment of the three rugs along the narrow corridor, the disposition of paperweights and candlesticks on the living-room mantelpiece, the chairs and table on the garden patio. In the front sitting room, he realigned one of the framed James Ensor posters – *Masks Confronting Death* – and Iseult's portrait of him with his back turned, his face averted. He didn't, however, unlock the mask room, nor did he take the new masks from his backpack.

At three in the morning, he gave up on the possibility of natural sleep. Not that his sleep was ever quite natural. Because of the Bell's palsy, his left eye never closed. The very absurdity of sleeping with one eye open often kept him awake. As if it mattered. As if anyone had actually seen him sleep for years now. Besides all of that, there was the prospect of more dog dreams.

When Helen Troy had told him about the dogs at the Argos Sanctuary, Leo was reminded of Charlie Llunga. He'd met the old man in a refugee camp in Angola and they'd struck up a friendship. You have the gift, Charlie used to tell him, but you got to learn to use it. The gift of premonition. Like last night's dog dreams. The trouble with premonition was that it warned you that shit was about to happen but never told you exactly what.

The house, left unheated for five days, had chilled him to the bone and the chill too kept him awake. He popped a sleeper. Relaxed. Waited. So much for the 8.30 a.m. meeting with the super. He'd pretend he hadn't got his text message. Battery down. Something like that. Superintendent Heaphy's bark was worse than his bite anyway. Besides, like any dog who knows you have a stick behind your back he barks merely to recover a little of his self-esteem. They went back a long way. Knew too much about each other. Their relationship was like a game of Snap neither of them could win.

Out at Attenboy House, Leo had tried ringing him but he'd been too busy with the Press Office people to answer. Well past nine it had been as he'd paced the walled garden in the dark. All the while, he had the sense of being in someone's sights. Next door, the modernist monstrosity seemed abandoned to the darkness. Yet, he knew that it was from there that he was being watched. Talk to the neighbour . . . what was her name? Kitty. Talk to Kitty Newman tomorrow, he reminded himself. And Sean Doran.

Detective Sergeant Helen Troy had wanted to head directly to Honeyvale Heights earlier. What if Doran does a runner, she'd protested when he decided against; the story was all over the evening news, wasn't it? She had had to make do with carrying out a background check. Maybe he should've let her go out to Hearnstown and not given in to instinct.

But no. A man driven to distraction by his wife's mental collapse might certainly have killed Dermot Brennan but wouldn't abandon her by doing a runner. And if he had murdered the developer, he'd already had two days to lose himself in. Besides, the kind of reckless passion that had drawn Doran into overt threats seemed to Leo to be absent at the scene of the crime. Yes, there were several blows, but, as the pathologist had noted, no sense of frenzy prevailed and great care seemed to have been taken to leave no traces in the outhouse. A couple of boot prints scuffed expertly over. Nothing touched but the crowbar, of which the grip end was wiped clean. The bruise on Dermot Brennan's left side was, the pathologist confirmed, certainly the result of a kick. But a measured one. And only one.

Sleep continued to resist him. He thought about ringing his supplier for something stronger or maybe something mellower to chill out on, but the last thing he needed now was a slow-motion conversation with Dripsy Scullion. He wandered around the house. Spent a while standing on the first landing, looking down on his cement garden that glittered with frost. Further off was the AIB Bank Centre, bright as a casino with its glow-worms of strip lighting.

He flicked in a desultory way through the papers from the International Mask Conference. *The Mask of the Fool: A Cross-Cultural Study. Lady Gaga, Madonna: the Modern Mask in Popular Culture.* Again, he dismissed the idea of hanging his new purchases in the mask room. Tomorrow maybe, if he could find the time between catching up with Sean Doran and Kitty Newman and tracking down Dermot Brennan's partners in the consortium. And figuring out why the hell Brennan kept a leather satchel containing 59,700 euro in fifty notes in his wardrobe.

Outside, the dawn chorus started up. Soon, the first of the Dart trains would rattle and hum on its track just thirty metres from his house. It was already tomorrow.

Tuesday, 23 November

10

At first, Leo couldn't put his finger on the change in Superintendent Aonghus Heaphy. The angry pallor of the cheeks, the frustrated busyness of the hands and the table-thumping were familiar. All part of the master–servant game they'd played with each other for the best part of thirty years now. Then a few minutes into the lecture on Leo's poor time-keeping, reality dawned. The super couldn't quite close his mouth any more. His teeth were too big. He looked like a man in constant pain who nevertheless found humour in the absurdity of life. Heaphy wasn't that kind of man.

'And another thing. For God's sake, Leo, when you're going somewhere foreign, make it your business to tell us where you're going and—'

'Your teeth,' Leo said.

Suddenly deflated, Heaphy sank back in his swivel chair, turned himself a few degrees east of Leo.

'Damn it,' he said. 'Are they that obvious?'

'Not at all.' Leo took another look at the row of ceramic tombstones in the super's mouth and thought he'd better offer more encouragement. 'You're a new man. Did you get them in Budapest?'

'Some town outside Budapest. I couldn't even pronounce the name *before* I got the teeth.' The superintendent put a hand to his mouth and grimaced. 'I'm in agony. And this cold weather isn't helping.'

'Takes time to get used to new dentures,' Leo assured him. 'And you can always go back and get a new set, can't you?'

Heaphy glanced up distrustingly at Leo, watching for signs of sarcasm.

'They're not dentures. They're bolted into my gums.'

Leo squirmed at the thought of all that drilling into the bone beneath the gum, imagined waking up to the pain of the aftermath.

'Why did you put yourself through it, Aonghus?'

'They told me my teeth clicked and clacked when I spoke in public,' the superintendent said.

'They?'

'The powers that be,' Heaphy said, glancing at the ceiling. 'There'll be a lot more television and radio to do if I get this promotion, you know. They said I'd have to sharpen up my act, so . . .'

'Ah.' Leo smiled. 'Speaking of politics, what's the story with the Brennan case? I hear one of our Junior Ministers is running scared?'

'There's no political angle to the Brennan case.' Heaphy swung back to face Leo. His teeth bared, he looked like a demented chimpanzee. While his mouth widened, his eyes narrowed. 'Not exactly. Who've you been talking to?'

Superintendent Heaphy was a true proponent of justice. Always looking for someone to hang. Leo said nothing.

'This business of the threats to Brennan,' Heaphy said.

'This Sean Doran fellow. We shouldn't be jumping to conclusions there. The fact is his wife already had psychiatric
problems before this flooding business. And she'd had a
previous miscarriage. So . . .'

'You've been a busy boy, haven't you? You found out all
this since you got back from Budapest last night?'

'Leo, my mouth is sore, I may have to get these teeth re-
done and the Junior Minister's on my back. So spare me the
wisecracks, will you?' The superintendent passed a hand
along the two outcrops of grey hair above his ears. 'Listen,
this group that Brennan built the houses out in Hearnstown
for. The Junior Minister's first cousin is involved. Pat Foley.
He's an auctioneer and mortgage consultant. He has a number of sub-offices but you'll find him in the Hearnstown
branch today.'

'So you've already made an arrangement with him, have
you, Aonghus?'

'No,' Superintendent Heaphy said. 'Here's a list of the
others in the group.'

Heaphy picked up an A4 page from his desk and studied
it. His ponderous delay was meant to underline the docu-
ment's importance, its confidential nature, such things.
Leo watched the clock. Half past ten already. Should've told
Helen to head out and track down Sean Doran. Don't let me
down by doing a runner, Doran, he thought.

He stood up, caught the super off guard.

'Where're you going? I'm not finished yet,' Heaphy said.

'Hundred and one things to do, Aonghus,' Leo told him.
'Have to see Doran, the Brennans again, the neighbour
and . . .' The gardener if there is one, he thought, catching
himself off guard this time. What was I thinking? Never
asked Anna Brennan if she hired someone to cut the grass,

trim the leylandii along the boundary of Attenboy House, tend the walled garden. 'And the boys on your list there.'

He leaned over and swept the page from Heaphy's hand. The door-handle was within reach of Leo's hand before the super found his voice.

'One of these days, Leo, you'll push me too far,' he said.

Leo thought he saw a flash of that old resentment in Heaphy's eyes. He hoped it was just his imagination. He hated to be reminded of that long-ago betrayal of his colleague.

'I'm putting Detective Garda Murphy on the team with you for this one, Leo. Great young lad. Destined for glory.' Heaphy was aware of the antipathy between Leo and the young man. 'And keep the new girl,' he added. 'That's fair enough, isn't it?'

Leo nodded. Sometimes he wondered if the young fellow had become, for Heaphy, the son he and his wife Mary had never had. He had to admit, at least to himself, that Ben Murphy was good. Energetic, a mind for patterns and logic, a cool head. Yet, Leo had never taken to him. He didn't quite know why. It wasn't the law degree or the fact that his father was a District Justice or the snappy suits or the unblemished face or the ironic distance in him . . . Or maybe it was all those things, all those advantages, all those prospects. And the fact that the young fellow had something Leo hadn't had for years.

A future.

The brisk half-hour walk from Glasnevin into Harcourt Street had left Detective Sergeant Helen Troy heavy-legged and in foul humour. She was badly out of shape. Three months of Chinese take-aways, cheap Chardonnays and no regular exercise had taken its toll. She wondered if she should go back to playing football again. Find a club here in Dublin. Or was she already too old for that, her best years spent trying to negotiate the slippery ladder of a male-dominated force? Maybe she could follow her father's footsteps and work towards a coaching cert? She'd have plenty of time on her hands now that Ricky had bailed out. His excuse, ironically, being that she spent so little time with him. The reality being, more than likely, that he'd found himself another bed to sleep in. She was glad to be busy.

Clocking in before seven, she'd driven out to Howth with Sergeant Martha Corrigan and set up the NBCI stall in the Incident Room. In truth, this involved little more than connecting half a dozen laptops and phones and hauling in a couple of flip-chart stands. Still, it had distracted her almost to the point of cheerfulness. So cheerful that she'd dared bring up the subject of Detective Inspector Woods as they worked.

'Why didn't you warn me what to expect when I met Leo?' she asked with a mock offendedness that put the ex-Rose of Tralee on the back foot. Then she pressed her advantage. 'How long has he had this Bell's palsy?'

'Eight, nine years.'

She could tell that Martha immediately regretted the revelation. She looked annoyedly at Helen, blaming her.

'I'm sorry, I shouldn't have asked,' Helen said.

The tall woman shook her head and sighed. She set another flip-chart on its easel.

'No one's sure of the exact details but it happened in Bosnia,' she said, then glanced over at Helen. 'This is strictly between ourselves, OK?'

'Of course.'

'Story is the UN had located this Bosnian Serb guy who

was on the wanted list for war crimes. Leo was called in because he knew the territory from his time there in the war. On the morning of the operation, someone noticed this odd twitch in Leo's eye. They wanted him to get it checked out but he insisted on taking his place in the operation. Which would have been fine if things had gone smoothly.'

'What happened?'

'The Serbs had been tipped off,' Martha explained. 'The unit was attacked and Leo got separated from the others in some deep forest area. No one knows whether he was taken hostage or got lost. He doesn't talk about it. One way or another, it was too late to do anything about the palsy when he showed up a week or so later.'

'How awful,' Helen said.

'Yeah. The strange thing is though that before all of this, Leo was the last man you could imagine feeling sympathy for. He was distant, full of himself, totally obnoxious actually. Now he's . . . well, put it this way, Leo has his idiosyncrasies but you won't meet a better guy to work with.' Martha's was the smile of happy memories. 'Grab yourself a seat now before someone else hangs their jacket on it. That plastic one in Leo's office must be a killer.'

Helen's own difficulties seemed less than tragic compared to Leo's. This thought and the cushioned chair she sat down on were small comforts but comforts nonetheless.

She'd been on the PC and the phone ever since. Not that her low-level access to the Pulse computer system had much to offer on Sean Doran beyond some traffic offences. Three speeding fines and one dangerous driving conviction two years before. Nothing since then.

From among the details, she discovered that he worked as a hotel maintenance man – though not in which hotel –

was thirty-one years old and drove a souped-up Fiesta. *Silver blue with customized white stripes,* the notes read. An ageing boy racer, in other words. Or a boy racer who'd had to grow up fast when his troubled wife introduced him to the more terrifying thrills and spills of real life.

When Helen had rung Lucan Garda Station, the closest one to Hearnstown, hoping for some further background on Doran, they promised to ring back. While she waited, Helen tried the numbers of hotels in the area from the list she'd drawn up. One after the next yielded nothing. Zombie hotels for the most part, built for the tax breaks they provided. As she put the phone down on yet another eternal ringing tone, the Incident Room door opened. Detective Sergeant Cooney cooed at the threshold.

'Ah, the new girl,' he said, somehow making the phrase sound vaguely offensive. 'Any sign of Leo yet?'

'I haven't seen him,' she said. 'But I've been stuck here all morning on the phone, so . . .'

Cooney squinted down at his watch, made some inscrutable calculation. Helen's work mobile rang. Lucan Garda Station. She recognized the voice at once. Brian O'Riordan, a classmate from Garda College and a decent type.

'Brian, how's it going? Yeah, settling in, you know. You have something for me? Great. The Hearnstown Regency Hotel? Closed in January? He's on the dole then? And what did the wife work at – I mean, how did they pay the mortgage? Ah, same hotel. So they really were landed in the shit when it closed.'

She savoured Cooney's irritated attempt at eavesdropping. He was the kid in kindergarten who wanted one of your sweets but you knew you'd never get one of his.

'Which means they lost their jobs, what, two months after the flooding?' Helen went on. 'Doran's got a lot to be angry about then, hasn't he? Do you reckon he's angry enough to . . . ? Yeah, I probably would be. Great, well . . . No, I hung up the boots, Brian.'

Detective Sergeant Cooney looked askance at her.

'Yeah, cheers.'

While she'd been speaking, Leo had entered the room so quietly that Helen hadn't heard him. The phone dropped from her hand when he spoke and proved slippery as a fish as she tried to return it to its cradle. She hated making an arse of herself like that. A young man stepped out from behind Leo, compounding her embarrassment.

'Right, lads,' Leo said. 'Better get things moving here. Helen, this is Detective Garda Ben Murphy.'

He was tall and dark-haired, trim and honey-tanned. His charcoal grey suit had an expensive cut about it. His handshake was cursory and damp. He gave the impression of having more important, more serious things on his mind. He either liked himself a lot or disliked other people a lot. It was hard to tell which. Something sombre about the eyes though, tired, as though he worked too much, or work meant too much to him.

'How are you, Helen?' Polite though, and oddly formal for a guy in his mid to late twenties.

Leo allowed no time for a reply. He launched into a series of instructions for each of them. Cooney, the local man, was to coordinate the local door-to-door enquiries and check out any recent break-ins. His team was also to follow up on the other members of the Honeyvale Heights consortium, see if any of them had been threatened, advise them on security precautions. The Junior Minister's auctioneering cousin Leo kept for himself.

'And we need more on the Brennans' background,' he continued. 'Where they're from, how long they've been in Howth, who doesn't like them, what they have for breakfast, everything, right? And see what you can dig up on their financial situation. Chances are he's stony broke. Find out what he owes and who he owes, that kind of thing. And talk to the people who worked for him. See what they made of him.'

Ben's task was to liaise with the Technical Bureau and the pathologist's office, make contact with the Latvian girl, Daina, set up another interview with her for this afternoon. Helen waited for her instructions. There weren't any.

'Right then,' he concluded. 'The super's holding a press conference at half past three. We'll meet back here at, say, two thirty and see what we've got.'

She felt stupidly jealous of Ben Murphy as he left the Incident Room. She was the more senior officer after all.

'I'm afraid you'll have to put up with me for the day, Helen,' Leo said.

11

Honeyvale Heights was the pits. An unfinished development of sixty houses, only a very few of which were occupied. Empty shells in the main, their timbers rotting greyly, window panes smashed. The roads had been left unfinished. Streetlight stanchions stood hollow, no globes at their peaks only the forked snake's tongue of unconnected wires. Everywhere were pools of stagnant water, high weeds and broken glass. Any fool seeing the great clusters of reeds in the adjoining fields would have known that the place was a floodplain.

'Honeyvale Heights,' Leo said. 'Great name for a hell-hole, isn't it?'

Helen Troy felt too depressed to answer, reminded as she was of her own situation. At least her riverbank apartment down in Tipperary stood in a completed and, more or less, fully occupied complex. And her floor was high enough off the ground not to have been affected when the river burst its banks last winter. However, the same stinking atmosphere of entrapment, of having somehow been cheated, prevailed. She'd never have thought she'd ever feel sorry for a boy racer, but looking at the dusty Fiesta in the sinking tarmac drive of No. 8 Honeyvale Heights, she did.

Along the abandoned street, only one other house had a car parked out front. All of the house-fronts were stained filthily up to the level of the ground-floor windowsills. Slowly it dawned on Helen. The sills measured precisely the high-water mark of the floods. She looked at Leo. His ill-favoured side. He was wiping an unbidden tear in that rough way he had. Why, she wondered, did he always seem to be punishing himself for something that was out of his control?

'Jesus wept,' Leo said as he opened the car door to be met by the sickening stench of raw sewage. 'If Sean Doran didn't kill Brennan, he's a bloody saint.'

The deepening cold attached itself to his flesh, dug beneath it. Only now did Leo realize he was still wearing the linen suit from yesterday. He hoped the shiver he felt inside him was just down to the weather and not those damn parasites stirring in his liver again.

A dog barked sporadically in the distance, amplifying the bleakness. The two police officers dodged puddles, jagged cracks and dogshit on the paving that led to Sean Doran's front door. The tax and insurance discs on the blue Fiesta were out of date. Leo wondered if Doran still brought it out on the road. He placed a hand on the bonnet. The metal sent a warm, pleasant wave through him that the cold air soon chased off.

As they neared the front door, Helen's attention was drawn back to the car. Something didn't quite gel. The number on the licence plate? No. Not the absence of the front left hubcap either. Something else that she couldn't put a finger on.

She caught up with Leo. There was no bell to ring, no door knocker to sound. Leo knuckled the PVC frame. Echoing footsteps in no great hurry advanced from inside.

'You're the police, I suppose, are you?' The young man's voice was sluggish, drugged perhaps, his tired expression unfazed by Leo's looks. Everything about him was a mess. Unwashed hair, sleep-wrinkled tracksuit, oily hands. 'Took youse long enough to find me.'

Leo and Helen's senses were assaulted by the vapours of a stench more insidious than that of the sewage. Something more corrupted, more pervasive, more likely to linger in your nostrils for days, maybe weeks. Helen knew the smell. When the ground floor of her building had been flooded twice back in the winter months, that smell had become one in her mind with her father's slow death. It crept in upon her now.

'Sean Doran?' Leo said. The young man nodded. Short, compact, stronger perhaps than at first sight he'd appeared. Leo showed him his ID. 'Detective Inspector Woods. And this is Detective Sergeant Troy. Can we come in?'

Doran led them into the front room. A living room, Helen guessed, though it contained nothing apart from a large flat-screen TV, a white-painted steel garden chair at the centre of the room and an overflowing ashtray. Damp stains created a map of some forbidding world on the bare floorboards. Take away the TV and you had the minimalist stage set for a Beckett play. Doran sat on the chair. It felt like an invitation to interrogate him. On second thoughts, Helen decided, the set for a Tarantino movie. The same tide mark she'd seen outside soiled the four walls of the room.

When Doran began to speak unbidden it sounded like a justification.

'I seen it on the news this morning. The house in Howth. Weird how the place looked more real on the telly. The big house, the Mercedes, the perfect garden. Probably some celebrity gardener done it. And every last bleedin' cent of it came out of our pockets. He deserved what he got. They all do.' He looked up at them, a smile on his face but not in his eyes. 'Maybe the revolution starts here, what d'ye reckon?'

A bright inner-city kid who'd come up in the world but not far enough to avoid getting sucked back down again fast.

'Where were you Friday night, Saturday morning, Sean?' Leo asked.

The young man laughed, turned his attention from them to the bare walls surrounding him.

'Over there, she had a four-seater couch,' he said with a nodding gesture. 'Leather, sort of a tan colour. And there was these controls to move the leg-rests up and down.' He did the actions. Pressed an imaginary button, raised his feet slowly from the ground. People crack in different ways, Leo knew. 'Cost three thousand euro but she loved it, she loved to lie there and . . . and along under the window there, we had this deadly sound system. Speakers up each side of the window. Something else, man, the sound of Snoop Dogg blasting out of them things.'

How romantic, Helen thought: an evening by the fire with a sexist rapper.

Doran looked at them again, but not as though he saw them.

'We were nearly there,' he said. 'Another couple of years and it would have got easier to pay for all this stuff, and we'd have had a good life. Then the hotel closes overnight and we don't even get the last pay-cheque.' He mussed up his untidy hair, careless of the greasy slick on his hand. 'If she'd had the child there might've been something, you know, something to hold on to. But she lost that too and it wrecked her head.'

'Friday night, Sean, where were you?' Leo asked again. 'Saturday morning?'

'Where was I? Let's see. Well, I went to dinner at L'Écrivain restaurant – champagne and snails, that kind of shit. And then I went over to the Shelbourne Hotel to meet some of my celebrity pals, and after a few bottles of red we headed off to Lillie's Bordello. VIP section of the night club, needless to say, and—'

'Did you kill Dermot Brennan?' Leo knew there was no easy way to stop the young man's rambling, jokey grief. He didn't like himself for having to cut to the chase but the smell of the house was getting to him.

'No way, man,' Doran said. 'Friday evening after I got back from visiting Lisa-Marie, I watched telly until around four in the morning. Drank a slab of some old piss from Lidl and got up, I don't know, three, four o'clock Saturday afternoon. And, before you ask, no, no one saw me because there's no one here but me. Not here in this house, not in this whole Godforsaken avenue.'

'Isn't there a car parked outside one of the houses opposite?' Helen said.

The flash of anger was brief but Helen noted it. She noted too that his tone was different with her than it had been with Leo. More aggressive, more bitterness in it.

'That's a repossessed car sitting in front of a repossessed house, love,' he said. 'Go and check it out if you don't believe me.'

'We need to take a look around the house, Sean, if that's OK with you,' Leo said, taking the heat off Helen. If Doran was going to blow up, it was better he blew up on Leo.

'For what?'

'Just routine, you know,' Leo said.

'Don't you need a warrant to do that?' Doran said.

'Technically, yes.'

Doran's momentary tetchiness evaporated. He shook his head, looked down at the palms of his hands. The lines of life and love and other destinies sullied with black oil.

'Look all you want,' he said. 'There's nothing here. We have nothing. Not a bleedin' thing do we own here.'

Leo gestured silently at Helen to take the upstairs rooms. She headed out into the hallway, began to slip on some latex gloves as she climbed the steps. Sometimes, she thought, you knew you were going to find something. At the landing window, she looked down at the Fiesta on the drive. At once, she saw what she'd missed earlier. The white stripes, mentioned in the case details on the Pulse computer system, had been sprayed over. Why?

Left alone with Doran, Leo drew out his cigarettes, offered him one, did the lighting up.

'When you went to visit your wife on Friday, did you drive to the hospital?' Leo asked.

'I don't use the car any more.'

Doran's right foot tricked around, finding little clumps of cigarette ash to scuff. He tried to give the impression that the task took all his attention.

'Listen, Sean,' Leo said, 'I'm not investigating traffic offences here, tax, insurance, all that stuff, right? So, be straight with me. We know you've threatened Dermot Brennan in the past, we know you've been to the house. Help me out here, Sean. Tell me why I shouldn't regard you as a suspect.'

The sound of Helen's feet crossing and recrossing the room directly above them bothered Doran. His jawbones were in lockdown, his teeth clenched.

'The engine's warm out there,' Leo said. 'Your hands are covered in motor oil. One and one is two, right, Sean?'

Doran stood up sharply. The steel chair tumbled and rang out and he helped it along with a kick. Upstairs, the footsteps came to an abrupt halt.

'I start up the car every day so's it won't fall asunder,' Doran said. 'My hands are like this because I'm trying to fix our oil-fired central heating so's I won't die of bloody hypothermia when this cold blast they keep warning us about comes along. Probably be better off if I did cop it. They say there's no pain when the ice gets you.'

He went to the door and out into the hallway. Leo followed. Short but bullish strides carried Doran along to a foul-smelling kitchen. Some new odour added itself to the mix of sewage and sour damp. Rotting food maybe. No, something dead – a mouse, perhaps. Or a rat. How in Christ's name does he live here? Leo thought. Then again, what choice did the poor bastard have? Beyond the kitchen was a utility room, its floor-to-ceiling shelving packed with the detritus of damaged possessions. And a central heating unit, its body parts spread across cracked floor tiles whose grouting had turned to dust.

'OK?' Doran said, pointing at the mess, white with anger but managing to keep a lid on it. Just. 'And you want to know how I get to the mental home, yeah? I walk into Hearnstown. It takes twenty minutes, give or take. Then I wait for a bus to the city centre. I'm there if I'm lucky in an hour. I get another bus out to Lisa-Marie. That's three quarters of an hour. And then it's vice fucking versa all the way home. I leave the house at five and I make it back in the door around midnight. Does that answer your question?'

While Doran spoke, Leo noticed on the shelf behind him

a tangled collection of beribboned medals and some cheap trophies, the faux-silver flaking off from the lone boxers atop them.

'Do you still box, Sean?' he asked. 'Great game. Did a bit of it myself back the years.'

The young man sized up Leo's frame sceptically.

'You don't have to tell me,' Leo said. 'I couldn't box my way out of a paper bag now. What weight did you fight at? Bantam?'

'Yeah.'

'Southpaw?'

'How did you know?'

Leo nodded towards the cigarette Doran held in his left hand. The boxer turned away, pretended an interest in the old trophies. Leo hadn't yet decided whether Doran's earlier outbursts were by way of camouflage. He knew this one was.

'That lot didn't do me any favours either, the boxing crowd. No way should I have lost the national final. An Olympic year too it was. I could've gone to Sydney, I could've . . . Only the once ever did I get to box for my country. One miserable green singlet was all I ever got for my trouble.'

Helen surprised them both, seeming to materialize in the doorway without a sound. She held out a digital camera so that Leo could see the photograph on its screen.

'Anna Brennan,' Leo said, and Helen nodded.

'There's more,' she told him.

81

12

When the back-up team arrived, Helen escorted Sean Doran to Howth Garda Station. Leo headed for Pat Foley's auctioneering sub-office in the centre of Hearnstown. Already this new urban centre looked like some redundant vision of a future that had turned out rather differently than expected. As futures always do, Leo mused. Twenty acres of glass and steel fleetingly captured the passage of clouds across a thousand acres of grey sky. The buildings were of the off-the-shelf kind, devoid of individual personality or imagination or any other worthwhile values. Like their makers. He drove by an empty shopping centre, a vacated hairdressing salon. The streets were similarly devoid of life. A rusting ten-year-old Audi sat on four cement blocks, its stolen wheels as distant a memory as the brochure promises of the developers.

He caught a brief glimpse of two women wearing chador veils and pushing prams as he steered his way into the main street where the sub-office stood. Further along, he saw three young women, two of them pretty and one very beautiful, lightly dressed for a different country in a different season.

Up ahead to the right, a squad car was parked below a sign declaring Foley and Son – Estate Agents, Auctioneers and Valuers. Leo hadn't ordered the official protection on the office. So it had to have been Superintendent Heaphy. By order of the Junior Minister, no doubt. Framed in a window above the office signage, a fat man in a black suit and a head full of gypsy black hair talked into his hand. Personal security. The auctioneer really was running scared then. Of Sean Doran? And, if not, of whom?

Next door to Foley's office stood a permanently shuttered turf accountants, RaceFair. You knew a country was fucked, Leo thought, when even the bookies closed up shop.

'Detective Sergeant Helen Troy commencing interview with Mr Sean Doran at one fifty-five p.m. Also present is Garda Pacelli Dempsey. Before we talk about your relationship with Dermot Brennan, can you confirm that this is your—'

'My *relationship*? He ruined my life, he put Lisa-Marie in the madhouse. That's the sum total of our *relationship*.'

'You threatened Mr Brennan. You called to his house.'

'Too right I threatened him. Wouldn't you? But I didn't kill him. I'm glad he's dead but I didn't kill him.'

'We have reason to believe that Mr Brennan wanted to work something out in relation to your mortgage, help you out. Is that the case?'

'That lot don't do charity.'

'Did he offer some kind of pay-out, some kind of financial assistance?'

'You're taking the piss, right?'

'OK. Is this your camera, Mr Doran?'

'No.'

'The camera was found in a box of CDs under your bed.'

'I told you, it's not mine.'

'So how did it get there?'

'Probably Santa Claus got pissed and mixed up the months.'

'Where were you on Friday night and during the early hours of Saturday morning?'

'I already told that ugly bastard back at the house.'

'And now you're going to tell me.'

'Go and shite.'

'That's enough of that talk, Doran. Answer the detective sergeant's question.'

'Are you screwing her, you muck savage? Is she any good?'

'You little—'

'Try her. They're all whores anyway. Especially the ones in uniform.'

'Mr Doran, when you're finished playing your boring little macho game, you might tell me why you resprayed your car. Were you trying to make it less identifiable so that you could drive out to Howth more anonymously?'

'I was trying to sell it. Stripes isn't everyone's cup of tea.'

'Where did you advertise it for sale? Newspapers? Internet?'

'I had a sign on the back window.'

'It's not there now.'

'The wind must've blown it away.'

'When did you have the car resprayed, Mr Doran?'

'I can't remember.'

'See if this photo helps. I take it you recognize yourself here standing beside a blue Fiesta with white stripes along the doors?'

'That's my twin brother. Identical, aren't we?'

'You don't have a brother, Mr Doran. You have three sisters.'

'Must be one of them in drag then.'

'The photo was taken on October twenty-seventh. That's less than a month ago. Who took the photo?'

'Answer her question, Doran.'

'Shut the fuck up, you lump of culchie dung.'

'Did you take the photo yourself, Mr Doran? . . . Mr Doran refuses to answer the question. And this photo was taken the following day. That's Dermot Brennan's house, isn't it? . . . OK. Can you tell me, Mr Doran, why you've got three photos of Mrs Anna Brennan on your camera? . . . No? . . . One at Attenboy House, another at the post office and a third in a café down at the harbour. Why? . . . Why, Mr Doran?'

'Silly bitch.'

'Me or Mrs Brennan? . . . Mr Doran refuses to answer. OK, these other photos then. Stephen Brennan leaving Attenboy House. And this one, Stephen at the Argos Sanctuary with a Ms Gudrun Remer. What are all these paparazzi shots about, Mr Doran?'

'Don't get smart with me. Hear me? I'll smash your pretty little—'

'Back away from her. Sit down on the chair, Doran.'

'Shut up, you big heap of—'

'Sit down on the chair, Doran. Sit down on the chair.'

'Just quit hassling me, will you? You're doing my skull in. I can't get that face out of my head.'

'Whose face, Mr Doran?'

'Sit down on the chair. Sit down on the chair.'

'That fucking face. Looking at me. Looking.'

'On the chair, Doran. Not on the floor.'

'Whose face?'

'Leave me alone. I can't take any more of this . . . this . . .'

'Interview with Mr Doran terminated . . .'

'I keep seeing his face, every time I close my eyes I see his face.'

'. . . at two fifteen p.m.'

13

Disgust. Not a sound basis for a relationship. Especially when it's mutual.

Leo sat opposite a squat, well-dressed man in his late fifties. His receding hair was too lustreless a black to be real and his skin too orange and oddly rubbery. His smiling mouth took up too much of his face. He looked like a man wearing a Silvio Berlusconi latex head mask. Not a pretty sight. Pat Foley, on the other hand, glanced with irritation at a wrinkled Hong Kong linen suit and a face that, from the off, had clearly reminded him of his own inner ugliness.

'I really can't imagine that Dermot's death has any connection to our company,' he said, swinging idly from side to side on his swivel chair. 'I mean, of course it's deeply upsetting on a personal level to lose a former colleague, but, really, my cousin's overreacted sending out a squad car to watch the place here.'

'Made your own security arrangements too, didn't you?' Leo asked, pointing at the ceiling.

'He's a client,' Foley said, and looked ostentatiously at his watch like his time was more valuable than Leo's. 'As a matter of fact, we've a meeting in five minutes.'

When the auctioneer's secretary had rung the inner office a few minutes earlier, Leo heard the slide of a bolt before Foley had emerged. He looked at the door now, saw a freshly screwed-in bolt and a little cluster of fresh shavings on the floor.

'Do you know Sean Doran?' he asked.

'The fellow you're taking into custody?' Foley said. 'Yes, I believe I do. Not in any personal sense, I mean. He was a customer, a client.'

Leo was surprised neither that the auctioneer had already been passed the information nor that he wanted to let Leo know how close his ear was to the ground. More significantly, it was clear that despite Doran's detention, Foley didn't yet feel safe enough to relax his security. For now, Leo kept his focus on the boxer. Whether or not Doran had killed Dermot Brennan, Leo felt sure he had some part to play in the story.

'Has he made any threats to you in the past?'

'No.'

'He's never approached you about the flooding problems at Honeyvale Heights?'

'Yes, he has.'

'And?'

'And I explained my limited role in the construction process,' Foley said. 'I told him how I'd been making every effort to have the drainage system completed as it should have been in the first place.'

'And he was satisfied with your . . . your explanations?'

'Hardly satisfied, Mr Woods. But appreciative of my efforts, yes.'

Leo began to sense what the auctioneer was up to. Hanging a dead man. He followed that slippery gaze, silently challenged Foley to look him straight in the eye. Foley tried. And slithered away again among some papers he tinkered with on his desk.

'Was he appreciative of Dermot Brennan's efforts?'

'What do you mean?'

'Sean Doran, so you tell me, was happy that you were doing the best you could for him in the circumstances, right? Was he happy that Dermot Brennan was doing his best?'

The answer was slow in coming. Even Judas, Leo supposed, had hesitated a moment or two before fingering Jesus. Probably shrugged too, like Foley did now, raised his palms outwards in a gesture of exculpation before folding them back into prayerfulness.

'What can I say? Honeyvale Heights was basically Dermot's project from day one. We were in, but he drove it.' Foley paused. 'But all that being said, I'm convinced that whatever happened to Dermot was . . . well, more than likely an intruder and Dermot confronting him. That'd be Dermot's style. I mean, in the sense that he wasn't one to back off in a fight.'

'Honeyvale Heights was Mr Brennan's project?' Leo said. 'Not everyone thinks so. In fact, my information is that he was dead set against the scheme, that he'd warned the rest of you the site was on a floodplain.'

'Your information is wrong.'

'We've good reason to believe there may be documented proof of Brennan's objections,' he bluffed.

The effect was spectacular. A vampire couldn't have sucked the blood out of the auctioneer so fast, Leo thought. Foley held on to the edge of his desk. His voice, when he responded, was defiant but tremulous.

'All you need to do, Inspector, is ask the other board

directors. They'll tell you the same story. This was Dermot's baby.'

'I bet they will,' Leo said, and switched his point of attack. 'Where were you late Friday night, early Saturday morning last, Mr Foley?'

Leo had expected a display of offendedness. Instead, he got, in quick succession, a sneer and a leer.

'My wife and I spent the weekend golfing in Connemara, Inspector,' Foley said. 'With my cousin, the Junior Minister, among others. I'm sure he'll verify that if you care to ask him.'

Meaning if you *dare* to ask him, Leo thought. He let his irritation subside, let the moments pass, let the auctioneer imagine they'd reached a stalemate.

'Right then, are there any other clients who've threatened you, or rather who are appreciative of your efforts in getting them out of the water? So to speak.'

'Don't take that tone with me, Inspector,' Foley warned. 'I've spent twenty-five years providing good, solid homes for people. Have I had complaints? Yes, I have. Everyone who deals with the public has had them. I'm damn well sure you do. Self-pitying whiners with no sense of personal responsibility, the most of them. And yes, of course they complain when their houses get flooded, but all of our schemes have gone through the planning process; the plans we submit have always met the most stringent standards.'

'But the plans you submit aren't always, let's say, followed through by the builders,' Leo said. 'Is that what you're saying? You're saying that Dermot Brennan was cutting corners, yeah?'

Foley did his Judas thing again. The shrug. The palms up. The prayerful steeple of fingers. Leo stared at the bolt on the door, let his gaze fall slowly towards the shavings on the floor, turned and looked at Foley.

'You've a new bolt on the door, Mr Foley. Looks like it went on today. If it's not some disillusioned customer, who is it you're afraid of?'

'Do you really imagine that bolt would keep a killer out?' Foley sneered. 'Yes, we've got disillusioned customers, customers who were crazy enough to take out loans they couldn't afford, customers who blame me for everything. Everything. They'll blame me for this Arctic weather when it comes too, when their pipes freeze, when they slip on their front paths and break their bones. These are emotional people, Inspector, living in emotional times and they pester me in here from time to time, but they're not killers. A bloody nuisance but not killers.'

'So, it's basically a pest control thing, is it?' Leo said. 'OK then, you're one hundred per cent certain you've nothing to fear from your customers. Which could only mean, *one*, that you know for sure it was an intruder who killed Dermot Brennan. Which is kind of unlikely, right, unless you were the intruder, or sent the intruder in?'

'How dare you accuse me of—'

'*Two*. You know for sure the murder was personal, domestic, whatever you like to call it. Again unlikely. *Three*. You know it wasn't an intruder and that it wasn't domestic because you know exactly who the killer actually is. Am I wrong? Am I missing something here?'

While Foley tried to cut his way through the brambles of Leo's logic, Leo took in the surroundings. The guy lived, no doubt, in some tastefully renovated manse much like the Brennans, but this office was probably a truer reflection of his soul. Or his lack of same. Banality incarnate, it seemed to Leo. An indifferent magnolia coloured the walls. MDF shelves and cabinets tricked up to look like mahogany. Faux-leatherbound *Reader's Digest* compendiums for that bookish effect. On the wall, one decoration: a large Ordnance Survey map of the Dublin area, fields and sites highlighted in dayglo pinks and yellows and greens. Most of us, Leo reflected, scratch around here at ground level. But these people? He looked at Foley. These people scratch around in the sky above us. Like vultures.

'I thought they put you on the case because you're discreet,' Foley said, disgruntled, unsettled.

Leo felt one of his Eric Cantona moments coming on.

'No, they put me on the case because I'm an old dog with nothing to lose. And I might shit all over the field but I'll find that bone and I'll find who buried it and I'll find out why, and when I do I'll chew him up and spit out the pieces.'

14

All twelve seats around the conference table had been claimed. Half a dozen or so uniformed officers stood, some as if to attention, others leaning against the walls. Halfway down the table, Detective Sergeant Helen Troy looked like she'd been crying. Leo felt a stab of guilt. Dempsey stood directly behind her, a bruise below his right eye turning into a real shiner. Detective Sergeant Cooney had grabbed himself a seat and divided his prurient attention between Helen and Martha Corrigan. Only Detective Garda Ben Murphy was missing. Leo looked forward to giving the fellow a polite bollocking when he arrived.

'OK then, bit of hush, please,' Leo said. 'So, this is where we stand. Dermot Brennan, builder and developer, aged fifty-six, six foot two, sixteen stone or thereabouts. A big man. Can't have been easy to take down. Not without a large slice of strength. Or luck.' He stood up and turned to the map of Howth on the wall behind. 'The victim lived here. Attenboy House. Electronically controlled front gates, an alarm system that wasn't in operation and no CCTV cameras on-site. Access to the grounds isn't difficult. A tree-lined border with the next house and no fencing. On the other side, an eight-foot wall flanking a public laneway. To the rear, a garden wall same height more or less. Out behind, a walking path. Below the path, the land slopes down to the sea and is covered in gorse and heather. It's pretty rough terrain and not likely to have been used by the killer. We're searching it anyway so's to rule it out more definitively.'

He went on to describe the murder site, the modus operandi, the estimated time of death, the absence so far of more detailed forensic evidence. As he spoke, he began to feel oppressed by the sense of lethargy in the Incident Room. The heating was on full blast because the cold outside was nearing full blast. Someone yawned, someone else sighed heavily.

'Right then, our main candidate for now is Sean Doran,' Leo continued. 'He lives in one of those ghost estates that Brennan and his pals built. Honeyvale Heights they call it, but there's precious little sweetness out there and shag-all elevation. The houses are wrecked from flood damage. Doran and his wife lost their jobs and couldn't keep up the mortgage. Then she loses the baby she was expecting. She's in a psychiatric hospital from the stress of it all.'

Someone had opened a window and Leo talked above the mutterings in the audience.

'Apart from the Doran angle, there are three other possibilities we need to investigate. First, a burglary gone wrong. We're looking at the pattern of burglaries out there – if there is one – any recent incidents of burglary with assault, any suspects that might fit the bill.'

Helen religiously noted down everything Leo said. She might have done so anyway, but in this instance her note-taking was an excuse to lower her reddened eyes and to distract herself from her incompetence. The interview with

Doran had been a disaster. She'd felt stage-struck; her mouth dry, her questions lame. Worst of all, she sensed that her fear had shown through and that Doran had taken advantage of it. She didn't believe in the wobbler he'd thrown. Even the punch he'd caught Dempsey off guard with had, she felt, not been spontaneous. This vague conclusion was all she'd had to offer Leo after the interview.

'On the domestic front,' Leo continued, 'we've got a son, Stephen, in his early twenties who didn't get on with his father. Seems a bit flakey and he's a big lad. Big enough to swing a crowbar, for sure. Anyway, he's lived out in Wicklow with some New Age animal rights mob for about two years. Gudrun Remer's the head honcho. Middle-aged hippy type. Says she slept with Stephen on Friday night but Helen's not convinced, are you, Helen?'

Some jokey mutterings on the subject of cougar relationships broke out before Helen found her voice. She was angry with Leo. Not for singling her out just now but, more absurdly, for having trusted her to tackle Doran without him. You didn't mess it up, Helen, I did, he'd told her afterwards.

'I wouldn't rule out a relationship between Gudrun Remer and Stephen Brennan,' she replied, 'but my feeling is that she's covering for him.'

'Anything on Ms Remer's background yet?' Leo said, surveying the audience, trying to remember whom he'd assigned to this task.

Sergeant Martha Corrigan stepped forward, her notebook open, and the room fell under her spell, her auburn hair, hazel eyes and lightly freckled, translucent skin almost doll-like in their perfection. The ex-Rose of Tralee's was the most unaffected kind of beauty, and for that reason she was only vaguely aware of the effect she had on most of the men around her.

'Well, she's German – from the old East, actually. Leipzig. Forty-two. Unmarried. She came to Ireland eight years ago and bought a cottage in County Wicklow. She set up this animal shelter a few months after she moved in. Since then, she's been involved in animal rights issues. She and her group, including Stephen, were charged with criminal damage to a pharmaceutical testing unit out in Kildare last November. Broken windows, slogans painted on the outside walls. She was given a twenty-thousand-euro fine and will get three months if she doesn't pay up by early next month. Some of the others got three-month suspended sentences. Stephen didn't show up in court last Friday for sentencing. Health reasons, which the court accepted. He's due back in court in two weeks' time.' Martha looked up from her notebook and caught Leo's lap-dog stare. She smiled. 'I've put in requests for information on Ms Remer from the Landespolizei and the Stadtpolizei.'

'*Danke schön*, Martha,' Leo said, and hid behind his hand as he always did when he felt he'd made a fool of himself.

The Incident Room door swung inwards and caught Garda Dempsey so sharply on the funny bone that he cried out. Detective Garda Ben Murphy's apology was as profuse as his blush was profound. Gerry Cooney led the tittering. He didn't like this Young Turk any more than Leo did.

'Grow up, Gerry,' Leo said sharply, shamed by his own inexplicable aversion to the young detective. 'Let's move on to strand three. The business strand. Anything on Dermot Brennan's finances yet?'

'We're not machines, Leo,' Cooney said, his sulky pout

confirming his infantile nature. 'My team's been chasing up his business partners all morning.'

'So, what have you got?'

'Well, the accountant on the Honeyvale project was Brian Mahoney. He's dead. Three strokes last year and third time unlucky, you might say.' Cooney didn't use a notebook. Like himself, Leo supposed, he didn't even have one. 'Philip Molloy's next. Runs a couple of food export businesses, has a major property portfolio, of course. And he's on the board of Anglo-Celtic Bank.'

Cooney savoured the intakes of breath that greeted the revelation. The bank had become one in the national psyche with corruption and economic collapse.

'Anglo-Zombie Bank – why am I not surprised?' Leo said, and shook his head.

'Mr Molloy says he never met Sean Doran or had any threats from him nor from anyone else. Claims he didn't know Brennan very well. Never met him socially but thought he was a decent enough type until the flooding problems started in Honeyvale Heights.'

'And he blames Dermot Brennan for what happened out there?'

'Yeah. He says Mr Foley told him that the drainage and sewage systems weren't finished according to plan. Something to do with the piping width and the capacity of the pumps that were used.'

'How did he react when he heard about the murder?' Leo asked. 'Shocked, surprised, not surprised?'

'Mr Molloy was pretty shaken by the news. Took a bit of a turn actually. He's got some kind of heart condition and he's pretty frail. Must be seventy-five if he's a day. I doubt he'll make his seventy-sixth.'

'Who else have we got in this consortium?' Leo asked.

'Brian Driscoll,' Cooney said, and every head turned towards him.

'The Irish international?' Garda Dempsey gasped. 'The rugby player?'

'Not Brian O'Driscoll. Just plain Brian Driscoll. This fellow was the main investor in the Hearnstown Urban Centre development and took the biggest hit financially when it ran into the ground,' Cooney said. 'His Irish assets are worth very little at this point. But he's got mining and engineering companies based outside the country and a host of other financial interests in South-East Asia and China. The reality is that any losses he's taken in the Hearnstown project barely register on the scale for him.'

'Have we located him yet?' Leo asked.

'He's one of these tax dodgers domiciled abroad,' the squat detective snapped. 'Been in Sierra Leone for the past six months.'

'So we're saying this guy's an unlikely suspect?' Leo surmised.

'I suppose,' Cooney had to admit. 'But we can't rule out the possibility.'

'And we won't, not just yet,' Leo said. 'But for now it looks like Driscoll and Molloy are in the clear. Yes?'

Heads nodded. Watches and mobile phones were surreptitiously checked. Stiffened spines stretched. Ben Murphy had been trying, one hand half raised, to get centre stage all this time but Leo had left him dangling in the corner of his eye. Now, the young detective spoke up.

'Sir,' he said, 'there's a problem with this Daina girl.'

'A problem?'

'One of her flatmates, a Ms Cepurnieks, says she hasn't

seen or heard from Daina or her sister Sonia since late last evening.'

'Her *cousin* Sonia, you mean,' Helen said.

'No, her sister,' Murphy responded. 'Seems Daina lied about that. I've no idea why. I spoke to Mrs Newman, but all she knows is that Sonia hasn't been answering her mobile all morning.'

Leo wondered if Daina had more to hide than her age. Had she seen or heard something as she worked at Attenboy House, something that implicated the killer or, at least, pointed to a likely suspect?

'And you've put out the word that they're missing?' Leo asked.

'Yeah, I got some photos from the flatmate and sent them out to all stations and we're liaising with some Latvian community groups they might have had contact with.'

'Good. Good stuff,' Leo said, though it stuck in his craw to praise the young hotshot. 'So let's move on to—'

'One other thing,' Ben Murphy said, flicking through the pages of his notebook.

Maybe this was his reason for not liking the young fellow. The fact that he always managed to come up with the goods. The fact that neither praise nor blame appeared to affect him. The arrogance lying just below his posture of deference. The sense that he was just passing through the rain clouds towards the upper atmosphere on his meteoric rise and would soon jettison all of them.

'As you know, Anna Brennan ran a charity shop in Howth which she closed recently. Three weeks ago it was trashed. Nothing was taken but the place was a mess, a serious mess. I mean, disgustingly messy, as in faecal matter spread along the walls, urine in the till. Plus the perpetrators tried to set fire to the place but failed. And the thing is, neither Anna nor Dermot Brennan informed the local station. They had the place cleaned out and shut up shop.'

'Where did you dig that up?' Cooney blurted out.

'I asked a lady in the hairdresser's alongside why the charity shop had been closed,' Murphy replied, his shrug indicating that he felt he was stating the obvious.

Leo looked at Detective Sergeant Cooney whose bullet head had grown so hot and sweaty it was disgusting in some vaguely phallic way.

'Missed that one, did you, Gerry?' Leo said. 'Were you in Bangkok at the time?'

Cooney remained tight-lipped but he stared at the spoon beside his coffee mug with such fierce intensity that he might have been a psychic bursting a gut to bend it.

15

Detective Sergeant Helen Troy sat on a lavatory seat in the Ladies at Howth Garda Station. Her ridiculous, embarrassing tearfulness had passed. In its place had come anger and obstinacy. She couldn't believe what Leo had suggested she do. Absolutely no way, she'd told him. Now, her resolve was weakening.

When Leo had called her back to the Incident Room ten minutes after the team meeting, she'd expected a dressing-down. As she'd approached him warily, it was clear to her that he'd had time to watch the interview video. She'd tried to deflect him.

'I've just had a call from the Technical Bureau people,' she said. 'They've not found any business-related files on the PC yet. And he didn't use it for emails. They're trying what they call a "brute force attack" on the laptop but they're not making any promises. I'll talk to Foley and the others, see if I can get an email address for Mr Brennan. Then again, he might well have a number of email addresses with different servers so—'

'Why didn't you tell me that Doran said he couldn't stop seeing Dermot Brennan's face?' Leo asked.

Strange how a situation could change, Helen thought, and you're suddenly no longer the supplicant but the one dishing out mercies. Trying to. Clumsily. Standing above him, she'd been offered too stark a view of the red raw well of his left eye.

'I didn't think it was important.'

'Are you serious?' he asked. 'Isn't this as close to a bloody admission as we're likely to get? Or am I missing something here?'

She'd delivered the blow in as kindly a way as she knew how. Her head tilted slightly to the side, leaning a fraction forward, muted tones.

'Doran wasn't referring to Dermot Brennan's face, sir.'

'So who the hell was he referring to?'

The truth dawned on Leo. He shook his head.

'Ah, it was *my* face he was talking about.'

'I really messed up that interview, didn't I?' Helen had said, redirecting the conversation.

'You did fine,' he'd told her. 'The cock-up was mine. I sent you in there because this guy's taken a dislike to you. I knew he'd lose the rag and I hoped he might let something slip. Instead of that, I put you and Dempsey in danger and I apologize, OK?'

Already utterly disarmed, Helen had been confounded by what followed.

'I've apologized to Dempsey,' Leo told her, 'and I think you should too.'

'But I didn't . . . it wasn't . . .'

'It's the right thing to do, Helen.'

'No way,' she said, burning with humiliation at the very thought of bowing before that gormless oaf. 'Absolutely no way.'

Leo had stood up and gathered his bits and pieces. His mind appeared to be elsewhere as he delivered his message. The message was no less clear for all that.

'You were the senior officer in the room,' he stated. 'Ergo, you take the responsibility. That's what you're paid for. Now, go away and think about it and get it done and I'll meet you down at the carpark in, say, twenty minutes. We're off to Attenboy House.'

Helen flushed the toilet for a third time. She remembered how in the dark days after her mother's death in a hit-and-run accident she could spend an hour sitting in the bathroom at home in protest over some perceived slight. Eight years old, angry and clueless as to why. She remembered how her father would wait patiently outside. Once in a while he might ask quietly if she was OK. There was no one to ask her if she was OK now. Not Ricky, not anyone. She thought of the physical humiliation of her father's last days fighting cancer. She thought of the humiliations Leo must endure with his palsied face. Apologizing to Pacelli Dempsey didn't seem such a big deal.

Pacelli. With a name like that, she thought, Dempsey must have known days of humiliation too. Maybe that was why his neck had grown so thick.

'How do they get away with this, Leo?' Superintendent Heaphy demanded to know as he stood by the desk in the office he'd borrowed at Howth Station. He indicated the tabloids and newspapers spread about there. 'This . . . this . . . scurrilous stuff, it is. Did you see these?'

'I've been working all morning, boss. Didn't have time to buy a paper never mind read one.'

'Well, maybe you should've made it your business to read

them because someone in here's been leaking information.' Still on his feet, Heaphy was building up a head of steam, the toothy grimace indicating that his suffering was both psychological and physical.

Leo sat by the desk. He picked up one of the tabloids. 'Speculator Slain'. He winced, imagined some shifty-eyed editor going, 'Good, yeah, we'll go with that and to hell with the family.' He glanced at some of the other front pages. The usual mix of mock-horror, self-righteousness and innuendo. One good one though: 'Death of a Builder'. A bit classier than usual for that particular rag, the Arthur Miller reference in the title. He scanned the piece. *Frenzied attack . . . Latvian au pair . . . the bankrupt builder . . .* Never going to win the Man Booker Prize with that kind of shite, Leo mused.

The superintendent's thick forefinger intruded, pointing up the closing paragraph.

'Read that bit,' he insisted. 'Imagine what the Junior Minister said when he saw that.'

A source close to the investigation stated that a revenge attack of this nature 'was always on the cards'. Insidious threats on the lives of rogue bankers, builders and developers have been on the increase in recent months. The burning question now is whether the dreaded consequences of our dire economic woes have taken a murderous turn?

'Too many adjectives,' Leo said. 'And that last question mark is redundant.'

'What?' Heaphy sputtered. He stood above Leo, attempting to loom large. He wasn't big enough to. People wondered how Heaphy had ever got into the Guards. Leo knew. Stacked two-inch heels; another inch gained from blow-dried hair; a last half inch courtesy of his county councillor uncle. 'You're not taking this matter seriously, Leo.'

'The murder I'm taking seriously. The rest is bullshit.'

'But this irresponsible journalism? I mean to say, this is putting people's lives in danger. People who failed, yes, but failed honestly. Mostly.'

'Not my problem,' Leo said.

'It's a dangerous game they're playing, these newspapers,' Heaphy insisted. 'Stirring people's emotions, planting the seeds of revenge. And where will it all lead? To riots on the streets. To another Argentina.'

'Ireland isn't Argentina.'

'It could be, Leo, I'm telling you. When people's passions are inflamed, anything can happen.'

'We don't have passions in Ireland, Aonghus,' Leo said. 'Argentina has Maradona and the tango. That's passion. What do we have? Bono and the fucking two-hand reel.'

Heaphy retreated behind his desk and sat, slumped beneath the weight of high office.

'Do you reckon Sean Doran did this, Leo?' he asked.

Leo understood his old colleague's desperation. If Doran was the killer, motivated by his suffering at the hands of developers and their political friends, then the spotlight would be on Pat Foley and, by extension, the Junior Minister. As a deputy head of Criminal Investigation, Heaphy would suffer the consequences and his promotion chances in the dying days of the regime would sink without trace.

'He's an angry man. He's basically lost everything. The wife's cracked up, his job's gone, his home's about to be repossessed. He's got no alibi. He's been lying through his teeth and acting up on us. Plus he's got snapshots of Atten-boy House and Anna Brennan on his camera. I can't tell you he didn't do it.'

'But your gut instinct?' Heaphy asked.

'I have my doubts, sure,' Leo said. 'But tell me this, boss. If you're convinced it's not Doran or some other unhappy client, why did you send out protection to this Foley fellow?'

Heaphy fulminated, fiddled with some files on his desk.

'Orders from on high,' Leo said, answering his own question.

'A precaution is all. And, listen here, take it easy with Foley, will you? No need to go antagonizing him like you did this morning.' The superintendent blushed and moved swiftly on. 'And another thing. Why in the name of the Divine Mother did you send that young one in to interview Doran? She's only just out of nappies, for God's sake, and you throw her in against a boxer. Now I have an assault on one of our officers to deal with. As if I didn't have—'

'I made a mistake,' Leo said.

The direct admission discomfited Heaphy. Direct admissions weren't the superintendent's style. He fished out an A4 page from under the tabloids. Went through his check list for the press conference. The paper shook in his hands. Heaphy was like a moth to the media limelight. He craved it though it burned him and he kept coming back for more.

'So,' he said. 'I'll ask for any potential witnesses to come forward, et cetera, et cetera. The usual. I'll say we're following several lines of inquiry and that we've no reason to believe at this . . . at this . . . what's the word I'm looking for?'

'Juncture, point, moment in time, crossroads in the history of mankind—'

'Juncture will do,' Heaphy interrupted sourly. 'I'll say we've no reason to believe at this juncture that it's anything whatsoever to do with this revenge business the papers are whipping up. And as for Doran, I'll tell them he's being held for assaulting a police officer. If they ask whether Doran was brought in for questioning about Mr Brennan's death, I'll tell them he's being detained in relation to traffic offences. That sound all right?'

'Pulled the wool over my eyes, anyway.'

To Leo's surprise, Heaphy didn't react. For half a minute or so, the super gave a decent impression of concentrating on amending his check list. Then Leo saw the eyelids flicker busily. Always a sure sign that the fellow was up to some trick. Would have made the world's worst poker player, Leo thought. Then again he was too poker-arsed in his aversion to vice of any kind ever to indulge.

'How are the teeth?' Leo asked, but the super wasn't to be distracted.

'Sore,' he said, and reached into the breast pocket of his uniform. He took out a small slip of paper and handed it to Leo. All of this without an upward glance from his check list. 'Another name for you.'

'Peter Prior?' Leo read aloud. An address in Ranelagh. A landline number.

'That accountant who died?' Heaphy said. 'Seems he wasn't the original accountant on the Honeyvale Heights project. Mr Prior was. You might want to look into that side of things.'

'Where'd you get this nugget?'

'From the Companies Register, Leo. I had it checked out seeing as no one else bothered to.'

Who're you kidding, Aonghus, Leo thought. And why

are you giving me this? Am I being steered like a bloody elephant? And who's my driver?

Through the small rectangle of glass in the door of the station's Medical Room, Garda Pacelli Dempsey could be seen assuming the foetal position on a treatment table. He appeared to be alone. Helen Troy began to count to ten, got to five and went inside. Dempsey sat up too quickly, dropping his Smartphone on the floor, the sounds of Modern Combat still bleeping on it. She picked it up and he snatched it embarrassedly from her.

'Are you OK?' she asked.

His right eye had begun to swell. Below it, a strip of plaster blazed vividly white among the poisonous colours of bruising. Sick yellows, purples, greens.

'He caught me off guard,' Dempsey said, and added accusingly, 'I was trying to get between the two of you.'

'Listen, Pacelli,' she began. Diving in, getting it over with. 'I—'

'Garda Dempsey,' he insisted. 'Not Pacelli, right?'

'Look, I pushed him too far. I should've been more careful and I'm sorry you got hit. I take full responsibility.'

Dempsey relented, unstiffened. He lay back down and turned on his side, facing away from her like a sulking child, drawing his knees up again. Helen stood at the centre of the room, her task completed but intrigued by the big boy's fall from his macho heights.

'I can't believe he decked me,' he said.

'Doran's a boxer. He's fought for Ireland apparently.'

'He's five foot four,' Dempsey muttered thickly. 'I'm six two.'

She wanted to tell him to grow up but didn't need any

more hassle. She didn't imagine either that he'd be impressed by the 'size doesn't matter' argument. Boys usually weren't.

'Well,' she said. 'Inspector Woods is waiting for me. I should go.'

'Yeah,' he grunted in that trademark tone that tried for toughness but achieved only hollowness.

As she opened the door to leave, she heard the creak of the treatment table. He was on his feet when she glanced back, a nervous, tentative expression on his face. The maddest thought passed through her mind. He's going to ask me out on a date. How ungrateful am I going to seem if I refuse? When I refuse.

'I was wondering . . .' He swallowed hard.

'I really have to—'

'Yeah, but I was wondering . . . how long has Doran's wife been in hospital?'

'Four months or so. Why?'

'And she hasn't been out in all that time?'

'She's been out for the afternoon three or four times,' Helen said, wondering what he was getting at. 'But the exact dates I don't know.'

'Only I thought maybe she might have taken those photos,' he said. 'The first photo, like, Sean Doran's actually *in* it. He could've used the timer and taken the shot himself but . . . maybe . . .' He was losing his nerve, thinking himself a fool. 'Ah, it's just a thought.'

'No,' Helen said. 'Why don't you check with Admissions at the hospital and see if she was out when those photos were taken? Ring me if the dates match up. I'll be out in Attenboy House.'

Dempsey's theory actually added up. Earlier, at the house

in Honeyvale Heights, she'd thought it oddly reckless of Doran to have kept the photos on the camera. What if he hadn't known where the camera was? Helen remembered the CDs that were in the box she'd found the camera in. Half a dozen Celine Dions, fistfuls of Westlife and Robbie Williams and, more unexpectedly, Elvis Presley. More than likely the CDs had been hers. Snoop Dogg's romantic classic 'Bitches Ain't Shit' was more to his taste.

All of which meant what? That Doran was protecting his wife? Against a charge of murder? But if he was some knight in shining armour, why did he give off such an unpleasant whiff of misogyny?

'It might make sense then?' Dempsey asked, brightening with unrestrained naivety.

'It's definitely worth chasing up,' Helen told him. 'Good thinking, Garda Dempsey.'

'You can call me Patch,' he said.

He felt so proud, he could have jumped for joy. When Helen left to find Leo, he punched the wall. It hurt. It hurt a lot.

16

Leo sat behind the walled garden of Attenboy House by the cliff walk, watching the sea churn and crash scarcely fifty metres away. The icy gusts blowing in from Greenland ripped into his tear ducts, emptying them – half a pack of tissues binned in his pocket already today. Along the slope leading down to the water, furze and heather bushes tossed about like seaweed in some ocean deep.

On the bench beside him, Anna Brennan was dressed neither for the weather nor for outdoor work. She shivered in a charcoal-grey cardigan and black dress. She wore gardening gloves and on her bared knees, spots of mud had dried to dust. Did her own gardening then, Leo concluded, some of it anyway. He saw that she hadn't slept much and had cried a lot. She'd aged more than a day since yesterday but still didn't look fifty-one.

'This is my hideaway,' she'd explained when Leo found her, one of the Guards on duty at the house having directed him there. For a moment, he mistook her high pitch for hysteria. Then she added, 'The sea's very loud but do you mind if we talk out here?'

'You're not too cold?' he'd asked.

'No, I don't feel anything much.'

They stared at the sea for a while. An infinity of grey swells, foamy breakers appearing and disappearing, events as brief and insignificant as the lives of men. Any old fool could become a tinpot philosopher when contemplating the sea, Leo mused. At some time or other, he knew, Dermot Brennan must have sat here too. Sat beside his wife here where he was sitting now. Seen the same bared legs, the same red-gold hair whipped around in the breeze. Man and wife, facing the elements.

He remembered Iseult, fairer, more pale-skinned than the woman at his side. The pain of losing her still speared through his insides. A self-inflicted loss, he knew, knew too damn well, but what must widowhood be like? And it occurred to him that for all he knew he might be a widower himself. Hardly likely but possible. Better chance of that than of ever seeing Iseult again after what he'd done.

Had betrayal and jealousy come between the Brennans too? Whose betrayal, whose jealousy? Had some other man sat here beside her once? Someone who'd confronted Dermot last Friday night? And at whose behest, his own or Anna's? Financially, she'd be the main beneficiary of Dermot's death. If there was anything left to inherit. Or had Dermot Brennan strayed and been dipping too liberally into his supply of condoms? Been confronted, perhaps, by a jealous husband or the representative of a jealous husband? Or the representative of his own jealous wife?

'Mrs Brennan,' he said, 'there are some more questions I need to ask. I'd prefer to wait, you know, give you more time, but the possibility remains that this person or persons may strike again. It might well not be the case but in this business we have to presume the worst.'

With a girlish toss of her hair, she turned his way. In the dun afternoon light, her eyes had lost much of their unique hue and their power to distract. She seemed more ordinary, more vulnerable.

'Last month, the charity shop you ran in the village was vandalized,' Leo said. 'More than vandalized. Defiled might be the more appropriate word, I'm told, and an attempt made to torch it. Do you think it was personal? Directed at you or at Dermot?'

'Of course I don't,' she said. 'This kind of thing happens all the time. It's the kind of disgusting world we live in now, isn't it?'

'You didn't report the damage. Why not?'

He sensed her disappointment with him. Couldn't be helped, Leo thought. A policeman was essentially a bollocks. Had to be. How else to ask the hard questions? How else to consider anyone and everyone capable of murder, or at least complicity in murder?

'It was a charity shop, Inspector,' Anna Brennan said, infected by his curtness. 'We had nothing of value. The till was empty.'

'All the more reason to suspect it might have been a personal attack. A warning, a punishment, revenge?'

'People don't need a reason. Not these kind of people. The point of vandalism is that it's pointless and random, isn't it?'

'A random break-in at the shop. A random burglary at your house,' Leo said. 'It's kind of unlikely.'

'But the shop wasn't Dermot's. He wasn't involved. And I wasn't involved in his business. The shop was mine. Mine and Kitty Newman's.'

'Your neighbour? The one who's fallen out with you?'

Leo wasn't quite sure if it was the mention of Kitty

Newman or his directness that sharpened the lines on the widow's face. One way or another, she was angry.

'She's been bad-mouthing me, I suppose?' Anna said. 'She's a spiteful woman. I don't know why I ever let her near the shop, near my bloody life, for that matter. What has she been saying about me?'

Leo delayed, feigned reticence in the hope of drawing her out. He could see that she was becoming annoyed now at her lack of access to his inner thoughts. Worried too.

'Some jealous fantasy, I imagine,' she said, and Leo didn't answer. 'Such a pathetic little woman. All this pretence of old-money grandeur when, actually, fucking and shopping is all she's got on her mind.'

Leo had to work hard not to look in her direction as her passion rose. He felt a vague, very nearly sexual excitement. He told himself to cop on.

'She can't conceive of a relationship with a man that isn't on the level of *Desperate Housewives*. As for conversation . . . Some mutual interest in anything that isn't completely brainless? Some kind of real empathy? Forget it. She sees you talking to someone and thinks it's the prelude or the aftermath of a shag.'

'She saw *you* talking to someone?' he asked.

'Please, Inspector,' she said. 'I'm pretty sure Kitty's already told you whom she imagines I'm bedding.'

'I haven't spoken to Kitty Newman,' he said. 'You'll appreciate I'll have to know who you're referring to so's we can eliminate him from our inquiries.'

Leo waited while she took off her gardening gloves and attended to the pebbles of clay that hadn't yet fallen from her bare knees. He was glad she'd stepped into his little trap. As long as he could believe in her naivety, he could believe in her innocence. He didn't want Dermot Brennan's death to have anything to do with her. Foolish, he knew, but there it was.

'Alan Cobbe,' she said. 'He and Kitty were seeing each other for a while, on and off. He lives down the country and used her place as a Dublin base when he needed one. Sometimes he'd call in here and we'd talk. I was interested in his work is all. He's a sculptor and we commissioned a piece from him for the garden. Which, of course, didn't go down well with Kitty.'

Ah, Leo thought, the Eggman.

'When he grew tired of her possessive carry-on and stopped seeing her, she blamed me,' Anna said. 'It's as simple as that.'

'And he stopped seeing her when?'

'Oh, I don't know. Weeks. Months.'

'Does he still call here?' Leo asked, and she shook her head. 'Where can I find him?'

'Why are you doing this?' she protested, suddenly plaintive. 'Why are you making this worse for me . . . implicating me?'

'I'm sorry but this is how it works, Mrs Brennan,' he said. 'Do you have an address, a phone number for Alan Cobbe?'

She swept the wisps of hair back from over her face and unpicked what matted clay she could from her gardening gloves. Her tone became dismissive.

'He lives in County Wexford,' she said. 'Outside Enniscorthy. Ballinlea. I've got his number inside somewhere.' She gestured vaguely towards the house.

Enniscorthy. Not a million miles from Passage East where she had the holiday cottage, Leo thought. Same direction out of Dublin at least.

115

'Did you meet Mr Cobbe at the weekend?' he asked.

'Yes,' she said irritably. 'On Saturday. For lunch. Dunbrody House Hotel. Ask them. They know me there.'

Her new disdain for him rankled, made it easier for him to push on. He felt as though the hand he held up to block the breeze was a Venetian mask – the Harlequin Columbino covering the eyes of a slow-witted Arlecchino.

'We found a bag of money in your husband's walk-in wardrobe,' he said. 'Fifty-nine thousand seven hundred euro. Do you know why he might have had so much cash lying around?'

She was less surprised than she ought to have been. She shrugged.

'Sometimes he paid his sub-contractors in cash, I presume. Or someone paid him in cash for work.'

'And he was working on something in recent weeks? Did he still have building work?'

'I don't know,' she said. 'He leaves every morning – left every morning – at the usual time, but the truth is I didn't know where he was going or what exactly he was doing. Even if we'd been talking, it isn't something we'd—'

'Was he in trouble financially, Mrs Brennan?'

'Isn't everyone these days?'

She wrapped her arms about herself. She was either beginning to feel the cold or looking for sympathy. Or both. The sea was getting rougher. Leo paddled on.

'Answer the question, please, Mrs Brennan.'

'Dermot was going to file for bankruptcy,' she said. 'The house is in my name now, the cottage in Passage East too. The apartment in Nice is up for sale. There's about two hundred thousand euro that he transferred into my bank account and I know nothing about any other accounts or assets. I was never involved in his business affairs, as I've already told you.'

'So, you wouldn't know whether Honeyvale Heights, for example, was his idea? Whether he set up the contract and all of that? Pat Foley tells me your husband drove the project.'

If Leo had sunk in her estimation, he'd never reach the depths to which Mr Foley, Auctioneer, had clearly been consigned by Anna Brennan. Her expression spoke of a contempt bordering on hate.

'Foley's a low-life,' she answered, a new determination awakening in her. 'Like I said, I know very little about Dermot's business dealings and normally he'd never burden me with this stuff, but six or seven weeks ago, I can't remember exactly when, he was suddenly so upbeat, so . . .' She bowed her head, descended briefly into regretfulness but came up stronger. 'You see, Foley had convinced Sean Doran and everyone else that Dermot was responsible for the problems in that scheme. Faulty construction of the drainage system, he claimed. He'd already turned the other directors against Dermot.' The widow took in a breath and looked at Leo. It was as if she'd crossed some line. 'But back in September my husband told me he'd soon have something on Foley that would force him to retract, force him to . . . I don't know . . . to absolve Dermot.'

'But you've no idea what this *something* might be?'

'I did ask,' she said. 'He didn't want to go into the details.'

'And you haven't spoken about the matter since September?'

'No. Like I told you yesterday, we hadn't spoken about anything, full stop.'

'You mentioned a misunderstanding,' Leo said. 'You didn't elaborate.'

She stood up and tossed the gardening gloves on the bench. She wrapped her arms tight, her fingers clutching the elbows. Leo caught a brief glimpse of that gem-like blue in her eyes again.

'Our *misunderstanding*, this one at least, was about our sex life, Inspector,' she said. 'A private difficulty.'

'Whose private difficulty, Dermot's or . . . ?' Leo asked and immediately regretted his directness.

She shook her head. Leo felt his face lightly peppered by sea spray. His eyes filled up, obscuring, first, the horizon line, then the sea itself and, finally, Anna Brennan. He forced both eyelids closed with a thumb and index finger.

'My husband's, Inspector. He's had the problem for some time and I wanted him to see someone about it,' she said. 'I mean, I just hinted at it. Probably once too often. And there was no stand-up row or anything like that. We just retreated from each other. That's what we always did when something came between us. Can you please keep this to yourself? I couldn't bear to see Dermot's personal difficulties aired in public.'

'Of course,' Leo promised, but wasn't sure if he meant to keep his word.

'Neither one of us was good at dealing with problems,' she said. 'We've always let things drift, hoped they'd sort themselves out. Even before we stopped talking to each other, we weren't good at opening up to each other. We were reticent. All of our life together, we were shy of each other. Does that make sense to you at all?'

'I believe it does,' Leo said.

'We should finish this inside,' the widow suggested and turned to go. 'You're shaking.'

17

Attenboy House had few pockets of untidiness. Stephen's bedroom, or rather the bedroom he'd occupied last night, was one. Helen stood before the mess and wondered where to start her search. She'd been shocked on her arrival at Attenboy earlier to find that Gudrun Remer had called for Stephen a few hours before. He'd left his mother alone in the house and gone back to the Argos Sanctuary. Had they perhaps argued? And if they had, what might they have argued about? Or was it simply par for the course in their fragile relationship? In telling them where Stephen had gone, Mrs Brennan showed no surprise, no measure of upset. She seemed to Helen the kind of woman who could, unlike herself, quite comfortably live alone.

Given their mutual antipathy, Stephen's bedroom seemed the least likely place to find Dermot Brennan's encryption password or any documents relating to his business. Without expectation, Helen began her search. There was no bed, only a hammock hanging from the ceiling. Sifting through the disorderly bookshelves and study desk, Helen saw that the young man had been reading Pure Maths at Trinity. A second-year timetable on the desk was assiduously marked and annotated up to the end of Michaelmas term two years ago. From then onwards, there was nothing. Why, she wondered, had he quit?

A letter pinned to his noticeboard gave details of a scholarship, the Minchin Prize, awarded for his performance in the first year of the course. So it wasn't a question of ability, at least in the academic sense; social ability was another matter. The room contained no evidence of friends or of a student life of any kind apart from study; no club membership cards, no party invitations, no madcap collage of photos depicting wild nights on the lash.

Had something happened in college or, perhaps, at home that led to his abandoning the course? Something that had further affected his relationship with his father? Something that pushed it beyond mere antipathy? Gudrun Remer had referred to some previous 'trauma' in Stephen's life. Could it be that this trauma had caused him to leave college? Or was it something from the more distant past?

When she climbed the folding stairs to the attic, Helen found another pocket of disorder. She made her way to the centre of the musty, cobwebby space in search of a light switch. Soon, her forehead and armpits were damp from the prickly heat, the bare light bulb close by burning poker-hot into her cheeks. Almost every scrap of paper she searched through related to lives more ancient than those of the Brennans. Photograph albums from the thirties and forties, thick ledgers from the twenties, a bundle of postcards and short letters from earlier still, stiff with formality and reticence. No secret cache of documents relating to Dermot Brennan's business affairs was to be found nor any cryptic grouping of letters and numbers that might constitute a password for Brennan's laptop.

Over by the attic hatch, fresher air gusted up from below. Helen crossed the makeshift floor dragging two boxes behind her. The smaller one, made of cardboard, was filled with yet more papers and photo albums. The other, an empty tea chest, she turned bottom side up and rested her legs, cramped from squatting too long.

The waters of her eyes and her sinuses had filled up with dust. Her scalp ached and her neck muscles had stiffened up. She needed a break. Her navy-blue Garda zip-up hung on a beam at the far end of the attic. She stepped around the water tank. The heavy metal sheet covering it had strayed off centre and she struggled to set it square. With a stifled scream, she leapt back and her stomach lurched.

She approached the tank again. Two dead and decomposing rats floated on the water's surface. She remembered making coffee in the kitchen below for Anna Brennan yesterday. And drinking a cup herself. She darted towards the attic hatch and vomited down through the well of the hatch and onto the landing.

'What the . . . ?' Garda Pacelli Dempsey roared from below. 'Oh, Jesus! Oh, God!'

'Lot of work, the garden,' Leo said as he held open the rear door of the walled garden for Anna Brennan. 'Do you do everything yourself?'

'More or less,' she said. 'Keeps me sane.'

Her smile was forced. She let her hand drift along the branches of trained apple and pear trees, pausing occasionally to detach a dead leaf.

'These things are hypersensitive to all kinds of disease and these colder winters we're getting don't help,' she said, examining the dry leaf. 'Comes from all that seed selection and manipulation. Sometimes I'm sorry I didn't get, you know, natural trees and let them just grow.' She discarded the leaf. The breeze took it further than Leo could see. 'Are you a gardener yourself, Inspector?'

They had reached the house end of the walled garden. Leo stepped aside as she went through into the cobbled yard.

'No, I'm not the green-fingered type,' he said. 'Grey-fingered more like. Grey as in cement, you know.'

Close by the stretch of scraggy leylandii between the garden and the first of the outhouses, Leo paused. Their recent thinning out had been effected with a chainsaw, he guessed from the thickness and smooth finish of the branch stubs. He wondered if her husband had cut them. The front lawn too. Anna had already turned towards the house.

'Messy old things those leylandii, aren't they?' he said. 'Who cut them for you? And the front lawn?'

Anna looked at the trees. She tried but couldn't disguise her unease.

'We hire someone for the heavy work,' she said. 'Skip Sheridan his name is. He was here for a few days last week.'

Still she stared at the clutch of trees. Leo followed her line of sight. She wasn't looking at the trees. She was staring through the trees at a petrol-blue SUV parked in Kitty Newman's drive.

'He's American,' she said distractedly. 'Skip Sheridan, I mean. He lives somewhere along the coast north of the city, I think.'

'Do you have his phone number?' Leo asked. 'Only we'll have to have a word with him.'

The sound of loose pebbles scuffed, of voices audible but indistinct, reached them from beyond the trees. Leo couldn't see clearly through the mesh of arthritic branches.

'Why?' Anna asked, moving deliberately, Leo thought, to block his view of the SUV next door.

'Well, he may have noticed some suspicious activity around the place or—'

'Wouldn't he already have reported it?' Anna said bitterly. 'Aren't we all over the bloody newspapers and the TV?' Tears she was scarcely aware of fell. 'I saw the newspaper front pages on TV3 this morning. Can't they just let us grieve in peace? Couldn't they have waited until after the funeral to start throwing the mud?'

'These people don't do sensitivity, Mrs Brennan,' Leo said.

The pot calling the kettle black, he thought, and asked:

'The SUV next door, is it Mrs Newman's?'

'No.'

'But you recognize it?'

'The country's full of SUVs,' she said.

'Whose SUV is it, Mrs Brennan?'

She turned from him and walked across the cobbled yard.

'Mrs Brennan?'

She tossed her answer over her shoulder at him like a bone for a pesky terrier: 'Alan Cobbe's.'

Leo chewed on it.

'I'm so sorry,' Detective Sergeant Helen Troy repeated as she dried Garda Dempsey's hair in the shower room off Anna Brennan's bedroom.

Dempsey raised himself and took command of the towel. His shirt off, he was well built if a bit pudgy around the waist.

'It's all right,' he said, his irritability at last soothed away. 'Thanks.'

Helen had volunteered to wash his hair. Well, it's my

sick, isn't it, she'd told him. Besides, she was grateful for his
assurance that the rats had been floating in a tank supplying
the central heating pipes rather than the kitchen taps, and
for the fact that he'd bagged them. Still, she hadn't expected
his nod of agreement. She'd rinsed his shirt too and hung it
in one of the upper bay windows to dry. He began to flatten
his hair with the palms of his hands.

'No,' Helen said. 'Spike it up.'

'Yeah?' he said doubtfully.

'Yeah. Just brush your hands back through it.'

He did as he was told. He wiped the steamed-up mirror.
His reflection impressed him. His eyes began to search
for hers in the spaces behind his mirrored self and she
retreated to the upper landing, pretending to check on the
damp shirt. Over beyond the outhouses and beyond Kitty
Newman's side lawn with its ovoid sculpture stood a blue
SUV. Child-like in size before a tall grey-haired man who
stood by the open door of the SUV, Mrs Newman was
giving a finger-wagging lecture. Helen couldn't see how the
man was taking it.

'What do you reckon about Mrs Doran then?' Dempsey
asked. 'Do you think she might have taken the photos?'

He leaned against the door-jamb of Mrs Brennan's
bedroom, sucking his stomach in. His hunch had come up
trumps. Mrs Doran had been out of hospital on both of the
days on which the photos had been taken. He'd come to
Attenboy to tell Helen of his discovery. And because he was
in love. Even her vomiting on him had come to feel like a
good omen as she'd massaged the shampoo into his scalp.

'We're going to have to tread very lightly there,' she said.
'Do we question her? *Can* we question her? I'll have to talk
to Leo about it.'

Dempsey came closer, and the shiver passing through Helen reminded her of the rats again.

'How long do you think they were in the tank?' she said. 'The rats.'

'A few weeks, I'd say. They didn't smell all that bad, like,' Dempsey said. 'They were dead before they hit the water though. Taken from traps they were. I saw the marks.'

'Who'd do a thing like that?'

Dempsey shrugged, advanced a little more. In her unease, Helen focused on the argument developing down below on the driveway next door.

'I wonder what that's all about?' she said lightly as she felt his breath at the nape of her neck.

The man beside the SUV stepped out from behind the open door he'd been leaning on. He punched Kitty Newman in the face and she fell to the ground.

'Jesus! The bastard!' Garda Dempsey exclaimed and, still naked from the waist up, ran towards the head of the stairs. He turned back, grabbed his damp shirt from the window and pulled it on as he ran.

Helen was on her work mobile to the Guard on duty down at the gate even as she slid the screeching lower half of the casement window upwards. The man standing over Kitty Newman looked up. He changed his mind about the follow-up kick he'd intended to deliver.

'Blue SUV next door,' she yelled at her mobile. 'Don't let him leave. Go, go, go! He's moving!'

18

'Get out of the vehicle!' Garda Dempsey shouted. 'Get out of the vehicle!'

At a loss for further words, he pounded the roof of the stalled SUV. Out of the squad car that had swung in to block the gateway, a middle-aged uniform emerged with fire in his eyes. The mud-spattered SUV had come within inches of ploughing into the driver's door. Joining Dempsey in his assault on the SUV, the uniform elbowed the glass of the passenger door. The driver revved his engine loudly once, twice, reversed and sent both men jumping to one side. A gap of three or four feet remained between the squad car and the left pillar of the entrance.

Helen, still a little way off, could see that the big man was thinking about trying his luck. His eyes were popping and Helen thought they might be cocaine eyes. She unzipped her jacket, reached in for her Walther P99c semi-automatic. Their eyes met. He seemed to be daring her. She drew the pistol and he went for the gap. The SUV made it through, sweeping the squad car aside with its bull fenders, and, swerving left, headed out of view.

Leo emerged from the entrance of Attenboy and stepped

into the moment of suspended animation left in Cobbe's wake.

'What in the name of Christ happened here?' he asked of a crouched, pistol-toting Helen.

'Some guy just planted Kitty Newman with a punch and he's done a runner,' she said.

'It's Alan Cobbe,' Leo told her. 'He did those sculptures in the garden, the eggs. Seems Mrs Newman and Mrs Brennan had words over him.'

'What kind of man punches a woman in the face like that?'

Leo looked down at his hands that had instinctively made fists of themselves.

Dempsey and the other uniform came to life and ran towards the squad car.

'Call Howth and Sutton Stations,' Leo shouted after them. 'Tell them to get down rapid to Sutton Cross and close it off.' He turned to Helen. 'This guy was armed, was he? No? I didn't think so.'

His mood had darkened visibly. There was an edge to his words, an irony bordering on sarcasm, and it wounded her.

She looked at the semi-automatic in her hand. It didn't feel like it was her pistol or her hand. She didn't know what to say but words came anyway. Irrelevant words.

'I found two dead rats in a water tank in the attic of Attenboy House,' she said, and Leo looked at her as though she'd completely lost the plot.

'And that explains the bloody gun, does it?'

She knew she'd made a mistake but the angry, seething change in him baffled her.

'We should be chasing the bastard,' she said defensively. 'He could be our man.'

'Put away the gun, Helen,' he said. 'I never saw it, right? You never drew it, right?'

'But—'

'And neither did the others see it. I'll talk to them,' he said. 'For Christ's sake, Helen, you do know the protocol, don't you? Or did you miss that class? Where's Kitty Newman?'

'She's . . . '

Helen looked back along the tarmac drive leading to the assortment of white boxes that made up Kitty Newman's home. Her flesh tightened; a rush of ice and fire touched the nape of her neck. The woman was nowhere to be seen.

'She can't have been . . .' Helen stuttered. 'She can't have been in the SUV. Can she?'

'You'd better hope not. Go and check the house.'

Over by the squad car, Dempsey and the other uniform carried on separate animated conversations with Howth and Sutton Garda Stations. Helen's heart pounded in her chest. She knew she wasn't thinking straight but she tried to think anyway.

'He's going to get away,' she objected as Dempsey tried and failed to start the damaged squad car.

It didn't make sense to her that they weren't already in pursuit of the SUV. At the very least someone should be racing back up to the unmarked car in the cobbled yard of Attenboy House. Leo wiped some moisture from the lower well of his twisted lips.

'The gun, Helen, will you put the damn thing away?' he said. 'Howth is a peninsula, remember? One way in and one way out. We block off Sutton Cross and he's a blue-arsed fly in a jam jar, nowhere to go except up his own arse.'

'But if he's got her in the SUV, we may have a hostage situation on our—'

'Go up to the house. Now. And ring me if you find her.' Leo called across to Dempsey. 'Get the unmarked car. Now. Now!'

He wondered what the hell the young Garda was doing with his shirt wrongly buttoned and his damp hair slicked back like some ageing, overweight boy-band singer.

Kitty Newman's house hadn't been built with acoustics in mind, Helen thought. Or perhaps the shrillness she heard as her own voice bounced back at her was simply down to panic. She'd found the front door open but no further trace of the woman as she moved up through the house. Landings, half landings proliferated. Then, on the white-painted and rough-grained wall, she saw two finger-wipes of blood.

'Mrs Newman!' she called out again. 'Detective Sergeant Troy here. You're quite safe now, he's gone.' More impatiently, she cried, 'Where are you?'

She'd reached the highest box in the modernist pile. Of the three doors only one was locked. She banged her fist repeatedly on the light frame. Some kind of box plywood, she thought, easily kicked in if needs must.

'Mrs Newman, open up, please,' she said, glad now of the short hair cut back from her streaming forehead. 'I'm going to have to force the door if you don't open up.'

No response came from inside. Helen worried that the woman had collapsed and knew she had to get in there fast. But what if Kitty Newman lay on the floor, her head just by the door? If it was Kitty Newman. Might be her Latvian housekeeper, Daina's sister or cousin or whatever, she thought. Couldn't be, for Christ's sake, Helen – the girl's gone missing.

A new realization hit her. Daina's sister – yes, sister – hadn't been working yesterday morning but Daina had. Why? Had no one thought to ask?

Some instinct kicked into gear in Helen's brain. She held the handle firmly as she threw her shoulder against the flimsy door. On her third attempt, the lock snapped. She eased the door inwards on a white-tiled bathroom with chrome fittings. Over by the toilet bowl lay a motionless Kitty Newman, face up, her eyes closed to the ceiling, her nose bloodied and awry.

Helen got the woman on to her side. She rolled out a fistful of toilet paper to staunch the flow of blood from the nose that had undoubtedly been broken. It was impossible not to pity the woman – even if she'd had her nose deliberately broken before for cosmetic reasons. Helen rang Leo. While the phone rang, she dabbed at Kitty's face, taking care not to do any further damage.

'Helen.'

'She's here. Broken nose, I think, and she's passed out. Have you got Cobbe yet?'

'Not yet. The local boys tell me the traffic's jammers at Sutton Cross every evening at this time. He's not going anywhere. Not in the SUV anyway.'

To Helen's relief, his earlier sharpness of tone had mellowed.

Below her, Kitty Newman began to stir. Helen tried to rub away a renewed flow of blood, which elicited something between a moan and a scream from the woman.

'Jesus, what was that?' Leo asked.

'She's coming to. Can you send an ambulance up here?'

'No problem. And don't worry, we'll have this shitbag in jig time,' Leo said, and to Helen it felt like absolution.

*

Shame was the burden of the beast, Leo mused, as Garda Dempsey sped the unmarked car along Abbey Street towards the junction with Howth harbour. The squall of the Tetra radio system, the wail of the siren and the flash of the blue light atop the dashboard were doing his head in. The past too, crowding in on him. Shaming him. Ever since Helen had told him about the punch to Kitty Newman's face, he'd felt sick to the pit of his stomach. He was no better than his Nazi father, the SS Wallonie man hiding out in Ireland after the war. Only hit Iseult that once, he silently protested, and he'd been pissed, doped up, strung out and paranoid from battling those IRA bastards.

Down at the harbour front the traffic was densely packed and irritatingly slow to make way.

'Greenfield Road, Howth Road and Dublin Road blockades in place.' The voice from Howth Station crackled through the radio static. 'Three cars heading to Station Road exit. We've stopped two petrol-blue SUVs so far on Greenfield Road. Two mothers taking their kids home from school.' The static took over for a minute or two. 'We've nothing on what this fellow's wearing.'

Dempsey snapped up the radio receiver.

'Green T-shirt, combats,' he said, a decibel short of a shout. 'Some kind of writing on the T-shirt, black print but small. The last word is "mark", over.'

Leo looked across at the young Garda. He was impressed. Most fellows remembered nothing of any consequence from these high-risk situations. Panic and fear blanked their memory banks. Pity he couldn't blank his own memory banks.

The car radio voice emerged briefly from its electric storm

– 'Station Road exit blockade in place' – and disappeared again.

They freed themselves from the traffic just beyond the turn-off into the working side of the harbour. Dempsey slammed his foot on the accelerator and they shot forward.

'Pull in, pull in to the right,' Leo shouted as he scanned the footpaths. 'Blue SUV over at the railway station.'

'Where? Where?' Dempsey cried, the jerking car adding to his sense of confusion.

'Swing right, over there.'

'That's the one,' Dempsey confirmed, savouring the screech of tyres as he pulled the unmarked car across the road into the small station carpark. 'Covered in mud. An L-plate on the back.'

Leo was out of the car before Dempsey had switched off. The SUV was empty, the doors locked. Dempsey ran to the entrance of the railway station – a set of ten, twelve steps divided by an iron rail and leading upwards to a double door. He took the steps three at a time. In his wake, a breathless Leo reached the foot of the steps. He thought he could kill or maim or at least hurt someone if given half a chance. He was.

No sooner had Dempsey disappeared inside the double doors than a broad-shouldered man in a green T-shirt emerged. The slogan read 'I Have Made My Mark'. Alan Cobbe, wide-eyed with panic, scanned the scene, saw no threat in the man with the disfigured face ascending on the left side of the iron rail. He set off down the steps and got halfway before Leo caught him off guard with a perfect right to the chin. As he sank to the seat of his combats and then on to his back, the man gave Leo a distant, puzzled look before drifting into unconsciousness.

Fate, Leo mused, often caught you unawares like that with its ugly face and its leaden fist. There was no point in asking why.

19

The largest of the three upstairs bedrooms was where Leo had his mask room. Because it lay to the front of the house, he never opened the curtains there. The windows he opened an inch or two now and then but not on nights as frosty as this one. He sat on his high-backed leatherette swivel chair and surveyed his collection. The masks almost filled the two main walls. Ten thousand euros' worth of them by now, Leo calculated. An absurd extravagance, but who or what else did he have to spend his money on? No one. Nothing.

Sometimes he sat here to let his thoughts on a case find some order, some direction. Sometimes he sat here to indulge himself in self-pity. Tonight, it was a little of both. The masks, from the wild and colourful African constructions and the dark-browed Eric Cantona rubberized head mask to the pale and subtle Noh ones, ran the gamut of human emotions. Fear, anger, doubt, panic, madness, elation, love, hurt, sadness, jealousy. Not forgetting shame, of course. And the gamut of human emotions was what you had to steer through in every new case. Always remembering that some masks expressed what the wearer really felt while others hid true feelings. The trick was to be able to tell the difference.

Who, for example, was the real Sean Doran? Was he protecting his wife or hiding behind her? The question had become even more difficult to answer now that Leo had discovered the ex-boxer had been in Attenboy at some point between late Friday night and Monday morning before the body of Dermot Brennan was found.

Earlier, in the holding cell at Howth Garda Station, Leo had set a trap for Doran. He recalled what he could of the interview. You never knew what you might have overlooked in the heat of the moment.

When Leo had peered in through the spy-hole of Doran's cell, he knew the fellow wasn't feigning sleep. The wayward abandonment of limbs was not a pose anyone could have consciously maintained for long. Leo might have left him alone if it hadn't been for the memory of Doran's interview with Detective Sergeant Troy. *Every time I close my eyes, I see his face* . . . Yeah, well, Leo thought, guess what you're going to see when you open your eyes now, son. On the ceiling, the light fixture was fitted with a metal surround like a dog muzzle.

The rattle of the key in the lock and the slam of the metal door sent Doran tossing and turning but didn't quite wake him. Leo kicked the metal frame of the bed. The dense walls absorbed the higher decibels of the sound. When Leo spoke, he had the curious feeling that his voice remained inside his head.

'Sean,' he said. 'Wakey, wakey, son.'

'What? Leave me alone. What do you want?'

Doran blinked under the caged light, found his bearings and then found Leo's face.

'You can't interview me here,' he said, shielding his eyes. 'I've a solicitor coming in the morning and he says not to talk to anyone.'

Leo leaned against the wall at the end of the bed wishing he could light a cigarette like in the old days.

'This isn't an interview, Sean,' he said. 'It's a courtesy call.'

Curiosity got the better of the ex-boxer. He dragged himself up to a sitting position.

'I can't remember the last time I fell asleep so quick,' Doran said. 'And now you . . . you . . .'

With a better view of the fellow's eyes, Leo could see he'd gone further along whatever despairing journey life was taking him on. But it was too late and, besides, not the time for misgivings, he told himself.

'Listen, Sean, you haven't cooperated with us. All you've done is messed us around, right? So, tomorrow I'll have to talk to your wife about these photos.'

'That can't be right,' Doran said. 'That can't be legal.'

'Those photos were taken on two specific afternoons when Lisa-Marie was on day release from the hospital. In your care. Help me out here, Sean. Convince me there's an innocent explanation for all this, or at least a plausible one.'

'I don't have to answer your questions. My solicitor will be here at eleven in the morning. You can ask me then.'

Doran's assertion might have come across as irate if there had been even an ounce of energy in it. There wasn't.

'Can't do that, son. I'll be with your wife at ten. It may take a while to get the truth out of her but what choice do you leave me?'

'Bastard.'

'I know. It comes with the territory.'

Doran drew his knees up, leaned his forehead on them.

His muscles were slack, that fighter's tautness in him gone to seed.

'I'm on your side, Sean, I *want* to believe you.'

'No you're not. No one's ever been on my side.'

'So? The photos?'

'A game,' Doran said, his head sinking further down so that it became more difficult to hear him. 'A game to . . .'

Leo didn't catch the rest.

'A game to do what?'

'A game to help Lisa-Marie from . . . from topping herself.'

Leo sat down at the end of the bed.

'Tell me more.'

Doran came up for air. It wasn't great air, Leo thought, stinking as it did of fifty years of the raging alcoholics and farting scumbags who'd overnighted there. The ex-boxer pulled in a few lungfuls of it anyway. He'd breathed in worse at Honeyvale Heights, no doubt.

'The psychiatrist in the mental, he says hope is the thing. Hope is what Lisa-Marie needs. Something to look forward to, and I tried. Got a shitload of brochures about emigrating to Canada and Australia and she just says they won't have the likes of us, Sean. Brought her a pile of stuff from the universities, mature student stuff, and the grant aid she might be able to get.'

He looked up at Leo. A kid who wants to be believed but knows he's going to get a wallop one way or the other.

'She was good at school, like, did her Leaving Cert and all. And she practically ran that bleedin' hotel single-handed when we were there. "Heartbreak Hotel" she calls it now. Did the accounts, managed the supplies, ran Reception, everything. But she don't give herself no credit for all that.

All she wants now is one thing. To see the Brennans suffer like we suffered.'

'Suffer in what way?'

'She got this crazy idea into her head that we stalk the Brennans. Take these snaps, like, and post them anonymously. She wanted to put the frighteners on them, let them know they were being watched and worry about who was watching them. That kind of thing.'

'Did you actually send any of these photos to the Brennans?'

'No. I pretended to Lisa-Marie I did.'

The story was daft enough to be true and elaborate enough to be a lie. Then again most stories were, Leo supposed. He might have left it at that if Doran had. If he hadn't dipped his gaze down again and gone all slippery on Leo again.

'She believed me for a while but now she's completely lost the plot. She's got her own game going now.'

'Which is? Look at me, Sean.'

'Which is telling the other women in her ward that I topped Brennan. That I done it for her. And I didn't. No way, man.'

'Didn't kill him or didn't do it for her?' Leo asked, a little more jokily than he'd meant to.

The ex-boxer didn't rise to the provocation. Leo wondered if the fellow was still trying to box clever. Only one way to find out. Cheat.

'I've been talking to the pathologist, Sean,' he lied. He'd put Ben Murphy on the post-mortem detail and not heard anything back yet. 'He tells me there's a good chance it was a left-handed shot that took Dermot Brennan out. And you're a southpaw, right?'

'You're full of crap.'

Leo stood up, acted out a casual readying-himself-to-go routine.

'I'm just telling you what he told me,' Leo said, fixing his tie and heading towards the metal door.

'Wouldn't matter if you were left- or right-handed,' Doran insisted. 'Swing a crowbar even on your weak side, you'd break a guy's skull.'

'A crowbar?' Leo said. 'How do you know he was killed with a crowbar, Sean?'

'Read it in the papers,' Doran answered uncertainly.

'We didn't release that information. It wasn't in the papers and it wasn't on the radio or TV. Which can only mean you actually saw the crowbar, Sean. So you called to the house between Friday night and Monday morning, right?'

Doran made himself small, folded himself into the corner at the head of the bed and clammed up. The corner he'd painted himself into. Draw him out, Leo thought, offer him a sweetener, soften him up.

'You haven't talked to Lisa-Marie since Sunday night, have you? She must be dead worried.' He felt like a louse. 'Would you like a chat with her? I can arrange it for you if—'

'If I give in and let you lot stitch me up, yeah? Confess to something I didn't do? Wouldn't be the first time you bastards did that, would it?'

'Probably not,' Leo said, and Doran, in momentary surprise, peered out from his corner.

'You wouldn't be trying to stitch me up if I was related to a government minister, would you? Guys like Foley live outside the law.'

'Do you seriously think Foley would have the balls to kill Dermot Brennan?'

'No,' Doran said. 'But ask him how he dumped the three

squatters out of number thirteen and sorted the problem at number nine.'

'Tell me.'

'I could hang the bastard. But he could hang us too.'

'Tell me, Sean, for Christ's sake.'

'Ask him yourself. Or maybe you're under orders to lay off him. Wouldn't surprise me.'

'I'll ask him.' Leo knew he wasn't going to get any further with the ex-boxer, who'd turned to face the wall. 'Talk to your wife tomorrow, son. No strings attached, OK?'

'Thanks for nothing,' Doran said.

The last train shuttled easefully by Serpentine Crescent. Leo checked his watch. 23.57. Two minutes late.

He hadn't been able to decide which mask best suited Sean Doran. He wondered if Alan Cobbe's true nature would prove as elusive. Out at the railway station in Howth, he'd taken the keys from the guy's combats and opened the boot of the SUV to find a few lumps of granite, an assortment of hammers, a pair of protective gloves and a canvas sleeve of chisels. The tools of the Eggman.

The sucker punch Leo delivered had proved too effective. Cobbe had had to be hospitalized overnight. Concussion. Kitty Newman lay in a private ward on the floor above him. Shock, loss of blood and a broken nose. The medical staff wouldn't let Leo near either of them. He hadn't minded at the time. He did now because he knew he faced another sleepless night bothered by this case, bothered by the image etched in his mind of Iseult's bruised face like a smudged Francis Bacon portrait. An image rather than a memory because he'd had no recollection even back then of hitting her, only of her telling him so over the phone before she vanished.

The ashtray at his side overflowed. He needed a different kind of smoke. He took up his mobile and rang his supplier. Dripsy Scullion, thirty-five going on eighty, a brain-addled, famine-thin wreck of a man but reliable. He spoke slowly as though he had to look up every word in a dictionary before he used it.

'Hey, Leo . . . how's the goin'?'

'For Christ's sake, Dripsy, how many times do I have to tell you? Don't use my name on the phone.'

'But . . . but you just used mine, man.'

'That's different,' Leo said. 'You're the fucking criminal.'

Wednesday, 24 November

20

At nine in the morning, the sky was still a cloudy mixture of day and night. The cold had a new rawness to it. Detective Inspector Leo Woods and Detective Garda Ben Murphy were headed to interview Alan Cobbe at Beaumont Hospital. Murphy, in the driving seat, spoke only when he was spoken to. Long silences left him unfazed. He seemed preoccupied, a deadly seriousness about him. Maybe that was his problem with the young detective: the absence of humour, the solemnity that was almost priestly.

'So, what's the story on the post-mortem?' Leo asked.

'The report is on your desk, sir,' Murphy said.

'There's a lot of reports on my desk, son,' Leo said. 'Just give me the headlines.'

'We can't say for sure yet if it was the fall rather than a punch that caused the split lip and cracked tooth,' the young detective began, calmly negotiating Leo's ire. 'Doesn't appear to have been much of a struggle if any at all, in fact, so no DNA samples under the fingernails or elsewhere. No prints anywhere, but the crowbar and the sliding bolts on the outhouse door had been wiped.'

'And the other outhouse doors?'

'No, just the outhouse we found him in,' Murphy said.

Leo felt he was still wandering in the mists of last night's weed. He wanted to open the window and clear his head but he knew the icy breeze would lash his dodgy eye.

'You asked the pathologist about the possibility that the attacker might have been left-handed?'

'Of course.' Murphy's tone was more matter-of-fact than offended. 'Inconclusive there too, though. The crowbar wasn't swung as such. I mean, wasn't swung from either the left or right side. It came straight down on Dermot Brennan's head. And the blows weren't especially powerful. But the fact that he was on his knees when he was hit—'

'He was on his knees? So, surely he must have taken a punch.'

'Or he was forced on to his knees by his killer – forced into an attitude of repentance before the blow was struck?'

'That's all a bit metaphorical, isn't it, son?' Leo said. 'You're a policeman not a poet.'

'It was just a thought.' Murphy shrugged.

'Anything else?'

'Yeah. Stomach contents. Seems he'd had a few shots of brandy.'

The young detective shifted in his seat and Leo detected a hint of irritation in him. He was tempted to pursue it but wasn't given the time to. As always, the young detective seemed about to play another trump card.

'There's more?' Leo asked.

'Not from the pathologist. But I've been looking through the items we took from Mr Brennan's bedroom,' Murphy said.

'And?'

'That packet of condoms in his bedside table? The use-by date is July two thousand.'

'So?'

'So, Helen's theory about Brennan's playing the field might be off the mark.'

Leo didn't appreciate Murphy's trying to put one over on Helen.

'Detective Sergeant Troy,' Leo insisted. 'And *her* theory had some grain of sense in it. Repentance, my arse.'

They turned on to Kilbarrack Road. Tree-lined though not leafy nor twee. Not for the idle or acquisitive rich these suburban semi-detached homes with their red-bricked ground floors and white-dashed uppers, their tidy lawns and mid-range cars. The kind of place Dermot Brennan belonged, Leo suspected, not out at stately Attenboy. His sense of the dead builder was that he'd been an ordinary, hard-working guy who'd got himself screwed over by the feral overclass.

'When will the body be released?' Leo snapped.

'Today, sir. Mrs Brennan's already made the funeral arrangements.' Murphy's voice was quaking with tamped-down fury. 'She's taking him to the church in Rathmines this evening. The cremation's tomorrow at Newlands Cross.'

'Would that be Mary Immaculate Church?'

'I think so.'

Anna Brennan's seeming alacrity proved less startling to Leo than the fact that she'd chosen the very church where his belief in God, music and his father had disappeared for ever in the course of a Bach chorale. He wondered who played the organ now at the Church of Mary Immaculate Refuge of Sinners, to give it its full and proper title.

Along Strand Road in Portmarnock, Detective Sergeant Gerry Cooney pressed his goggled snout forward as he drove. Beside him, Helen Troy tried to make the best of the diminished sea view. A grey expanse of water mirroring a grey expanse of sky, the horizon line too lightly pencilled in. Further ahead, a Martello tower reminded her of her solitary, abandoned state.

Demotion always hurt, and every instance of demotion in your life embedded itself in your memory, never to be forgotten. Switched from the lead to a supporting role in that long-ago school production of *Annie*. Taken off after fifty minutes that first time your father had come to see you play in the Irish jersey. Dropped without explanation by Ricky after two years of cohabitation. Now she faced the chop again. She'd submitted a report to Leo on her breach of the firearms regulations. Hers might well be the shortest detective sergeant career in history. Leo, it seemed, already had reservations about her. Pairing her with Cooney was evidence enough of that. Half an hour it had taken them to get from Howth to Portmarnock. All that time, Helen had resisted his every effort to start up a conversation. She had feigned a couple of yawning fits and then sleep.

A futile day loomed ahead. A pair of peripheral witnesses to be interviewed. Peter Prior, the accountant who'd dropped out of the Honeyvale Heights project early on and lived in Ranelagh. And here at work in Portmarnock, the guy who'd culled the trees at Attenboy. Skip Sheridan.

They pulled into the driveway of a large two-storey house that aspired to the regal with its crenellations and its heavy iron-banded front door.

The man wielding a chainsaw one-handed in the upper reaches of a silver birch tree in the side garden wore no protective gear of any kind. Helen had never seen anyone handle a chainsaw as carelessly as Skip Sheridan or take such chances with his footing on thin and pliable branches. Earphone wires hung down the front of his workshirt. He had to be either into extremely loud heavy metal or deliberately ignoring their repeated calls and arm-waving.

'To hell with this,' Cooney said and wiped his forehead and bald pate of sweat. 'There's only one way to get him down out of it.'

He picked up two fistfuls of loose pebbles from the drive and advanced on the birch tree.

'But what if he's startled and falls?' Helen objected. She held his arm as he was about to throw. 'I can't let you do this.'

Cooney was not a happy camper. The man in the tree had made him even more unhappy.

'Listen, love,' he seethed. 'If he falls, I didn't throw a pile of stones at him, right? And you didn't pull a gun on an unarmed man yesterday. Call it *tit* for tat.'

He pulled free of her and let fly. The pebbles fell back down through the tree, peppering the leaves with a hard rain. The chainsaw puttered to a halt. Skip Sheridan removed his earphones and waved at them good-humouredly. At the sight of his hard-muscled arms some primitive species of admiration stirred in Helen, but only briefly. Her innate suspicion of men who worked out and went in for cock-a-doodle-do display kicked back in.

She flashed her ID but, sensing the pointlessness of doing so at such a distance, called out, 'Police.'

'Sure. Been expecting you,' he said quite casually. 'Coming down.'

Helen tried to place his accent. A southern drawl it seemed to her. Tennessee? Passed through it when she'd travelled the States for three months in her student days. Now that her life seemed claustrophobically small as it did these days, she regretted ever having come back. Never have met that bastard Ricky if she'd stayed on.

Sheridan's descent proved as reckless as his working methods. He slid, fell, jumped, and seemed to enjoy the buffeting he took on his way groundwards. Cooney's face had gone heart-attack puce.

'Bloody Tarzan,' he muttered as Sheridan picked up a red zip-up jacket from the car trailer at the base of the tree and got his arms into the sleeves as he approached.

The American was neither quite as tall nor as young as Helen had at first thought. Five seven, five eight, and some-where in his mid-thirties. A stiff brush of red hair, deeply freckled face and forearms and dimpled, foursquare chin gave the impression of a military type. A certain formality of bearing and manner too now that he was close enough to offer her his hand.

'Ma'am,' he said, and turned to a perplexed Cooney. 'Sir.' Then, addressing both of them, he added, 'I'll be glad to help if I can.'

'You nearly gave me a heart attack,' Cooney snarled. 'Don't you realize how dangerous those bloody things are?'

'I been using chainsaws since I was a kid,' Sheridan said.

'From Texas then, are you?' Helen said, and he gave her a quizzical look before breaking into a smile. He got the joke. Cooney didn't, and didn't like the fact that he didn't.

'This here chainsaw's got a great safety mechanism. You just gotta let go of the trigger and it cuts out.' Sheridan shrugged, zipped up his jacket. 'I can't believe what happened to Mr Brennan.'

Helen unpocketed her notebook and fished around for a pen.

'So, Mr Sheridan,' she began. 'You did some work out at Attenboy House recently. How long were you there for? A couple of days?'

'Three days, yeah, early last week,' Sheridan said. 'But I'd been out there a coupla times before that. Cleared some brush from out back the walled garden. Cut back the bushes along the front lawn. That kind of thing.'

'And the trees between the Brennans and their next-door neighbour.'

'Yeah.' Sheridan gave a wry grin. 'Mrs Newman. I guess she figured I was from Texas too.'

'She had words with you?'

'No, ma'am, not with me. With Anna Brennan. See, I was pruning them conifers and trying to keep the deadwood from falling into Mrs Newman's lot like Anna'd asked me to.'

Mr Brennan, but *Anna* for his wife, Helen noted. Meaning he'd dealt with her rather than with Dermot Brennan? At her side, Cooney eyed the American with a mixture of suspicion and irritation. Helen suspected that irritation was the major ingredient.

'Course, y'all know, some of it's gotta fall in there,' Sheridan continued. 'And this lady, she freaks, claims I been doing this deliberately and, well, end of story. Couldn't finish the job. Been waiting on a call from Anna since then. She was gonna sort things with Mrs Newman.'

'And you haven't been back there since then?'

'No, ma'am.'

'Did you have any contact with Mr Brennan or was it his wife you dealt with?'

'Met the feller once or twice but he didn't have a lot to say.'

'And you didn't notice anything untoward out there? Any

151

visitors confronting Mr Brennan? Any sense that he was expecting trouble?'

'No, ma'am. But like I said, I didn't see a whole lot of the guy.'

Helen had run out of questions. She glanced with lowered eyes at Detective Sergeant Cooney for rescue or inspiration. She got neither. He was too busy scrutinizing the American, seeking some justification for his dislike of the fellow. Over beyond Sheridan stood a dusty, beaten-up blue Opel Kadett. 1998 registration. County Louth. A pretty wide range for a one-man operation. Or maybe not. She couldn't honestly tell. But she could ask.

'Where do you live, Mr Sheridan?' she asked.

'Clogherhead,' he told her. ''Bout an hour from here.'

'That's in County Louth, isn't it? So, how do you come to be working down here in Dublin?'

'The work don't just happen, you gotta go find it.' Sheridan was growing impatient, though not ill-humouredly. 'I advertise all the way down to Dublin. In stores, community centres, churches. In Howth, I advertised in the HeadUp shop, which is how I got the gig at Attenboy House. Simple as that.'

'HeadUp?'

'Mrs Brennan's charity shop,' he said. 'I best be getting back to work here. I'm way behind schedule already. OK?'

'Sure,' Helen said, distracted by the thought that neither she nor anyone else had asked which charity the shop had been dedicated to.

Sheridan turned to go back to his manic branch-cutting, but Detective Sergeant Cooney had found a rationale for his distrust of the American.

'How long have you been living in Ireland, Mr Sheridan?'

he asked. 'I'm assuming from that accent of yours that you're not Irish.'

'You're assuming wrong, sir,' Sheridan said, sharper now, annoyed. 'I was born here. I lived outside Clogherhead for two years before my folks emigrated. My dad's business went under and—'

'What kind of business?'

Cooney's question was meaningless, Helen knew, pointless. He was a dog fighting for a bone he had no interest in eating.

'Automobiles.'

'So what brought you back to Ireland, Mr Sheridan?'

'I came over here with my mom's ashes.' The American's eyes glistened over and Helen could see that he focused on her because he didn't want to lose the rag with Cooney. 'I wanted to see what it might be like to give things a shot over here so I stayed on.'

'And what about your father, is he still alive?'

'No, sir. What's this got to do with—'

'Thank you, Mr Sheridan,' Helen interjected. She handed him a calling card. 'Ring us if anything occurs to you. Sometimes the smallest detail can help.'

'Sure. Y'all have a nice day now,' Skip Sheridan said, like they'd ruined his.

They watched him retreat to the car trailer. He lifted out the chainsaw and pulled roughly on the starting cord, twice, three times. The chainsaw sputtered and failed to kick into life. With a barely suppressed snicker, Detective Sergeant Cooney registered his pleasure. Helen headed for the unmarked car.

'Something fishy about that guy,' Cooney insisted as he followed in her wake. 'He's over here a year and he's already set up in business? Stinks to high heaven, if you ask me.'

'It's called *initiative*,' Helen said, and swung the car door open. 'Some people have it, some people don't.'

Cooney bristled at the insinuation. He turned sour, his lips curdling. He lapsed into default mode. Sex-starved prick mode.

'I don't believe it,' he said. 'You fancy the guy.'

'You can be a real arsehole, Cooney.'

'Sergeant to you.'

'Yeah. Sergeant Arsehole.'

21

Black-eyed, her head bandaged and a length of white gauze reaching vertically down from her forehead and over her nose, the nostrils packed with wadding, Kitty Newman had managed until Leo's arrival to avoid seeing her reflection. She'd averted her eyes from her image in the bathroom mirror of the private ward, the dressing mirror in the white pine wardrobe, the stainless-steel cereal bowl at breakfast time, the spoons, the buttering knife. For that reason she'd been able to withstand the pressure of Detective Garda Ben Murphy's questions.

Leo had listened from outside the ward door that Murphy left slightly ajar. She had no idea, she insisted, why Alan Cobbe had done a runner yesterday evening. The blow to her nose had been a silly accident with the door of the SUV. She knew nothing about any possible *dalliance* – the word was hers – between Cobbe and Anna Brennan. When Leo entered the private ward, Kitty fell silent. He let her sweat for a minute or two, let her unease fester.

'Why was Sonia not working on Monday? Had you given her the morning off?'

'Oh God,' she cried. 'Such a mess, such a terrible, terrible mess.'

The bitter tears of Kitty Newman had been waiting a long time to come. No, Leo told himself – waiting a long time to be displayed. The tears you cried alone merely tightened the cords that bound you. Those you cried in front of others offered the possibility of release. He approached her, took a paper tissue from the box on her bedside table and proffered it to her. Her piteous and pitying smile seemed to ask if either of them would ever look normal again. He sat on the side of the bed.

'Can you tell me why you gave Sonia the morning off on Monday?' he asked, then tested some of the theories Helen had offered earlier this morning. 'You didn't expect that you'd be at home, did you? You'd planned to spend the weekend away maybe? With whom?'

Kitty Newman nodded amid an outburst of sobs which Leo patiently waited for her to contain.

'You were going to spend the weekend with Alan Cobbe?'

More child-like than ever in her fearfulness, she glanced over at the door as though expecting the big bluff sculptor to barge in. She nodded again.

'And he cancelled the arrangement?' Leo said.

'Yes.'

'Why? Because he was meeting Anna at her holiday cottage? In Passage East?'

Her tears spent, Kitty sat herself up higher on the bank of pillows. She smoothed out the contours of the bedspread with busy, tremulous hands. At the other side of the bed from Leo, Ben Murphy was still taking notes. Leo wondered what the young detective had to write about, so little had been said. Always like this Murphy had been. Page after page of notes during even the most unproductive of interviews. And always had not one but two notebooks. The official one and a second, art-shop version with a Miró cover. Have to sneak a look at one of those notebooks some time, Leo reminded himself again. The Miró one especially.

'So, he was meeting Anna then?' he repeated.

'Yes.'

'How do you know this?'

'I saw them together on Friday evening,' she said. 'At the cottage.'

'You followed her down to Passage East?'

'I did. I know it sounds pathetic and it probably is.' Kitty surprised Leo by grasping his hand, holding on too desperately. 'But you have to understand. My husband abandoned me ten years ago and I'm . . . Sometimes it's hard to be alone. You do understand, don't you?'

He didn't like this intimate tone, this assumption that he knew too well what loneliness was. Especially in Ben Murphy's presence. Christ alone knew what he'd make of that in his bloody Miró notebook.

'And you what? You confronted them?' he asked, and her bony grip tightened.

'Oh God, I wish I had,' the woman moaned. 'I so wish I'd done that instead of . . . Oh, Jesus, I've been so stupid, criminally stupid.'

'What *did* you do, Kitty?'

'I . . . I rang Dermot,' she said. 'I told him they were at the cottage.'

Her bandaged head and the perpendicular strip of gauze over her nose put Leo in mind of the Schandmaske, the mask of shame dating back to the sixteenth century. The Scots called it the scold's bridle. A kind of iron muzzle, it was placed over the heads of troublesome women; gossips, naggers and shrews. Unfortunately for Alan Cobbe, the punishment hadn't worked in this case. Kitty Newman had more and more to say.

The Eggman was boiling. And it wasn't only because he'd lain on a hospital trolley in an alcove off the busy A&E corridor, watched over by two uniformed officers, all night. It didn't help that the trolley was made for a smaller man and required some effort on his part to stay aloft. Leo let the two uniforms take a break. They looked like they'd had enough of the sculptor.

The dust of Alan Cobbe's profession had greyed his skin, adding years to him when seen from afar. Leo revised his age estimate of the guy. Closer to fifty than sixty. More vigour there too now that the deathly pallor of his concussion had passed to reveal a ruddy complexion. His grey hair, careless and full, tended to fall over his eyes and he left it there like a man with things to hide.

'I'm fully aware of my rights. You can't harass me like this while I'm under medical care. And you can't question me in front of all these . . . these people.'

He meant *plebs*. You could tell.

'They can't hear us, and anyway, they've got their own problems, Mr Cobbe,' Leo said. 'I doubt they're interested in yours.'

'You won't get away with this, you know. I'm not without connections.'

The sculptor's accent was upper-crust, the delivery crusty. A man who'd walk all over you given half a chance and beat up on you given half an excuse. He watched Leo with a mixture of surprise, professional interest and, finally, the stirrings of some vague recognition.

'They kept you overnight as a precaution because of the concussion, Mr Cobbe,' Leo said. 'There's nothing wrong with you now. I've spoken to the senior registrar.'

'The wog? Who can't actually speak passable English? Did he manage to communicate to you the fact that I have no memory of what happened yesterday and that I'm still having dizzy spells?'

'I'll ask you one more time, Mr Cobbe,' Leo said. 'Why did you assault Mrs Newman? An assault that was witnessed by two of my officers. And why the reckless getaway effort?'

'I don't remember hitting anyone. I don't remember any-thing from yesterday,' Cobbe insisted from below his untidy fringe and waited defiantly for Leo's next move.

Leo turned his back on the sculptor and leaned against the end rail of the hospital bed. Ben Murphy still scribbled in his notebook over by the water dispenser that didn't work.

'Detective Murphy,' Leo began, 'can you get Dr Ahmed to sign off on the release form and ring Howth Garda Station for back-up. Tell them we may need serious restraint measures bringing this guy in. Cuffs, tasers, a bit of brawn, OK?'

'Yes, sir,' Murphy said, pocketing his notebook and buttoning his suit jacket. 'We're not bringing him in to Howth Station, are we?'

'Why not?'

'We're running out of room there. We could go to Coolock or Raheny.'

'We'll find room.' Leo knew he was being stubborn, which only made him more stubborn. 'Ring Sergeant Corrigan.

She'll sort it. And ask her to do a background check on our friend here, see if he makes a habit of trouncing women.'

The young detective set off through the trolleys towards the A&E reception area. Meanwhile, Cobbe had let the trace of a sneer filter through his obstinate block of a face. Time to squeeze some balls, Leo thought. Knock him off guard first though.

'Did you ever hit Anna Brennan?' he asked.

The question, out of left-field, first baffled and then enraged Cobbe, as it was intended to. Leo didn't give him time to articulate either emotion. He laid Mrs Newman's account on the Eggman.

'You were with Anna Brennan on Friday evening at her holiday cottage,' he said. 'While you were there you got a text from Kitty Newman. She'd informed Mr Brennan that you and his wife were an item, that you'd been carrying on an affair for some time. You rang Mrs Newman from your mobile and told her you were on your way to Howth to have it out with her. Mrs Newman told you she wasn't at home but you insisted that you'd find her.'

Cobbe made no response.

'So,' Leo continued, 'an hour or so after your first call to Mrs Newman, you rang again. You were at her house but she'd vamoosed. You became even more agitated and told her you were going to talk to Dermot Brennan. Clear the air, you said. So, did you talk to him?'

'I didn't go to Howth.' Cobbe remained stony-faced but a light mist had descended on the stone.

'Listen, Mr Cobbe, you're about to be charged with assault causing grievous bodily harm to Mrs Newman, with fleeing the scene of a crime, causing criminal damage to a police vehicle and with recklessly endangering the lives of my officers. You're looking at up to three years on that lot alone. Be straight with me and I'll see what we can do in the sentencing process.'

'You're offering me some kind of deal?' Cobbe was torn between sarcasm and self-interest.

'I wouldn't offer you a ham sandwich in a famine, Mr Cobbe,' Leo said. 'I've no intention of helping to minimize your sentence but I'll damn well work to maximize it if you keep messing me about.'

For a man with no memory and plagued with dizzy spells, the Eggman appeared to have retained the art of calculation. The rattle of medicine trolleys, the despairing complaints of an old woman further down the corridor and the buzz and squeak of the PA system from the A&E foyer grew louder as Cobbe's silent concentration deepened. He looked up at Leo, trying to gauge the seriousness of the inspector's intent. Leo presented his more inscrutable profile.

'I told Brennan what he already knew. That Kitty is a fantasizing old wagon. That there was nothing untoward going on between Anna and me.'

'And he accepted your word on this?'

'Yes, he did.'

'And where did this conversation take place?' Leo asked. 'In the yard, in the house?'

'In the house.'

'Which room?'

'The kitchen.'

'And Anna? Where was she all this time?'

'I didn't tell Anna about the text message. She was in Passage East.'

'So, Anna knew nothing about all of this? Knows nothing about all of this?' Leo asked sceptically.

'No.'

'You just up and leave the cottage and she doesn't even ask you why?'

'I was leaving anyway, Inspector,' Cobbe insisted. 'I told her I was going back home to Enniscorthy.'

'But you met her again on Saturday,' Leo said. 'And you expect me to believe the subject didn't come up?'

'It didn't come up because Brennan and I agreed that she didn't need to know about this silly bitch's paranoid delusions.'

Leo watched Detective Garda Murphy negotiate the trolleys at the far end of the corridor. To his surprise, the young detective paused occasionally, bestowing smiles and a few comforting words on some of the patients lying there. Didn't think the guy did caring any more than he'd thought Cobbe did protectiveness. And yet. Hadn't he himself felt something very like protectiveness from his first conversation with Anna? Hadn't her husband felt it too, if she was to be believed, keeping her at arm's length from his business affairs?

There were, Leo speculated, some women whom men felt compelled to protect. And it wasn't, he believed, altogether down to gaining brownie points from a desirable woman. Nor, in Anna's case, was it down to any sense that she was naive or especially vulnerable. He struggled to find a precise explanation. Something to do, perhaps, with the knowledge that she'd suffered in the past and didn't deserve to suffer any more? The relevance of all this to the investigation eluded him for the moment. It was no more than a solitary piece of blue sky among many in a jigsaw puzzle. But somewhere, it fitted.

'The form's been signed. Sir?' Murphy said, drawing Leo

back to the reality of a hospital corridor full of trolleys. 'Support cars should be here shortly.'

'Yeah,' Leo said. His eye leaked; the cool air of the corridor found a tributary of drool along the side of his chin. He wiped it on a sleeve. Cobbe looked out from his hairy hideaway in fascination.

'And your showdown with Dermot Brennan,' Leo said, leaning in closer to the Eggman and startling the young detective with his sudden belligerence. 'No punches thrown, no? Or do you keep those for the women?'

'You won't frighten me with your bad cop routine, Inspector,' Cobbe said, though he was clearly fearful now.

'You know what I'm thinking, Mr Cobbe? I'm thinking you wouldn't risk your neck with a man like Dermot Brennan. I'm thinking you're the kind of lad who'd hit a woman in the face but hit a man like that from behind. And I'm thinking you wouldn't trust your fist to do the damage either. You'd need something in your hand. Something heavy, something—'

'Are you hearing this?' the Eggman asked of Ben Murphy. 'You're a witness to this intimidation.'

The young detective walked away. Fair dues to you, son, Leo thought, maybe I've been too hard on you. He pressed closer still to the sculptor.

'What time did you arrive at Attenboy House?'

'Eight, half eight, something like that.'

'And you left at?'

'I was with Brennan for no more than twenty minutes,' Cobbe insisted, apparently having found a new lease of courage. 'I got back home to Enniscorthy before eleven. Quarter to eleven. Which Caroline can verify.'

'Caroline?'

'Caroline Hunt,' Cobbe said, his eyes narrowing. 'My partner.'

Leo withdrew a little, seeming to relent. Further off, Ben Murphy took possession of a bundle of clothes from a young nurse he was sharing a quiet joke with, like they were old friends. Leo let the Eggman grab a few relieving breaths before catching him unawares again.

'Brennan,' he said, and Cobbe was flummoxed. 'You never refer to him as Dermot. Always Brennan. You didn't like him, did you? No?' Leo pushed on. 'Something tells me he didn't like you either. Didn't like some arty-farty he-man sniffing around Attenboy, did he? Bet he didn't like your stone egg either.'

'He was a philistine,' Cobbe blustered. 'Much like yourself, I imagine.'

'And Anna Brennan deserved better. She deserved Ireland's answer to Michelangelo, right?' Anna's talk of loyalty came to mind. 'But that was never going to happen while Dermot was alive because, unlike you, Anna's not the kind who'd kick a man when he was down.'

Cobbe let his fringe fall lower still, concealing his eyes. What he couldn't conceal was the hard, nervous swallow that followed.

'Now we're getting places,' Leo said as Detective Garda Murphy arrived with the sculptor's dusty threads. 'Throw on those rags and we'll take you out to Howth for afternoon tea.'

22

The Priors' house on upmarket Morehampton Grove was a wreck. Everything that distinguished its neighbours was missing there. Pristine front rails and lawns, manicured shrubs and trees, red-brick façades whose limestone ornamentation stood intact, and airy, revelatory long windows displaying artworks and the plusher, creamy comforts of the bourgeoisie. Where St Judes differed most, however, was in its absence of light. The house was concealed within a circle of evergreen trees that stood like mourners around a graveside. Along the driveway, clutches of weeds and tufts of grass held sway. The wrong kind of abundance filled the empty lives of the Priors.

'Bloody shame letting a house like this go to rack and ruin,' Detective Sergeant Gerry Cooney muttered as they waited at the top of the steps that led to the front door. 'I'll do the talking this time.'

Peter Prior was a creature of the half light, mushroom-fleshed, an odour of neglect rising from his well-tailored but greasy-shouldered suit. White-haired, his tanned skin long yellowed, he was in Helen Troy's estimation around the sixty mark. A man for whom life had already gone on too long.

His mild-manneredness seemed like the last vestige of respectability in him. And even that was easily compromised. A stubbornness entered his tone and expression when he heard Dermot Brennan's name mentioned.

'I can't say I regret his passing,' he told Cooney.

'And why is that, Mr Prior?' the detective asked.

'Why? Because that cursed family destroyed us.'

'Would you like to elaborate?'

'Can you please just leave us alone? My wife isn't well. Nor am I.'

'Can't do that, Mr Prior,' Cooney insisted.

Peter Prior looked at the shaven-headed detective as if he saw no end to the intolerable cruelty that life continued to inflict on him. He retreated into the hallway and went through an open door to his left. They followed him.

The high-ceilinged sitting room was not untidy but neither was it clean. Thick layers of dust lay undisturbed on the furniture and along the shade of the standard lamp that Prior switched on. He gestured vaguely towards a sofa they might sit on if they wished. He sat on the armrest of a chair by the fireplace. Helen could tell from the sooty must of the room that the fire hadn't been lit for a long time.

'"Destroyed us", you said. What exactly do you mean by that? Financially?' Cooney asked as he took sceptical measure of the sitting room's dusty but clearly valuable contents.

Prior turned, his ear attuned to the open door. From outside came a woman's spiritless voice.

'They took our only son, our only child from us.'

Mrs Prior had the gaunt, weathered features of a woman who'd been drinking too much for too many years. Her hair, blonde tending to grey, was tied back so severely that it stretched her eyes to a slant. She wore a much-faded pink towelling tracksuit. Helen could hardly bear to look, so pained was the woman's bearing. Cooney, out of his depth in the midst of all this emotional intensity, made silent appeal to Helen.

'They got what was coming to them,' the woman went on.

Her husband stared at the carpeted floor whose pattern clearly made more sense to him than his life did.

'And if they think that time will heal and all that nonsense, they'll soon learn better.'

'What happened to your son, Mrs Prior?' Helen asked.

Peter Prior stood up, pointing a warning finger at Helen which he withdrew and raised indecisively again.

'*They*'ve sent you here,' he said. 'I can't believe this. *They* have the nerve to accuse *us* of murder.'

'They?' Helen asked.

'The Brennans.'

'We've come here because you were a partner in the Honeyvale Heights project with Mr Brennan,' Helen said. 'I can assure you we know nothing about your son.'

'Frankie was driven to suicide by that family,' Mrs Prior said as she floated across from the door and went by her husband as though he were a beggar on the street for whom she had little sympathy and much contempt.

In the long mirror above the fireplace, Mrs Prior, motionless now, couldn't stop herself from looking at her image.

'We can do this another time,' Helen said.

'No,' Peter Prior said. 'Now is fine. Now will be fine in a minute.'

He sat in the chair by the fireplace. Helen and Cooney sat too but more tentatively as they watched the woman come to terms with herself again, calmed by whatever prayer or exhortation she was clearly repeating in her mind. Soon, she was sitting opposite her husband and with her back to the two detectives.

'Honeyvale Heights,' Prior began. 'I withdrew from the project and from several others because of Dermot Brennan, because of what he did to Frankie.'

'It was *her* fault,' his wife insisted. 'Anna's. And Stephen's.'

'When did your son die, Mr Prior?' Helen asked.

'Two years ago. January. It was cold. Very cold.' Prior said this as though his bones had never warmed up again. 'My son was a sensitive child. Not up to the rough and tumble of this world. And, well, life can be difficult for kids like Frankie. He never fitted in, had no friends and no interest in sport or the outdoors. We tried to help, you know, brought his classmates round here, encouraged him to try rugby at school, or at least cricket or karate or—'

'Karate?' Helen asked nonplussed.

'Believe it or not, I used to be a black belt,' Prior said as though apologizing for his physical deterioration.

'Encouraged him to try?' his wife said accusingly. 'Corralled, threatened him is what you did.'

Helen could see that he'd heard all her accusations before and grown immune to them. He went on undeterred.

'Naturally all of this made for a pretty tempestuous home life.'

'About which you knew next to zilch,' Mrs Prior spat. 'Because you were never bloody here. You were out chasing the Celtic bloody Tiger. Fiddling the books for the crooks.'

Peter Prior shrugged a mea-culpa shrug. In the tree-shrouded afternoon light that eked into the sitting room, a photo, presumably of their son, on the mantelpiece revealed itself more clearly to Helen. A child, winter-dressed, his hands clasped behind his back in an oddly adult pose as he contemplated a snowy slope. Prior's voice was like the muted commentary of some biographical documentary. One that would end in tears.

'Children can be the cruellest of creatures, you know. Like vultures, and even the least unkind of them steer a wide berth of kids like Frankie. A child alone is a terrible thing to see. Especially when it's your own child.'

Prior paused. He'd already decided that Helen was the more empathic of the two detectives and directed his attention to her.

'When Frankie made friends with Stephen we were so relieved, not to say delighted, that we went out of our way to make the friendship last.'

'We surrendered our son,' Mrs Prior said. She was like someone who'd strayed into the midst of a church choir and persisted with singing the wrong hymn.

'Hanora,' her husband said, 'please don't upset yourself.'

'They met at school?' Helen asked.

'Tell her how they met, Peter,' Hanora sneered. 'Tell them who brought this bloody catastrophe down on us.'

Prior stared at his wife. He may still have loved her, Helen thought, but he didn't like her much any more.

'Dermot Brennan built an extension for us here,' he said. 'It was summertime . . . July, I think . . . five years ago . . .'

'Six,' his wife said. 'Six.'

'Dermot sent his son along to help and he and Frankie—'

'They weren't homosexuals,' Hanora Prior insisted. She'd turned so abruptly to face the detectives that Cooney sat back with a start. 'Not Frankie anyway.' The comically raised arch of her right eyebrow pointed up the dreadful absurdity of even the greatest pain.

169

'Frankie began to spend more and more of his time out in Attenboy,' Prior said. 'Stayed over at weekends, went down to their cottage in Passage East. Even brought the dog.'

'What dog?' Cooney blurted out in his exasperation with the oblique turns in the conversation.

'Rover,' Prior said. 'Frankie's dog. After Frankie died, Stephen kept it. We tried to get the dog back but Stephen claimed it had died in that animal welfare home he works at. When I went out there I saw the dog. He and that German tramp tried to convince me it wasn't Rover but I knew. Rover was all we had left of our son and Stephen stole him from us too.'

The Argos Sanctuary, Helen thought. So this was where Gudrun Remer entered the picture then.

'Back up the truck there now,' Detective Sergeant Cooney interrupted with all the subtlety of a man in an after-hours pub debate. 'Your son killed himself because of something the Brennans did to him, yeah? So what did they do?'

Stunned by the shaven-headed detective's insensitivity, Peter Prior faltered. His lips moved but the words he meant to speak failed him until he cleared his throat and gulped so hard it must have been bile he swallowed, Helen thought.

'They claimed that an . . . an incident of a sexual nature took place at Attenboy,' he said. 'I say *claimed* because I don't believe for one minute that anything of the kind happened because if it did, wouldn't they have called the Guards? But they didn't, and why? Because nothing happened. Because Dermot got it into his head that Frankie fancied his son and threw him out, literally threw him out, banished him from Attenboy. And did Frankie's so-called friend intervene? No. Stephen cut him off, isolated him and . . .'

The two detectives exchanged glances. Cooney's suggested that they get the hell out of there fast. Helen wasn't so sure. Most murders were domestics, the results of family disputes. Frankie Prior had once been, in all but name it now seemed, part of the Brennan family. So, by extension, were his parents. She wondered how long it had been since Peter Prior practised his karate skills.

Detective Sergeant Cooney stood up, dusted off the cuffs of his jacket. Helen rose too.

'We'll leave it at that for now, Mr Prior,' Cooney said.

'In relation to the Honeyvale project,' Helen intervened, to his annoyance, 'were you aware of the flooding out there last winter?'

'Yes, I was. Terrible business that.'

'Were you aware that the houses were to be built on a floodplain? Your decision to back out of the project, it wasn't influenced by that consideration, was it?'

'I knew it was an issue but it didn't concern me. Pat Foley negotiated the planning permits with the council officials.' He paused. 'I'll show you out.'

'One last thing,' Helen said as they left the sitting room. 'You'll understand we have to ask. A formality really, but where were you late Friday night, early Saturday morning last?'

In the hallway, Helen noticed a coat-stand in the space under the stairs. Among the coats was a freshly dry-cleaned karate outfit still in its plastic covering. She simply couldn't square the taut energy required for martial arts with this small, slope-shouldered, white-haired man who was leading them to the front door.

'I was here on Friday night,' he said. 'I never go out.'

'Except to your karate club?' Helen suggested.

He looked back at the alcove where the coat-stand stood. He smiled.

'Ah, the karate gi,' he said. 'If you're passing by St Mary's Church in Donnybrook, you'll find this week's newsletter and there's an ad in there for a charity jumble sale we're holding. This gi is one of our offerings. It was Frankie's. He used it four or five times at most.'

Helen wanted to press the rewind button and take back her too-clever suggestion. But life didn't have a rewind button, she told herself.

23

Detective Inspector Leo Woods felt knackered. He leaned against the stone wall of the small carpark out behind Howth Garda Station. To his right, a spectacular view beckoned: the hook-shaped harbour and the sea beyond and, among the waves, the sleeping giant of Ireland's Eye island. To his left, a team of telecom technicians came and went by the fire escape as they worked on the cabling from the radio tower to the rear of the station. A communications problem apparently. Like most problems in life are, Leo thought.

Inside the station, Sean Doran and his solicitor, and Alan Cobbe, awaited his arrival. Cobbe's solicitor too was due shortly. Leo wasn't ready for any of them yet. He slipped out by the archway in the cut-stone wall, strolled down St Lawrence's Road and turned right into Church Street. There, he found the window ledge of an abandoned Chinese restaurant to sit on. The red paint flaked away when he brushed the ledge. He snapped the tip off a cigarette, lit up and closed his eyes. The accumulation of sleepless nights weighed heavily on him. After a minute or two he tossed the half-smoked weed away and leaned back against the chipboard sheet that filled the glassless frame of the restaurant window.

At the foot of Church Street, an elderly man was making his way up the steep climb. Bent over and wielding a walking stick, he moved at a snail's pace. He lugged a canvas shopping bag in his free hand. On his head sat the kind of black beret Leo hadn't seen men wear for years, the kind his father used to wear. The man's face, ancient and anonymous, became visible only when occasionally he looked up to see how far he'd got. His crooked features suggested he'd had a stroke at some point in the past. Sometimes the world was one great mirror you couldn't turn from, Leo thought. Everywhere you looked you saw yourself growing old and dying. Sleep was the only escape, and he found a modicum of it as he sat there on the sill.

In his dream, the old man reached him after an eternity, stopped, stared at Leo for a further eternity and said: '*Ich kannte deinen Vater während des Zweiten Weltkriegs. Je vous reconnais. Vous êtes Leopold Dubois, non?*'

A hand gripped Leo's shoulder as he made to stand up from his window perch and he shook it off roughly.

'Sir?' Detective Sergeant Helen Troy said. 'Are you OK, sir?'

Leo looked at her, looked along Church Street. The old man had gone.

'Sorry, Helen,' he said, and a wave of relief began to radiate through his bones. It didn't get far. Helen's face was flushed and her short hair spiked awry.

'Sean Doran's escaped,' she said.

He stared at her. He didn't think why or how. He thought, Where to?

'Go up to Attenboy House, Helen,' he said. 'Take a few uniforms with you. And stay with Anna Brennan. They're taking the body to the church this evening. Stay with her and get her back to Attenboy after the service, right?'

174

'You think he might come for her?'

'I don't know,' Leo said. 'But leaving her unguarded isn't a chance we can afford to take. Are you carrying?'

'No, I . . . I'm sorry about this mess I created with the gun yesterday. I've left a report on your desk taking responsibility for—'

'Helen, there's no mess, there's no report, there's no time for this crap. Go get yourself a gun.'

Two hours later, Superintendent Aonghus Heaphy arrived at Howth Station breathing fire. His mood wasn't helped by the gathering of reporters, photographers and cameramen who'd been tipped off about the calamity. He pushed through the crowded forecourt maintaining what he imagined was a stoical silence. In reality, his pained, toothy expression spoke of comical despair. In the station lobby, he dismissed Sergeant Martha Corrigan's soothing, placatory noises. He looked around for someone to berate.

'Where's Leo?' he demanded of the tall officer, stepping back from her to seem less insignificant a little man.

'He's waiting for you in the Incident Room, sir.'

'Send up that young one . . . what's-her-name. Send her up as well.'

'Helen? Helen Troy,' Martha told him. 'Leo sent her out to Attenboy House.'

'First chance she gets, I want to see her,' the super insisted. 'She's got questions to answer.'

In the Incident Room, Leo moved over to the long window so that he could take the call Martha Corrigan was waiting to connect. Bedlam surrounded him. Officers came and went, shouting into phones to make themselves heard. In the far corner, a nurse and an ambulance operative sporting a yellow dayglo jacket attended to the groggy officer Sean Doran had knocked unconscious with the toilet cistern lid. Garda Dempsey. If a comet ever plummets down on Ireland, Leo thought, it'll surely land on that unfortunate bastard's head.

'OK, Martha, I can hear you now. Who is it?'

'Dr MacNamara at St Martin's Psychiatric Hospital.'

'Hold on a second.'

Leo covered the mouthpiece of the phone and scanned the crowd in search of Cooney's sweaty scalp. A group of officers stood deep in debate at the far end of the conference table. Behind them, Cooney comforted the young solicitor who'd found Garda Dempsey and raised the alarm. The girl was in shock and appeared neither to hear nor to see her comforter. Just as well for her, Leo thought.

'Gerry,' he called, 'are the squads in place outside St Martin's?'

'They've been there half an hour or more,' Cooney said. He switched to sage-like mode for the solicitor's benefit. 'No way is Doran heading for the hospital, and even if he is, he can't have got there yet.'

'And Honeyvale Heights?'

'Covered,' Cooney said.

Neither location was a likely one for Sean Doran but better to be safe than sorry. Where are you running to, son? Why are you running? Leo feared that the ex-boxer had outmanoeuvred him. Had he laid on the victimhood so thickly that his true nature had been expertly masked? The faint nausea that came with the realization of failure started up in Leo's stomach. He uncovered the phone.

'Martha, I'm snowed under here,' he said. 'Tell him the area around the hospital's well guarded and that I'll get back to him as soon as I've any info on Doran's whereabouts.'

'He says it's urgent, Leo. Very urgent,' Martha said. 'I think you need to take the call. And, Leo, the super's on his way up.'

Leo felt a wave of bile hotly approaching his throat. He got it back down. He hated psychiatrists and he didn't like bad news. Now it looked like he was about to get a dose of both. He shouted across the room.

'Shut the hell up! I can't hear myself think.'

The silence that followed was a resentful one and wasn't improved by Superintendent Aonghus Heaphy's walking into it.

'Put him through, Martha,' Leo said before the super had time to launch into a rant.

'Inspector Woods?' Dr MacNamara's voice bore an unexpected timidity. The kind of timidity you heard when a mistake had been made.

'Speaking. Listen, we've circled the hospital so there's no danger Doran will get in there, OK? I very much doubt he'll even try.'

'Inspector, Lisa-Marie Doran has left the building.'

'She's dead? She's topped herself?'

The resentment in the Incident Room dissolved. All eyes were on Leo. An air of foreboding had set in.

'We don't use euphemisms in here, Inspector. Especially not of the pejorative kind.'

'Sorry, sorry. So she's literally left the building? How can that be? How can she just walk out of a place like that?'

'We don't lock people up and throw away the key, you know.' A tentative assertiveness now in the psychiatrist's tone. 'We develop an individual recovery programme for each of our patients depending on their needs. So, Mrs

Doran had free access to the grounds and was encouraged to occasionally – and I mean very occasionally – leave the hospital. To be taken for a drive by her husband, for example, or go to a shop directly across the road from us, which is where she went today. Resocialization is an important part of—'

'You let her out to the shop unsupervised?' Leo said. 'A woman whose husband was being detained as a murder suspect? A woman who—'

'Mrs Doran wasn't sectioned, Inspector. She was here because she wanted to be here and we have no powers of enforcement in—'

'How long has she been gone?' Leo asked, his patience running thin.

'It appears that she took a phone call from her brother about two hours ago and was last seen in the grounds a short time later. So, you're probably talking an hour and a half or so.'

'That wasn't her brother, that was her husband,' Leo said. 'Don't you screen their calls?'

For answer, Leo got a shuffling flurry of noise and imagined the psychiatrist covering the phone so he could curse at the ceiling. Bloody psychiatrists, Leo thought, useless bast.rds with their talk of drives and complexes dreamed up by that coke-head Freud. Everything was about sex with those clowns. Except sex. Which was about death. Idiots. He was about to hang up when he heard a clearing of the throat at the other end of the line.

'It's not our policy to screen calls in all cases,' Dr MacNamara said.

'Listen,' Leo said, hoping he'd get something useful from the conversation, 'Sean Doran claimed his wife had been telling the other patients that he killed Dermot Brennan, that he did it for her. Can you confirm that?'

More hesitation followed and Leo was near breaking point. He shot stop-looking-at-me glances around the room.

'This is a murder investigation, Doctor. I need an answer and I need it now.'

'Mrs Doran has made that claim, yes. But . . .' The nature of Dr MacNamara's hesitation changed subtly. This, Leo sensed, was the prelude to a new revelation. 'Inspector, I'm stepping slightly beyond the bounds of confidentiality here but . . . today one of our nursing staff returned to duty after a trip to Morocco. He hadn't been aware of the murder out in Howth or of Mr Doran's detention and . . . and, well, he informed me a short time ago that before he went off duty last Thursday, he heard Mrs Doran say that her husband was, in her words, "going to sort out matters with Mr Brennan at the weekend".'

'And he didn't report this before he left?' Leo asked in exasperation. 'Surely to Christ a statement as specific as that would've been followed up? Surely to Christ we should've been told about this?'

'Mrs Doran lives on the borderline between fantasy and reality, Inspector. We don't, for example, assume she's a prostitute even if she constantly propositions members of staff.'

'Propositions?'

'In the sexual sense,' the psychiatrist said. 'She displays a degree of obsession in that regard. Lewd talk, inappropriate touching, that kind of thing. It's a relatively common manifestation of low self-esteem.'

'You might have told us this before now.'

'But it's entirely irrelevant to—'

'*We* decide what's relevant, Doc.'

'Don't blame us for your own incompetence, Inspector, and don't call me Doc.'

'Ah, fuck off,' Leo said. 'Doc.'

He slammed down the phone. Superintendent Heaphy advanced on him. A pointing finger conveyed the meaning of his inarticulate mutterings. Leo despaired at his own misjudgement of the ex-boxer. The Incident Room was emptying rapidly of its denizens. None of them fancied getting caught in the crossfire between Leo and his boss.

'Leo,' Heaphy said, nodding towards the door. 'A word.'

'Later,' Leo said. 'There's not a free room in the station at the minute.'

'We'll find somewhere.'

It was less a promise than a threat.

24

In the kitchenette at Howth Garda Station, Superintendent Heaphy pulled out a high stool for himself, took off his braided cap and placed it resignedly on the blistered faux-marble worktop. His anger had abated. He looked at Leo like a man on the point of giving up on a jigsaw puzzle.

'Why didn't you bring Cobbe to another station?' he asked. 'You could've brought him to Raheny or Coolock.'

'I know, I know. I messed up.' Leo was angry at himself for his irrational resistance to Ben Murphy's suggestion earlier.

'Sergeant Corrigan should've thought of it too,' Heaphy said.

Leo felt shivery. Fatigue, he speculated, not to speak of falling asleep in the cold earlier.

'It was my call, right? Leave Martha out of it,' he said. 'Anyway, Doran and his solicitor were up there on the top floor and these telecom people were working on the cabling. They needed to go in and out from the top floor to the fire escape stairs and the door up there was unlatched. Doran spots this as he's being taken to talk to his solicitor. He goes in and, first, he gets to make the call to his wife I promised him last night.'

'You promised him . . . What were you thinking, Leo?'

'I was trying to soften him up. He hadn't spoken to the woman for a few days. I didn't promise he could make the call in private. That was down to the solicitor, but I wouldn't blame her for that. It was an ordinary kindness. Doran took advantage of her. So, call over and he talks to the solicitor for a while. Then he asks to go to the jacks. Garda Dempsey takes him there. Doran pretends it's a serious toilet visit, locks himself in, says he can't unlock the door. Dempsey finds something to stand on so he can look down into the jacks and Doran clocks him with the lid of the cistern. Then he waits for the technicians to move away, slips out on to the fire escape and he's gone. Dempsey's out cold and the solicitor's waiting ten, fifteen minutes, she's not sure how long, but suspects something's up and rings the switchboard and . . . the rest is history.'

'And no sightings yet?'

'Not a dicky-bird,' Leo said. 'Depending on how well he knows Howth, he might have got to the railway station in less than five minutes without breaking sweat.'

Heaphy shook his bald head and sighed deeply. Leo fetched a paper hankie from his pocket and dabbed the perspiration from his brow, blaming the stuffy, soured-milk atmosphere of the kitchenette.

'So Doran's our man after all,' the superintendent said. 'To tell you the truth, I thought from the start that it was him only I had to be careful not to say so. With the Junior Minister on my back and all, you know.'

'I'm still not convinced,' Leo told him.

'But why would he break out if he was innocent?'

'Half a dozen reasons. Number one being that he believed we were going to stitch him up,' Leo said. 'He's been at the wrong end of bad luck all his life. Positive outcomes are not what he's come to expect.'

'Well, we need an outcome, positive or negative, pretty fast,' Heaphy said.

Leo leafed distractedly through the papers he'd brought with him from the Incident Room. Sometimes you had to think about other things so that your subconscious might get to work on the problem at hand. The autopsy report. Nothing there that Ben Murphy hadn't already told him, he supposed. He scanned it anyway.

'What about this Cobbe fellow? Any prospect he might fit the bill?' Heaphy asked.

'He has a lot of questions to answer,' Leo said without looking up from his papers.

He set the report aside to reveal the next item. One of those curious moments of synchronicity followed when two minds separately alight upon the same subject.

'Talking about questions to answer,' the superintendent said, and lowered his voice further, 'did that young detective sergeant pull a gun on Cobbe yesterday?'

Leo, speed-reading Helen's report and its admission of culpability, realized that the story had moved on. Denial was no longer an option. Love to know who shopped her, though. The jealous elder lemon, Cooney? Or that zealous Young Turk, Ben Murphy?

'Are you listening to me, Leo? She's a liability, that one. First, she mucks up the interview with Doran and—'

'She saved my life,' Leo said. 'If she hadn't been thinking on her feet, I wouldn't be standing on mine.' You're sitting down, Leo, you clown, he told himself. He blundered on. 'Cobbe was heading straight at me in his SUV and swerved away when he saw the gun. I don't think he meant to mow me down or anything but my guess is he was running on autopilot until the gun appeared.'

Superintendent Heaphy looked at him doubtfully. Leo knew his boss had heard plenty of these spontaneously concocted stories over the years. Back in the early days, they'd both invented their fair share of them. Actually, it was mostly Leo. Heaphy had always had too many qualms in that area. Still, in the end, he'd invariably been won over by Leo's assurances.

'Of course, Cobbe doesn't remember any of this,' Leo reassured him. 'The concussion, you know.'

'But he might get his memory back,' a weakening Heaphy objected. 'And where do we stand then? What if he complains to the Garda Ombudsman?'

'He can't afford to. His only defence in the assault on Mrs Newman is that he can't remember what happened,' Leo said and, placing Helen's letter face down on the autopsy report, switched the subject. 'We've sent out extra security on Attenboy House, on Mr Foley's home, and on Mary Immaculate Refuge of Sinners. Can you give me clearance on that? It's maybe twenty officers and some overtime.'

'Mary Immaculate Refuge of Sinners?'

'The church in Rathmines. Dermot Brennan's being taken there this evening. We don't know what Doran's state of mind is, so we have to cover even the unlikeliest places he might turn up.'

'Of course,' Heaphy said, and wandered away nursing a vague resentment as he often did after his encounters with Leo, the sense that he'd gone in with fists flying and left with his arse kicked and his world-view turned on its head.

Meanwhile, Leo had just uncovered Sergeant Martha

Corrigan's report on what she'd gleaned from the German police about Gudrun Remer. And from Interpol.

The woman had form. Form, the evidence suggested, might well have been encoded in her DNA. Her mother, a Red Army Faction member, had abandoned the five-year-old Gudrun and was jailed for her involvement in a 1972 bombing of US Military Intelligence HQ in Heidelberg which left three dead and five injured. As a teenager Gudrun had fallen out with her engineer father and left home. In her twenties she'd taken to anarchist pyromania, and in more recent years to animal rights activism. Short prison spells in Germany and Britain marked her passage through the nineties and into the noughties. Since 2002 she'd lived in Wicklow at what was to become the Argos Sanctuary.

Like Stephen Brennan, the German woman had despised her father, left home, become radicalized. Hardly a significant link, Leo decided, since it was essentially the story of his own early life too, the early lives of many. But Gudrun Remer's passion for pyrotechnics? Was there some connection there to the failed attempt at setting Anna Brennan's charity shop alight after it had been trashed?

Maybe this interest in Gudrun Remer was merely a signal of his despair. A clutching at straws or, perhaps, a pathetic attempt to stave off the feeling of foreboding that overtook him whenever Sean Doran came to mind. Killer or not, the ex-boxer seemed to him to be hurtling through some deep, enshrouded forest. No map, no compass, no logic, only the last fraying threads of sanity holding his mind and body together. Leo knew the feeling.

He put away the Rose of Tralee's report. The last item was a preliminary report from the Technical Bureau. Nothing he didn't already know, and the 'brute force attack' on Dermot

Brennan's encrypted laptop had failed. Often does, Leo thought. From his forehead, the sweat streamed down, sent tributaries to the corners of his eyes, burning into them, joining up with the tears to run acidic along his cheeks. His armpits burned too though he shivered uncontrollably.

Not the fucking malaria, Leo thought, not now. Not before I make sense of Dermot Brennan's death.

25

'**D**o not hide your face from me now that I am in distress. Turn your ear to me; when I call, answer me quickly. For my days vanish like smoke . . .'

From her perch in the organ loft, Detective Sergeant Helen Troy counted forty-two people in the Church of Mary Immaculate Refuge of Sinners while the elderly priest read from Psalm 102:2. Including herself, Detective Garda Ben Murphy and the dead man. Among the others, she saw just one familiar face apart from Anna Brennan's. Alongside her, Murphy had finished with his private and, it seemed, intensely genuine prayer and blessed himself. Now he displayed a broad-brush knowledge of the mourners. 'Neighbours,' he'd whispered annoyingly a number of times as a few well-dressed couples entered sporadically before the service started. 'Worked for him,' he'd averred as a group of two middle-aged and three younger men took up a pew near the back; 'not one of them has a bad word to say about him apparently'. She wasn't in the mood to be impressed.

'I lie awake and moan, like a lone sparrow on the roof.

'All day long my enemies taunt me; in their rage, they make my name a curse . . .'

Alone in the front pew, Anna Brennan stared vacantly ahead. She wore a simple black jacket and skirt. Her red hair coming gradually loose from a carelessly clipped bun was the only suggestion of disarray in her. Her son Stephen was absent not only from her side but from the church. Had he hated his father so much? Helen thought. Or was it possible that guilt kept him away? And if so, was it a murderer's guilt or just the regrets of an ungrateful or spiteful child? The kind of child who would put dead rats in a water tank in his parents' home?

The scent of lilies, sweet at first but soon overpowering, had plunged Helen back into memories of her father's funeral three years before. The bleakness of the Psalm didn't help, and Helen wondered if Anna Brennan had chosen it herself. Her brother's text message, sent half an hour earlier as she'd waited outside the church, played on her mind. It seemed oddly to make her mobile weigh more heavily in the breast pocket of her jacket. *We have to sell the house. I want my cut. Jamie.* He hadn't texted her for weeks and she'd been wondering why. Now she knew.

Apart from the fact that putting the house on the market now would mean accepting a pittance for it, Helen had a promise to keep. Through his last days, her father had worried what Jamie might do with his share of the money should the house be sold. By then, her brother had already been before the courts twice on charges of possession and once on a public disorder charge. Helen had vowed that she'd never sell. 'Never say never,' her father had told her, 'but hold out as long as you can, pet.' In the intervening months, Jamie and his seemingly endless string of boyfriends had let the small terraced house become a tip. As straitened as her circumstances had become this past while, it had never occurred to her to go back on her word to her father.

The old priest had more than a touch of New York in his guttural County Meath drawl. Probably spent his working life over there and would pass his retirement filling a gap left by the lack of priests in Ireland. His accent brought to mind the one mourner she'd recognized. Skip Sheridan. She turned her attention to him. He still wore denims and a lumber shirt but freshly laundered. She wondered if, like hers, his mind had been cast back to his own loss. His expression, which she'd noted as he arrived at the church earlier, suggested it had. Sad, a hint of the troubled in the wrinkling of his forehead.

'Because of your furious wrath, you lifted me up just to cast me down.

'My days are like a lengthening shadow . . .'

The sweeping swing of a door and the unrestrained clatter of footsteps advancing from beneath the organ loft startled Helen and Ben Murphy. They peered over the balcony rail, gun hands reaching inside their jackets. It wasn't Doran. She didn't know the diminutive Gucci-suited man with the Jaffa orange suntan. Murphy did. The man found himself a pew close to the front of the church. He worked on his hair, his tie and his cuffs for a minute or so before folding his arms and settling in for an irritated wait.

'Pat Foley,' Murphy told her. 'The auctioneer guy in the Honeyvale Heights project. The Junior Minister's cousin.'

Helen nodded but didn't engage in the eye contact she sensed Murphy was inviting. How would Anna Brennan react to Foley's presence? Would he dare stand before her and offer his sympathies?

The starting breaths of the church organ and the elderly organist sounded beside them.

MARK O'SULLIVAN

The piece was neither familiar nor conventional. It offered no melodic consolation. Strangely sustained and dissonant chords followed by a carnival-like outburst eerily suggested the Gothic absurdity of death. Helen looked in over the organist's bent shoulders at the sheet music. 'La Vierge et l'Enfant' by Olivier Messiaen. Recalling her schooldays French: the Virgin and the Infant, a mother and her child. She looked down at Anna Brennan. The piece had to have been her choice, and how ironic that was. But Anna's child wasn't there, only an auctioneer, a gardener, a couple of detectives, and a scattering of neighbours and workmen.

When the service ended, a small queue of sympathizers formed along the aisle. Pat Foley grabbed a place in the vanguard. Skip Sheridan was among the last few. Hands were extended to Anna Brennan and she shook them firmly but briefly. There was an embrace or two, similarly brief. An occasional word was spoken but not from her. Helen watched transfixed as Foley drew near to the widow. He held out his hand. The widow didn't take it. He left it there, said something. The plea in his expression rang false. Anna turned her head for the first time. She smiled sadly at the next person in the line and Foley moved away feeling, Helen imagined, like a spider flushed down a bath-hole.

Soon, it was Sheridan's turn to sympathize. Murphy nudged her as the widow unexpectedly raised her arms and drew the gardener closer than she had any of the others. Sheridan, looking out over Anna's shoulder, was surprised by this special treatment. When he caught Detective Sergeant Helen Troy's eye, he seemed to be desperately pleading for release.

'What was all that about?' Murphy whispered.

*

The Incident Room in Howth Garda Station throbbed with life. A team of uniforms took calls of possible sightings, reports from house-to-house enquiries at the inner-city block of flats where Doran had grown up, the uncooperative statements of his sisters, neighbours, his old boxing mates. The team out at Honeyvale Heights checked in regularly too. None of them had anything of substance to report. Helen Troy when she'd rung in did have something interesting to say, though not concerning Sean Doran. The incident at the church that she'd relayed to Leo surprised him but he didn't have time to dwell on it.

Meanwhile, Alan Cobbe continued to kick and punch the walls and metal door of the holding cell in his frustration. Leo had fobbed off the Eggman's celebrity solicitor earlier, bogged him down in the details of the charge sheet for a while. The trick had worked. Vincent Rice was a tired, late-middle-aged man, gaunt from his young bride's demands. In the end, the guy, all togged out in a dangerously loose-fitting dress suit, had left, gratefully accepting Leo's promise to ring him as soon as he was ready to interview the sculptor.

Cobbe's partner waited in the outer office downstairs. He'd got a quick glimpse of her a short while before. Caroline Hunt was in her mid-thirties, careworn and very nervous. He'd let her stew for half an hour, put in a call to Enniscorthy Station hoping to get some background info on Cobbe. He got more than he could have hoped for. It was time to confront Ms Hunt.

She was terrified of him. She stood up from the bench she'd been sitting on in the outer office, stepped back from his outstretched hand. Lowered head, tightly folded arms, a sideways-on stance. Her default position, Leo thought, making herself small, covering her soft spots from life's assaults. And Alan Cobbe's.

'Inspector Leo Woods,' he said. 'I've some questions for you, Caroline.'

'I want to see Alan. I've got every right to see him,' she said. English, Leo decided, Sussex. South anyway. Somewhere below London.

'I'm afraid that won't be possible. Not tonight anyway.'

'You can't do this to him,' she insisted. 'He's quite claustrophobic, you know. You have no idea how badly this will affect him, being locked up like this.'

'It isn't some medieval dungeon he's in. Now, sit down please. You can help him if you're straight with me.'

Caroline Hunt sat on the bench and her face emerged from its hiding place. She smelled of cats. A lot of cats. He imagined she took comfort in them. Lonely people often did. Even the ones who weren't alone. Below the mousy, unwashed hair her eyes were bloodshot, the bags beneath them shaded with fatigue. At the outer edge of her left eye, an inch-long scar had some rawness left in it yet.

'Back in March, you were discovered close to where you live by some neighbours. You'd been beaten severely,' Leo said. 'You were bleeding from a face wound. The muscles of your right forearm were bruised and in spasm. Was Alan Cobbe responsible for this assault? Whoever it was that rang the Garda Station anonymously a few days later certainly thought so.'

'I told the police that I'd been out walking and been attacked by someone I didn't recognize.'

'I know what you told them. What I want to know is the truth.'

'That *is* the truth.'

'Alan Cobbe has a previous conviction for assault,' Leo

went on. 'His ex-wife, nineteen ninety-three, in Waterford. Three years suspended after the woman entered a plea for mitigation on his behalf. And yesterday two of my officers witnessed him punching a woman to the ground in Howth. So, can you understand why I don't believe you, Caroline?'

She clutched the sleeves of her long grey shapeless cardigan with white-knuckled fists.

'Stupid, jealous women,' she said. 'What could they know about the . . . the pressures of being an artist, the turmoil of being blocked, of not knowing if new work will ever come and, if it does, whether it'll sell?'

'And you do? You're an artist too?'

'Was. Thought I was.'

'And now you're what? The sculptor's muse? Or his skivvy?'

Her technique for resisting interrogation was a familiar one. Find a point in the middle distance to stare at and beam yourself up from the reality of the moment.

'Was Mr Cobbe conducting an affair with Kitty Newman or Anna Brennan or with both of them maybe?'

'Alan's only interest in these people was commercial. There was nothing else to it, except in their tiny minds. They don't know the difference between a salesman and a lover.'

'Not always easy to tell, is it?' Leo said, and her gaze lingered on his face for a little longer, her aversion overcome. This was her story in a nutshell, he thought. Flinch from the first blow but then accept and rationalize. What she would never understand was that this was simply an invitation to further abuse.

'Was Mr Cobbe with you last Friday night, early Saturday morning?'

'Yes, he was.'

'What time did he arrive home on Friday night?'

'Quarter to eleven.'

'Your recollection is very precise.'

'I was at my laptop. I checked the time when he came in.'

'Why would you do that? And, even if you did, how would you remember?' Leo asked, and had one of his Eric Cantona moments. 'Most minutes and seconds of our lives pass us by like a river. It's only the rocks that capsize us that we remember.'

Nonplussed, the young English woman returned to her contemplation of the floor tiles. The trick wasn't working quite so well now. She tried building a wall of stubbornness instead but there's not a lot you can build when your hands are shaking and your eyes are watering.

'He was with me all night,' she said.

'Like he is every night?'

'Yes. Apart from the occasional trip here and there.'

'Sales trip or love trip?'

'Bully me all you want, Inspector, but you won't break me,' she said.

'You're already broken, girl,' Leo told her. 'All I've got to do is wait until the pieces start falling. Listen to me now and listen well. Mr Cobbe will more than likely march out of here tomorrow with his solicitor and then it's just him and you again. We'll be on his case big time, watching every move he makes, and he'll take it out on you because that's his form and all either of us can do is hope he doesn't go too far again.' He took his calling card from his jacket. 'Take it, Caroline, you're going to need it.'

She took the card, fumbled around in her handbag to find a place for it. Leo felt sorry for her. He wished he didn't have to keep whipping at her.

'This is a murder investigation, Caroline,' he said. 'One

lie, one half truth can easily deflect us, waste valuable resources and give the killer time to run or to strike again. Do you want to be responsible for that?'

A picture of despairing angst, she snapped her handbag shut. The gesture briefly emboldened her. She stood up from the bench. It occurred to Leo that she dressed so dowdily – that bedraggled, colourless cardigan, the insipid browns of her blouse and skirt – because of Cobbe's possessiveness, his controlling nature. It wouldn't be easy to wrest her free from him so that the truth, in turn, could be wrested free. Or rather, confirmation of the truth. Leo was already quite certain that Cobbe hadn't been with her on the night of the murder.

The questions he needed to ask Anna Brennan were mounting. Questions that, unfortunately, would have to wait until the day of the funeral had passed.

'Sir. Leo. Sir.'

Leo, asleep at his temporary desk in Howth Garda Station, stirred reluctantly. The voice didn't rouse so much as coax him from sleep. It was Sergeant Martha Corrigan, her voice as sweet and fair as her looks. Imagine waking up every morning to the Rose of Tralee, Leo thought drowsily. Then he remembered where he was. He snapped to attention.

'Detective Garda Murphy on the line, sir,' she said. 'There's trouble in Hearnstown.'

'Thanks, Martha.'

'Are you OK? You seem feverish.'

'Do I?'

He wiped his damp forehead with his fingers. The unease within him took on a worrying momentum. He took the phone.

'Inspector Leo Woods here,' he said, overdoing the sour formality.

'Detective Garda Murphy here, sir,' Murphy said, lobbing the formality ball back into Leo's side of the court. 'I'm in Hearnstown, outside Foley's office. Someone just drove a JCB through the front window. Driver's gone but—'

'Weren't we supposed to be watching his office?'

'Couple of kids started throwing rocks at the squad car there,' Murphy explained. 'Car went chasing them and whoever did this was clearly just waiting his chance. Probably paid off the kids.'

'Right, he was waiting unobtrusively in a bloody great JCB,' Leo said. 'And where were you?'

'I was keeping a watch on Honeyvale Heights, sir.' Murphy's voice remained even. 'Sir, it gets worse.'

'How can it get any worse?'

'There's a body inside the building. A woman, we think.'

26

Darkness and fog and the flashing blue lights of squad cars lent Hearnstown an almost festive air. Better than the blandness of its daytime manifestation, Leo thought. But not much better. He raised the white plastic strip that marked the police cordon and headed down the main street. Distended voices, the crack and splinter of glass, and the thud of broken blocks guided him towards Foley's office. A swirl of yellow light insinuated itself into the blue. The colours didn't mix. That was Hearnstown for you, Leo mused, a sociopath's paradise.

Out of the fog, a couple of uniforms emerged and pointed him in the direction of Foley's office. He heard Ben Murphy's voice from somewhere up ahead.

'Of course I do, love,' the young detective said. 'Tomorrow night, yes. All night, I promise.'

Just as Leo saw that Murphy was talking on the phone, the young man saw him.

'Have to go now, sweetheart.'

He looked at Leo defiantly and didn't explain himself. Instead, he got down to business.

'The Technical Bureau should be here in ten minutes or

197

so, sir,' he said. 'But the building's not safe enough to get inside and ID the body yet, so I'm not sure what they can do.'

'Who says it's not safe? We have an engineer on site, have we?'

'I tried to get in but part of the roof came down and covered the body. It's still coming down.' Murphy was his usual detached self though more tired in the blue light and looking less healthy when he crossed into the yellow light.

'Let's have a look,' Leo said.

Murphy led the way. The sight of the JCB parked in the lobby of Foley's office brought Leo back to the reality he now realized he'd been avoiding since he left Howth Garda Station. He thought he knew who the dead woman might be. When Murphy spoke again, he might have been reading Leo's mind.

'Do you reckon Sean Doran did this, sir?' the young detective asked.

'It's a real possibility,' Leo said.

'So, if it was Doran, then . . .'

'Then maybe the body is Lisa-Marie Doran's, yeah.'

'But why would he kill her?' Murphy said. 'And why would he leave her here? Is he implying that Foley and his Golden Circle pals are ultimately responsible for what happened to her?'

'More bloody metaphors,' Leo said hotly. 'Your Miró notebook must be filled with this shite by now.'

Murphy gave him a questioning look but didn't respond.

The façade of Foley's office and of the bookmaker's next door had entirely collapsed. All of the ceilings and most of the roof had tumbled inward. In the spinning yellow light, Leo glimpsed a naked thigh, the hint of a bare arm. The rest of her was covered in rubble and broken glass. He felt bitterly angry with Doran.

'She'd been telling the other patients that he planned to sort things out with Dermot Brennan last weekend, and after the murder she claimed that Sean had done it,' he told Murphy. 'If he did kill Brennan then he may have reckoned he had to shut her up. Or it might just be down to offended masculinity. His wife was fixated on sex when she was in the psychiatric hospital. Maybe he couldn't hack it any more.'

The young detective shook his head, shuffled a stray lump of pebbled cement away from his left foot. Though he didn't feel convinced of the scenario he'd painted, Leo bristled at Murphy's implied dismissal of it. He wished Helen was there. He thought about ringing her but let it go. How could he justify saddling her with his longing for female company? Even if it was merely work-related. The edge had gone off his irritation with Murphy.

'I talked to Sean Doran in the holding cell last night,' Leo said as another sheet of plate glass fell from the upper floor of the building. The loud crash set his heart racing. 'I told him he could ring his wife and he basically didn't want to know. "Thanks for nothing" was his response.'

'So what does he do now?' the young detective asked.

'Christ knows.' Leo gestured towards the ruined office. 'Maybe he'll try to get Foley. We have to be aware of that possibility. Better put more men on Foley's house and send a car with him wherever he goes, OK?'

'I spoke to that bastard half an hour ago,' Murphy said, his expression taking on the bitterness of the insulted. Leo had never heard the young fellow swear before. 'He's decided to beef up his own security arrangements. Says he doesn't trust us to protect him.'

Bells rang across the landscape of Leo's brain. He tried to locate them, follow where they led. Detective Garda Murphy made to speak but Leo raised a halting hand. The young detective listened to the sounds he imagined Leo was listening to. The shattered building caved in some more, the woman's body almost entirely buried by now. Leo was listening to Sean Doran. *Ask him how he dumped the three squatters out of number thirteen and sorted the problem at number nine.* How do you send a bunch of squatters packing? You hire a few heavies. Like the fat man with the black ringlets in the room above Foley's office when Leo had dropped by the other day?

'Check out Foley's security people,' Leo said. 'He may have used some hired muscle to clear some houses in Honeyvale Heights of squatters. Maybe he makes a habit of sub-contracting his dirty work. See what you can dig up.'

'Will do,' Murphy said. 'By the way, sir, I've had some thoughts on these missing Latvian girls. Should've copped it before, but that second job Daina worked, it was in an Indian restaurant on the southside.'

'And?'

Murphy shifted from one foot to the other uneasily. His gaze didn't have its usual directness about it. Always had an extra bullet in the gun this guy, Leo thought, always one step ahead of the posse.

'I don't mean to be xenophobic or whatever,' he said, 'but it's at least a possibility that . . . well, you've heard about these sham marriages between Eastern European women and non-EU nationals who want to get residency rights in Europe. Indians, Pakistanis, Sri Lankans usually. The girls get paid anything from two to five thousand euro, which is major money for them and for their families back home.'

'Go on,' Leo said.

'The thing is that to marry at a registry office, you have to present in person your passport, PPS number and birth cert three months before the ceremony.'

Murphy had got his confidence back. Trouble was it looked like arrogance.

'And?'

'And Mrs Brennan said that Daina had been working at Attenboy since she arrived in Ireland two months ago. But the interpreter's notes from the interview with the girl suggested three months. I checked with the interpreter. He clarified things. Daina hadn't said she'd been in Ireland three months. She'd said that she intended to stay here only for three months.' In the absence of any encouragement or a reply of any kind from Leo, he went on. 'I've emailed all of the registry offices in the country, asking them to check on all marriage applications made in recent months.'

Leo remained silent, though not in an effort to be un- pleasant. He remembered Daina's repeated insistence that she was nineteen years old. Maybe the girl hadn't after all been afraid of being sent back home as a minor. Maybe she'd merely been insisting that she was of marriageable age from fear of losing out on the pay-out for a sham marriage.

'Stay on it,' he said peremptorily, and waited for Murphy to move away. The young detective didn't oblige him just yet.

'Sergeant Corrigan is following it up, sir,' he said.

Over by the plastic strip of cordon, a white minibus had pulled up. The driver, a middle-aged woman, remonstrated with the uniform on duty there.

'Sort that, will you?' Leo told Murphy but the young detective was already headed in that direction.

Leo stared grimly at the ruins before him. The JCB held its bucket up towards the heavens like it was pleading with the gods to accept this human sacrifice. How many more silent sacrifices would be laid at that altar in the coming months and years? Jobless mortgage defaulters driven to madness or suicide. Broken marriages, homes and hearts. A lost generation paying for the sins of the rich.

'Sir!' Detective Garda Murphy shouted, and in that very moment Leo looked towards the body in the rubble and saw a hand move. Leo was in among the fallen steel and blocks and glass in a flash, scrabbling away the detritus from the woman's body, already hearing her moan. A twisted sword of aluminium speared down from the roof.

'Sir!' Murphy called again as he ran from the cordon. 'Watch out above!'

Leo ducked left and the aluminium missed him by inches. Tenderly, he brushed the debris from the woman's swollen mouth, from the deep gashes on her cheeks and from her eyes. It occurred to him that he had no idea what Lisa-Marie Doran looked like.

'You're OK, Lisa-Marie,' he said. 'You're going to be OK.'

'*Socorro!*' the woman cried feebly. '*Socorro!*'

'What language is that?' Leo asked of Murphy, who had now reached his side.

'No idea, sir.'

'*Ajude me!*' the woman moaned again from out of her bloated mask of blood and dust.

'Could it be Latvian?'

Daina? he thought. Or the sister? What was her name? Sonia. It was impossible to know.

With Murphy's help, he scrabbled at the duvet of rubble that covered the woman.

'Get out of here,' Leo said, glancing up at the unstable remains of the roof.

'No, sir,' Murphy said.

The woman's eyes closed and she fell silent. Murphy found a wrist below the rubble and then found a pulse. He nodded at an expectant Leo. They worked together, the young detective gradually freeing the woman's limbs, Leo concentrating on her head. Soon, he had unmasked her.

Thursday, 25 November

27

Each element of the Newlands Cross Crematorium had been designed and constructed to soften the blow of death. The hushed greys of limestone, Wicklow granite and board-marked concrete. The light a shade more spacious than gloom. The complete absence of religion's cruel imagery. A high-roofed circular amphitheatre, its stone-tiled floor sloped towards the point of exit beyond which the flames awaited. Detective Sergeant Helen Troy sat alone in the back row wondering if Stephen Brennan was going to show up. The crowd was already down on last night's ceremony at the Refuge of Sinners church in Rathmines.

Hardly surprising that Foley had given the crematorium a miss but Skip Sheridan hadn't appeared either, and that gave Helen more pause for thought. What was the nature of Anna's relationship with the American? The guy hadn't worked at Attenboy House very often. Even if she'd succumbed to his charms or vice versa, what could have developed between them beyond a stolen kiss or two? Perhaps Anna's embracing Sheridan had been some irrational and spontaneous expression of her guilt at betraying the dead man. Or might it be something altogether more innocent than that. Had the American somehow penetrated that reserve of hers? Had they simply become friends of a sort, clicked on some platonic, conversational level that in Helen's experience was an all too rare occurrence across the genders?

The music started up, scattering her speculations.

Down below, the coffin began its last journey. Helen couldn't bear to look at the aperture opening to receive it while Anna Brennan sat as stiffly as ever, apparently un-moved as her husband was returned to dust. Not a woman, Helen thought, who believed she'd lost everything.

A second and, she presumed, final piece of music was playing. Some generic, synthesized dirge without lows or highs. Discomfort spread through the gathering. A polite cough here, a soft shoe shuffle there, heads almost imper-ceptibly moving to see who might decide it appropriate to make the first move. Helen obliged them. She had to go out-side anyway. Leo would be waiting for her call. She was glad to escape.

Outside the crematorium doors, a circle of pillars held up the great weight of a concrete disc. In the shadows of the cloister, the breeze carried an edge of excoriating ice in it. The drastic weather predictions were beginning to stack up. It wasn't just getting colder by the day but by the hour. The phone reception was crap too. She scrolled down on the work phone to Leo's number as she headed in the direction of the carpark. The text messages she'd received on her own phone would have to wait. Two from Jamie. One from the other bastard, Ricky.

'Helen.'

Leo's voice, oddly frail, almost ancient, bothered her.

'Leo, are you all right? You sound—'

'Knackered, I know. Coming down with something.' He

sighed. 'So, how's Mrs Brennan doing? Has she talked to you at all?'

'Not a word,' Helen said. 'Should I do some probing?'

'No, not today,' he said. 'Not unless she decides to open up to you. Which is possible. She's got to break some time.'

'I don't know. She's not showing a lot of emotion.'

'Which means precisely nothing,' Leo said, roused from his lethargy to an unexpected sharpness. 'Emotion doesn't have to consist of weeping and gnashing of teeth, you know. Life's more subtle than that. You'll learn that in time.'

Helen wasn't sure if she was being berated for being young or for being foolish. Either way, it didn't feel good.

'So, did the son show up?' Leo asked.

'Not a sign of him. Nor of Foley,' she said, swallowing her pride.

'Foley won't show,' Leo said. 'He's holed up in his house. I'm on my way over there now.'

'Do we know who the girl in Hearnstown is yet?'

'Brazilian, apparently. Works as a cleaner and lived in an apartment above the bookie's next door to Foley's office. Lucky to come out of it alive. Even if she is in a coma.'

'Was it Doran, do you think?'

'Can't think who else it might be,' Leo said.

A tired pause followed. She'd reached the edge of the carpark. There were ten or twelve cars at most, an ancient but well-preserved green Mercedes among them. The glare of the sun on the windscreen masked the occupant. A slow, deep intake of breath at the other end of the phone line gave the impression of a tired man working up his resolve to go on.

'I'll head out to the Argos Sanctuary when I've finished with Foley,' Leo said. 'Young Brennan won't be expecting to see me. Maybe I can catch him off guard. And listen, Helen, I'll be having a chat with Mr Cobbe this afternoon. I want you to sit in on it with me.'

'Are you sure that's a good idea?' Helen asked. 'I mean, that business with the gun and all.'

'His only defence to the assault charge is amnesia so he can't admit to seeing you pull the gun,' Leo said. 'Give me the low-down on that kid who committed suicide and his parents, will you? I need to push Stephen Brennan hard with everything we've got.'

As she spoke, Helen wandered along the grass margin of the carpark and kept a watchful eye on the Temple building where the cremation had taken place. People had begun to drift out. Five, six of them. By the side window of the Mercedes ten metres distant, she saw what appeared to be a child dressed in white jumping around on the back seat. She felt she was being watched. She scanned the crematorium and the bare, newly planted landscape around her. Nothing. She turned to the green Mercedes again, walked towards it.

A pair of petrified eyes peered out at her from the side mirror of the green Mercedes. Her phone hand fell to her side. There was no child in the car. Just a white karate gi swinging on its hanger in the breeze from the open driver's-side window. Peter Prior's gaze went skulking down and disappeared from the mirror. Instinctively, Helen turned back towards the crematorium. Was Prior waiting for his wife? If so, what the hell was she doing at Dermot Brennan's cremation? If not, what the hell was Prior doing there? She could feel the vibrations of Leo's voice in the palm of her hand.

The sudden, unexpected conjunction of Peter Prior and Dermot Brennan in her mind struck a spark. The kick they'd noted to the victim's side. Prior's black belt status. A karate kick stood a better chance of taking a big man down than a southpaw punch from a boxer with a modest reach.

She lifted the mobile.

'Leo, that blow Dermot Brennan took . . .' But the phone coverage had faded and the line gone dead.

Most of the mourners had emerged from the Temple building. Mrs Prior wasn't among them. Helen went inside. Only three people remained. A couple Ben Murphy had described as neighbours last evening, and Anna Brennan. A wave of panic came over Helen. Had she done the wrong thing? Should she have confronted Prior outside? But confronted him with what, and for what reason? She knew only that she had to get Anna Brennan out to the unmarked car, join up with the squad car out at the front gate and get her back to Attenboy House.

She went over and sat behind the widow.

'Whenever you're ready, Mrs Brennan,' she said.

'I'm ready.'

'But if you'd prefer to wait a—'

'There's nothing to wait for,' Anna said, and stood up. She looked at Helen as though she were seeing her for the first time. 'Aren't you very young to be a detective?'

'Not especially,' Helen said. 'I'm thirty-four.'

'Thirty-four?'

The widow's stunningly blue eyes remained fixed on Helen for what seemed like an age. Helen sensed that there was more behind the hint of mild surprise in her expression than met the eye.

She walked to the side and a step ahead of the widow as they left the godless Temple. From the circular cloister outside, she once again had a clear view of the carpark below. The Mercedes had gone.

28

A tree-lined avenue of red-brick embassies and diplomatic residences, a private school and stately pads for the rich to hide in, Ailesbury Road was the second most expensive street in the Dublin version of Monopoly. Unlike the board game, there was no Jail, and while the residents might occasionally lose a school tie or two, they would never lose their shirts. No matter how the dice fell, Leo reflected as Garda Dempsey parked on the street by the railings of Pat Foley's house, these people always won. The best an ugly detective could hope for on a street like this was some kind of pyrrhic victory. Some psychological equivalent of pissing on their roses.

'Welcome to the Land of the Point Zero One Percentiles, Dempsey,' Leo declared, and opened the passenger door of the squad car.

'The what?'

'Where the other half lives,' Leo said.

'The other half of what?' Dempsey asked, and Leo gave up.

'Tell you what, son. Get out your Cleverphone there and play a game for yourself. I won't be long.'

'I don't play games when I'm on duty, sir,' Dempsey objected. 'And it's an Android Smartphone actually.'

'Ah, an android. Does it dream of electric sheep?'

'Electric sheep?'

'Google it, son,' Leo said, and closed the car door behind him.

He felt too high-spirited, and knew that high-spiritedness marked the onset of a malarial bout as surely as it marked its end.

At the gate, a burly black-suited man with a straggle of curly black hair awaited him. The fat man in the attic. In his skittish mood, Leo adopted Eric Cantona's straight-backed swagger, even turned up the collar of his jacket. He reached the gate. Closer up he could see that much of the fellow's bulk was down to steroids, the muscles unnaturally thick in his neck.

'Are you looking for something?' the heavy asked, his accent raw, guttural. North Cork, he thought, or maybe Limerick.

'Aren't we all?' Leo said. 'Isn't that the essence of the human condition?'

The big fellow didn't appreciate Leo's sense of humour. Some days, Leo reflected, no one appreciates your sense of humour but yourself. He flashed his ID and trumped the big man's obstinacy. 'Open the gate, sunshine, Mr Foley's expecting me.'

The earpiece squawked somewhere inside the fellow's hair. He turned from Leo and muttered into his left hand. Another squawk. He opened the gate. Leo crossed the pebble-strewn drive. He negotiated the channel between a black Mercedes SUV and a silver Alfa Romeo Spider convertible and climbed the ten steps to an open front door.

A smaller dark-suited man with the same squawk in his ear guided him silently to a sitting room where he pointed at the only hard chair in a room full of sofas.

'Wait here,' he said. Another gruff Limerick accent.

'No thanks,' Leo said, and went back out into the hallway. 'Paddy!'

He felt a hand on his arm and turned to see what was at the end of it.

'Did you just touch me?' he asked the small man.

'I asked you to wait. Which ear are you deaf in?'

'The one I'll put to your chest to see if your heart's still beating after I hit you,' Leo said. 'Listen, son, go and fetch Mr Foley pronto and I won't write your name in my little black book, all right?'

The small man gave the matter some thought but not much. He went along the hallway to a door at the end and knocked on it. A muffled reply emerged but the door stayed closed. Leo sneaked up on the small man, brushed him aside and went inside. The auctioneer was eating breakfast. Startled, he looked up from his newspaper. He wore a purple paisley dressing gown. He'd just showered. It didn't make him seem any cleaner. He swallowed down whatever it was that filled his mouth.

Leo gestured at the broadsheet propped against the sugar bowl. They were still running with the photo of Chopra the Chopper from the IMF walking past a beggar in Dame Street on his way to the Central Bank.

'Wouldn't you think he'd throw him a few bob, all the same,' Leo said.

Pat Foley folded the newspaper and set it aside haughtily.

'Are they still running the Fantasy Property Supplement on Thursdays?' Leo joked. 'Bespoke residences in the Vale of Honey. All mod cons. Gold taps and enough water to drown in. What d'you reckon, Pat? Would they give me a job writing shite like that?'

'Have you found Doran?' Foley asked, ignoring the jibe and quickly adding, 'Whatever he might have told you, it's all rubbish.'

'We haven't found Sean, actually. What might he have told us then, Mr Foley?'

'The usual nonsense. These people have a victim mentality. The concept of individual responsibility is alien to them.' He pushed away his plate. 'They sicken me.'

'*These people* or the sausages?' Leo asked, nodding at the discarded plate.

'If you'd a few less comedians in the ranks you might be able to do your job properly,' the auctioneer said. 'Weren't you people supposed to be protecting my property out in Hearnstown?'

'Your property is the priority, is it? What about the Brazilian girl who's lying in a coma over in Beaumont Hospital? Doesn't that bother you?'

'She wouldn't be there,' Foley retorted, 'if it wasn't for your men's incompetence.'

'Do you own the bookie shop premises too? Was she renting the apartment from you?'

'The place was leased to RaceFair. What they do with it is their business,' Foley said. 'And the premises isn't mine. Or not only mine. It belongs to Hearnstown Enterprises Ltd. I'm on the board.'

'But the bookie shop is closed.'

'The lease has been paid up to the end of this year. It's still theirs to use as they see fit.'

Leo took out his cigarettes and popped the filter from one.

215

'We don't smoke in the house, Inspector.'

Leo lit up. He wasn't surprised that smoking was the kind of issue a man with no morals might take a moral stand over. He felt tired. Life wasn't so funny all of a sudden. Another sign of the oncoming relapse. One minute you were having a laugh with a fellow, next minute you wanted to knife him.

'Complain to the Junior Minister,' he said. 'But you'd want to hurry. This government will be out on its arse pretty soon.'

The kitchen strove for a rustic Provençal look. Open shelves, pots and pans hanging from hooks, subtle clutter. Pat Berlusconi hopped up and drew a soiled plate from beneath a potted plant. He tossed it on the table by Leo's elbow. He stood with hands on hips, tapped a slippered foot on the kitchen floor tiles, waited. On the far wall was a photograph of Foley playing happy families with a woman who looked too sophisticated for him and two daughters whose good looks came from the maternal line. Leo continued to stare at it until Foley took umbrage.

'Now, Inspector,' Foley said, 'I've a busy day ahead of me, sorting out the insurance on my premises, thanks to you lot.'

'A few more questions,' Leo said. 'If Sean Doran was, as you claim, satisfied with your efforts on his behalf, why would you believe he's the one who wrecked your offices? Why would he want to?'

'Because he's a loose cannon,' Foley replied defensively. 'Because he's hardly a master of logic, given his situation, is he?'

'If he was driving that JCB last night, he had a reason,' Leo said. 'And another thing. You had problems with squatters at Honeyvale Heights earlier this year. How did you sort them? Was it the Boys of Limerick out there?'

Foley paled. His hands left his hips and found refuge in the pockets of his dressing gown. He sat down at the table again, composed himself, and then composed a reply. A careful reply. All the while he wore that wary look of a man trying to judge how much his adversary knew.

'Squatters, yes, it's an ongoing problem in all unsold properties, and ours are no exception. But I can assure you that any actions we took were above board. No unnecessary force was used. No one was hurt. You'll find no complaints of ill-treatment were made to the Guards.'

'I'll bet I won't,' Leo said. 'How many houses were involved?'

'Just the one.'

'And the address?'

'If memory serves me, it was thirteen Honeyvale Heights.'

'What about number nine? Any squatters in there?'

'No.'

'You sure?'

Foley leaned his elbows on the table and let a wry smile form below his hard little eyes.

'Let me guess, Inspector,' he said. 'You don't like me. You don't like my profession. You don't like the fact that my cousin is a Junior Minister. You have a problem with anyone who actually makes money, who makes some actual contribution to the economy. So, you desperately want to find some connection between Dermot Brennan's murder and me. There is none, Inspector. Except in your overactive imagination. You're wasting my time and yours trying to find things that aren't there.'

'You blamed Dermot Brennan for the flooding problems

at Honeyvale Heights but we have reason to believe he had information that would force you to retract this allegation.'

Foley kept his weak smile together with a minimum of twitching. He brushed back his coal-black hair in a gesture that was alarmingly similar to the real Berlusconi. Leo felt himself slide towards the fantasy world of malarial fever. He stood up abruptly, faltered when he reached the heights. Foley gloated, his arms crossed high on his chest just like the rogue Italian PM.

'So, let's say Dermot lays this info on you,' Leo said. 'And you send Dumb and Dumber out to Attenboy House and things get out of hand.'

Foley settled into a comfortable smugness. Leo felt as though they were playing Charades and his guesses were way off the mark. What am I missing here? he asked himself. But couldn't find an answer. He took a shot in the dark.

'These heavies, did you hire them from a security firm or are they on your payroll?'

'They're my employees,' Foley said. 'And they're not heavies, they're—'

'How long have they been working for you?'

'Two, three years. I can't remember exactly.'

'So, you've needed bodyguards for quite some time then. Why would that be, Mr Foley?'

'They're not bodyguards, Inspector,' Foley insisted. 'I took them on to work security at the hotel while it was still in operation. We had regular break-ins and, besides, a night club brings its own problems. And, needless to say, we had little or no Garda presence out in Hearnstown.'

'You owned the hotel? The Hearnstown Regency?'

'Hearnstown Enterprises did. Like I've already told you, I

was on the board of directors. I—' Foley shut himself up at that point.

The smile and the smugness had disappeared from his face. He placed a hand over his mouth. All that was left was a mask. A Venetian mask, Leo decided. The Bauta. Square-jawed, an obstinate chin line, no mouth, featureless.

'But you were doing the hiring and firing. You ran the show. So it was you who closed it down and left the Dorans jobless. What did Sean make of that, Mr Foley? Or was he grateful for your efforts in this regard too?'

The auctioneer shrugged.

'I kept it going as long as I could. They both knew that.'

'Sean Doran told me they could hang you but that you could hang them too. What did he mean by that, do you think?'

'I've no idea.'

'Dodgy goings-on at the hotel? Or at the night club, maybe?'

'Absolutely not.'

The collar of Foley's pyjama T-shirt was a loose one but it was still too tight for him at this moment.

'I'm asking you to leave now, Inspector,' he said. 'And you can rest assured that every detail of our conversation will be relayed to your superiors. So take your vendetta, Inspector Woods, and piss off out of here.'

'Ah, the mask of urbane reticence slips,' Leo said. He wished he had more energy for the fight. The air around Foley was astringent with fake lavender fumes. He headed for the door. 'Next time you shower, Mr Foley, forget the deodorant and try some disinfectant instead.'

29

Clondalkin took an eternity to negotiate. A monotony of industrial estates, motor outlets, commercial warehouses. The wrong kind of world, it seemed to Helen, to return to after burying your dead. Spiritless, anonymous, utterly material. Along Ballymount Road and Belgard Road, she felt her pity grow inexplicably for Anna Brennan. When they'd reached the slow filtering lane on to the M50, Helen knew the reason why. She knew what it was like to be regarded as cold and unfeeling. Jamie had flung the accusation at her often enough. Ricky too. But that was how the world worked. A man made sacrifices to reach the top and he was a workaholic. A woman did the same and was judged a bitch.

She wished she could find something to say but guessed that the widow sitting in the back seat didn't want to talk anyway. Then the first text message came in. The phone on silent, only the lightly vibrating thrum audible. She assumed it was her personal mobile on the passenger seat and checked. It wasn't.

Helen sneaked glances in the rear-view mirror as she drove. During the twenty minutes it took to reach yet another standstill of traffic at the turn-off from Malahide Road, Anna Brennan had received and answered three text messages. She'd made no attempt to hide the ongoing exchange. Not once did she check the rear-view mirror to see if she was being watched. Helen felt certain that the texts all came from the same person. The widow's look of weary forbearance suggested it might be her son, Stephen.

As they passed slowly by Fingal Cemetery, Anna stared at the bland grey wall there with a kind of troubled longing. Coming from out of this trance, her question was all the more unexpected.

'Is Kitty Newman OK?' she asked, her gaze still on the cemetery.

'She's got a broken nose,' Helen told her. 'I think they're letting her out of hospital tomorrow once the brain scan results are in.'

Still new to the city, Helen hadn't intentionally taken this round-about route by the cemetery, but wondered if her mistake might have unsettled the widow. She wanted to test Anna Brennan, probe a little that inscrutable façade. When they got a clear run beyond the cemetery, she did.

'Were you surprised by what your friend Mr Cobbe did to her?' she asked. 'He might have done more damage if we hadn't been watching.'

She had the widow's attention now. Her appalled attention.

'You saw this happen?'

'Yes,' Helen said. 'Two of us did, actually.' She pushed harder. 'It was disgusting, really revolting. Did you know he was that kind of man?'

'What men are capable of has never surprised me,' the widow said, and added pointedly, 'Or women, for that matter.'

'Has he ever assaulted you, Mrs Brennan?'

'Of course not,' the widow said, resentful now.

'Why "of course"? Why wouldn't he assault you like he's assaulted his ex-wife and Mrs Newman and—'

'Is this normal procedure?' Anna asked. 'Interrogating a widow on her way home from her husband's funeral?'

'You started the conversation, Mrs Brennan.'

She wanted to push on, confront the widow with Cobbe's admission that he'd gone directly from the holiday cottage in Passage East to Attenboy House on the night of the murder.

They stared at each other in the rear-view mirror, re-assessing each other. Then Helen mimed an unsubtle glance at the mobile phone in Anna Brennan's hand. The widow put the phone in her handbag. For the rest of the journey to Howth, she remained silent. Obstinately silent.

The dogs howled and yelped in the yard at Argos Sanctuary. Leo wished he had their energy and their indifference to the cold. His shivering would soon be uncontrollable, the only consolation being that the fever rarely lasted more than a day. Not a great consolation because after the shakes came the vomiting and the marrow-deep pain in the bones and the weird, hallucinatory hours before the parasites went back to hibernating in his liver.

'That's an awful bad dose you have, sir,' Garda Dempsey said. 'I hope I don't catch it off you.'

The squad car was buffeted by waves of small dogs throwing themselves at the doors and windows. Beads of cold sweat broke out on Leo's forehead.

'If it was contagious, I've no doubt but you'd catch it,' he said. 'But it isn't. Do you like dogs, Dempsey?'

'Can't stand them, sir.'

'You'll be staying in the car then?'

'I will, sir, if I'm let.'

'How's the head today?' Leo asked, noting the plaster on the top of the young Garda's scalp.

'A bit sore is all,' Dempsey said, but his concerns clearly lay elsewhere. 'It wouldn't be swine flu you have, sir, would it? There's talk of an epidemic.'

He'd sneaked the driver's-side window open a little and appeared to be trying desperately to breathe the fresh air from outside.

The door of the cottage opened. Stephen Brennan stood there looking sleep-befuddled in his black T-shirt, jeans and unlaced climbing boots. He looked at the squad car and shook his head, but a double-take had him staring at Leo with the same obsessive fascination as when they'd first met. Leo wasn't in the mood for being ogled.

'Roll that window down further, Dempsey, will you?' Leo said. He leaned across and called out, 'Put those dogs out of harm's way, son. I need to talk to you.'

'They won't bite you,' Stephen said, trying not to stare but unable to resist.

'If those dogs come near me, I'll kick seven colours of shite out of them,' Leo told him. 'The choice is yours, son.'

Leo expected to be faced down but the young fellow shrugged, called to the dogs, cajoled them along towards an outhouse to the left of the cottage. They ran in and out among three mongrel cars all of which shared a colourful variety of door and body panels. Eventually he got all but one of the dogs inside the outhouse door whose lower edge was either rotten or had been gnawed by rats. Leo wondered if there were rat-traps around the place.

Over by the side wall of the cottage, taking the sun, lay a shaggy German Shepherd just like the ones that had been haunting Leo's dreams for going on fifty years. Leo stepped gingerly out of the car but stayed on the safe side of the open door.

'What about that one?' he asked of Stephen Brennan. 'Those Alsatians are lethal.'

'Rover has got cancer. Every move he makes, he suffers.'

'Why don't you have him put down then?'

'Gudrun doesn't believe in that kind of thing,' Stephen replied without conviction.

'In what kind of thing?' Leo asked. 'Mercy?'

'She thinks it should die a natural death.' Stephen glanced at the cottage like he'd been caught telling tales, picked up a bucket of meat scraps and headed around the corner of the cottage and out of sight.

'Do you want me to come with you, sir?' Dempsey asked.

'No need,' Leo said.

Over at the cottage a curtain twitched. Gudrun Remer, he supposed. Though he kept a wide berth of Rover, the nausea rising in him had reached his throat. The dog barked threateningly, made to lunge at Leo, but age and pain pulled it back. Leo felt an unexpected and overwhelming pity for the thing.

He went after Stephen Brennan and found him fiddling with the lock of an opening into a chain-linked pound. Inside, a pack of menacing pitbull terriers pissed themselves with wild anticipation.

'You're not going to open that gate, are you?' Leo said.

'Feed my lambs, feed my sheep,' the lanky young man answered obliquely.

'Yeah, well, Christ didn't mention pitbull terriers.'

'We can't help what we look like, can we?'

Stephen Brennan was growing in confidence now that he'd picked up the scent of Leo's fear. He undid the lock and was about to pull back the gate when a woman's voice interrupted.

'What do you want from us?' the middle-aged woman in gypsy finery said. 'We have spoken to the police. We have nothing more to say.'

The woman's raw attractiveness and her Marlene Dietrich tones were only slightly compromised by her furious expression. As she hurried towards them, Leo noted the young man's irritation. Peace didn't reign in this New Age household, Leo thought.

When she had come within a few yards of him, Leo turned to face her.

'*Bitte*,' she murmured.

Leo held out his hand and she felt obliged to take it.

'Inspector Leo Woods,' he said. 'And you'd be Gudrun Remer?'

'*Ja* . . . yes.'

'I need to talk to the both of you,' he went on. 'Inside would be better.'

'I've got to finish feeding the dogs,' Stephen said, and reached again for the gate, but Leo got there first. He slammed the lock tight.

'Now.'

Inside wasn't better. The cottage stank. A vast skillet pot with two gas rings burning beneath it. A bubbling brew of sheep's heads, innards, pigs' feet and God knew what else. Leo felt hot, spaced out. He sat down heavily at the rustic kitchen table. He gestured at young Brennan to sit opposite him. Gudrun Remer went and stirred the pot.

225

'*Rieche ich Hundefutter?*' Leo asked, and Gudrun turned sharply from the cooker.

'*Ja*,' she said, her voice curt with suspicion.

Did she feel her secrets would be harder to keep from one who spoke her mother tongue? Stephen Brennan seemed to be getting nervous too. Leo noticed that the couple avoided each other's glance.

'*Mein Vater hatte einen Hund*,' he said with a smile as though sharing an intimacy with Gudrun. '*Ich habe immer diesen Geruch gehasst.*'

'Nothing wrong with a natural smell,' she said. 'You speak good German.'

'*Ich besuchte eine Deutsche Schule.*'

'*In Deutschland?*'

'*Nein, in Irland.*'

The trick worked. Stephen treated the German woman to a hateful look and turned on Leo. Good stuff, Leo thought, let him rant a bit and then stick it to him.

'What do you want from me? You should be out there looking for Sean Doran, for Christ's sake, instead of hassling me just because your pious middle-class sensibilities are offended by the fact that I didn't go to my father's funeral. I hated him. He hated me. That's all there is to it. You expect me to act the hypocrite and show up all in black like I give a shit. Well, I'm sorry, Inspector, but I don't.'

Stephen leaned closer to Leo, making fists on the table.

'I'm sick of you bastards. Pig bastards.' He spat out the words like a kid at the front of some protest march in the face of a visored riot-policeman. So, Leo gave him a dirty dig.

'Tell me about your friend Frankie Prior,' Leo said. 'Tell me why he killed himself.'

Stephen Brennan reeled back on his chair. His lips moved but his vocal cords were on mute. A flush rose from his long neck, touching his cheeks, gathering at the peaks of his sculpted cheekbones. He looked like Leo felt. Ablaze.

'Your father threw Frankie out of Attenboy,' Leo went on. 'There was an incident of some kind. What happened out there, son?'

Over by the gas cooker, Gudrun Remer set her ladle aside, wiped her hands on her red gypsy skirt and took a chair at the young fellow's side. She thought about placing a hand on his shoulder but clearly changed her mind.

'None of that has anything to do with Dad's murder,' Stephen said.

'We have to examine every possible angle,' Leo responded. 'It's as simple as this. Frankie's suicide means that you and Mr Prior both must be considered as suspects. Until we know the precise details of that incident at Attenboy House and what followed, we can rule neither of you out. What we've got here is a son who hates his father so much he didn't even show up at the funeral. And we've got Mr Prior who blames your father for his son's suicide. Both of you have motives and neither of you has the strongest of alibis.'

'But Stephen was with me on the night of the murder,' Gudrun Remer objected.

'Like I said, not the strongest of alibis, Ms Remer, not unless we've an independent witness to the fact.' Leo turned back on Stephen Brennan. 'Frankie was obsessed with your mother. I'm guessing this was a sexual obsession, right?'

The young fellow made to stand up. Leo placed a firm hand on his shoulder and held him down.

'This is an outrage,' Gudrun Remer said. 'You cannot speak to the boy like this.'

'The boy?' the boy said. 'Don't call me a boy.'

'Listen, son, we can do this here, nice and cosy, or we can take the both of you out to a dark room at Howth Garda Station. Make up your mind fast because I'm not feeling the best and that smell is getting to me and I'm liable to lose the run of myself any minute now.'

Stephen Brennan held his head in his long-fingered hands. He pulled so hard at the strands of his straggly fair hair that Leo expected lumps of it to fall on the table. The German woman could no longer hold herself back from comforting him. The young fellow swept her hand away roughly.

'Are you happy now?' she asked of Leo. 'Look at what you have done to him. Can you not see the pain you are giving him?'

'Ms Remer, I saw what was done to Dermot Brennan.' Leo shrugged. 'This doesn't seem so bad in comparison.'

'Dad found Frankie dressing up in Mam's clothes,' Stephen said, his head lowered to the table. 'I'd gone down to the shops for . . . I can't even remember what for. And Mam was . . . I don't know where but she wasn't there either. Frankie had stayed over and when he woke he thought Dad was out too. He went into Mam's room and . . . I didn't know he was like that. I mean, I knew he was weird in some ways but I never thought he was, like, a total weirdo.'

'And your father, did he hit him? Was that it, did he beat him up?'

The young fellow nodded, his eyes still lowered.

'Which is kind of understandable,' Leo said provocatively. 'In the circumstances, like. If I saw some young lad prancing around in my wife's stuff . . .'

A wave of nausea swept over him. He thought he was about to throw up.

'You are not well, Inspector,' Gudrun said.

'I'm fine, I'm grand,' Leo countered, annoyed at the distraction.

He searched his pocket for a tissue. A dozen snapped-off cigarette tips fell out on to the floor. A long stringy lump of tissue followed them and he bent down towards it, wiped his forehead and the leaking eye, and nearly didn't make it back up. Stephen Brennan watched Leo, taking in these signs of collapse that seemed to confirm his tragic view of humanity. The kid actually feels sorry for me, Leo thought. To hell with that.

'So, you left home because your father trounced Frankie?' Leo said. 'I don't get it. You leave home but you cut yourself off from Frankie too.'

'I left because Dad wouldn't believe I wasn't into the same weird shit as Frankie. He thought I was a tranny.' The plea for pity, for understanding in his voice irritated Leo. 'All my life he's dissed me. I wasn't what he expected from a son and he never let me forget it.'

'Gave you a hard time, did he? Made life intolerable for you, yeah?'

The anger rising in Leo didn't immediately reveal its source to him.

'Yeah.'

'Such as? Beat you as a child, did he?'

'No,' Stephen answered warily.

'Punched you to the floor and kicked your head so hard that he burst your eardrum?'

The young fellow shared a perplexed shrug with Gudrun Remer. Leo was sweating like a pig. His cheeks burned. His brain floated somewhere near the ceiling. Things didn't look any better from up there.

'Told you that because you were tone-deaf, you had no soul, did he? Made you scrub dog shit from the kitchen floor and kicked your arse when you missed the smallest spot? Walked out the door when you were eight years old and said it was your fault he'd never be back?'

Leo closed his eyes on the dizzy spell that threatened to unseat him. He pressed his fingers hard into the raw, leaking wells. Pull yourself together, Leo, or get the hell out of here now.

Stephen Brennan and the German woman came back into starry focus. They seemed to be awaiting an explanation.

'Another case,' he said. 'One I dealt with years ago. So, we were where? Your father thought you were a tranny. And your mother? Did she think you were a tranny too?'

'She did not help,' Gudrun said.

Stephen Brennan stood up and shook a fist in her face. 'Don't you rubbish my mother! I've heard enough of that crap from you!'

She didn't like it, but she didn't flinch. A tough little cookie, Leo thought. He'd expected not to like her. Old revolutionaries pissed him off, even the ones who hadn't bloodied their hands. And yet, he took to Gudrun Remer. More than just took to her. Felt a stirring for her.

Go home, Leo, he told himself.

'I rescued you from all of that,' Gudrun told Stephen calmly. 'I helped you to—'

'If you're so concerned about your mother, son,' Leo intervened, 'why did you leave her standing alone in the church and at the crematorium? What kind of son does that to his grieving mother? A guilty one maybe?'

Leo steeled himself as well as he could in his condition for

Stephen Brennan's attack. It didn't come. The young fellow pulled a sneer from his infantile repertoire.

'How do you live with a face like that, Inspector?' he asked.

Gudrun Remer turned away in embarrassment.

'If you think this is ugly, son,' Leo said, 'wait until you hear what happened at Attenboy. Your father is kneeling on the ground in a stone shed. Behind him, someone is standing with a crowbar in his hand. Could be a *her*, I suppose, or some kind of in-between species like yourself. Anyway, this someone raises the crowbar. Remember it? The one your father played his macho game with? Did you ever play? I doubt it somehow. But you've enough strength in those weedy bones to swing it all the same and you've enough of the sneak in you to hit him from behind. So this fine specimen cracks open your father's skull, throws in a few more shots so's to be sure, like. Then he kicks your father in the ribs as he lies dying. That's ugly, isn't it, son?'

'It wasn't me,' Stephen said.

'You know what I reckon?' Leo continued. 'I reckon that whoever swung that crowbar also trashed your mother's charity shop.' He turned to Gudrun Remer. 'Trashed the shop and tried to set it on fire. You'd be an expert in that area, wouldn't you, Ms Remer, if your CV is anything to go by. What do you reckon?'

Stephen Brennan sneaked a look at her. She grew defensive.

'My fires always ignite, Inspector,' Gudrun said. 'And this charity shop? It was for nothing but to clear her conscience. She did not love the son she had and so she wanted another. This boy Frankie misunderstood.'

'And little Stevie here wanted a new mammy, right?' Leo

said. 'What's he going to do if you can't pay the twenty-thousand-euro fine? Three months without a mammy, Stevie boy. Can you hack it?'

The young fellow made to swing a fist but Leo caught hold of it. Then, absurdly, they were arm-wrestling each other, their elbows resting on the table. Leo was having to work harder than he'd expected. The rising fever burned away his strength and Stephen Brennan grew in confidence. All Leo had left in him was his doggedness. It got him through until a distraction came along. From inside the hallway beyond the kitchen came the crinkling sound of paper. Leo let go of the young fellow's hand.

'Who's that?' he asked of the German woman.

'A dog, Inspector. This *is* a dog sanctuary.'

'I was thinking it might be a rat,' Leo said. 'Or maybe even two rats. What do you reckon, son? You seem to have a problem with rats out here. Do you set traps for them?'

'Stop calling me *son*,' Stephen said. 'I'm not your son.'

'Did you put the rats in the water tank in Attenboy House, son?'

The young fellow blushed madly. An admission. Leo wanted to test him some more. He knew that the contempt he felt for the kid wasn't entirely fair or reasonable and that much of it was down to the parasites in his liver and the rotten memories they stirred in him. Still, Leo thought, you use whatever you've got. Even if you've only got recurring malaria.

'I know the story,' Leo said. 'Your nobody's child, right? Ever hear that old song? Awful, self-pitying old crap.'

The fight had gone out of Stephen Brennan.

'Is this really necessary?' Gudrun said. 'This intimidation?'

'The truth is necessary,' Leo told her. 'The path to the truth is necessary. Therefore I must walk it, shoes or no shoes, shit or no shit.'

They both looked at him in confusion. It was time to abandon ship.

'I'll see myself out,' he said. 'But I'll be back.'

In the chain-linked enclosure behind the cottage, the pitbull terriers raged. Ugly pugs on them, vicious eyes, death-trap teeth. Poor bastards, trained to maim and kill, and when they do what they're trained to do, they're abandoned. Who'd want to be a dog? he thought. Or an ugly detective?

He stumbled past the dying Alsatian, who was looking at the world like he didn't give a damn any more, and got himself to the squad car. Fell into the passenger seat, dead on his feet. Helen Troy and Ben Murphy would have to take the Cobbe interview, he told Dempsey.

'Sir, are you all right?' Garda Dempsey said, so frightened by Leo's sickly appearance that he'd forgotten to hide his Smartphone or turn off the ping-ping of the game he'd been playing.

'Take me home,' Leo said, and closed his eyes.

There were dogs in there too but he fell asleep anyway.

Friday, 26 November

30

The worlds inside and outside Leo's brain speeded up, teemed with amplified voices and obscure objects, and meanings that eluded him. It was a world that no longer required his presence but he hung in there anyway because he knew he had things to do even if he couldn't remember what those things were. He sat against the kitchen wall, hid under the duvet on his bed, lay on the mask room floor counting the masks and getting a different total each time. Sometimes it seemed like he was in all three places at the same time.

Close to dawn, the fever tossed him aside like a wet rag and left him for dead. His work mobile hadn't stopped ringing and buzzing with incoming texts all day. Next time it rang he'd answer, Leo thought. Then the memories began to filter through the fog. He'd already answered his phone, and more than once through the long fevered hours. He sat in his armchair facing his wall of masks. Like a hostile crowd, they watched him. Though it was still dark outside the suburban trains had begun to roll. With each one, a further cargo of memory was delivered to him though none was quite intact. They came too without a timetable so that the actual sequence of the calls remained obscure.

Detective Sergeant Troy's call was the first one to reconstruct itself in Leo's mind. She'd been solicitous. Her concern had been real and he'd appreciated it. He hoped she hadn't been too offended by his reaction to what she had to say. Or too freaked out by his precarious state of mind.

'Cobbe's been released? For Christ's sake, Helen, that should have been my call.'

'It was Superintendent Heaphy's decision, with a little smarmy persuasion from that celebrity solicitor guy. The file on Cobbe's assault of Kitty Newman is ready to go to the Director of Public Prosecutions and with this Caroline Hunt woman vouching for Cobbe's whereabouts on the night of the murder the super reckoned we had nothing to hold him on. But we did. I mean, Cobbe was so blatantly pointing the finger at Skip Sheridan, it was obvious he had stuff to hide.'

'Sheridan? This is the gardener? The American?'

'Yeah. And Cobbe claims that when he went to Attenboy House on the evening of the murder, Dermot Brennan was upstairs somewhere. So Cobbe knocks on the back door a couple of times until Brennan calls down, "Is that you, Sheridan?" And, according to Cobbe, there was real venom in the way he shouted it. I don't believe a word of it.'

'But how does Cobbe even know of Sheridan's existence?'

'The guy was working at Attenboy House when Cobbe visited some time back. Anna introduced them. Listen, Leo, as soon as I walked into the interview room, I knew that Cobbe recognized me, maybe even remembered that I pulled the gun. OK, he may have had concussion but it's well gone by now. Everything he says is bullshit.'

Leo thought there may have been more to the conversation but couldn't be sure.

The call from Detective Garda Ben Murphy must have come later because Helen would surely have referred to the young detective's latest success. He'd found Daina and Sonia, the missing Latvian girls, in an apartment building on Mountjoy Square near the city centre. The rising star had taken off big time, Leo thought. In one raid, he'd hit an array of targets. An immigration case, human trafficking and double kidnap, and an identity theft scam. What he hadn't yet got was so much as one word from either girl. Leo remembered almost embarrassedly the resentful exchange that ensued.

'Get back to me when Daina starts talking.'

'About what precisely, sir?'

'How the hell do I know? Something she's seen or heard up at Attenboy. Something out of the ordinary.'

'Such as?'

'Such as, go away and do your job, son. I'm sick, I'm tired, the masks are dancing on my wall.'

'Masks?'

'Who said anything about masks?'

'You just did, sir.'

'Look, don't be annoying me. I'll be in early tomorrow morning and I'll be expecting real progress.'

'You don't like me, do you, sir?'

'No, I don't.'

'Might I ask why?'

'You might, but you won't get an answer any time soon. So fuck off and do what you're paid for.'

'I'm not finished reporting to you yet, sir.'

'You have something else? How come you always have something else, Murphy? Are you trying to prove something or what?'

'Yes, sir, I am. I'm trying to prove I can do my job.'

'Just give me the something else.'

'The girl we found at Foley's office.'

'Is she OK? Don't tell me we have a second corpse.'

'Still in a coma, sir, but the prognosis is positive so far. The thing is, we found a backpack of hers. Some interesting stuff in there. Not what you'd be expecting a cleaner to pack for a night's work.'

'Such as?'

'An assortment of exotic underwear, a set of handcuffs . . . Let's see . . . A strap-on dildo, two packets of condoms, one edible, and a sort of, I don't know, eye-mask thing.'

'Don't take the piss. Are you taking the piss?'

'Sir? I'm telling you what's in the backpack. I'm telling you this girl is no cleaning lady, sir.'

Leo squirmed at the memory of his fevered rantings. He drank a litre of water from the plastic bottle by the armchair. He lopped the tip from a menthol cigarette, lit up and inhaled deeply. The smoke went down a treat but came back up a cough. He inhaled some more and won the battle over his protesting lungs. The wrong kind of fight, Leo thought, was the kind of fight he always won.

He surveyed the masks. He saw what it was that had so confused his counting of them earlier. At some point during the feverish day he'd hung the two new purchases made in Paris last week. Put them centre stage. Two left-side, partial masks, at once more ordinary and extraordinary than all of the others.

At last year's International Mask Conference in Liège, Leo had heard for the first time of Francis Derwent-Wood. A sculptor in civilian life, the fellow had put his art to practical use making masks for soldiers facially disfigured in World War One. He'd use photographs of the men to return to them something of their old selves with full or half or quarter masks depending on the scale of damage. For Leo, it was the beginning of another mild obsession, which eventually brought him to Marcel the mask-maker's shop. The old man in his eyrie at the end of a courtyard in Montparnasse asked no questions and seemed fascinated by this odd commission.

The first mask was based on a photo taken at the Garda College in Templemore on Leo's graduation day. The second, on a snapshot from his early days with the UN in Angola. The twenty-two-year-old and the thirty-five-year-old half faces were like brothers. One naive, the other cock-of-the-walk. Leo stood up and his head spun. He took the older brother from the wall. The papier-mâché was lightweight but firm. Its coldness surprised Leo. There was no mirror to check himself out in. He kept the half mask on and left the mask room.

He was feeling better. The dizziness had passed, the racing thoughts too. He'd forgotten that he'd meet himself in the long window of the landing since it was still dark outside. It didn't prove too great a shock. The slightly blurred reflection was kind enough to him. Considering he was mad as a fucking hatter, he thought amusedly. He stood there for a while. What was madness anyway? Wasn't it merely what others judged you to be? How many crazy bastards had he met in his work over the years who were perfectly rational or, at least, whose madness seemed perfectly rational to them. And that was just the police officers he'd worked with.

Yes, he was feeling better. Funny how you could be walking downstairs into a sombre pre-dawn house and feel like you were floating upwards into the light. He knew it was just the post-malarial high but any high would do after what he'd been through.

At precisely the same moment as he switched on the hallway light, one of the mobiles in his pocket began to ring. Not the work phone, thank Christ. Number withheld. He answered it.

'Yeah, who is this?' The half mask muffled his voice.

'How's the goin', Eric? You sound kind of weird.'

'Dripsy, you rang the wrong number,' Leo said, sweeping off the mask. 'Who the hell is Eric anyway?'

'It's your code name, like,' Dripsy whispered. 'You said you didn't want me using your real name, man.'

'Why the hell are you ringing me at this hour of the morning?'

'You're an ungrateful bastard, do you know that? I'm over here in Sherrif Street busting my arse for you the last four hours and this is the thanks I get.'

'You've lost me, Dripsy. What are you on about?'

At the other end of the line, a hurricane blew in. Leo could hear the uneven shuffle of Dripsy's stride. Dripsy had a limp when he was sober. Leo's head was beginning to hurt again. What had he asked the skinny junkie to do for him among the inner-city flats complexes? Find something heavier than weed for him? Leo ambled along the hallway and waited for Dripsy.

'You still there?' Dripsy asked. 'Leo? Eh . . . I mean Eric.'

'Yeah, yeah.'

'I tried everywhere, every pub I was let into, every squat I could find, and nothing. Asked a couple of heads who know the lie of the land in the flats and some of the girls who work the territory. Nobody seen sight nor sound of Seanie Doran.'

He'd sent a heroin addict searching for a murder suspect? Christ, he really was losing it.

'Then I met Torrid,' Dripsy added.

'Torrid?'

'Yeah. Torrid used to be in the same boxing club as Seanie. And, get this. He seen him Wednesday lunchtime in that new pharmacy down the bottom of Talbot Street. And Torrid's so out of it, man, he didn't even know Seanie was in the shit over that murder in Howth. So he just says, How's the goin', man, any chance of a few bob? And Seanie had nothing to give him so Torrid leaves it at that and fucks off with himself.'

It wasn't much to go on but it was something. Maybe Doran had been getting his wife's medication. Maybe they could pick up his trail or some hint of his trail from the people at the pharmacy.

'Good stuff,' Leo said. 'I owe you one.'

'You owe me two,' Dripsy said. 'I dropped some shit in your door like you asked me to, remember?'

On the floor by the front door was a white envelope. Leo couldn't believe he'd asked Dripsy to deliver the hash to the house. You're getting bloody careless, Leo, son.

'Yeah, thanks,' he said, and cut the call.

Leo picked up the envelope. The barely legible scrawl read *Erik*.

His work mobile rang and he went hunting for it in his jacket, littering the floor tiles with balls of tissue paper and cigarette tips. Detective Sergeant Helen Troy. Her breath was punched. In the background, dogs howled.

'I'm out at the Argos Sanctuary,' she said. 'We have another body and it's . . . Jesus, Leo, it's monstrous . . . and the dogs are everywhere—'

Leo heard two gunshots ring out at the other end of the line. A throaty gasp. And then nothing.

244

31

Detective Sergeant Helen Troy leaned against the side wall of the Sanctuary cottage in the early light of dawn, learning how to breathe again. A little way off, the front passenger window of Gudrun Remer's ramshackle Toyota Corolla looked like one great spider's web surrounding a clean entry hole. Whose wayward shot had that been? Hers or Detective Garda Murphy's? The laneway below her was strewn with the corpses of pitbull terriers they'd had to shoot or be ripped to pieces by them. She counted seven, eight. Murphy still stalked the field opposite the Sanctuary. The whiff of cordite hung in the raw air, mingling with the smell of dogshit. And blood. She looked at her watch. Time hadn't accelerated this past half hour. It only felt that way.

The image of Gudrun Remer's naked, ravaged flesh played on Helen's mind. The headless Alsatian too. She felt as though she'd stepped into some ancient mythological world where gods ripped living things to pieces, feasted on them, tossed the bloodied bones aside and returned to their sky, staining it red with dawn. She looked at the distant horizon, barbaric in its roseate beauty. A couple of squad cars came into view, half a mile away. The plaintive wail of their sirens rang through the narrow valley.

Down at the road, Ben Murphy climbed the ditch and waited for the cars that seemed to take for ever to reach him. When they did, Inspector Leo Woods was the first to emerge. From where Helen waited, there seemed to be a new sharpness in his movements, a quickening in his pace. She found it impossible to square this aura of well-being with his weirdness on the phone last night. He didn't stop to talk to Murphy. Rather, he strode up the laneway while the young detective followed in his wake, filling him in on the details. Murphy's expensive suit was a sodden mess, his hair damply awry, his pallor tending to green. She could see that he was unhappy with this lapse in his usual self-control. It soured him.

'Helen,' Leo called to her as he approached. 'You OK?'

'Fine, I'm fine,' she said. She guessed he hadn't asked the same of Murphy. The tear rolling down Leo's cheek might not be for her but she found empathy in his eyes nonetheless and it lifted her. 'The cottage is empty. We've been through every room and through the outhouses. No sign of Stephen Brennan or anyone else.'

'Looks like she was attacked in the shower room,' Murphy said. 'There's blood but not a lot. Signs of strangulation, or at least an attempt at strangulation. Then she was carried rather than dragged outside, it looks like, and dumped into the dog pen. Five or six hours ago, I'm guessing.'

'We'll let the pathologist work that one out, Murphy,' Leo said. 'So, who raised the alarm?'

'Farmer down the way about quarter of a mile,' Helen said. 'Apparently he came up here breathing fire at six this morning when he spotted some of the pitbulls chasing his sheep. He couldn't get out of his jeep because of the dogs and drove up behind the cottage and . . . well, you'll see what he found there.'

Some more sirens sounded in the distance. The trembling inside Helen had ceased. She felt less fearful, the visceral dread receding. Strange, she thought, how we can face these terrors so much better when we crowd around them.

'Christ, what a job we have, eh, Helen?' Leo said. 'Isn't it just as well they pay us such big bucks?'

Ben Murphy walked on ahead of them. He'd taken a notebook from his inside pocket, a silver Parker pen. He scribbled as he turned the corner. Maybe it was his way of preparing himself for what awaited them there, Helen thought. She let Leo advance a stride or two ahead so that his bulk shielded her. Maybe that was her way of preparing herself, she thought.

'Oh, Mother of the Lord Sweet Jesus Christ Almighty,' Leo said.

The Alsatian lay not too far from where it had rested yesterday. What was it called again? Rover. A great deal of the dog's innards had poured out through the hole left when its head had been lopped off. A rough enough lopping off it had been too.

'Any sign of the head?' he asked.

'No, sir,' Murphy said. 'We found the axe that was used. May have been used on the victim too. One of those long heavy-duty ones. Dog must have attacked our killer and—'

'Maybe, maybe not. When I was here yesterday, they told me that dog was on its last legs. And it didn't have the energy to make a lunge at me even though I'm pretty damn sure it wanted to.'

Leo caught sight of the naked body in the pitbull terrier

enclosure. Every step he took required a separate command from his brain. The gate of the enclosure stood open. All the dogs had gone. Behind him, the back door of the cottage was open too and the stewy stench of yesterday's cooking wafted his way.

Gudrun Remer lay on her stomach in a soup of mud and blood. A colourfully beaded anklet was all she wore. The flesh along her arms had been torn, chunks ripped from it. Along her back and across her neck were bite-marks. Her hair, matted with blood, covered much of her face but not, unfortunately, the horrified eyes. Leo felt sick at the possibility that if Stephen Brennan had killed her, then it was he himself who'd left her at the young fellow's mercy. He remembered their argument, Brennan's repressed fury.

'I wonder,' Detective Murphy said, 'whether she was dead before the dogs got to her.'

'I hope so,' Leo said. 'I'll take a look around the cottage before the Tech Bureau arrive.'

An excuse to escape the gypsy curse of the German woman's stare, but he tried to sound purposeful, focused.

'Get the cordon sorted down at the road, Murphy. And Helen, send a few uniforms to the fields up behind. We don't want the neighbours or the press wandering in the back way. Anyone got a pair of latex gloves?'

Murphy had. Leo should have known. He took the gloves so gracelessly that Helen felt embarrassed for her colleague.

When Leo had gone into the cottage, the young detectives headed towards the road. As they passed the pitbull terriers' enclosure, neither one looked at the corpse. The knot in Helen's stomach felt like a repressed scream, an obscure rage in her demanding release. Halfway down the lane her personal mobile rang. Her brother.

'I need to take this, Ben,' she said, but he kept on walking as though he hadn't heard.

She felt glad of the strong breeze that cooled her flaming cheeks and swept her angry voice in the other direction from the squad cars and the uniforms on the road below.

'You're ringing me at eight in the morning?' she said.

'You told me you get up at seven every morning,' Jamie said, booze-hoarse, cigarette-wheezy. 'Remember? That lecture you gave me after Dad's funeral?'

'I'm surprised you remember, you were so pissed.'

In her mind's eye, Helen saw her brother lying in his self-imposed squalor. When she'd gone back home for the funeral, it had taken her two hours to tidy the house, and that was just a quick skim to make the place respectable enough to receive her father's neighbours and friends.

'Look, I'm busy here,' she said. 'If you've rung to ask me to sell the house, the answer is no.'

'It's not a question any more, Helen.'

'What?'

'I mean, I'm not asking whether or not you want to sell. If I want to sell my share then the house has to be sold. I got legal advice.'

'From who? From Ricky? He never got past second year in Law. He doesn't know his arse from a hole in the ground when it comes to these things.'

Helen wanted desperately to ask her brother what Ricky was up to and whom he'd abandoned her for. She couldn't bring herself to.

'I have a buyer,' her brother said.

Four more squad cars entered the valley, the keening of their sirens spreading across bare, rocky fields. Out of sync with one another, the sirens clashed and overlapped, the Doppler effect unsettling her.

'No one's buying in this market,' she said. 'Unless it's one of your shady pals. Is that it? You want to hand over the house Dad worked his butt off to buy and renovate to some druggie? Like you didn't cause him enough trouble when he was around?'

'I'm not the one who shagged off to an interview the day he died. I hope the fucking job was worth it, sis.'

She cut the call, half ran, half walked towards the road. Garda Dempsey stood by the squad car closest to the front gate. He wore a gormless and overly sympathetic expression.

'Bad up there, is it?' he asked.

'You, O'Neill and Twomey, stand guard up behind the cottage,' Helen ordered. 'And while you're up there, keep your eyes peeled for a dog's head, an Alsatian's, right?'

The three uniforms looked at her like she'd lost the run of herself.

'Sorry, Helen . . . Sergeant Troy, but I've to take Leo up to Howth when he's done here,' Dempsey said.

He watched her walk back up to the cottage with Detective Garda Ben Murphy. He sighed. He wondered if she had a tattoo and, if she had, where it might be.

The trouble with post-malarial euphoria was that it didn't always hit Leo at the most appropriate time or place. Sometimes, it came within minutes of the fever's end in the privacy of his home. Sometimes, a day or two might pass before it hit and he'd have to make some excuse, get himself out of the office in Harcourt Street and head to the sea or some other place that was vast enough to contain the surge of wild optimism in him. Sometimes, however, the euphoria reared its foolish head at a murder scene. Elation and horror made a strange mix. It was like having one hand immersed in icy water and the other held over a flame. It hurt. But in a good way.

Painterly blood splashes marked his passage through the cottage kitchen, along the dank, littered corridor and into the minuscule flat-roofed extension that comprised the bathroom. Walls and ceiling, spotted black with damp. The cutting cold a built-in extra, Leo thought, not just a product of the evil that had taken place there. A few hand-slides of blood streaked the cream ceramic tiles, a hand-print clutched the rim of the toilet bowl. There was shit on the floor and it wasn't dogshit. Pools of yellowish liquid too. He turned away and continued his tour of the cottage.

In every room, the air had a stagnant quality about it. Curtains, it seemed, were rarely opened, and windows, never. He went through three bedrooms before he found a bed. There were plenty of mattresses, though even a wino would have had scruples about lying on most of them. The one bed which almost filled the smallest bedroom, on the other hand, was a rather grand affair. One of those dark mahogany sleigh beds, and relatively new. Alongside it stood a neat but fragile Regency chair with a red velvet seat. Something familiar about the looped figure-of-eight shape of the back rest, Leo thought.

Some posters had been torn from the wall, strips hanging on where the thumb tacks had remained secure, the rest tossed on the floor. He pulled on the latex gloves. Their chalky interiors numbed his fingerpads. He turned over one of the paper slivers. The image of a small, tortured dog hurt his bones. Its hellish expression was one with Gudrun

Remer's. Footsteps along the papery debris in the corridor outside sent the shiver into his scalp.

'Sir?'

Detective Sergeant Helen Troy peered around the door. Red-eyed and pale. She was learning the hard way, Leo thought.

'The Technical Bureau are on their way,' she said.

Ben Murphy entered the bedroom. He didn't look at Leo. He looked at the room instead. Helen considered the torn posters on the floor, trying to make sense of their destruction.

'No blood on them,' she said. 'So they were ripped from the wall before the attack? Which points to an argument in here maybe? Then she goes to take a shower and Stephen follows her in there and—'

'But why?' Murphy said. 'Because he can't trust her any more? She gave him his alibi for Dermot Brennan's murder and she's had second thoughts, is that it?'

'Could be,' Helen said. 'One way or another, it's not looking good for Stephen. And no surprise he's done a runner, but where to?'

'Attenboy House?' Murphy suggested.

'Hardly, he'll know we've still got a squad car on the gate out there,' she said. 'Maybe he went to the holiday cottage in Passage East. Are we still watching that?'

Murphy shrugged, went to his pocket for the mobile. Helen turned to Leo, but his mind was elsewhere. He was staring at a dog's face in the poster at his feet. She wondered if, in that pained grimace, he saw something of the cruel experiment that chance had carried out on him. Last night she'd been Googling his condition and discovered that fewer than four per cent of sufferers failed to make a full recovery. Discovered a lot more. Symptoms, physical and psychological. Now that search felt intrusive and it embarrassed her.

'Why would he kill Rover?' Leo asked aloud of himself. 'Apart from the unlikely possibility that the dog might have been attempting to defend Gudrun Remer, I mean. What other . . . significance could . . . ?'

'The dog's name was Rover?' Helen said.

'Yeah.'

'Frankie Prior's dog was called Rover. The dog Stephen Brennan brought here. The dog he refused to return to the Priors.'

'Go on,' Leo encouraged her.

'Stephen insisted the dog was dead but Prior told me he'd been out here, that he'd seen Rover. Didn't much like Gudrun Remer either. Plus he's a karate black belt and I wondered about that kick to Dermot Brennan's ribs.'

In his post-malarial elation, Leo recalled the illusion of movement he'd experienced on the walkway at Dublin Airport the other day. He surrendered to it. At once, he remembered where he'd seen the chair before.

'That chair,' he said. 'There's one just like it in the library at Attenboy House. And this is the only bed in the cottage. What're the odds that it came from Attenboy too?'

'And Stephen's bedroom in Howth,' Helen recalled. 'It's the only bedroom that doesn't have a bed in it.'

'So, how did these things get here?' Leo said, the words almost falling over themselves as they emerged. 'Who brought them? The chair you could throw in the back of a car. But those bed ends? You'd need a lorry, a trailer, an SUV . . .'

'Dermot Brennan was a builder,' Murphy said sceptically. 'He or any of his men could have delivered them here.'

'Well, let's ask them,' Leo said.

'I don't see the logic of your—'

'Look, I'm just taking this bed, this chair here as examples, right? What I'm saying is that what we're after are the possibilities, the threads leading from Dermot Brennan's murder to Gudrun's. Details that might link the two, even the smallest details. The killer is in the details.'

Helen had no idea where this was leading either. She exchanged a befuddled glance with Murphy.

'When I was in Angola, I came down with some kind of an old bug,' he said. 'I was on the flat of my back for the best part of a week. And this old guy, Charlie Llunga, he took care of me. Used to do this fortune-telling stuff. Had this basket and he'd put things in there. You know, trinkets, little symbols and stuff. Then he'd fling them out and he'd read your fortune from how these bits and pieces fell. Things know more about us than we know about them, he'd say. That's what we need to do. Look at every little thing. Read what they're trying to tell us. Am I making sense?'

'Yeah,' Helen said.

'Not exactly,' Murphy said.

Leo let it go. He was still buzzing. He led the way out of the bedroom and through the cottage, speculating as he went, dishing out the orders, snapping off a cigarette filter and lighting up, talking his way past the bodies of the woman and the dog, pulling at every loose thread that came to mind, hoping this buzz would last another while, that he wouldn't hit the next brick wall too hard or too fast.

'OK, I'll head out to Attenboy House, see if Stephen Brennan's been in touch with his mother. Have to push her on her relationship with Cobbe too. That guy's still in the mix here, I'm sure of it. Why's he implicating this Sheridan fellow?'

'He didn't mention Sheridan when we spoke to him at the hospital,' Murphy said.

'Exactly. Maybe he's developing a new angle for himself,' Leo said. 'Listen, Murphy, see if you can find out where Cobbe stayed last night after his release. If he headed back to Enniscorthy, he was moving in the same direction as the Argos Sanctuary. His solicitor might know. If not, get our lads in Enniscorthy to check his house. See if you can speak to him and the partner separately. We're looking for a link from Cobbe to Gudrun, a reason he might want to do away with her. Maybe there's none. But if there is, we have to shake it out of him.'

'Yes, sir,' Murphy said.

'And Helen? Check out Peter Prior. He'd damn good reason to hate Dermot Brennan and if he didn't like Gudrun Remer then maybe he flipped, maybe one murder led to another. He's got a screwed-up wife and a messed-up life, so it's a possibility. Go in mad urgent, see if he cracks. It's a case of having to be cruel to be kind. We want to rule him out, but rule him out fast.'

They'd reached the first of the squad cars that filled the narrow country road. Inside, Garda Dempsey had got himself twenty-three allies in the Nations at War game on his Smartphone, his arched eyebrows excitedly remarking his achievements. Leo knocked on the window. The squad car flustered and swayed. The window slid down.

'We're off to Howth, Dempsey, top speed, siren all the way,' Leo said, and Garda Dempsey, relieved at not being bollocked and happy with his mission, sat bolt upright and stiffened tight as though he'd become one with the metal of his machine.

Helen Troy looked back up at the cottage. From this

255

distance, its tawdry bleakness and the bloody secret it concealed were lost in the clear, cold light that had broken out across the sky. A picture-postcard Irish idyll. No wonder the German woman had been drawn to the place. She must have walked that field to the front on summer days and thought she was in heaven. Then, Helen remembered the photograph.

'Sir?' she said. 'That photo the Dorans took of Gudrun and Stephen. We can't rule them out either.'

'Yeah,' Leo said. 'I've had a tip-off of a possible sighting at a pharmacy in Talbot Street. Have someone check it out, will you?'

'A tip-off? From?'

'Don't ask,' Leo said.

Detective Garda Murphy stood a little way off, making notes and looking peeved. Another problem with euphoria, Leo knew, was that it was a first cousin to paranoia. What's he writing in there? Why's he always writing when I'm talking and not when others are? Not true, Leo told himself. Might be true though, the other Leo countered.

'Murphy,' Leo said, 'anything from Daina or the sister yet?'

The young fellow gave him a grumpy shrug.

'Who's talking to them?'

'Martha Corrigan.'

'Sergeant. Corrigan. Sir,' Leo corrected the young detective. 'What about the girl in the ruins? Anything more on that?'

Detective Garda Murphy shook his head.

'You've been a busy lad, haven't you, son?'

'I've been taken off that element of the investigation, sir.'

'By?' Leo asked.

'By the boss, sir. By Superintendent Heaphy. Sir. He wants the investigation into the demolition job at Hearnstown ring-fenced. Says it might be a distraction from the Brennan case.'

'So, who's on it now?'

'Detective Sergeant Cooney, sir.'

'Ah, who better to put on the case of a girl with a strap-on dildo in her backpack than a filthy-minded joker?' Leo said as he opened the passenger door of the squad car. 'Right then, Murphy. Hold the fort here until the Technical Bureau and the pathologist come. And ring me if anything comes to light.'

Nothing was left of his euphoria but the sticky sweat on the back of his shirt, and even that was turning to ice.

32

At first, Detective Sergeant Helen Troy thought that Hanora Prior might be dead. In the shadows of the densely overgrown drive at Morehampton Grove, she paused. Her right hand went instinctively to the Walther semi-automatic in her jacket. The front door of the red-bricked house stood open. Closer by, in the passenger seat of the green Mercedes, Mrs Prior sat stock-still, goggle-eyed and unblinking. Helen heard a glassy crash from inside the house and the woman's head snapped in her direction. She fixed Helen with a stare, at once terrified and terrifying.

Helen approached the car, her right hand inside the zip-up jacket. She knocked on the passenger-side window but Mrs Prior had returned to her catatonic state. Another crashing sound emerged from the house. More metallic this time, echoing longer and louder. Helen opened the door of the Mercedes.

'Are you OK, Mrs Prior?' she asked of the woman who she now realized wore a see-through nightdress beneath her ankle-length sable coat.

No answer came. Helen noted that Mrs Prior wore no shoes and that her feet were caked in mud. And blood. Her hands were muddied too. Helen looked across to see if the key was in the ignition. It was. She closed the passenger door and walked around the front of the car. The house erupted again. A large, collective smashing of ceramics. Helen took the key from the car and, as quietly as she could, rang for back-up. Sergeant Martha Corrigan answered.

'Martha, I'm at the Priors' place in Morehampton Grove,' she whispered and told her what she'd just seen and heard.

'Get back out to your car and wait,' Martha said. 'Now. We'll have back-up there in, say, ten minutes. Hopefully less.'

'But what if—' She had no time to articulate the speculation. Peter Prior stood in the arched doorway of the house. His expression manic, a length of two-by-four timber in his hand.

'Helen? What's happening?' Martha asked.

'Too late, Martha, he's . . .'

She put away the mobile so as to free her right hand for the gun. You don't need to pull it, she told herself, you won't need to. The street was no more than twenty yards back up the drive. She heard the traffic, heard the footfall on the pavement. Ordinary people going to ordinary jobs. You should be one of them, she told herself. She tried to calculate her chances of reaching the gate before Peter Prior caught up with her. For a moment or two, he seemed to be making the same calculation. Then he went back inside. She followed him, palm to the grip of her hidden gun.

'Mr Prior?' she called from the threshold of the front door.

Helen listened. Nothing. She called again. Something fell. Something insubstantial lightly tossed aside. Police sirens sharpened the early morning city soundtrack but distantly as yet.

At the far end of the hallway and beyond the stairway, a kitchen etched itself out of the shadows as Helen edged her way inwards. A long American fridge lay on its side there, its door open, its contents leaking out on to a tiled floor covered in broken delph. From inside a door to the left she heard the breathy panting of a dog. No, not a dog, she thought. She eased the solid door inwards, looked in by the gap opening at the architrave to see if Peter Prior hid behind it.

'Mr Prior?' she called again, more softly.

The man wasn't hiding. He sat on the same armchair as he'd done last time. He looked somehow as if he always sat in the same chair here, and perhaps in the same spot in the kitchen at every mealtime too, and on the same side of the bed every night. She wondered if such small habits made his life seem normal to him. She doubted, though, that he made a habit of crying so unashamedly in front of others as he did now.

'You'd think there was enough wreckage in our lives without my adding to it,' he said. 'But there's only so much a man can take.'

'What happened to your wife? Her feet. Where has she been?'

Peter Prior crouched in his armchair, hedgehog tight, his head lowered almost to his knees.

'Yesterday,' he moaned, his pitch so high that for a bizarre moment Helen thought he might be attempting to sing the old Beatles song.

The flesh of Helen's scalp tightened as she heard the chunky slamming of a car door. She moved into the room, took a sideways step and got her back to the wallpaper with its brushed velvet flowers. She listened for the pad of bare feet from the hallway but all she heard was Prior repeat, an octave lower, 'Yesterday.'

'Tell me what happened, Mr Prior,' Helen said.

He looked up at her, his long neck gristly with age, despair in his eyes.

'Yesterday was Frankie's birthday,' he said. 'His twenty-first.'

The red sky Leo had seen in the Dublin Mountains had failed to live up to its promise. Howth had frosted over, the sky gone snow-grey. As they sat in the traffic, he watched the boats bob and sway in the large quadrangle of the enclosed harbour. On the near side were the pleasure boats, further off, the working ones. Only one light shone that he could see and that was in the wheelhouse of a small fishing vessel. A shadowy figure moved around in it. Leo wished it could be him.

Yet another apoplectic text message came in on his work phone from Superintendent Heaphy.

Garda Dempsey glanced across at Leo. The young man had been getting more and more uncomfortable this past hour. Leo hadn't been answering the phone though it rang time and again. Instead, he'd been staring sullenly and all too silently ahead. Dempsey wasn't good at silences. He was inclined to take responsibility for them, blame himself.

Leo scrolled up the super's number.

'Leo,' Heaphy said, 'I hear it's an awful mess out there at the Sanctuary.'

'I've seen worse,' Leo said. 'But not much worse.'

'Is young Brennan a psychopath, do you reckon? Because all we need in the papers now is a bloody axeman frenzy.'

'It's looking that way.'

'And the dogs? I'm hearing we shot at least fifteen dogs dead up there. The RSPCA will love that one, Leo. What on earth was that about?'

'Whoever killed Gudrun Remer let them loose. We're talking pitbull terriers who've been locked up for God knows how long. Basically they went apeshit and our officers couldn't get to the body. They had no choice but to shoot them.'

'I don't know, Leo,' Heaphy said. 'I'm hearing that this young Troy girl lost the run of herself. I've a feeling we have a Calamity Jane on our hands.'

'More like a Wild Ben Murphy on our hands, Aonghus,' Leo said. 'He did most of the shooting.'

Dempsey got them through Harbour Road and on up to Abbey Street. All the while, he glanced Leo's way, gobsmacked at the sarcasm and hostility he was hearing.

'Let me tell you something, Leo,' Superintendent Heaphy said. 'And this is between ourselves because it came up in my assessment meeting with Ben Murphy so it's confidential. That young fellow actually thinks you're the best detective he's ever worked with. He admires you, Leo, and you make his life a misery.'

Dempsey hadn't heard what the superintendent had said but he knew Leo had been stopped in his tracks.

'And let me tell you something else while I'm at it,' Heaphy went on. 'He admires the fact that you get on with your job, with your life, in spite of . . . well, you know, in spite of your . . . your misfortune . . . on the facial front, so to speak. He's a good, decent lad, Leo, and—'

'If he's so wonderful, why did you take him off the Hearnstown demolition investigation?'

A pause followed. About the length of an Our Father, Leo guessed. About as long as it took Heaphy to apologize to his God for some moral lapse.

'We don't need to involve ourselves any further in that matter,' the super said eventually. 'It doesn't relate directly to the murders so it's not the Bureau's business. We'll be letting the local boys deal with it from here on in.'

'What you mean is, hands off Foley,' Leo said. 'Well, let *me* tell *you* something now, boss. That vulture has not and will not leave my thoughts until we find who killed Dermot Brennan and Gudrun Remer and why. I'll rule him in or out when *I* decide, full stop.'

'Detective Sergeant Cooney will deal with any and all matters relating to Mr Foley,' Heaphy insisted. 'And that's an order. And not from me, Leo. Not from the chief superintendent or even the assistant commissioner. And more than that, I'm not at liberty to say. For God's sake, Leo, I'm only carrying out orders. What else am I to do with this promotion still hanging in the balance?'

Dempsey swung the squad car down the tree-lined lane towards Attenboy House.

'Have to go now, Aonghus. I've a widow waiting for me.'

Garda Dempsey chuckled aloud and Leo gave him a friendly but warning glance.

'Leo, I know you,' Superintendent Heaphy said. 'You don't just want to get to the bottom of these murders. You want to pin something on Foley because you don't like the colour of his money. You want to be judge, jury and executioner just like in the old days. These are ordinary decent businessmen trying to survive in a worldwide recession.'

'Ordinary, yes. Decent, no.'

'When are you going to stop trying to play God, Leo?'

'When the real God shows up, Aonghus,' Leo said, and cut the call.

The gates of Attenboy came into view and his stomach sank at the prospect that lay ahead, not so much for him but for Anna Brennan. He knew what he was like when he turned nasty. He hoped the widow wouldn't have to find out.

'How do you get away with talking to the superintendent like that, sir?' Dempsey asked with genuine bemusement.

'In the words of the great French philosopher Eric Cantona, it doesn't matter if you're sitting in a ditch at the side of the road or on a throne, you still have to sit on your arse,' Leo told him.

'Helen?'

She'd never been so glad to hear her colleague's voice.

'Yeah,' she called. 'In here.'

Detective Garda Ben Murphy, when he appeared, was paler than ever. He looked from Helen to Peter Prior and back, a question in his pinched expression. She shrugged. She removed her hand from the semi-automatic hidden inside her zip-up and went to sit opposite Prior. The clumping sound of the Mercedes door closing came again. Murphy looked back along the hallway and, after a moment or two, shook his head at someone. A uniform, Helen supposed.

'She won't get out of the car,' he told Helen. 'It's bloody awful cold out there. What should we—'

'Leave her,' Peter Prior said abruptly. His voice shook. His entire body shook. 'I'm taking her for . . . for a rest.' He looked at the two young detectives. 'You know.' They didn't. 'Respite care? A chance for her to calm down again.'

But he was the one needed calming down rather than the

woman sitting madly indifferent to the cold and the filth of her extremities, and to the chaos reigning in her home.

'Where has your wife been walking, Mr Prior?' Helen asked.

'Just up the road. Herbert Park.' He gestured with a vague nod. 'She spent the night wandering about in the park refusing to come home. I sat in the car and waited.'

'But you could have called someone,' Murphy said, as astonished as Helen was at the image of a man waiting in his car as his half-naked wife roamed a darkened suburban park.

'This happens all the time,' Prior said. 'I used to ring the hospital or your good selves but, to be honest, when I leave her alone and let her do as she feels driven to do, well, it's less distressing for her. Strange, I know, but such is life. Such is our life, at any rate.'

'And yesterday?' Helen asked. 'You were at the crematorium in the morning, right? Why did you go there and why did you do a runner when you saw me?'

Some colour returned to Prior's cheeks, but it was the colour of shame.

'I went there to see Anna Brennan suffer,' he said. 'To see her cry and fall apart like Hanora did. But I couldn't make myself go inside.'

'And after the crematorium?'

'Nowhere.' Prior's sudden abruptness came unexpectedly.

'We really need to know where you both were yesterday, Mr Prior,' Murphy said.

'Why?'

'Were you at the Argos Sanctuary?' Helen asked.

'No.'

Helen leaned towards the trembling man. Prior retreated.

He didn't want to be touched. She knew the feeling. Grief had done the same kind of thing to her.

'We really need to know where you and—'

'Why? Why can't you just leave us alone?' Prior exclaimed. 'Aren't our lives miserable enough without these insinuations, these accusations of yours? We had nothing to do with Dermot Brennan's death. Nothing.'

'There's been another murder, Mr Prior,' Murphy said. 'At the Argos Sanctuary yesterday. Gudrun Remer. I believe you know her?'

The revelation had a curious effect on Peter Prior. He seemed to uncoil, his inner tension released. He sat back in the armchair as though a great weight had been lifted from him. He spoke more evenly now.

'The woman did us no favours but I wouldn't have wished this on her all the same,' he said. He let his eyelids have the brief rest they craved and went on. 'Yesterday, after I left the crematorium, I drove back here and we did what we always do on Frankie's birthday – well, since he died, that is. This would be the third one. Are you aware of how my son died?'

Neither Helen nor Ben Murphy knew. He looked from one to the other in a state almost of wonderment.

'My son's death is the central fact of my life, of our life,' Prior said. 'But one tends to forget that it means little or nothing to anyone else.'

'Every family has its tragedies, Mr Prior,' Murphy said, and now it was Helen's turn to wonder at the depth of feeling in her colleague's words.

'You're right, of course,' Prior said and sat up straight, collected his thoughts and continued. 'My son walked into the sea at Passage East not far from the Brennan cottage. No one was in the cottage at the time so they can't be blamed in that sense for what happened. Anyway, his body was washed ashore a week later up the coast at Rosslare harbour. So, what we do, my wife and I, what we did yesterday, was that we pack some lunch and some flasks and we drive down there and sit in the car and watch the waves. There's quite a bit of traffic there, what with the lorries. CCTV cameras too I should imagine. We stay there all day, all evening, until Hanora is so drunk that she falls asleep or what passes for sleep, and last night she dropped off just after ten o'clock. Then I drove her home and put her to bed, and when I woke around three, she'd gone. But, of course, I knew where she'd gone because Herbert Park is where she always goes. Herbert Park is where she used to take Frankie as a child.'

He stood up and buttoned the jacket of his muddied suit. He negotiated the fine line between dignity and absurdity, brushing dried mud from his sleeve, wiping his hands together.

'Now, I really should be going, Hanora needs me.' He turned to Helen and almost pleadingly added, 'What I don't understand is how that woman can still use the cottage, how she can look out of that long window and see the very spot where Frankie left his clothes. What kind of woman is she? Does she have a soul? And if she does, what's happened to it?'

33

Because he'd lived in the same house for most of his life, Leo Woods had never experienced that common disappointment upon returning in adulthood to the childhood home. Often encountered it in novels though, when he'd still bothered to read novels. All was diminished. Rooms seemed minuscule, less bright, altogether more dowdy and sparsely furnished. Beyond the physical, there lay an even deeper absence. Whatever force, whatever energy had once inspirited those rooms had expired. What remained was the corpse of the past in the tomb of memory. Such were the sensations that enveloped Leo as he waited for Anna Brennan in the library of Attenboy House. The house was not what it had been and, when she appeared, neither was Anna Brennan.

She wore a cream silk dressing gown carelessly and unevenly tied. Beneath it, a matching nightdress revealed the slight wrinkle at the join above her breasts. Her lapis lazuli eyes were dull with fatigue.

He stood up from his seat at the oval table. Whatever expression or lack of expression his face betrayed, Anna

Brennan took fright at it. She folded her arms tightly, stood stock-still at the centre of the room as though suddenly awakened from a sleepwalk.

'You'd better sit down, Mrs Brennan,' Leo said, gesturing at the Regency chair with the red velvet seat.

'Why? What is it?'

She spoke groggily. Probably downed a few sleeping tablets last night, Leo thought. Her red hair was a tumbleweed mess and she tried to do something with it but in an abstracted way.

'Your son's not here. No?'

'My son?' she said vacantly.

'Gudrun Remer has been murdered at the Argos Sanctuary,' Leo said. 'We need to speak to Stephen. Has he been in touch with you since yesterday afternoon?'

She stared at him. Stared in his direction at least for there was no sense that she saw either him or anything else in the room.

'I spoke to him yesterday evening,' she said.

'And how did he sound?'

'He was perfectly fine. A little upset maybe but only because he hadn't shown up at the funeral and wanted to explain himself.'

'Why didn't he go to the crematorium?' Leo asked. 'OK, they never got on. But isn't it pretty extreme not turning up at all, not even briefly? Not even for your sake?'

'Extreme, yes. Stephen's always been like that. Overreacting, taking offence too easily, all that. He's emotional, passionate. The young are like that.'

'And he's been before the court for violent protests with this animal rights mob?'

'Only because they were provoked by bully-boy police tactics,' Anna countered. 'Seems to go with the territory, doesn't it, Inspector?'

'Often does, yeah,' Leo said with a shrug. 'Speaking of which, mightn't Stephen have regarded your husband's treatment of Frankie Prior as bully-boy tactics? Mightn't that have provoked him into seeking revenge?'

'If Stephen had wanted revenge for Frankie's suicide, it's Hanora Prior he'd have blamed.'

'Why would he blame Frankie's mother?'

Anna observed him with annoyance. She was clearly coming to some unwelcome decision and blamed Leo for forcing her into it.

'Hanora Prior has never been a stable woman, Inspector,' she said, sitting down at the table and choosing her words with some care. 'Her relationship with Frankie was always peculiar, to say the least. I mean, I do pity her. I know how difficult these last few years have been for her.'

'Difficult to put it mildly,' Leo said. 'I'm told she's an out-and-out alcoholic now and a nervous wreck by all accounts.'

'I'm sorry to say that she was both of those things long before Frankie died,' the widow said. 'Frankie was her second child. Her first was a girl, Frances, who died of pneumonia when she was two years old. Hanora never got over that. The drinking started back then, and with the drinking came the . . . the strangeness. There was a period early on when she indulged the fantasy that Frankie was . . . She still had the little girl's clothes, the dresses, the . . .'

She paused, fussed at her hair again. Leo could guess the rest.

'You spoke to Stephen at what time?'

'Six, half past six,' she said. 'He rang from some pub in the city centre, I don't know where. He may have told me but I don't remember.'

'Did he tell you where he was headed to, where he planned to stay the night?' Leo asked.

Anna Brennan gave up on her hair and worked her fingers on the stitched end of a tapestry table runner instead. Only now did Leo realize that she had clay under her fingernails. She seemed altogether unaware of the fact. He wasn't sure where to go next but she took him somewhere he hadn't foreseen.

'He stayed with Skip Sheridan,' she said, her attention still on the tapestry.

'The gardener? He's a friend of Stephen's?'

'Skip was kind enough to take some furniture over to the Sanctuary for me, some things I wanted Stephen to have,' she said. 'They met, they got friendly. Sometimes they meet up for a drink in town, that kind of thing. Clubs, I suppose, and all of that. Whatever people do to enjoy themselves these days.'

She smiled faintly.

Friendly? Leo thought. As in . . . as in Skip Sheridan was the new Frankie Prior in Stephen's life? He wondered if Dermot Brennan had been aware of this development. Hadn't Alan Cobbe claimed that when he'd called to Attenboy on the evening of the murder, Brennan had thought it was Skip Sheridan and hadn't been happy about the fact?

'Mrs Brennan, did you know that Alan Cobbe called here on Friday evening? After he'd been with you in Passage East.'

She didn't know. She was appalled. Leo believed in her unspoken reaction because her hands dropped to her sides and her dressing gown and nightdress fell away enough to expose her left nipple while she, unaware, stared at him. Leo lowered his eyes.

'He claims to have come here to assure your husband that he wasn't having an affair with you. He says that he called out when he didn't get an answer at the door and that your husband at first thought it was Skip Sheridan. He says that your husband didn't seem to like Mr Sheridan.'

'Dermot had no reason not to like Skip,' she said, her breath fluttering audibly.

'Was Sheridan working here on Friday?'

Anna Brennan shook her head.

'Mrs Brennan, what is the nature of your relationship with Mr Sheridan?'

'He's done some work for me . . . for us,' she said. 'That's all there is to it.'

'At the church the other night, you responded to Mr Sheridan as though there were more to your relationship than—'

'I *responded* to him? Don't you know what grief is like? The irrational, silly things you do and say in these situations? You're not *thinking* at moments like that, you're on auto-pilot.'

The cold air of the library had hardened her exposed nipple. She looked down at herself. Unhurriedly and without embarrassment, she covered her breast. Leo searched for the work mobile in his jacket. He got through three pockets before he found it.

'Give me a minute,' he said. 'And Mrs Brennan? Don't call or text your son while I'm out of the room, please.'

'I don't have my phone with me,' she said, bitterness wrinkling her upper lip unflatteringly. 'Do you mind if I make some coffee in the kitchen? You can come and watch if you like.'

She didn't wait for permission. She pulled the lapels of her dressing gown together and glided barefoot along the cold floorboards. Leo let her advance into the kitchen and, from the hallway, watched her movements. He rang Helen.

'Leo?'

'Anna Brennan says her son stayed at Skip Sheridan's house last night. You know where Sheridan lives, don't you?'

'Yeah, Clogherhead. You want me to go—'

'Yeah, pronto. Take plenty of back-up. Plenty. This has all the makings of a siege, if Stephen's our man. So tread carefully, OK? What's the story with the Priors?'

He kept an eye on the kitchen. She'd filled the kettle and was now taking down a glass cafetière from a wall-mounted cupboard by the sink. Three or four feet further along the black granite work surface from the sink, a mobile phone lay between a wooden block containing four knives and a half-empty bottle of brandy. They caught each other looking at the phone.

'I think we can safely rule them out,' Helen said. 'Terrible what life can do to people, isn't it?'

'If you'd a tune, you could sing that one.'

'Ben's here with me. He's got some news on Sean Doran.'

'Put him on,' Leo said, maintaining a moderate tone for her sake, but she'd already handed over the phone to her colleague.

'Sir, we have Sean Doran on CCTV carrying out the demolition job on Foley's offices in Hearnstown,' Murphy said. 'They've got a pretty elaborate system out there. Intelligent auto tracking CCTV with auto focus zoom. Expensive stuff, and the picture's crystal clear.'

'A bit over-the-top for monitoring a ghost town, isn't it?'

'Yeah. Good for us though. Doran doesn't even try to hide.

Walks up to where he knows the camera is. He's popped up on something, I'm pretty sure of that, cocaine maybe, and it's like he's making some kind of speech or . . . I mean, there's no sound obviously, but something about his stance, his gestures makes me think . . . Look, this may sound strange—'

'Come on, man, I'm in the middle of something bloody important here,' Leo whispered furiously.

'I think Doran may have been singing, sir.'

'Singing? Singing what?'

'I don't know, sir,' Murphy said. 'Maybe I could get someone who lip-reads to check it out.'

'Yeah right. It'll take you longer to find a fucking lip-reader than to find Sean Doran.'

'My sister is profoundly deaf, sir, she's a pretty good *fucking lip-reader.*'

'OK. Sorry, son, I'm under pressure,' Leo said. He hated making excuses. Never came up with a decent one. Never could. 'See if your sister can help.'

'Will do, sir.'

'What about Alan Cobbe? Anything on his movements yesterday after we released him?'

'He and his partner stayed at Bewley's Hotel in Ballsbridge. They checked in around four in the afternoon. The night porter says he went out alone and rolled back into the hotel at about three in the morning and was pretty pissed. This morning, they checked out at eight. They may be on their way back down to Enniscorthy. We've put a watch on his house down there.'

'Checked out at eight? After a night on the piss?'

'Yes, sir,' Murphy said. 'And sir?'

Here he goes again, Leo thought, always the extra card to play. He waited to be trumped.

'The Technical Bureau got into Dermot Brennan's laptop, sir.'

'And?'

'And they ran into another snag,' Murphy said. 'A dummy password manager that took a while to crack but was empty. Now they're checking through the System 32 directory to see if—'

'Can you translate all this into English?'

'They haven't got into his email or any hidden business files. The System 32 directory check will run for twenty-four hours and might throw something up.'

'Surely Brennan didn't set up all this on the laptop himself?'

'It's actually quite simple to do,' Murphy told him. 'You just go online, Google "encryption" and download whatever software—'

'All of which gets us where precisely?'

'Nowhere, sir. Not yet anyway.'

Leo ended the call. So, likely as it was that Stephen Brennan was their man, Alan Cobbe was still in the picture. But what possible reason could you have to kill Gudrun Remer, Cobbe? And where are you, Doran? What the hell are you up to? Why did you flatten Foley's offices? Because you couldn't get close to Foley himself? And what next? Or have you already made your next move? Out at the Argos Sanctuary? But why would *you* want to kill that German woman?

Leo entered the designer kitchen in Attenboy House and sat at the table. Anna Brennan brought over two coffee mugs and a carton of milk. Both mugs were clean but stained on the inside. The one she'd placed before Leo had a name on it. *Dermot*. Some long-ago gift – from Anna or Stephen? Leo didn't know if he should point this out to her. She poured the boiling water into the cafetière. The aroma of fresh rich coffee filled the kitchen. A purely momentary bliss. He'd have to drink the coffee from a dead man's mug. He took note of the brandy bottle on the kitchen counter again. He wondered if this explained her earlier state of disarray.

As she waited for the coffee to brew, Anna Brennan looked out through the kitchen window at the cobbled yard and the outhouses whose doors were still sealed with white plastic Do Not Enter ribbons. She placed her hands on the hot and cold sink taps as though the kitchen were some kind of launch and she controlled its imperceptible movements. On the windowsill stood a sleek black Roberts internet radio. She turned it on. Some kind of chamber music. Straining, high-pitched scratchings interspersed with a tune of sorts. Severity and tenderness. Good cop, bad cop. Must have been written by a detective, Leo thought.

She brought the cafetière and a bowl of sugar to the table and sat down.

'I can't bear silence,' she said. 'I never could.'

Leo didn't tell her that he couldn't bear music.

Anna Brennan poured the coffee shakily. She didn't recognize her husband's coffee mug. Her eyes were bloodshot and Leo wondered if that explained their lack of lustre. She slid the sugar bowl towards Leo and turned an ear to the music.

'Janáček's Kreutzer Sonata string quartet,' she said with that distracted, half-mad air of someone who knows they're speaking inappropriately but can't stop themselves. 'Strange how that piece came about. First Beethoven writes a violin sonata called the Kreutzer. Then Tolstoy uses the piece in a novella about a man who kills his wife out of jealousy. And calls the story *The Kreutzer Sonata*. Thirty years or so later, Janáček comes along and writes this quartet based on the novella. Strange, isn't it?'

Leo shrugged. Was she trying to tell him something with this talk of a story about jealousy leading to murder? Sometimes people began to reveal what they really knew in this oblique, even subconscious way.

'You think I'm some kind of monster,' she said. 'Everyone does.'

'I know the feeling,' he said.

'I'm so sorry, I didn't mean to offend you,' she told him, her hand going instinctively to her cheek as though to the mirror image of Leo's. 'People expect to see tears, wailing, all that. I'm just not like that. I've always kept a lid on my emotions. I've had to. It doesn't mean I'm not completely devastated at losing Dermot.'

'Of course it doesn't.'

'And Stephen's reaction to Dermot's death, that isn't what it seems either,' she insisted. 'If you knew how he really felt, you wouldn't suspect him like you obviously do. That distance you see in him, that seeming not to care? All of that comes from my example. There's always been a part of me I've withheld, Inspector. A part of me that holds back. It's helped me survive but it hasn't helped me to be a good mother. Or wife.'

'If I suspect Stephen, it's purely down to facts,' Leo said. 'As of now, he's the most plausible link we can find between the murders of your husband and Gudrun Remer. He's the only one who had a major problem with Dermot as well as being, let's say, unhappy with Ms Remer.' He saw that Anna was genuinely taken aback. 'I spoke to them yesterday morning at the Sanctuary and you could've cut the atmosphere with a knife. They may have been close but there was a lot of hostility there. On your son's part, for sure.'

'But that's typical of Stephen,' she said pleadingly. 'He's like that with everyone he's close to.'

'Your charity shop was in aid of a mental health organization helping young people,' Leo said. 'I have to ask you if Stephen has had, let's say, psychiatric problems in the past. Is that why you got involved in the charity?'

The widow swirled the coffee in her mug, washed away the line of brown scum just below the rim, watched another one form.

'I opened the shop because of what happened to Frankie,' she said. 'I wanted to . . . to do something, and this HeadUp organization focuses on suicide in young men.'

'But Stephen hasn't needed psychiatric help?' Leo asked.

'No,' Anna answered curtly.

'He's clearly had problems dealing with Frankie's death,' Leo said. 'He dropped out of college, didn't he? Left home. And he seems pretty rudderless, to say the least.'

'Stephen has always been vulnerable, Inspector. Always been too bright for his own good, too sensitive. And since Frankie died, I've been terrified, terrified that he might . . . You know how it is with suicide. It's like a virus. Especially among young people. And God knows how he'll react to being accused of . . . of killing his own father, of killing this woman.'

She bowed her head. The Noh mask she'd brought to mind before had been of an attractive and, perhaps, calculating woman. Now he was reminded of an altogether different Noh mask in his collection. The Uba mask was indented on the forehead with three wave-like wrinkles. Below each eye were two deep crescent-shapes denoting their weariness.

And the mouth, half open, teeth bared, suggested pained despair.

'I shouldn't say it, but that Gudrun was no good for him. I don't know why we ever went to that bloody sanctuary. I wish—'

Anna Brennan stopped short. She looked to Leo like someone stunned by a sudden realization. She was.

'The dog,' she said.

She'd been holding her coffee mug halfway between the table and her mouth for some minutes now. The mug tilted dangerously. Coffee lapped against the lowered edge, threatened to spill over at any moment. Leo wasn't sure whether he should tell her of the Alsatian's fate. She set the mug down carelessly and coffee splashed out on to the surface of the table. Leo found some tissues in his pocket and soaked it up, which left him with none to soak up the unbidden tears that came when he drank or ate. Crocodile Tears Syndrome they called it. He hadn't yet sipped the coffee, and now he couldn't. Another simple pleasure denied him.

'Frankie Prior's dog,' she said.

'Rover?'

'Yes,' she answered, and wondered, it seemed to Leo, how much more he knew. 'After Frankie died, his parents didn't want the dog around. So, even though Stephen couldn't stand dogs, he brought it here. But the dog didn't settle and we had to think about what we might do with it.'

'Peter Prior tells us he wanted the dog back,' Leo said. 'He'd been up at the Sanctuary a number of times trying to—'

'That was later, after the first shock of Frankie's death had passed. I wanted Stephen to let them have the dog but he dug his heels in. He said they'd never cared for the dog and had done everything they could to get rid of it long before Frankie died and made him miserable in the process. More miserable. Such an unhappy boy.'

Briefly sidetracked at the memory of Frankie Prior, she shook her head and went on.

'Anyway, what I'm trying to tell you is that we didn't just pull out the Yellow Pages and find the Argos Sanctuary. The whole business came up in conversation when Alan Cobbe was visiting one day and it was he who recommended it. Gudrun Remer was a friend of his partner's. They're both involved in one of those animal rights groups.'

'Gudrun Remer was a friend of Caroline Hunt's?'

'Yes,' Anna Brennan said.

Leo remembered the smell of cats on the young English woman. He had another call to make, another major search to set in motion. Find Cobbe fast. Drag him in again, kicking and screaming if need be.

He rang Sergeant Martha Corrigan, told her what he wanted done.

'And I'll have some pronto with that,' Leo added, warming to the task.

'Pronto you shall have,' Martha said. 'Meanwhile, that young Latvian girl we're holding?'

'Daina?'

'Yeah, Daina Klaviňš. She's dead, Leo. In a manner of speaking.'

34

The convoy of squad cars passed through the fishing village of Clogherhead, veered out beyond its disproportionately large and mostly empty housing estates, and on to the more human scale of Chapel Road where Skip Sheridan lived. The sky out in the countryside had that high, liquid quality of seaside air though the sea itself was hidden from view.

'The chapel,' Detective Garda Ben Murphy said, lifting a finger from the steering wheel.

Up ahead and at the point where the road swept to the left stood the old chapel. Long and narrow, clad with a mix of grey and russet stone, a bell tower at the front end. Remote and silent as a chapel should be. Sheridan's cottage was, they'd learned, just past the bend. They went by a two-storey house and a long-since unfinished bungalow. Murphy slowed down below forty. Theirs was the lead car of five and Helen could sense the build-up of tension from behind as they coasted to a stop twenty metres back from the cottage. Helen radioed back to the other cars.

'Stick to the plan, OK, everyone? He's unlikely to be armed so there's not going to be a problem.'

Murphy looked at her. She was expecting some hint of annoyance from him. She'd pulled rank and done all the talking earlier while they'd planned the swoop, more from nerves than any conscious attempt to rule the roost. But he wasn't annoyed. He was too busy checking his iPhone and finding a message that clearly bothered him.

'It'll be fine,' he said, like he was trying to convince himself of something.

Before today, Ben Murphy had seemed to her the kind who'd be bright-eyed and bushy-tailed in the morning, ready to kick on his career when others were nursing hangovers and other regrets. A very different Murphy rubbed the cramp from around his neck and sighed at the momentary release. She clipped a magazine into her semi-automatic. She hoped she wasn't going to have to use it.

'Let's go talk to Stephen Brennan then,' Murphy said.

As they walked along by the bare hedgerows to the left of the road, Helen tucked away the gun.

'No car over there,' she whispered as they paused within first sight of the cottage.

Helen peered around the end of the hedgerow where a low stone wall, pebble-dashed in the not-too-distant past, began. The cottage and its surrounds gave a tidy impression. Inside the wall was a well-kept concrete yard. The cottage stood no more than thirty feet back from the wall and had been newly painted. There was no side access to the left of the cottage, and to the right, high trees blocked the passage.

'No trailer either,' Murphy said quietly. 'Sheridan's not here. Must've already gone to work.'

They took the last stretch along by the front wall as casually as any normal couple out for an early-morning stroll. Of the three windows, two had their curtains closed and a third looked in on an empty kitchen. No gate hung on the front pillars. Murphy stepped back out on to the centre of the road and signalled to the cars. Uniforms piled out. They followed Murphy's urgent semaphore. Five officers climbed into the field beside the cars and made for the back garden of the cottage. Two stayed on the road to deal with any traffic that came along from Clogherhead. Two more passed by the cottage to cut off traffic from the Castlebellingham direction as Helen and Murphy went in by the open gateway.

Helen rang the faux-brass bell before realizing that the door was off the latch. She pulled the zip of her jacket down a couple of inches.

'Hello?' she called as Murphy eased the door inwards. 'Stephen? Stephen Brennan?'

The hallway had been swept clean and, to their right, the kitchen and living area had an organized air about it. Skip Sheridan was clearly the house-proud type, Helen thought, which seemed at odds with his cavalier attitude to the dangers of a chainsaw. Only one of four doors along the hallway was closed. From the others, daylight filtered out. They heard a sudden stirring that was like the flutter and sweep of bedsheets followed by faint cries. Then the noise grew louder and seemed to have moved above them. They both looked back at the front door just as a flock of gulls went sweeping overhead, veered around by the stone chapel and headed for the sea beyond. Helen and Murphy shared a sigh of relief and, off-guard, jumped back when the door beside them opened.

'What . . . ? What are you doing in here?'

Stephen Brennan wore only a T-shirt and boxer shorts, his skinny body shaking, his fair hair in a mad tangle. There was a drowsy limpness about his voice and movements.

Helen caught a glimpse of tattoos on his arms but the light was poor and then he folded them tight against the cold. He stank of alcohol.

'If you're Jehovah's Witnesses or Mormons or something, you can bail out right now,' he told Ben Murphy, his voice slurred, his gaze unfocused as he examined the spruce young detective's charcoal grey suit.

Helen showed him her ID. He glanced at it briefly then looked slowly up at her. He'd recognized Helen from their earlier encounters.

'When are you people going to get off my back?' he complained as he took a shaky step back into the shade of the curtained bedroom. 'This Doran guy is still on the loose and you're out here hassling me?'

'Get dressed, Mr Brennan,' Murphy said.

'I'm not going anywhere.'

Stephen Brennan was trying hard to keep himself awake and standing.

'Get dressed, Mr Brennan,' Murphy repeated. 'We have questions to ask and it may take a while. We don't want you catching cold, do we?'

'Piss off,' Stephen said, and made to close the door in their faces but Murphy got his foot in to stop it.

He was in Stephen Brennan's face. Not a trace of fire in her colleague though, Helen thought. Ice, more like. The younger man tried a sneer but the tremor in his cheek undid it.

'Gudrun Remer has been murdered,' Murphy said evenly. 'Attacked in the shower. Her brain pulped, her body thrown to the pitbull terriers. Get dressed.'

The half-naked young man staggered back in a kind of demented moonwalk. When the backs of his legs touched the double bed, he sat, bounced briefly and slumped forward. He was searching for something in his hair. Maybe he was after the words that wouldn't come though his lips prattled on indistinctly without them.

'Can you tell us where you were yesterday, Stephen?' Helen asked. 'Inspector Woods spoke to you and Ms Remer in the morning. What then?'

'I can't believe this is happening to me,' Stephen said.

Helen and Murphy shared a disbelieving glance. His father and his New Age mentor lay dead but Stephen Brennan remained the exclusive centre of his own universe. She was reminded of her younger brother, his morbid self-pity. At least Jamie had some excuse. Lost his mother at five, never had the silver spoon this skinny little runt had all his life. Then she remembered that her brother's self-pitying outbursts were always calculated. Jamie had never craved sympathy for its own sake. He used it to cover his lies and deceptions.

Detective Garda Murphy picked up a red plaid work shirt from the chair by the door and flung it at Brennan.

'Put this on,' he said disgustedly. 'And answer the question.'

'It's not mine,' Stephen said, but he put it on, his hands slow and clumsy.

Helen had seen Skip Sheridan wear the shirt. She surveyed the bedroom. In cottage terms, this was a large room. Probably the main bedroom, she guessed. Double bed too. Four pillows. The American's clothes on the chair. She felt as though she stood before a stream and there were three rocks across which she could step, three conclusions she could jump to.

Skip Sheridan and Stephen Brennan were lovers. They were in on the murders together. Sheridan had done a runner.

Slow down, she thought. The links were tenuous but, at the very least, there were a whole lot more questions for Stephen to answer than she'd carried in here with her.

'We're waiting, Mr Brennan,' Murphy said.

'I was on the lash with Skip,' Stephen told him. 'I can't even remember getting here last night.' He gave Murphy a dizzy, puzzled look from under his lank fringe. 'We must've got a taxi because he was locked too, man.'

'Where is he now?'

'He's not here?'

'What time exactly did you meet Mr Sheridan yesterday?' Helen asked.

'Half past six or . . . I'm not sure . . . seven? There was a mix-up, like.'

'What kind of mix-up?'

'I was supposed to meet him at six o'clock in O'Donoghue's. You know, near the Shelbourne Hotel? But, I don't know, I was kind of confused. I ended up in the other O'Donoghue's. The one on Suffolk Street.'

'Kind of confused? You'd already been drinking before you went into town?'

'A few cans.' Stephen shrugged.

'And this was at the Sanctuary?' Murphy asked. 'What time did you leave?'

'I was out there until, I don't know, four? Half four? Until I headed into town. Whatever happened must've happened after that because she was still—'

'How did you get into town?'

'I got the bus . . . I must have got the bus. The forty-four from Enniskerry. There's one at five. Takes about an hour to . . . My head . . . it's so hazy, man, I can't remember anything, and I don't feel right.'

He seemed to be examining his hands and wondering why the fingers moved so slowly. Must have been doing drugs last night, Helen thought. She couldn't think what cocktail of drugs would leave him so listless and, if he was to be believed, so compromised on the memory front.

'What were you on last night, Stephen, besides the beer?' she asked. 'You're totally out of it.'

'Nothing,' he said uncertainly. 'Just Guinness. Nothing else.'

'You seem very certain of that,' Murphy said. 'Maybe your memory is coming back, eh?'

'Let's see if you can remember anything else, like how did you get to Enniskerry?' Helen asked.

'I walked. I suppose.'

'That's, what? A half-hour walk from the Sanctuary? Would Gudrun not have given you a lift? Or maybe she was already—'

Stephen Brennan suddenly burst into sobs.

'Gudrun . . . Oh, Christ . . . Gudrun . . .'

The reality of the German woman's murder had struck him. Or he'd remembered he should be grieving. It was hard to tell which. He disguised himself with strands of hair, long fingers, a clump of work shirt. Ben Murphy sat on the chair a couple of feet away from the bed. He looked like he needed the rest.

'You and the victim argued yesterday when the inspector called,' he said. 'Seems you were pretty aggressive towards her. So? The fight went on after he left, was that it? You lost control just like you lost control with your father? What was the problem with Ms Remer? She didn't want to cover for you any more? And you lost it and attacked her?'

'No way, man,' Stephen insisted, then immediately

contradicted himself. 'He provoked me deliberately, that ugly—'

In one movement, Murphy grabbed hold of the plaid work shirt, stood up and dragged the ragged-haired young man to his feet.

'You killed her,' Murphy said. 'Then you went on the lash. Is that what you did after you murdered your father too?'

'I never killed anyone . . . any thing,' Stephen wailed, and Murphy flung him back on the bed. 'This is police brutality. This is—'

Murphy did a double-take, stared at the young fellow's right arm and swept up the unbuttoned right sleeve of the work shirt.

'Open the curtains, Helen,' he said, and she did.

Stephen Brennan, his eyes averted from the blinding light, tried in vain to pull away from Murphy. What Helen had imagined to be tattoos were, she now saw, teeth marks. Dog bites. Most of them had healed and begun to fade. Two were more recent. Very recent.

'What's the story here, son? The Alsatian bit you, so you cut its fucking head off?'

Helen realized Murphy was doing an Inspector Leo Woods impersonation.

Stillness descended on Stephen and on the bedroom. For Helen and her colleague it felt like the stillness of an impasse. Stephen gave the impression that for him the stillness was one of recollection, of reconnecting the broken synapses of his recent memory and of hoping that among those lost connections he wasn't about to find himself feeding Gudrun Remer to the dogs. Helen needed to kick-start this process with a jolt.

'Did Skip Sheridan help you?' Helen asked, then threw in

an even wilder jolt. 'Did he help you kill your father too?'

'What? Help me? You're crazy. None of this has anything to do with me or Skip.'

'You're just good friends?' Helen said.

'Yeah.'

'Share a bed, do you?' Murphy asked.

'No way.'

'This is his bedroom,' Helen said. 'That's his shirt you're wearing.'

'You told me to put it on, remember? Why are you doing this to me? Why?'

She saw fearful anticipation in Stephen Brennan's eyes. She knew she had to keep pushing. Stephen knew it too.

'Did you wear Frankie Prior's shirts too?' she asked, and all hell broke loose.

Stephen sprang from the bed, swinging a wild palm that caught Helen on the right ear so hard she hit the floor while Murphy whipped his right fist into Stephen's jawbone, sending him down on to Helen, and she offloaded the young fellow with a sharp elbow to the nose, taking a spray of his blood on her cheek for her troubles before Murphy took her hand and yanked her up, pulled her close for a moment and let her go as if they were dancing, and when they swung round, Skip Sheridan was standing beside a uniform in the doorway. Wrapped in a quilted lumber jacket and wool hat, he was feeling the cold today and looked the worse for wear. Looked, Helen thought, ten years older. And more.

The American swept his wool cap off and Helen could almost hear the static zipping along his scalp. He looked at her as if the bloody scene before him was all her fault.

'You OK, Steve?' he said, but his gaze stayed on Helen.

35

The young Latvian girl had dyed her hair again. Or undyed it? Inspector Leo Woods had no idea which. The technicalities of hairdressing were beyond him. In any case, the girl was closer to her real self. Her hair was red again, her face less caked with make-up. The problem was that the self she'd returned to wasn't named Daina Klavinš. All the same, he wished he didn't have to psych her out. He had no choice, knowing he wasn't going to be able to psych her older sister out.

He'd taken one look at Sonia Leipinš and retreated from the holding room at Raheny Garda Station. Black hair dyed blonde and gelled into punky spikes, tight-fitting leather jacket, stone-washed jeans, long and bony fingers with two or three rings on each one. Her cold-diamond eyes met his with a withering calm, a young woman gone beyond disillusionment. She'd been in tighter spots than this and wasn't for breaking any time soon.

The girl who called herself Daina was Laima Leipinš. She sat in the interview room, chewing what remained of the flesh around her fingernails between outbursts of tearful rants against the interpreter. When she wasn't complaining or gnawing, she cast terrified glances at Leo who stood outside the open door, speaking in lowered tones with Inspector Eamon Selby from Immigration and Sergeant Martha Corrigan.

'These kids are up shit creek, Leo,' Selby said. 'And they've got bigger problems than us to deal with.'

Selby and Leo had served together with UNPROFOR in Bosnia. He was mid-forties, average height, average face, average intelligence. He'd met Martha an hour before. Like many average men before him, he'd fallen in love and realized he didn't have a chance with her in more or less the same moment. This left the immigration officer regretful though not bitter. Happens to all of us, Leo thought. Selby related the Latvian girls' dilemma.

'Back in their home town there's a branch of whatever the hell they call the Mafia over there and, apparently, they link up with these Asian guys to set up fake marriages in EU countries with loopholes in the law.'

'Such as Ireland,' Leo said.

'Yeah, unfortunately we've got more than most, but we've been tightening up. In the past, a girl could come on over, sign up for an intended marriage in some local registry office and go back home. After three months, she could come back, go through with the marriage and then head home where she'd get her cut of the money. Used to be they could make eight or nine thousand euro. Now it's nearer three or four, which is still major money for them. Plus these days they have to stay in Ireland while they're waiting to marry. Some of them, like Laima and Sonia, get work and it's a bonus.'

'Laima and Sonia are sisters for sure, are they?' Leo asked.

'Yeah, and this Daina girl was actually a cousin who died as an infant,' Selby said, turning from the ex-Rose of Tralee to Leo. Turning, his deflated expression implied, from the beauty to the beast. 'The plan was Laima's. Her sister had already committed herself to one of these fake marriages and Laima . . . well, she's a bright kid, it seems, and wants to go on to college and there wasn't much chance of that the way things stood. The family's got very little. The father's dead, the mother's remarried and abandoned them years ago.'

'So, what's the story now? You send them back?'

Selby shrugged. He glanced at Laima who'd slumped forward so that her forehead rested defeatedly on her arms. He shrugged again.

'Sonia told us she's been in touch with this Mafia lot,' Martha Corrigan said. 'They want their investment repaid. Two thousand euro. They've offered the girls an alternative, of course, another way to pay back the debt. And I don't mean housework.'

'What about the Indian guys who were holding Laima and Sonia?' Leo asked of Selby. 'Can't they pay up?'

'They weren't holding them, Leo, they were helping them to hide,' Selby said. 'The girls have admitted as much. Long-term we'll be deporting these guys. Short-term they'll probably leave anyway.'

The young girl's heaving sobs had subsided. So quiet was it in there that she might be sleeping. He wished he could think of some way to help her out of her dilemma. He turned towards the open door. The interpreter shook his head, checked his watch impatiently, raised his eyes to the ceiling.

'Do you reckon she knows anything about the murder?' Leo asked Martha Corrigan.

'Not the actual murder, sir, but I've tested her on Mrs

Brennan's . . . well, on Mrs Brennan's fidelity. And my instinct is Laima might have seen something she shouldn't have. When I mentioned Alan Cobbe, she clammed up. But . . . could I make a suggestion? No, an observation. Maybe I'm way off beam.'

'Go ahead.'

'The interpreter,' she said in a whisper. 'Laima won't talk while he's around is my guess. He's got this sneering tone and a horribly patronizing attitude. Towards me too, I have to say. But that's not the problem. The problem is that he's from Latvia, yes, and speaks the language. But he's ethnic Russian and looks down his nose at Latvians.'

'How did you figure all this out?' Leo asked in wonder.

'His given name is Boris,' Martha said brightly as though this were explanation enough. 'I think I could get through to her if we had someone more sympathetic, or at least more neutral. I've got a list here.'

'You know what, Martha?' Leo told her after a short pause for thought. 'I think you've got it in one.'

He crooked a beckoning finger at the interpreter who stood up with an exaggerated weariness. The girl raised her head and watched as Leo hoped she would. The young man reached the door and stood there, gritting his teeth in irritation.

'You forgot something,' Leo said.

'Are we now finished here?'

Leo gestured towards the jacket hanging on the chair the young man had occupied.

'*You* are. Grab your overcoat, Gogol, and get out of here.' He spoke loudly and sharply, and jerked his thumb back so that the girl might understand that the dismissal was final.

'You can't speak to me like that,' the interpreter protested.

293

'I just did. Get your coat.'

'You will hear more of this.'

'The coat.'

Leo went into the interview room. As he passed by Laima with his back to the interpreter, he gave her a wink. Her lips approached a smile but backed away from it. Leo grabbed the jacket and brought it back to the astonished young man.

'But why?' the interpreter asked.

'Your English is good, son,' Leo said. 'But your manners are appalling.'

He looked back at the young girl. Under her sad but trusting, wide-eyed gaze, Leo wondered if this was what it felt like to be a father whose child has gone from his protective arms, out into the cold world.

36

'Care for some coffee?' Skip Sheridan asked. 'Or tea? Can't take to the stuff myself but—'

'Sit down, Mr Sheridan,' Detective Garda Ben Murphy said.

The kitchen area with its breakfast counter looked like a cheap but clean take-away espresso bar. Murphy pulled out a high stool for himself. The American had already filled the kettle and held it aloft. He was trying too hard for normality. Helen intervened. She didn't yet dislike him in spite of her new suspicions.

'I'll do it,' she said. 'Take a seat.'

When she took the kettle from him, he had no further props to fiddle with. He'd taken off his lumber jacket and boots. There was nothing left to do but sit. His hands and feet seemed to work independently and without apparent rhythm or coordination. Fingers tapping the Formica surface of the counter, toes brushing across and back along the floor tiles. The sirens of the squad cars taking Stephen Brennan away had faded. A few cars still stood outside on the Chapel Road, Sheridan's dusty old Opel Kadett among them.

'From the beginning again then, Mr Sheridan,' Murphy said, notebook at the ready. 'Yesterday afternoon, you were working on the southside of the city. Rock Road in Booterstown. A small apartment block with communal gardens, right?'

'Yes, sir.'

There was more formality than respect in Sheridan's reply. Murphy took no notice. He was busy flicking through the pages of his notebook. Sheridan avoided looking Helen's way, disappointed with the results of his earlier efforts. She wasn't about to rescue him and he seemed hurt by her silent refusal. Murphy took a less oblique tack than he had first time round.

'But when you spoke to Detective Sergeant Troy and her colleague the other day, you stated that you worked the northside of the city and upwards into County Louth. Booterstown to the Argos Sanctuary, that would be what? Half an hour? A quicker spin than if you'd been working on the northside. You could make your way out to the Sanctuary and back and hardly be missed, couldn't you? Are we to believe this is just a coincidence?'

The American looked at Murphy incredulously, his hands and feet shocked into stillness.

'I'm a suspect?' he said.

He half turned towards Helen but changed his mind. She made the instant coffee. Two cups. Murphy had brought a small bottle of spring water in from the car and took a shot from it.

'Just answer the question,' he said.

'I got me a couple of clients south of the city, yeah. Black-rock, Dun Laoghaire, Booterstown. I go where the work is. I don't have no government cheque.'

Helen brought the cups to the breakfast counter and played good cop.

'Milk? Sugar?'

Sheridan didn't acknowledge the question. He took a sip of the coffee, didn't like the taste and set the cup aside. Helen could see that Murphy was getting to him with his endless rifling through the pages of his notebook. Murphy knew it too because, just then, he fished out a second, the Miró notebook, from his inside pocket and flicked through that one also. *We know more about you than you can imagine*, his actions implied.

'You worked there all afternoon and finished up at what time? Three thirty, four o'clock?'

'I worked from eight in the morning until late afternoon. I can't say what time exactly. Enough time to make it back here, shower and head on in to meet Stephen.'

'But there's just the one witness,' Murphy went on. 'A Ms Coughlan. You spoke with her for a little while at around three. No others?'

'I guess you'll have to ask in the apartments. I don't see no one else don't mean they've not seen me.'

'We'll certainly ask, Mr Sheridan,' Murphy said. 'Right then, this date with Stephen Brennan. When was it arranged?'

'*Date*?' The hurt turned to threat in Sheridan's tone.

'He was sleeping in your room, in your bed. He used to have a transvestite friend. He—'

'If you weren't hiding behind a badge, I'd smash your doggone face in.'

Helen didn't like the homophobic turn in the conversation but had to concede that it rattled the American, and rattle him was what they needed to do.

'Are you threatening me, Mr Sheridan?' Murphy said.

'Hypothetically, yes.'

'So where did you sleep last night?'

'I don't sleep,' Sheridan said, and indicated a long, off-green, high-winged sofa that took up too much of the living area. 'Behind the couch, if you care to look, you'll find a blanket and two pillows. I rested there.'

'You suffer from insomnia?' Murphy asked. 'Even after a night on the town?'

'Especially after a night on the town. I don't figure you'll understand that.'

'You don't?'

'No. Folks generally don't get it when it comes to these kinds of problems. Not unless they've had first-hand experience. They're pretty dumb that way,' he added pointedly.

'You think so? You think you're the only—'

The confrontation between the two men was beginning to feel as churlish as a schoolyard row. Helen stepped in.

'Tell us about the mix-up. Stephen went to the wrong pub. You waited, he waited. When did the penny drop? Did you ring him, text him? Or did he make contact with you?'

'He rang me,' Sheridan said. 'I'd been there a while but I guess folks are more relaxed about time over here. That's been my experience. So, it wasn't a problem. And it wasn't like I had any other plans.'

The image of his waiting alone in a crowded city-centre pub reminded Helen of her own isolation. She hadn't had any other plans that night either.

'And when Stephen arrived he didn't seem upset, hyped up, bothered?' she asked.

'Not so's you could tell.'

'So you went from there to the other O'Donoghue's pub,

the one near the Shelbourne? Stayed there until closing time?'

'Yes, ma'am.'

'Then you went to this club . . . Capers? Did you meet anyone there? Talk to anyone who might verify your story?'

'Like I said, I spoke to some lady but not for long enough to get beyond first-name terms,' Sheridan told her. 'Polly. She may have been taking me for a ride. I guess I was pretty tanked.'

'Tanked on what?' Helen asked. 'Beer? And? Cocaine, Ecstasy?'

'I don't do any of that shit,' Sheridan insisted.

'Does Stephen?'

'I don't know. I don't think so.'

'But you can't be sure,' Murphy said. 'That's not a problem, Mr Sheridan. We'll be doing a toxicology and DNA test on Stephen. On you too.'

'On me? Why?'

'My earlier question, Mr Sheridan. How did this arrangement to meet last evening come about? Was it your idea or his?'

'I don't remember. I mean, we've gone for a drink before. He's been showing me round the city. The pubs, clubs, you know. I guess I don't know anyone else to hang out with. I been so busy getting myself sorted, I haven't been moving out a lot.'

'You drove into the city even though you knew you'd be drinking all evening?' Helen interrupted.

This time Sheridan's hesitation was peppered with irritation. His fingers had stopped their tapping because he'd made them into fists. Helen and her colleague watched him, retreating imperceptibly from arm's reach. Who is this man?

Helen wondered, and at once a further question came to her, but she held it back for the moment.

'I brought the motor because I can't afford a cab both ways,' Sheridan said. 'Not at eighty euro a shot.'

'So this morning you headed into town to collect the car?' Murphy asked.

'Yes, sir.'

'You got a bus from Clogherhead to Drogheda and a connection into the city?'

'At eight a.m., yes,' Sheridan said. 'Got there about ten.'

'And you'd parked your car where?'

'I've already told you. Why don't you go check it in your goddamn book?'

'Tell me again.'

Sheridan changed his mind about the coffee and knocked back half the cup. The bitter liquid soured his expression further. He set down the cup too forcefully on the breakfast counter. The spillage annoyed him.

'A twenty-four-hour parking lot round the block from Jervis Street,' he said, and segued quickly into an extended and very weary complaint. 'From day one I been getting this crap over here. Suspicious goddamn minds everywhere I go, everything I try to do. I was born here. I got an Irish passport but it don't mean shit to you people. You don't accept my driver's licence. You won't give me a bank loan. I pay for all these improvements in the cottage here outta my own pocket and the jerk who owns the place won't take a dime off the rent. Makes me so mad I could die. What is it with you folks? Hasn't anyone here ever heard of making a new start? That's what I'm trying to do here, and what do I get? I get questions about the murders of people I don't even know. Some guy I've seen three or four times in my entire goddamn life. This German lady I've met once. Once. Ever. For Christ's sake, give me a break here.'

'We haven't mentioned Dermot Brennan's murder,' Helen said.

'Yeah, well, I'm pretty goddamn sure you were going to get around to it.'

'So, where were you late Friday night last, early Saturday morning?' Murphy put in, and the American gave Helen a told-you-so shrug.

'I was right here. Alone. I live alone.'

His sudden despondency made the American seem less dangerous. Detective Garda Murphy put away one of his notebooks as if making some concession to Sheridan's frustration.

'I come over here wanting to scatter Momma's ashes in these fields,' Sheridan added. 'And I walk into a goddamn minefield.'

'All we want to do at this point in the investigation is verify Stephen's story,' Helen said. 'He's implicated in both murders. We need to know if he's telling us the truth. We need to know especially how and where he spent the hours from early afternoon yesterday. Did he talk about that? Did he mention any problems he'd had with Gudrun Remer yesterday? Did he talk about her at all?'

Sheridan fisted the grain from his bloodshot eyes. Down to four or five hours' sleep at best most nights herself, Helen wondered how anyone could survive with none, with no rest from the night-thoughts that were darker and deeper than the worst of daylight imaginings. She pitied him. To her surprise, Ben Murphy did too. He put away the second notebook. There was something laboured about her colleague's movements as if tiredness had crept up on him

301

too and blunted the edges of his enthusiasm. Sheridan took note of the fact and mellowed.

'Yes, he talked about her,' he said. 'And, yes, they'd argued. She had this thing about him not going to his daddy's funeral. She felt he shouldn't go, that he shouldn't get sucked into remorse. And maybe she was right. Except it was too much for him to deal with. He's ... whatever ... twenty-two years old, but he's a kid. And, for sure, he's no killer.'

'You'd know a killer if you saw one?' Murphy asked.

Sheridan shrugged. The question tired him.

Just beyond the breakfast counter was a shelf of CDs. Twenty-five or thirty in all. Johnny Cash, Johnny Cash, Johnny Cash, Richmond Fontaine, John Mellencamp. Familiar names and styles. Country, country rock. Hard knocks, hard liquor, hard times. This morning, Skip Sheridan looked like he'd lived these songs all his life. Roseanne Cash. Lyle Lovett. Skip Ewing. *Skip Ewing*?

Sheridan saw her scanning the shelf.

'Not your bag, I guess?' he said, forcing a smile.

'Not all of them,' she said. 'Skip Ewing?'

'Liked him when I was a kid. Got my nickname that way.'

She remembered the question that had come to her a few minutes before.

'What's your real name, Mr Sheridan?'

'My real name?'

'Your Christian name, I mean. Your given name.'

'James Robert. James Robert Sheridan.'

'Can we see your passport, please?'

'Why?'

'Routine check,' Helen said. 'We'll need the details. Passport number. All of that.'

'Sure.'

302

Sheridan dismounted his high stool and came around the breakfast counter. Helen stood back to let him pass. He crossed to the living area of the room and searched through a small cabinet under the flat-screen TV. He returned to Murphy's side and handed over the passport.

'Both of your passports,' Murphy said. 'Irish and American.'

'I don't carry the American one.'

'Why not?'

'It came up for renewal a few months back,' Sheridan said. 'I didn't renew it.'

'Why?' Helen asked.

'Because I don't need it no more. Because I'm Irish. Because I won't be edged out of this goddamn country like my dad was.'

Ben Murphy's iPhone vibrated on the breakfast counter. He snatched at it, flicked down through the incoming message. He grasped the edge of the breakfast counter. His pallor disturbed Helen. She caught her colleague's eye and nodded at the door. Murphy stood and aimed himself at the gap. The message, she sensed, wasn't work-related.

37

Considering the plunge in temperatures outside, the room Inspector Leo Woods had nabbed for himself in Raheny Garda Station wasn't especially cold. He felt nonetheless chilled as he put the phone down. The news from the Enniscorthy desk sergeant troubled him. Yes, they'd found Alan Cobbe at his house and taken him into custody. And yes, he'd kicked up a fuss and had had to be physically subdued. And yes, he was at this moment being driven in the back of a Black Maria to be questioned in Raheny by Leo. But there was a problem. Caroline Hunt's whereabouts were unknown. The Eggman claimed he'd dropped her off in the city centre this morning and that she planned to travel down by train later in the day. She wasn't answering her mobile.

Leo asked the God he didn't believe in to deliver some good news. But God wasn't taking calls from strangers either, he supposed. Someone knocked on the door. He didn't want to answer, didn't want to go on. Always happened a few hours after the post-malarial high. The plunge, the inner sickening, the loneliness. He heard a voice whose timbre if not its sense he recognized. The ex-Rose of Tralee. He looked at the ceiling. Fair dues to you, he thought.

He unlocked the door and Martha Corrigan beamed at him. He felt like he'd stepped into some warm, sunny place.

'Laima talked?' he said.

'Yes, sir. She saw Anna Brennan in compromising situations with the same guy on two different occasions last month,' Martha said. 'Once embracing in the kitchen. Then one morning a week or so later, Dermot Brennan was in Manchester on business and she saw them sitting on Anna's bed. Anna was still in her nightdress, this guy was dressed but his shirt was loose and—'

'Alan Cobbe?' Leo asked.

'No, sir, it was the gardener. Skip Sheridan.'

'Martha, you've made my day,' he said. 'As you often do.'

She laughed. They went back a long way, knew each other's form.

'My Aunt Bridie had a very sensible take on flattery, Leo,' Martha said as she left. 'It's pleasant to chew on but not to be swallowed.'

'Good sense obviously runs in the family. Never ran in mine.'

Leo rang Helen and told her what he'd just heard.

'We're still at the cottage,' she said. 'I'll put it to him straight up. See how he takes it.'

'Do that,' Leo said. 'What about Stephen Brennan?'

Helen gave him the details of Stephen's prevarications. And his bite marks.

'You're bringing him in?' Leo asked.

'When he's discharged from hospital, which shouldn't take too long.'

'Hospital? For the bite marks?'

'There was a bit of a scuffle. We thought his nose was broken but it's nothing.'

'Who hit him?'

Helen didn't answer.

'You hit him?'

'Accidentally . . . sort of . . . self-defence, you know.'

Leo chuckled.

'You're a dark one, Helen,' he said.

At the wheel of the squad car, Helen Troy negotiated the narrow eFlow barrier on the M1 toll plaza at too great a speed. Clear of the toll booths, she flicked on the siren and blasted a couple of cars from her path in the outer lane in her efforts to keep up with the car carrying Skip Sheridan to Howth Garda Station. Ben Murphy lay back on the passenger seat. Eyes closed, skin an unearthly white with too much yellow in it. Helen slowed down the car.

'What's wrong, Ben?' she asked as lightly as she could. 'You look like shit.'

'Thanks, Helen,' he mumbled, and a weak smile began to form on his lips. 'Tired is all.'

'Tired isn't all,' she said. 'Whatever it is, you shouldn't be at work.'

He sat himself up on the passenger seat and looked straight ahead. Helen too kept her eyes on the road. She hadn't meant to sound as though she were pulling rank.

'I'm doing my job,' Murphy said. 'If you've any complaints to make about me, bring them to Leo. He'll be happy to hear them.'

'I'm not complaining, for Christ's sake. I'm concerned, right?'

He was watching her now, she knew, deciding whether or not to confide in her. Part of her hoped he wouldn't. Even the Good Samaritan, she thought, must from time to time have got pissed off with his burdensome capacity for empathy.

'My daughter's in hospital,' he said. 'Third time this year.'

'I'm sorry,' was all that Helen could say, so taken aback was she.

'Her name is Millie. She's got cystic fibrosis so she picks up every infection going. This one's the worst so far.'

'What age is she?' Helen asked.

'She's five. I've been staying overnight at Crumlin Children's Hospital for the last week and, to be honest, I haven't been getting a lot of sleep. My mother just texted me to say they'll be keeping Millie in for at least two more weeks. I may have to take leave.'

'But Millie's mother . . . ?' Helen began and chided herself for overstepping the mark.

'She's not in the picture. Can we leave it at that, please?' he asked. 'It's Sheridan we need to talk about.'

With some effort, Helen's thoughts turned to the American. When she'd gone back into the cottage after Leo's call, Sheridan was at the kitchen sink washing the coffee mugs. Scrubbing them diligently again and again until he was satisfied with the result. His failure to acknowledge her presence just three feet away had seemed almost juvenile. While he dried the mugs, his back to her still, she'd told him of Laima Leipins's revelations. He'd set the mugs upside down in an orderly cupboard. She'd asked him to explain what it was that the girl had witnessed. He'd folded the damp tea towel and placed it by the sink. From that moment until she and Ben Murphy saw him into a squad car bound for Howth Garda Station, the gardener had uttered only two words. 'Ask Anna,' he'd said.

'We need to check out this guy's background in the States,'

Murphy said, a renewed determination in him that he had to fight to maintain. Helen knew the feeling. Sometimes just forcing yourself through the motions brought you back to some kind of functioning normality. 'We could start with the Passport Office here in town and work back through the documentation he needed to file. And maybe the American Embassy could help out on his original passport, the one that's lapsed.'

'And the story about bringing his mother's ashes back here,' Helen said. 'That shouldn't be too difficult to verify, should it?'

Soon, they'd reached the northside of the city. They passed along the endless ribbon of semi-detached houses on Tonlegee Road and on to Kilbarrack Road, and the list of questions Ben Murphy entered in his notebook seemed without end too.

Where did Sheridan live immediately prior to his departure for Ireland? When and where had his mother died? Did Sheridan have a police record of any kind? What had he worked at, and for whom, and where? Where had Sheridan lived all those years since his parents had emigrated to the States? Always in the same place or had they moved around? How long had his relationship with Anna been going on? Had Cobbe been telling the truth after all when he spoke of Dermot Brennan's antipathy towards Sheridan?

They continued to swap questions until Ben's mobile rang. They were on the Dublin Road, quarter of a mile from Howth village. The icy breeze was rippling the low waters between the sandbanks of Bull Island, setting clusters of reeds on edge. Helen shivered in spite of the heat blowing through the car's interior.

'Mum,' Murphy said, turning from Helen, lowering his

voice. 'She'll be fine . . . Don't, Mum. I know . . . I know . . .'
He went on calming his mother down for another minute
or so. 'I really have to go now. Listen, did Angie get a chance
to watch the CCTV? She did? And? So, I was right. Tell her
thanks. Tell her I'll see her tomorrow. And tell Millie I'll be
there tonight with a big surprise . . . Yeah. Bye.'

He turned to Helen, bright-eyed, lightly flushed, smiling
broadly. He scrolled his mobile, got up a number and pressed
green to go.

'My sister had a look at the CCTV clip of Sean Doran,' he
told Helen as he waited to be connected. 'I was convinced he
was singing something or other. And he was. He was— Sir?'

Murphy's tone had become tentative. Leo was on the line.
'Sir?'

'What've you got for me?'

Murphy filled him in on the details of Skip Sheridan's
reaction to Laima's revelation.

'Ask Anna? And that was it?' Leo repeated. 'He refused to
say anything more?'

'Yes, sir,' Murphy said. 'Do you want to talk to her? Or,
well, we're already in Howth, so we could go over there if
you like.'

'Tell Helen to go talk to her,' Leo said. 'Woman to woman
might be better here. Anything else, Murphy?'

He knew there would be. He wasn't wrong. He wasn't
wrong either that the news would be delivered in a flat,
offended tone.

'The CCTV footage of Sean Doran?' Murphy said. 'My
sister watched it. Seems he was singing after all.'

'Singing what?'

'Singing "Heartbreak Hotel".'

*

309

Detective Inspector Leo Woods cut the call on his mobile. 'Heartbreak Hotel'. Sure as Christ, they were holed up in that God-awful hotel out in Hearnstown. His skin crawled. He feared the worst, imagined Sean Doran way up there on the top of the building, sitting on the edge. He felt the dizzy spin of vertigo just thinking about it. Then he told himself to calm down, think it through, think what to do. He left the office and slipped out by the rear exit of Raheny Garda Station. There, among the squad cars and the paddy wagons, he snapped off the tip of a menthol cigarette and lit up. The nicotine hit his brain with its usual combination of elation and defeat. He had to choose between the right thing to do and the *right* thing to do.

In official terms, the right thing to do was to hand this over to Detective Sergeant Cooney, call in the Emergency Response Unit and have a couple of negotiators on stand-by. All of which, Leo decided, would more than likely push Doran over the edge and end in disaster. On the other hand, what felt in his gut like the right thing to do was to confront the ex-boxer alone, convince him that he had nothing to fear from handing himself in, that he was no longer a suspect in the Brennan case nor in the murder of Gudrun Remer. He felt certain of Doran's innocence. Almost certain.

He took a last long drag from his cigarette and dumped it.

Around by the side of the station, Leo found Garda Dempsey at the driver's seat of a squad car fiddling madly with his Smartphone. He looked like he was masturbating. Leo slapped the roof of the car and heard a muffled squeal from inside. He might have laughed away the cramp in his gut but for the surprise that greeted him when he looked out by the side passage of the station. Pale and lank-haired in a limp grey anorak, Caroline Hunt stood at the corner of the building. She hadn't yet noticed him. She craned her neck the better to see along the front of the station. Leo made as soft-shoed an approach as possible so as not to scare her off.

'Ms Hunt,' he said, slowly, evenly. 'Can I help you?'

Startled, the young woman backed away. Her hands busied themselves with her hair, the zip of her anorak. Leo noted a fresh bruise high on her left cheekbone.

'I looked for you in Howth and they said . . . I gave a false name. I'm sorry. I'm just . . .'

'Is this about Gudrun Remer?' Leo asked.

It hardly seemed possible that the young English woman could get any paler, but she did. Leo raised a hand to steady her. She shrank from him.

'Oh, God,' she said. 'Oh, good God.'

She turned away from Leo, took a few tottering steps and held herself up with a hand on the gable-end of the Garda Station. He didn't have time to indulge her theatrics. He had to get out to Hearnstown fast.

'Caroline, I'm under pressure here,' he said. 'Tell me what you know.'

'But if Alan finds out I've—'

'We've already got Mr Cobbe in custody, Caroline,' he told her. 'So you've nothing to be afraid of.'

'You have?'

Caroline Hunt took a deep breath, flicked back her hair and faced him. Her eyes had become more steely and attractive than he could have imagined. She reminded Leo of his wife that day back in 1984 when she'd had enough of his constant explosive edginess. Iseult had gone from loud despair to quiet resolve in the blink of an eye. He remembered the strange sense of having missed what came between the extremes. A page ripped from his autobiography. Not the first nor the last to go missing.

'You'd better come inside and—'

'I'd rather not, Inspector,' she said. 'This won't take long and I've a taxi waiting.'

Outside the school across the street, the taxi purred, its driver deep in the shallows of a tabloid.

'Last Friday night,' she began, 'Alan didn't come home at a quarter to eleven. It was half past three in the morning when he arrived. He told me he'd stopped at Duncannon on his way back and went walking on the beach. Sometimes he does that. Goes walking by the sea at night when he's trying to work through some new idea.'

'But you no longer believe him. Why?'

'This morning I took a break from shopping in town and went to a café off Grafton Street. They had a radio playing and I caught the eleven o'clock news. The murder at the Argos Sanctuary was the first item.'

Caroline looked imploringly at Leo, craving absolution.

'I could've prevented this. I should've told you before.'

'Tell me now.'

'Gudrun and I . . . we were friends but I haven't spoken to her for months. I cut myself off from her because of what she did, because I was afraid of how Alan would react if he found out.'

'What did Ms Remer do?'

'Some months back when our neighbours found me by the side of the road . . .' Caroline said. 'Well, I hadn't been attacked by strangers. And while I was in hospital I rang Gudrun. I hadn't meant to but I told her everything. I pleaded with her not to go further with it. In the end, I agreed to a compromise. She'd make an anonymous call to the police in Enniscorthy. After Alan had been questioned, he accused me of reporting him and wanted to throw me out and I couldn't let that happen. I still loved him. You think I'm a fool, I know.'

'Love makes fools and worse of all of us,' Leo said. 'Did you tell Mr Cobbe who'd made the anonymous call?'

'Yes. I did.'

'When did you tell him?'

'Yesterday,' she said. 'I had a bad feeling about Dermot Brennan's murder. I didn't say anything to Alan, of course, but things had gotten very tense at home. You know how silences can be.'

'I do.'

'When he was released yesterday, I knew it was just a matter of time before he'd turn on me. And he did. Said I suspected him of being the killer, that I wanted to be rid of him. Said I'd been talking to the police about him and that it wasn't the first time. He brought up that anonymous call again. Which is when I . . . when I told him it was Gudrun. "That German bitch will be sorry she ever came to Ireland," he said. And now she's . . .'

'So, you can't vouch for his whereabouts yesterday afternoon and evening?'

Caroline Hunt shook her head.

'But he slept with you later at the hotel?'

'He didn't sleep. He drank, nodded off for an hour or so and wanted to drive down home. We checked out but I didn't go in the SUV with him. I grabbed a taxi into town while he was at the reception desk. He tried to ring me but I switched off my mobile.'

'We'll have to take a statement, Caroline.'

'But the taxi . . .'

313

Leo took hold of her upper arms and gently raised her from the slouch she'd fallen into.

'Caroline,' he said, 'you're a brave woman but you have to see it through now. We'll take your statement. Then you can disappear from his life once and for all. He doesn't deserve any better.'

38

Garda Dempsey turned the squad car in among the squashed beer cans and the deflated condoms scattered along the lane behind the Hearnstown Regency Hotel. He hadn't felt this excited and terrified since the All-Ireland Basketball Junior B cup final in 1999 when he'd lined out for Ballina Colts. Girls screaming on the benches all around, the air high and loud and suffocating, the scoreboard drifting inexorably the wrong way. Those crucial free shots towards the end of the game. Go on, Patch! Missed. Missed. Missed. Never played another game of basketball.

'Are you sure about this, sir?' he asked Leo as he cut the engine. 'Doesn't feel right.'

'From this moment on, Dempsey,' Leo said, 'time is suspended until I say otherwise, right? Stay in the car. Don't answer the radio or your Smartphone.'

'I should go in with you,' Dempsey said. 'If anything happens, how am I going to explain why I sat out here?'

'Simple,' Leo told him as he got out of the car. 'You were following orders. It's an old excuse, son, but in this force it still works.'

Dempsey's unease was catching. The hard knot in Leo's

315

stomach began to ache. The lane stank of a late night out with the wrong kind of people and he'd had too many of those. He opened the unlocked rear gate to the hotel. A large container had been overturned and had spilt its load of empty bottles across the enclosed yard. Leo stepped gingerly through the blitzed glass and made his way to what looked like a service entrance. Its double doors had already been jimmied. On the ground nearby was a discarded lock and spliced chain.

Leo pulled the doors open.

The storage area he found inside was empty but for a few large cardboard boxes of paper napkins. Then the reality and, very soon, the sheer stupidity of what he was doing struck him. How many rooms did the hotel have on its seven floors? Sixty, seventy, maybe more? If Sean Doran and his wife were alive they could elude him all day in this bloody place. And yet he knew by some blind instinct that he was meant to do this alone. Whatever it was that Sean Doran had to say, Leo should be the first to hear it.

He passed through yet another storage room filled with crockery and cutlery, shelves of the stuff. Every item reflected the same bland design, functional, institutional. At mealtimes, Lisa-Marie Doran probably couldn't tell whether she was in Heartbreak Hotel or the mental institution. When he pushed on, he found himself in a darkened kitchen. It smelled of rotted food scraps. He threw a switch or two to no avail. Still, there was enough light for him to see that no one had bothered to wash up after the last banquet. Pity, he mused, that Detective Garda Murphy wasn't there to file the metaphor in his Miró notebook.

In the lobby area, the air, too bright and too cold, had a kind of sharp-edged solidity to it. Leo sensed that it hadn't been disturbed for many hours, perhaps even a day or two. Maybe the Dorans weren't here after all. He stood at the centre of the lobby, looked around, listened. He heard nothing. Around him stood leatherette sofas that were too big to sit comfortably in and too small to sleep on, glass-topped coffee tables resting on faux-tigerskin rugs, factory-made Jackson Pollocks hanging on the walls.

Leo didn't know what to do next. Then he thought, What do you do when you arrive in a hotel lobby? You go to the reception desk, he told himself. There, propped against a stack of leaflets advertising the 'boutique joys' of the Hearn-stown Regency, stood an envelope. The handwriting fell exhaustedly from the horizontal line. It read simply, *Room 502*. Whatever hope he'd clung to this last hour began to fade.

The lift didn't work. Only when he'd stopped kicking the silvered aluminium door did it occur to him that he'd given up on keeping silent. He set off on the long climb and pulled out his work mobile to get his mind off what he might find. There was nowhere for the clatter of Leo's footsteps to go except to hit the damp-spotted walls and echo back at him again and again until they sounded like a dozen dead men walking behind the living one.

He felt weary. The prospect of interviewing Alan Cobbe in the coming hours had lost its charm for him. He rang Ben Murphy and repeated Caroline Hunt's story. He told the young detective to head to Raheny and put the screws on the Eggman. Then he returned a missed call from Martha Corrigan.

'Leo, I've some details from the pathologist out at the Argos Sanctuary. Very unpleasant details.'

'I thought they might be,' Leo said.

'The killer tried to strangle her but failed, it seems,'

Martha said. 'It was the blow from the axe that finished her.'

'Do we have a time of death?'

'Factoring in the low temperatures, they're suggesting midnight to two in the morning. But the attack may have happened earlier, possibly much earlier. They're having problems assessing the possible survival period.'

'You mean she could have lain dying there for hours? Why can't they tell?'

'Again, because of the cold, the damp and muddy environment, but also because the stomach contents were, eh, compromised.'

'Compromised?'

'The axe sliced her front open.'

'Oh, sweet Jesus . . .'

At the third-floor landing, a shortness of breath dizzied Leo. He moved closer to the long window there. He couldn't find a catch to open it and had to make do with more light in place of more air.

'Lost you there, Martha, sorry,' Leo said breathily. 'Coverage isn't great here.'

'Where are you?' Her light tone had a hint of worry in it. 'Sounds like you're inside a biscuit tin.'

'Yeah, that's me. Last biscuit in the tin. The plain broken one nobody wants to eat.'

The joke rang hollow.

'Where did you say you were?' Martha asked, more worried still.

'I didn't say. Anything else, Martha?'

'There were signs of recent and possibly consensual sexual activity. Of the, eh, anal variety.'

'Interesting,' Leo said. 'And the Bureau, have they dusted for prints in the cottage yet?'

'There are prints from ten, fifteen people, maybe more, out there. And that's just the kitchen and one of the bedrooms. It may be futile to—'

'Tell them to keep dusting, Martha. Stephen Brennan's will be all over the shop anyway but we're looking for matches with Alan Cobbe, right?'

'And Sean Doran?'

'I doubt they'll find his prints out there,' Leo said.

'I'll ring if they come up with anything,' Martha said, then, to his surprise, added, 'Wherever you are, Leo, take care.'

He switched off and resumed the climb. His legs dragged. He blamed the recent bout of malaria but knew he'd have to come up with a better excuse than that. On the fourth-floor landing, he stopped for a smoke. Or, at least, had a smoke in mind until he checked his pockets and found he had no cigarettes. Nor had he any tissues, but he supposed he'd find some in Room 502. He went on.

The view on to the rear of the surrounding buildings revealed smashed plate glass, pitted lanes and stacks of rubble that no one had got around to moving, such had been the pace of construction in the halcyon days. Leo's sweat dried and froze as soon as it emerged. When he took the last short flight of steps to the fifth floor, he remembered reading some time back about a writer who'd died after climbing a long stairs because the lifts had been out of order in the building where he worked. Couldn't think who it was.

He stepped into the unlit corridor.

Odd numbers on the left, even numbers on the right. Why was that? Did all hotels have this numbering system? And, if so, why? Room 528. Room 526. Every door he passed was closed. Swipe card units on each one; Leo wondered if Room

502 would be off-limits to him after all. He turned a corner, followed to the left. Up ahead to the right, a single chalk-mark of diagonal light. Room 512. Room 510. He wondered if there was any significance in Sean Doran's choice of room or room number. He thought not.

The smell reached him. Or he reached the smell. It hung in the corrupted air, invaded his clothes, his flesh, his innards. Could be worse, Leo thought, could be me.

Room 502.

Leo eased the door in with the tip of his shoe. Gazing at the strange tableau that greeted him, he stepped into the room and sat wearily on a chair by the door. The room was a large one. The sitting area to the right contained a boxy sofa, a coffee table, a TV and a writing desk. The dressing area to the left contained an open wardrobe, a long mirror and a folded ironing board. The king-sized double bed, directly facing the door, contained the bodies of Sean and Lisa-Marie Doran.

There had been no struggle, nor had any blood been spilled. Five small tablet bottles varying in height stood in a neat line on one of the bedside tables like a Giorgio Morandi still-life. The carpet still held the swirling stripes of the vacuum cleaner. From out of the fug of bodily decay, Leo picked up faint scents of wood polish, lavender joss sticks, sharp-perfumed toiletries. He wanted to open a window but couldn't bring himself to stand just yet.

He looked at the bodies again.

They lay in state. Side by side. Arms linked. A distant smile on her face, a mask of defeat on his. But all of this was ordinary compared to their dress. She wore what must have once been her receptionist's outfit, a smart olive-coloured two-piece suit. Around her neck and over her white blouse was a scarf of subtle autumnal colours. On the lapel of her jacket, a name tag. *Lisa-Marie – Reception.* Above his denims, Sean Doran had on a green sleeveless boxing singlet, emblazoned with a white shamrock. Neither one wore socks or shoes and the soles of their feet had begun to marble.

Leo dragged himself up from the chair and surveyed the room. On the bedside table at the young woman's side he saw a set of keys on a Mercedes key ring, a laptop notebook and a long white envelope like the one at the reception desk. From where he stood, Leo could see that this envelope had a name on it, and he knew the name was his. He braved the thickening stench closer to the bed and picked up the envelope.

Detective Inspector Woods.

Inside was a typed letter and a memory stick. He read the letter and took the laptop across to the writing desk. A pink tissue blossomed like a flower from a fancy box on the desk. He took the tissue and the one that grew in its place. He switched on the laptop.

No password protection. One hour and twenty minutes of battery left. The two folders on the memory stick opened without difficulty. Ten photographs taken, Leo guessed, from the upstairs front bedroom of Doran's house in Honeyvale Heights of the activities outside a house across the way. Number 13. A scanned tabloid front page from two months back. Had to hand it to the sweaty anorak brigade for coming up with such a humdinger of a headline. He read the letter again and wondered how the hell he was going to answer its contradictory pleas. All he knew was that he had to try. The last line of the letter read, 'I had no right to call you an ugly bastard and I'm ashamed I did.'

Think, Leo told himself. Don't let this tragic couple down. Everyone else has.

39

By the gates of Attenboy House, a middle-aged Garda who'd been leaning against the high wall came to attention when he saw the squad car approach. He wore his peaked cap back on the poll of his head. Helen never understood why so many of the older uniforms did this. Made them look like buffoons. Even the ones who weren't buffoons. Closer to the gates, she recognized the man. She couldn't remember his name but he was a likeable man and she felt guilty for having thought ill of him. So guilty that she stopped the car and rolled down the window. Later, she would reflect on how even our faults can sometimes lead us on the right path.

'You must be freezing, are you?' she said, offering a smile instead of the name which still eluded her.

'Not at all. I'm well used to it,' he said, leaning in to the window. She could tell he was mad for chat. 'I work on the lifeboats in my spare time. That's real cold for you. Cold you could eat if you had a knife and a fork with you.'

'The lifeboats, really?' she said. 'Are you ever afraid out there?'

'Ever?' He smiled. 'Always. Keeps you on your toes it does, being afraid.'

She couldn't think of anything else to say to the man so she improvised.

'Nothing much happening here, I suppose?'

'Well, actually,' the middle-aged Guard said, to her surprise, 'the next-door neighbour's been acting . . .' He searched for the appropriate word. 'Oddly.'

'Mrs Newman?'

'Yeah. She's been watching from behind the boundary trees up there,' he said. 'And twice she's asked me if "that poor disfigured man" is coming here today.'

'Leo,' Helen said, and the older man nodded.

'She obviously wants to talk to him but won't admit it,' he said. 'And I can't get an answer from Leo's phone.'

'Interesting,' Helen said. 'Thanks.'

'Denis,' he said. 'Denis Maher. I'm not the best at remembering names myself, girl.'

'Thanks, Denis.'

Helen rolled up her window. She didn't want to look indecisive but couldn't think which of the two neighbours to call on first. Anna Brennan, her head told her. Kitty Newman, her gut insisted. She reversed the squad car from between the pillars of the Attenboy House entrance and drove in along the ribbon of tarmac to the modernist pile next door.

Leo looked across Room 502 at his reflection in the long dressing mirror. The left side of his face seemed to have fallen further. Into his mind sprang the image of the most grotesque mask in his collection. The one most closely resembling his own face, the mouth twisted down on one side. An Iroquois Indian mask, the mask of the False Face Society. Its wearers were healers who would descend on the abode of the sick, dancing and chanting and driving away the evil spirits. Too late for healing in Room 502, Leo reflected, but maybe not too late to teach the evil spirits a lesson or two.

I could hang the bastard, but he could hang us too. That's what Sean Doran had said when they talked in the holding cell in Howth Garda Station. Leo knew what all that was about now. Doran, the letter explained, had tried to blackmail Foley with the photographs taken at Honeyvale Heights and the tabloid front page, but the scheme backfired. Leo knew what lay behind Lisa-Marie's sexual high-jinks at the psychiatric hospital too. The young woman's involuntary descent into prostitution, brief as it was, left Leo flushed and angry with the world.

He picked up the letter again.

I had to find a way to make Foley suffer for all he done without ruining Lisa-Marie's good name, which she don't deserve no matter what. So, I done a deal with Dermot Brennan. I give him the photos, he gets me a whack of money. I don't know what he got out of it but he must have got something because he was happy when he rang me to call to the house on Friday evening. When I found him dead up there, I lost the plot. I went through his sheds to see if there was anything worth stealing but there wasn't. Nothing except his fancy phone and I dumped that when I realized I could be caught with it. I thought about taking the car but I didn't. I done worse. I kicked his body. My ribs are aching ever since. But not any more.

324

So, Leo thought, the money in the leather satchel in Dermot Brennan's dressing room was for the Dorans. What Brennan had 'got out of it' was the means to stop Foley badmouthing him. And yet, whatever way he cut the deck, Leo couldn't see how Foley or his minions could have risked killing Dermot Brennan. For one, Brennan had presumably kept copies of the photos and the news-page. More importantly, neither of the Dorans, volatile in their distress, could be depended on to keep their knowledge a secret for ever.

The dilemma Leo faced was summed up in Sean Doran's penultimate paragraph.

We're dead now so it shouldn't matter but it does. Lisa-Marie was the only good thing that ever happened all my life. She was always there for me until she wasn't able to be herself no more and even then she done her best. Make Foley pay, Inspector, but don't make Lisa-Marie pay all over again. Don't let her name be dragged through the mud.

The letter went on to name the pimp, Theo Russell, who lived in Glasnevin, which for the northside of the city passed as leafy. The girl found in the ruins of Foley's office, Doran asserted, worked for the same guy. 'She's the one in the photos on the memory stick,' the letter read. Leo examined the photographs on the laptop more closely. Standing behind the two men carrying the body from the house in Honeyvale Heights was a young woman, knee-length black coat over her shoulders, the fingers of one hand splayed over her lips, her dark hair frenzied. The Brazilian girl. 'I never meant to hurt her,' Doran wrote. The two men were Pat Foley's bouncers.

Leo read Doran's personal apology again: 'I had no right to call you an ugly bastard and I'm ashamed I did.' He took out his personal mobile and a folded sheet of headed paper. Patrick Foley MIPAV. He'd scribbled the auctioneer's mobile number below the office number. The digits were just about legible except for the last of them. It might have been a three or a five. He tried the five and got a baker in a Grafton Street deli who thought he was ringing to arrange collection of a birthday cake. Then he tried the three.

'Mr Foley?'

'Who wants to know?'

'Detective Inspector Leo Woods. I need you to come out here to the Hearnstown Regency Hotel and pronto.'

'I'm in a meeting. I can send someone.'

'It has to be you. Alone. The rear entrance is open. Come up to room five-oh-two.'

'Look, Inspector, as far as I'm aware you're not involved in any investigation relating to Hearnstown. I'm going to have to ring the assistant commissioner and the Minister about this. I've had enough of this—'

'Before you do that, Mr Foley, I'm going to read the headline from an old red-top rag for you. Then I'm going to put down the phone and you can decide whether you want to ring your pals or get your arse out here so we can talk this thing through, right? I'm doing you a big favour here, Mr Foley. I've uncovered some evidence of an incident that took place two months ago. Some very specific evidence linking you to this incident. And out of the goodness of my heart and in the interests of fairness – fairness: you remember that concept, don't you? – in the interests of fairness, I'd like to offer you the opportunity to explain yourself.'

'This is . . . unbelievable. This is—'

'Look, it's a simple choice. In less than half an hour I can have a fleet of squad cars here, a couple of TV crews and a rake of sweaty anoraks from the tabloids. Or it can be you and me, all on our ownio. And, listen, on your way over here, buy me a packet of Consulate.'

'You want me to buy you a pack of cigarettes? Are you out of your mind?'

'Probably.'

'No way.'

'Ready for the headline then? Here it is. "Dead Pink Perv in a Blue Beamer". Remember that one? I have to say it's a classic.'

The sound he heard at the other end might have been Foley or his phone hitting the floor. He hoped it was the former. One way or the other, he cut the call. He looked over at the young man in the Irish international boxing singlet.

'I think you may have floored him, Sean,' Leo said aloud.

40

A few impatient minutes passed as Helen tried the door-bell of Kitty Newman's house and wandered around the building, peeping in through the windows at the clinical interior. Out by the conservatory, she caught a whiff of recent cigarette smoke. Further off, in an area skirted by high squared-off hedging, a little tell-tale blue cloud rose. She found an opening in the hedge and went inside to where another, similarly high hedge formed a passage to left and right.

'Mrs Newman? Mrs Newman?' she called. 'Detective Sergeant Helen Troy here. I need to talk to you.'

She heard a rustling nearby.

'Mrs Newman!' she shouted. 'Can you please—'

'Coming.' The voice was timid, fearful. 'Just a minute.'

Brisk footsteps across a gravel path announced Kitty Newman's arrival at the far end of the inner hedge. As she came into view, she lit another cigarette. She used her cigarette hand to camouflage the triangle of bandage on her nose. The flesh around her eyes had turned to green. She wasn't happy to see the young detective.

'What is it now?' she said. 'I don't see what else I can—'

'You've been looking to speak with Inspector Woods,' Helen said. 'Can I help?'

'No. It's . . . it's a sensitive matter.'

Kitty Newman shivered in spite of the fur-lined jacket that hung loosely on her small frame.

'The inspector is very busy right now,' Helen said, and decided to take a chance on pushing the woman harder. Gudrun Remer's murder had headlined the morning news though the victim's name hadn't been given. 'You've heard about the killing at the Argos Sanctuary?'

'Was it Gudrun Remer?' Kitty asked, tentative, terrified, no longer covering her bandaged nose.

'Yes,' Helen said. 'Is there something you should tell me, Mrs Newman?'

Kitty nervously tossed away her cigarette, then fetched another from the packet. She tried the lighter but her fingers shook too much. Helen took it from her and lit the cigarette.

'I want to speak to the inspector,' she said, but less insistently.

'Like I said, he's busy,' Helen said. 'This is a double murder, Mrs Newman, we need all the help we can get. And quickly.'

Without warning, the small woman darted swiftly by Helen and headed for the conservatory at the rear of the house. Helen followed, her patience at an end. She reached out and grabbed Kitty Newman by the shoulder.

'Did you know that Alan Cobbe was acquainted with Gudrun Remer?' she asked, and resisted the woman's attempt to shrug her off. 'Did you? Is that what you wanted to tell Inspector Woods?'

'This murder has nothing to do with Alan. And neither has Dermot Brennan's death. I would never have told him that Dermot knew about the affair with Anna if I thought he was capable of . . . I'm not to blame. None of this is my fault.'

Helen had assumed that Kitty Newman had been defending Alan Cobbe. She saw now that she'd been defending herself. The woman struggled free of Helen's grasp and ran. She reached the conservatory and slipped inside but Helen got a foot in the door before it was slammed in her face. She bundled her way in, furious now. She backed the trembling woman against the long glass.

'Did Alan Cobbe talk to you about Gudrun? Did he tell you that she reported his assault on Caroline Hunt to the Guards down in Enniscorthy?'

Kitty Newman slid down the glass wall and, crouching low, began to weep. Helen backed off. She sat back against a wicker table and let the woman indulge herself. It wasn't a strategy exactly but it worked nonetheless. Kitty dabbed her face with a stringy ball of tissue. She looked up at the young detective.

'What I wanted to speak to the inspector about doesn't relate to Alan Cobbe,' she said. 'It relates to Stephen. I've nothing against the boy. Please believe me. Nothing. He's always been remote but I never disliked him. I've only ever felt pity for him because he's always seemed so maladjusted. But now that Dermot and this German woman have been murdered, I . . . I . . .'

She paused, as though reconsidering what she'd set out to say. She lowered her head, then raised it again.

'When our charity shop was vandalized, I couldn't understand why Anna and Dermot refused to go to the police. She said that Dermot had told her there was some issue in relation to insurance on the shop. But when I confronted Dermot, he asked me to let it drop. Then he said

. . . he said it was a family matter and, for Anna's sake, he wanted to keep it that way.'

'Meaning that Stephen wrecked the shop,' Helen stated.

The small brittle woman nodded her head and stared almost longingly into the middle distance.

'Dermot was such a kind man,' she said. 'A little rough around the edges sometimes but not in any vulgar way.' With a quick, bird-like movement of the head she turned to Helen. 'She dragged him down, you know. Anna, I mean. Always so distant. No sense of fun in her. Stephen was the same. Dark. And all that business with Frankie Prior. So murky. And yet, Dermot took the responsibility for that too when it had nothing to do with him.'

'Dermot didn't beat up Frankie Prior?' Helen speculated aloud.

Kitty Newman stood up and crossed her impossibly thin arms as she gazed across at the thinned-out, scrappy line of conifers bordering the two houses.

'I was upstairs,' she said. 'And I happened to be looking over there. I saw everything. It was insane. It was almost as laughable as it was awful. The boy dressed in Anna's clothes . . . I recognized the blue dress . . . he ran out of the house and towards the walled garden. I thought it was some weird game they were playing. But when Frankie fell on the path in there and Stephen got to him, I knew it was no game.'

'Was Anna in the house when this happened?'

'She was in town,' Kitty said. 'I tried to ring her and couldn't get through. And before I had a chance to ring the Guards, I saw Dermot's Mercedes arrive. He'd been down for the newspapers, it was a Saturday morning. He heard Frankie's screams and . . . you know, it was plain to see,

Stephen was clutching Frankie's throat and the poor boy was kicking and—'

'Are you sure of that?' Helen asked. 'Can you really have seen so clearly? It's quite a distance.'

'I saw what I saw,' Kitty insisted. 'Dermot came to Frankie's rescue but not before having to fight off Stephen. Literally fight him off. It was dreadful. I could hardly bear to watch.'

But you did, Helen thought. Is this what you did when you were rich and idle and loveless and had no life? Watched the neighbours, watched life happening to other people, hoping it might explode into action?

'Have you ever spoken to Anna about this? Or Dermot?'

Kitty Newman shook her head. Her sigh, like the sighs of most martyrs, was for herself.

'What's a person supposed to do?' she asked desperately. 'You say what you've seen and you're perceived as an interfering busybody. You don't say what you've seen and you're still in the wrong.'

The woman's self-pity goaded Helen. She stood up from the table she'd been leaning on, ready to tell Mrs Bloody Newman that what a person should do is tell the truth before it's too fucking late. Instead, she took in a deep breath of the outside air that was cold but less chilling and infinitely more vital than the air in the rich woman's forbidding abode.

'I'll be sending someone over to take a statement,' she said. 'Please, don't leave until he comes.'

'I wasn't going anywhere,' Kitty Newman said bitterly.

No, Helen thought, just downhill fast. Then she thought, Don't be cruel. Anyone could be this way given enough time and disappointment.

41

The black-topped convertible, an Alfa Romeo Spider, inched its way into the lane behind the Hearnstown Regency Hotel. Leo watched from the fifth-floor landing as Pat Foley emerged and scanned the lane. The squad car was nowhere to be seen. Leo had sent Garda Dempsey away to the other end of Hearnstown. The auctioneer's tonsure of spreading baldness, Leo mused, presented the perfect target for a sniper. A flash of indicators and the convertible was locked. Foley entered the yard behind the hotel and was soon lost from view.

The clangour of footfall Leo was expecting to hear from the pit of the stairwell didn't come. Instead, the building itself began to twitch and crackle. Over at the lift, a red-lit number 1 flashed up and a bell tinkled. Foley had switched on the power. Leo watched as the flashing numeral reversed to 0 and then swiftly progressed to 5. The lift door opened and Foley stepped out. His tanned skin was dull and blotchy as a bruised fruit. Neither man spoke. Foley had nothing to say and Leo too much. Leo watched the auctioneer closely, waited for the smell of death to dawn upon the fellow. He savoured the eyes widening in terror, the fright and flight responses in Foley cancelling each other out and paralysing him.

'Did you bring the cigarettes?' Leo asked, and Foley handed over the Consulates.

Leo ripped off the plastic and took out a cigarette. He snapped off the tip and lit up.

'But the smoke alarms,' Foley said weakly.

'Never mind the smoke alarms,' Leo said. 'Follow me.'

'No . . . no way . . . I should never have come here,' Foley spluttered but, taking a firm grip of his shoulder, Leo guided him along the corridor towards Room 502.

'That guy in the Beamer,' Foley protested. 'I know nothing about him.'

'Of course you don't,' Leo said. 'You're an honest God-fearing man, aren't you? A family man. How many kids have you got, Mr Foley?'

'Leave my children out of this.'

Always pissed them off big time, that did. Mention their kids to some pimp or paedo, some greedy bankster or corrupt official, some slum landlord or gang boss, and suddenly they were filled with righteous anger. Only later, if at all, did it dawn on them that in destroying the lives of others, they destroyed their own children's lives too.

Leo steered the auctioneer round the corner.

They were soon within feet of Room 502. Leo pushed Foley in by the door, slammed it shut. Dumbstruck, Foley gaped at the bodies on the bed. He gagged, his stomach heaved repeatedly, his cheeks filling out and sinking back, filling out again. The sharp tie and stiff white collar he wore became too much for him and he pulled them loose. No matter where he looked he saw the dead bodies, mirrored, double-mirrored into eternity.

'What do you make of that then?' Leo asked, taking a deep pull from his cigarette. 'What was it you called them that first time we chatted? Bloody whingers, wasn't it? Taking on the kind of mortgage a couple of inner-city skangers were never going to be able to keep up with. Out of their depth, that's how you described them, remember? Then they go and top themselves just because their house got flooded and they lost their jobs and she went loo-lah and he tried to blackmail you – him and Dermot Brennan – and mucked that up too.'

'I don't know what you're talking about.'

Leo grabbed the auctioneer's arm and guided him roughly to the dressing table where the laptop sat idling.

'Sit down and enjoy the show,' he said, and hit the return key.

Beads of sweat peppered Foley's scalp as the small machine whined breathily and the screen lit up. Leo reached over the auctioneer's shoulder, slid his finger over the touchpad and tapped once, and the slide-show began. Ten shots in quick succession, like a jumpy old newsreel. Two men carrying the body of a fat man from 13 Honeyvale Heights to a blue BMW. The number plate was perfectly legible, the faces of the two men readily identifiable – along with the Brazilian girl who ended up in the ruins of Foley's office.

'You've seen these shots before, haven't you, Mr Foley?'

'No,' Foley replied, and almost tossed himself from his seat as Leo's right hand flashed by on its way back to the touchpad.

'Relax, sunshine,' Leo said. He opened another file on the laptop. 'Just refreshing your memory.'

A tabloid front page. In the bottom left-hand corner, a minuscule column headlined 'IMF Wolves at the Door'. Above, a long and narrow column featured a long, narrow and stoned young woman holding herself aloft with the help of a street-lamp stanchion outside a Leeson Street night club. 'Pole Model'. The main item, however, concerned the dead perv in the blue beamer.

'Je vous présente Redmond Flanagan,' Leo said. 'I'm sure you know him, yeah?'

'No,' Foley insisted. 'That is, I don't know him personally. Didn't. I've seen him on TV.'

Plump, smug and shaven-headed in his pin-striped suit, the pink shirt unbuttoned down to his hairless chest, Flanagan smiled at the camera. A publicity shot from a few years back when he'd hosted a weekly dogfight between a group of deluded young hopefuls vying to become managing director of some entrepreneur's new technology company. *Who's the Boss?* Unfortunately for him, the production company's boss fired Flanagan for some sexist remarks he made about a female contestant off-camera, for which he suffered vengeance by way of YouTube. Two years later, he went bankrupt. Two months back, he'd left this mortal coil clad in ladies' underwear.

'How ironic is that?' Leo said. 'Always wore pink shirts, found dead in pink panties. What beats me is where the hell he found a pair big enough to cover that arse.'

'You're a sick man, Inspector,' Foley said.

Leo snapped the laptop shut. Foley couldn't find the courage to look up from his cramped crouch.

'Enough of the faffing around,' Leo said. 'September twentieth, early evening. Redmond Flanagan drives from his mock-Tudor manse in Foxrock to one of your company's unsold houses at Honeyvale Heights. There, he meets a young Brazilian woman – the same young woman we found in the wreckage of your office.'

'She wasn't in my office,' the auctioneer insisted. 'She was in the bookie's next door.'

'Which was leased from you, or let's say from one of the companies in which you have an interest,' Leo said. 'So anyway, while this young woman is making friends with Mr Pinkie here, he gets a massive heart attack. She panics, rings her pimp – Theo Russell, in all likelihood. You know? The guy you've been hiring out rooms to?'

'*I* don't hire out rooms,' Foley said, his courage and his bantam chest puffed up as he pounced on the technicality like a barrister in a lost cause. 'Our rental division deals in short-term leases and holiday rentals.'

'Holiday rentals in Hearnstown?' Leo laughed.

Foley's brief recovery faded. He sank beneath Leo's gaze like a stone.

'So, where was I? Yeah, this pimp rings a friend, and before you know it a couple of heavies arrive at Honeyvale Heights. A little birdie has told him that no one lives in Honeyvale now but the Dorans. I wonder who that little birdie was?'

Foley shifted in his seat. He couldn't make himself stop looking in the mirror at the dead couple.

'Anyway, there's no car in the Dorans' drive but they go banging on the door just to be sure before they carry Mr Pinkie to his car. Only Lisa-Marie here is hiding upstairs all this time. And she's got a camera and a bit of an obsession with taking snaps. Mr Pinkie is found next day in his blue Beamer seventy miles away in County Longford. Sean Doran tries to blackmail you but, somehow, you know that Lisa-Marie has tried her hand at the game so she can keep up her mortgage payments. Your pal Theo the Pimp told you, I suppose?'

The auctioneer stood up suddenly and made for the window.

'I can't breathe,' he gasped as he grappled with the opening mechanism.

Leo wished there was a next world from which the dead couple could watch their tormentor's humiliation. The window slid open only a couple of inches. Suicide-proofed. More bloody irony, Leo thought, as Foley stuck his nose into the gap.

'My heart bleeds for you,' Leo said. 'So. Sean never knew of his wife's – what'll we call it? – her lapse until you told him. Like a knife in the stomach it must have been when you said . . .' Leo took the letter from his pocket and found the words. 'You said, "Your wife's a whore, Doran, and I can prove it." But then Dermot Brennan comes knocking and that's a different ball game, right? How much did you pay him?'

'We can talk outside in the corridor, can't we?' Foley pleaded.

'How much?'

'Sixty thousand euro,' Foley said. 'And a demolition contract. Now, please let me out of here.'

'A demolition contract?'

'We're clearing the Honeyvale Heights site. Cutting our losses. You'll find a signed and sealed contract at his solicitor's office. Now, can we please go outside?'

As he spoke, the auctioneer approached Leo, tentatively eyeing the hotel room door.

'The money,' Foley said, eyes narrowing on a last-ditch scheme. 'I don't expect to get it back. You know what I mean? Do with it as you will, Inspector.'

A twitchy half smile broke across the tanned face.

'I should probably beat the bejaysus out of you for trying to bribe me but I can't be bothered,' Leo said. He nodded towards the door. 'And just so you'll know, fifteen thousand of your blood money will go towards a reward for information on the murder of Dermot Brennan and the rest will go back into the state coffers where it probably came from in the first place. I'll address it to your cousin, the Junior Minister, for his personal attention. Now fuck off back to Ailesbury Road before I change my mind.'

'But how do I know you won't use this against me some time in the future?' Foley dared to ask.

'You don't,' Leo told him. 'Get out.'

Leo took a last look at the Dorans. Maybe it was the edge of iced air cutting in by the open window or the nicotine from yet another cigarette hitting his synapses but the hotel room didn't feel like a tomb any more. Lisa-Marie's despairing choice would never come to public attention. Pat Foley would pass some sleepless nights getting the image of the couple whose lives he'd ruined out of his head. And when that image had lost its horror, the auctioneer would have his own personal Sword of Damocles hanging over him as long as Leo was alive and kicking. And there was a bonus: two young Latvian girls would be released from a future of white slavery. It was a lot. It was a kind of justice. But it didn't seem like enough.

He picked up the laptop and left the room. He closed the door as though not to wake them. Out in the long dark corridor, he rang Detective Sergeant Cooney.

'Just had a tip-off, Gerry,' he said. 'Hearnstown Regency Hotel. Room 502. You'll find the Dorans there . . . No need. They won't be putting up a fight.'

42

From the back door of Attenboy House, Detective Sergeant Helen Troy followed the trail of the music. Violin sounds, cello, piano. A piano trio or quartet, Helen supposed. The rhythm slow and pained and, as she passed through the kitchen and into the hallway, seeming almost to break down completely. One plaintively pitched violin cried quietly as it detached itself from the pulse of the other instruments. Alone, it belonged, for a few moments, nowhere. Helen reached the library door. Inside, Anna Brennan stood at the bay window staring out at the lawn.

'Mrs Brennan?' she said.

The woman neither moved nor spoke in response. The music drifted towards its desolate conclusion. Helen crossed to the streamlined music system. She took brief note of the rolling digital display: Schumann, Piano Quartet in E flat, Op. 47, Andante Cantabile. Beautiful, melancholy. She made to switch off the music but saw that only thirty or so seconds remained of it and waited for the piece to end. It felt like she was doing the widow one last favour. Then she pressed the stop button.

'Mrs Brennan?'

The widow raised her shoulders and faced the young detective. It occurred to Helen that they were dressed almost exactly alike except for the Garda zip-up. Denims, knitted sweater, hiking boots. A new depth of sadness resided in those remarkably blue eyes. Or maybe it was the fact that the eyes were no longer the blue of morning or even of afternoon but the blue of evening. Late evening. Less dazzling, more profound, closer to the end.

'Have you found Stephen?' Anna asked, her voice tired and flat. 'Is he OK?'

'We've taken him into custody,' Helen said. 'He hasn't been able to account for his movements yesterday afternoon. Plus he hasn't helped his case by resisting arrest. I have to tell you it doesn't look good for him.'

'Where is he now? I want to see him. I demand to see him.'

Anna Brennan was an exhausted fighter throwing loose punches without conviction.

'You will. Right now he's on his way from hospital to Howth Garda Station.'

'Hospital? Why?'

'We thought his nose might be broken but he's been X-rayed and got the all-clear.'

'I'm calling a solicitor this minute,' Anna said, taking a mobile from the pocket of her denims. 'It's Alan Cobbe you should be taking into custody, not my son.'

'Mr Cobbe's being held too,' she said. 'And Skip Sheridan.'

Anna placed the mobile phone on the oval table that stood between them. A light flush touched her cheeks. She struggled to conceal the ferment that clearly lay just below the surface.

'You and Skip Sheridan, are you close?' Helen asked.

'He's done some gardening work for me,' Anna said. 'Nothing more.'

Helen approached the table, pulled out a chair and sat. She dug out a notebook from inside her jacket. She flipped through the pages as though searching for something specific. Her real intention was to unsettle the widow further.

'This is ridiculous,' Anna said. 'Am I being presumed to have slept with every man that's ever passed through my gate?'

'Would you like to take a seat, Mrs Brennan? I think you may need to.'

'I want to speak with Inspector Woods.'

'He's tied up at the moment,' Helen said. 'He's just been talking to Daina Klaviņš. Actually her name is Laima Leipiņš and she's sixteen years old.'

'Really?' Anna seemed genuinely surprised rather than concerned. She clearly wasn't aware that the young girl had spied on her.

'She's had some things to tell us about you and Mr Sheridan – about some, let's say, compromising situations involving the both of you. In the kitchen, in your bedroom.'

Anna wilted visibly, held herself up on flatted palms rooted to the surface of the table. She looked at the chair on her side of the table. Two sidelong steps might have taken her to it but she seemed afraid to risk the abyss she saw there.

'Mrs Brennan, if you want to help your son, you have to tell us everything,' Helen said.

'But it's not relevant to—'

'Everything is relevant. I think you know that. Please. Sit down.'

The widow sidled weak-kneed to the red velvet chair and sat. She leaned forward on her elbows and pressed her fingers to her temples. Her distress was palpable, ageing her shockingly. Anna Brennan might just have strayed, Helen thought, beyond the borders of Tír na nÓg.

'You were having an affair with Skip Sheridan?'

'Oh God,' the widow moaned.

'Sheridan's a young guy, handsome, you're flattered by his interest in you and he hasn't been getting out much, meeting people, finding love or whatever, and he's lonely over here in a strange country. So it's perfectly understandable that you'd both—'

The calmness spreading across Anna Brennan's features silenced Helen. Outside, the grey sky had that milky distance about it that presaged snow. When it fell, Helen thought, the contours of the world would be softened, sanitized, but only briefly. In the end, every little white lie melted away.

'Skip Sheridan is my son,' Anna said.

The biro poised above Helen's notebook slipped to the table. Her fingers went scrabbling after it though her astonished gaze never left the widow.

'I was only just seventeen, a very naive seventeen,' the woman went on. 'I'd never been away from home for as much as one night alone. My mother ruled my life and I was no rebel, believe me. I'll never understand why she let me go to university at such a ridiculously young age. Anyway, there I was, full of childish notions about becoming a musician or a music teacher at least. And, of course, about becoming involved with some radical composer type. I did. One of our tutors swooped down on me. He was going to be the next great Irish composer, or so he told anyone who'd listen. Married. About forty. I suppose the older man thing was part of it too. My father died when I was two years old and

I've no memory of . . . You don't need all this detail, I'm sure.'

'It's fine, it's OK,' Helen said.

'He's dead now – my composer,' Anna said. 'Two years ago he died. He'd spent his life composing advertising jingles. He was seventy-two. I found it impossible to comprehend that he was so . . . so old.'

Anna surveyed the table's French-polished surface as though there were images there among the lines and whorls of the grain she'd never noticed before.

'He made me believe that all his pieces were for me or inspired by me. Made little of my own efforts, of course, which I accepted as the verdict of the Master.' Anna swept her hair back with a careless hand, raised herself. 'Anyway, this is all beside the point. I got pregnant. He didn't want to know. My mother took charge of the situation and packed me off to a nunnery. I kid you not. A convent down in Cork. I had the baby and, after four days, they took him from me.'

The widow addressed the far wall beyond Helen. She wept in a curiously placid way, almost as though her tears were shed for someone else's story and not her own.

'I didn't have the courage or the strength to hold on to him. I watched them take him away that last time. They didn't tell me it was to be the last time but in my heart I knew and I did nothing. That must seem pathetic to a young woman like you but—'

'No, it doesn't,' Helen said.

'I was a small-town girl, full of romantic delusions. But so . . . so passive. It's the story of my life, this bloody passivity, this waiting for things to work out, hoping against hope. And now it's too late . . .'

The pause lengthened, and Helen was glad of it. She felt

an odd sense of relief now that the suspicion surrounding Skip Sheridan had been cleared up. A relief that didn't last because a new possibility had raised itself. The murders, or Dermot Brennan's at least, might still be related to this sad tale of a long-ago adoption. She tried to formulate the questions that needed asking and their sequence in ways that were not too insistent or merciless. But there were, she knew, no soft options. Except perhaps to find some indirect route.

She picked up her stray biro, hid behind the formality of her notebook, its demand to be filled with truths.

'This would have been when? The baby – what year was he born, Mrs Brennan?'

'Twelfth of September, nineteen seventy-six,' the widow said. 'I called him Robert. You know, after the composer Robert Schumann. That'll tell you how naive I was even after the birth. I still fancied I was Clara, the woman who gave up her musical ambitions and devoted herself to serving her husband's genius.'

Helen remembered Sheridan's given names. James Robert. The adoptive parents, she presumed, had had the kindness to at least acknowledge the young girl's choice of name for her stolen child. But Helen had more practical matters than kindness to consider.

'When did you make contact with Mr Sheridan?' she asked.

'Four years ago I put my name on a register of adopted children and mothers who'd given their kids up for adoption,' Anna replied. 'Stephen had started at college and was spending a lot of time with Frankie. So, most of the time, I was home alone and there was more time, too much time, to think about the baby I'd given up. And, I suppose, I decided I'd waited long enough to go looking for him.'

Snow began to fall outside the three long panes of the bay window. It felt to Helen like they were inside one of those old snow globes that you shook to see the flakes fall around a cottage or some religious shrine. She had never seen a woman so utterly defeated, her dreams so clearly unfulfilled. Helen had been through every room in this house and in none of them was there a musical instrument of any kind. Not a piano, a guitar, a violin, nothing. All the widow had was beauty, and beauty wasn't enough. Beauty, it seemed to Helen, was an instrument that other people played.

'Skip had already signed on to the register a few years before. In a matter of weeks, we were told of each other's existence. We exchanged emails for a while and then . . . then there was Frankie's suicide and I was so concerned for Stephen's state of mind that I couldn't go through with telling him about Skip. I didn't know how he'd react. I explained all of this to Skip and he agreed to put off the reunion.'

'But he forced the issue by coming to live in Ireland?' Helen speculated.

'No,' Anna said. 'He'd been planning to come to Ireland for some time. Ever since his mother – his adoptive mother – died five years ago.'

'And he called on you when he arrived in Ireland?'

'I hadn't told him where I lived and I asked him not to tell me where he was.'

'Why?' Helen asked.

'I didn't want to lose control of the situation,' the widow said. 'I was afraid. Afraid of all the things that might go wrong. So, we . . . I put off meeting until a few months back. I thought Stephen had found a new kind of equilibrium, even if it had to be with Gudrun Remer. And Dermot had sorted out the bankruptcy details and things didn't look quite so impossible. He'd lost a lot but we still had enough to live a more comfortable life than most.'

'Did you tell Stephen?'

'No,' Anna said. 'I always knew it was going to be difficult but I had no idea of just how complicated things would get. Like when Stephen and Skip became friendly. It should have made things easier for me but it didn't. Another complication was all I saw. I thought I was ready for all of this, as ready as anyone can be in these situations. I wasn't.'

'So you didn't tell your husband either? Skip Sheridan was here working in your garden and you never told Dermot?'

Anna Brennan shook her head.

'You've never told anyone?' Helen asked. 'Mrs Newman, maybe, when you were still on good terms?'

'No, she's not exactly the kind of person who can safely be confided in,' Anna said, but a certain hesitancy arose in her. She looked at Helen. 'I did tell someone. Not specifically that Skip was my son but that I'd given a child up for adoption. I imagined I was telling some kind of soul-mate.'

'Alan Cobbe?' Helen said, and saw from the widow's reaction that she'd got it in one. Inspired, she came to another conclusion. 'And he tried to use this knowledge to . . . to what? To force you into an affair?'

Anna stood up and, observing the snowfall, stepped into the curve of the bay window. There was something childish, almost eccentric about her as she took melancholic delight in the snow. A woman, Helen thought, who'd spent her life avoiding too much reality, dreaming instead of some idyllic alternative.

'All these years and I still hadn't grown up,' Anna said. 'First I fall for a would-be composer. Then, over thirty years later, I confide in a second-rate sculptor with an anger management problem.'

'Do you think Mr Cobbe might have told your husband about the baby?' Helen asked.

The widow stiffened.

'Mrs Brennan?'

Deliberately hiding her face now, Anna pressed closer to the glass of the central window.

'I don't know. I truly don't,' she said despairingly. 'I just pray that he didn't. Dermot deserved better than that – deserved better than me for that matter.'

The library was darkening, the windows turning to mirrors. Helen glanced at the time on her mobile and wondered how she was going to end this conversation without seeming to be abrupt. At the window, Anna continued to stare dismally at her reflection like a child does when she wants to indulge herself with tears.

'He loved me. There was nothing he wouldn't have done for me, no lengths he wouldn't go to to make me happy. And what did he get in return? Dark moods, long unexplained silences. When they took my child from me, they tore my heart out. I never loved again. Not even when Stephen came along. I could hardly bear to touch him at first and I never truly . . .'

Helen capped her biro, put it in the inside pocket of her zip-up. 'I never loved again' – did that statement include Skip Sheridan, her long-lost son? It was a long shot and perhaps not relevant, perhaps even cruel, but she somehow knew that she had to ask.

'Don't you love the son you've found?'

The question rattled the widow, rendered her momentarily speechless. When she did speak, what came out had an obstinate assertiveness about it that failed to ring true.

'Of course I do. How can I not, after all I've put him through? All that time I've left him waiting. How can I refuse him . . . not give him what he needs from me?'

Anna floundered. Probably happened more often than is admitted, Helen thought, this equivocation once a child and his birth mother were reunited. The weight of expectation had to be colossal, the sense of failure indescribable. She was sorry she'd raised the matter.

'I shouldn't have asked,' she said.

'It's all right, it doesn't matter,' Anna said. 'Stephen's going to find out about Skip now, isn't he?'

'I'm afraid so,' Helen said.

Anna leaned almost halfway across the oval table as she pleaded, 'Let me be the one to tell him. I've failed him in so many ways. Let me do that much for him at least.'

Even as she nodded in assent, Helen realized that the widow believed she'd made a killer of her second son.

'I'll have to run it by Inspector Woods but I'm sure it can be arranged.'

'Thank you,' the widow said, her fingers idling among the grey roots of her hair. 'And Daina . . . what did you say her real name was?'

'Laima.'

'Laima,' Anna repeated. 'She's OK, is she? I mean, she hasn't been harmed in any way, has she? I was worried for her. You hear such terrible stories.'

'She's fine,' Helen said as she rose from the table and tucked away her notebook in a zip-up pocket. 'Probably be repatriated to Latvia though.'

Anna Brennan lowered her head.

'Wasn't she very brave to venture out into the world so

young?' she said. 'Where do people get that kind of courage from?'

'From desperation, I suppose,' Helen said.

'No,' Anna said. 'Desperation only makes you weak, makes you do things you'll spend your life regretting.'

43

The whiff of death still assailed Leo's nostrils as he sat in the Incident Room of Howth Garda Station and listened to Detective Sergeant Helen Troy. He wondered if she and Ben Murphy could smell it too; from his clothes, his flesh, from his very breath. In his mind, the lights refused to come down on the cruel last act in the lives of Sean and Lisa-Marie Doran. He felt sour, edgy, self-conscious. He reminded himself that he always got like this when a case seemed close to resolution. The fact that he knew the reason why didn't help a great deal. Never does. Every closed case opened up a vast, empty vista before him; weeks, perhaps months of thumb-twiddling back at the Harcourt Street HQ, scratching around at old cases and hoping to draw blood.

'So, to sum up,' Helen said. 'Anna and Skip Sheridan first made contact in two thousand and six. He still lived in the States back then. New York. We've a Midtown Manhattan address that checks out and he worked in some of those communal gardens they've got over there. We've confirmed his late mother's address in Spartanburg, North Carolina too.'

'North Carolina?' Leo said, his interest stirred. He had a Cherokee mask from that state in his collection.

'Yeah. Seems he grew up there. I figured the accent was a southern one,' Helen said. 'And what else? Oh, yes, his Irish passport is kosher and we're following up on the American one he hasn't renewed. Anyway, because of Frankie's suicide and her fears for Stephen, Anna pulled back at that time. They maintained contact by email and he moved to Ireland a year back. They didn't exchange addresses until last July – Anna's idea that. Since that time he's done occasional gardening work at Attenboy. He was last there on Wednesday seventeenth when Kitty Newman objected to the boundary trees being cut and he was still waiting for a call to complete the job when he heard of Dermot Brennan's murder.'

The unease Helen felt had nothing to do with Skip Sheridan. Her personal mobile had vibrated for the fourth time in her jacket pocket. There had been a missed call from Ricky earlier. No, an ignored call. Somehow, she knew it had to be him again.

'So Dermot and Stephen were completely in the dark about Sheridan?' Leo said.

'She never told anyone about the child except Cobbe.'

'But didn't tell him it was Sheridan,' Leo said. 'I wonder how Sheridan feels about all this. He's got to be pretty pissed off that he's still Anna's little secret, that she hasn't acknowledged him publicly after all this time.'

'From what I can gather, Sheridan's got the patience of Job,' Helen said. 'Even tried on Anna's behalf to persuade Stephen to go to the funeral. It didn't work out, but he made the effort. It seems like he'll do anything so's not to lose her again. I suspect he might be covering for Stephen for that very reason. I mean, if he says anything that might implicate

Stephen in Gudrun Remer's murder, it's got to jeopardize his relationship with Anna. He was quite evasive on Stephen's state of mind last evening, wasn't he, Ben?'

Sitting further along the conference table from them than he needed to, Ben Murphy made no response. He stared blankly at the notebook before him. Only now did Leo observe the young fellow's weary pallor, the uncharacteristic disorder of that normally crisp white collar and narrow tie, the absence of that precise quarter inch of white cuff at the wrists, the hair flattened unflatteringly with damp.

'Are you with us, Ben?' he said. 'You're like a poisoned pup over there.'

The young detective's smile was weak and soon fell apart.

'Sorry, I didn't catch that,' he said. 'Late night, early morning, you know.'

'Yeah, well, perk up, son. We all have late nights and early mornings while there's a case on.'

Out of the corner of his eye, Leo caught Helen's disapproving glance and moved swiftly on.

'What's the story with Alan Cobbe then?' he asked of Murphy, allowing a pretence of mellowness in his tone. 'Have we verified his movements yesterday?'

Murphy didn't do his usual notebook shuffle, just sat there, unable to muster the energy to do more than speak haltingly. Leo was reminded of one of those Magritte paintings of disembodied suits draped on chairs.

'He's given us a list of five pubs and two restaurants, all of which he claims to have visited before returning to the hotel last night,' Murphy explained. 'Also a list of the dozen or so people he met. Or those of them he can remember.'

'Another lapse of memory? He should've been a politician,' Leo said. Helen didn't crack a smile. In the bad books there, Leo thought. He wondered if she'd taken a fancy to the liverish young detective. Nothing like the consumptive look to draw the women in.

'So far, three of the pubs and both of the restaurants check out. All of them in the city centre. We've spoken to seven of the twelve names he gave us and all of them say they met him. Four of them confirm that he was already well tanked up by mid-afternoon. Or gave that impression, in any case.'

'Any major gaps in the timeline?' Leo asked.

'Yeah,' Murphy said. 'Five until seven in the evening. Plus he claims to have fallen asleep in the SUV for a couple of hours before he returned to the hotel at around three in the morning. Says the SUV was parked somewhere in the vicinity of Parnell Square. We're sussing out CCTV in the area but nothing's come up yet.'

'And what has Cobbe got to say about Gudrun Remer?'

The small adjustment that the young detective made in his slack repose was effected with too much effort. Leo saw the concern on Helen's face and acknowledged it with a questioning glance. She shrugged almost imperceptibly. Her mobile had just vibrated again. *Leave me alone, Ricky, you arsehole.*

'He said, "The only good German is a dead German",' Murphy told Leo. 'Being obnoxious seems to be his default mode of self-defence. We had to pin the bugger down to get a DNA swab from him.'

'It's an outside shot,' Helen speculated, 'but Cobbe's the kind of guy who'd be suspicious of anyone who was hanging around the woman he was trying to bed. So, for the sake of argument, let's say that Cobbe somehow makes the connection between Anna's long-lost kid and Sheridan. Then, when he calls on Dermot Brennan, there's a shouting match and he spills this out.'

'So how does this add to the case against Cobbe?' Leo asked.

'He drops his little bombshell and then realizes that he's blown his chance with Anna,' Helen said. 'I mean, Dermot's bound to confront her with this information and tell her where it came from. So, maybe Cobbe felt he couldn't let that happen?'

Leo nodded as though he were half convinced. Helen kept on picking at the loose threads of her theory.

'Then, by claiming that Dermot had called out Sheridan's name, he actually manages to kill two birds with the one stone . . . sorry, not a good choice of words. But he's got rid of Dermot, and if Sheridan is implicated in the killing then Anna's basically got no one to turn to. I mean, she'd already lost Stephen to Gudrun Remer in a manner of speaking, hadn't she?'

'If that was the case,' Murphy said, 'why would he go and kill Gudrun?'

'Because Stephen would be the number-one suspect,' Helen said. 'Because if Stephen's convicted of both murders then Anna's going to need a lot of comforting, right?'

Leo shook his head.

'Seems to me that if Cobbe had gone out to the Argos Sanctuary yesterday, he'd have to have assumed Stephen would be there too. How could he possibly have known otherwise?'

The Incident Room fell silent. The wall clock there was angling towards ten. It had been too long a day for all of them. Especially, Leo suspected, for the party-boy Murphy. He decided to let Stephen Brennan in the cell below stairs and Alan Cobbe in the holding room over at Raheny sweat it out for the night. Barge in on them fresh and early in the morning. Have a word with Sheridan tonight though. Hadn't met the guy face-to-face yet and another possibility had suggested itself to him that he wanted to test on the American.

Leo called it a night. He told them to go home if the iced-up roads allowed, and Helen and Murphy to head over to Raheny Garda Station for eight in the morning. Helen wanted to tell him she had no home to go to and that if she didn't have more work to do she'd have to talk to Ricky, and she knew he was going to tell her who he'd dumped her for.

'But we should interview Stephen when Anna's finished talking to him,' Helen said in desperation. 'She's with him now upstairs. And he's going to be at his most vulnerable tonight.'

'And he won't be able to sleep,' Leo added, 'and he'll be in bits come the morning. The longer he stews, the better the chance that he'll break.'

'What about Cobbe?' Helen objected. 'And Sheridan?'

'We'll let Cobbe climb the walls all night too. And I'll talk to our American friend,' Leo said. 'When do we expect some results from the DNA and toxicology tests?'

'Monday or Tuesday for the DNA from Cobbe, Sheridan and Brennan,' Helen replied. 'Toxicology for Stephen and Sheridan on Wednesday if we're lucky.'

Her strained features bothered Leo.

'You need to rest, Helen,' he said, and, to take the edge from the cutting look she gave him, added, 'You too, Ben.'

He left the Incident Room. At the long table, Ben Murphy sat perfectly still, chin leaning on one hand, the other hand holding his silver pen a quarter of an inch above the note-book page.

Helen took out her phone. Four missed calls from Ricky. She went outside and down to the landing below the Incident Room and pressed green to call. Stuck somewhere between grief and fury, she let him have the first say.

'Hey, Helen love, how are you doing? Not keeping you from your work, am I?'

'Don't call me "love" and don't ask stupid questions,' she said. 'What do you want?'

'You changed the locks on the apartment and I need to get my blue guitar and my amp and stuff. I'm going to have to break in the door if you don't—'

'Do that, you prick, and I'll have you arrested in five minutes flat.'

'But my gear . . . and some of Jamie's ukuleles are there too.'

'It's coming up to Christmas, Ricky. Make a list, check it twice and send it to Santa Claus. Or maybe your new girl-friend will buy you a new guitar?'

'There is no new girlfriend.'

'Spare me the crap.'

'Jeez, Helen, we've a couple of gigs over Christmas and we need the money, man,' Ricky pleaded.

Muffled sounds in the background suggested that he wasn't alone. Then his voice returned and Helen knew that it had to be her brother alongside him.

'You have to let Jamie sell the house, Helen. He's in deep trouble, very deep.'

'When has he ever not been in trouble?'

'This time it's different,' Ricky said.

Helen laughed, but not because she was amused. A sudden sense of foreboding threatened her fragile equilibrium.

'This time he owes major shillings to a dangerous man,' Ricky continued. 'And I mean *major* shillings.'

'Listen, Ricky, he can screw up his own life all he wants but he won't screw up mine.'

'Won't screw up your career is what you mean. That's all that matters to you, Helen. Everything and everyone else takes second place. I followed you down to Cork when you got the transfer you wanted. I followed you up to Tipperary when you got promoted. Then—'

'You followed me because you're a fucking parasite.'

'I followed you because I love you, Helen. Is that so hard for you to grasp?'

'So why didn't you come to Dublin with me?'

'Because that was all about you,' Ricky said. The emotion was real, too real. The intensity too. 'You come home one day and tell me you got this job in Criminal Investigation, that you're moving to Dublin. No discussion. No, like, "What do you think, Ricky? You don't mind leaving the band, starting up all over again, Ricky, do you?" No, it's more like, "Here, throw this lead around your neck and I'll take you for a long frigging walk, Ricky."'

The sound of mounting footsteps reached her from the stairs below. From the mobile, a scuffling noise emerged, a heated but indecipherable exchange. For a terrifying moment, she thought it might be the 'dangerous man' Ricky had mentioned. Then she heard her brother's voice. Level, a crust of hardness to it.

'Listen, sis,' he said, 'it's a simple equation. This guy gets his money and our lives go on. Your life and my life. He doesn't get the money, I'm dead and your career is over because how are you ever going to get another promotion with a black mark like that on your file?'

Now, the footsteps rising towards her were joined by a descending shuffle from above. She leaned dizzily against the wall.

'You have no shame, Jamie,' she said weakly.

Heading up the stairs towards her were Skip Sheridan and Garda Dempsey. Heading down, and now in full view, was Anna Brennan followed by Stephen and two uniforms.

'And you have? All the times you left Dad waiting when you'd promised to come see him. Or if you did come, you'd stay half an hour and piss off again.'

Jamie was up to his old manipulative tricks. Always knew the right buttons to press, always merciless in pressing them. She resisted him, kicked back.

'Dad understood. He knew I had to fight twice as hard as any man to get ahead in the force,' she said. 'That's the difference between us, Jamie. Dad was a fighter. I'm a fighter. You've spent your life running from the fight. You and Ricky both.'

She cut the call with such force that the mobile fell from her hand and didn't survive the fall. She looked down at the pieces and saw two pairs of hands hovering about on the bare boards, picking up a battery here, a skin there. Skip Sheridan and Anna Brennan were on their knees before her. An odd moment occurred, as though in a dream. Sheridan's hand came accidentally upon Anna's and she pulled instinctively away, stood up and looked down at him with something approaching real contempt while he looked up in bewildered supplication. The incident passed Garda Dempsey by, so concerned was he with Helen's state of shock.

'Are you OK, Helen?' he asked.

'Yeah, yeah. Just . . . I don't know . . .'

'You should go sit down,' Sheridan told her.

Stephen Brennan stood before the American, wide-eyed and anguished.

'Why didn't you tell me, Skip? Why did you have to put on that big pretence of being my friend?'

Sheridan shrugged. He looked to Anna for some help but she had none to offer.

'Stephen, please,' she said.

'Did she put you up to it? "Make friends with my freaky son because he can't make friends of his own except with other freaks like Frankie Prior." Was that it?'

'Don't talk about the poor boy like that,' his mother said.

The landing was too cramped. The widow, her two sons and four police officers, all so close to one another that the cold air quickly heated up. Helen felt like she was stuck in a crowded and stalled lift. And one of the occupants had started to lose the plot.

'Poor boy?' Stephen seethed. 'He topped himself because of you, Mum. He was obsessed with you and he hung around with me just to be near you.'

'You know that isn't true,' Anna said, but uncertainly.

'We need to move along here now,' Helen intervened, and placed a hand on the young man's shoulder.

Stephen pushed her away and Garda Dempsey stepped in, shoved him against the wall. But Stephen hadn't finished yet.

'Of course it's not true. Why would you believe me when you never have? Ever. All my life, all those times I got messed about in school, all that stuff they said I did . . . I could see it in your face. The doubt.'

'I always stood by you, Stephen, you know that.'

'It's not the same thing!' he shouted. 'Can't you fucking see that? No, you can't, because you live in a fucking bubble with your Mahler and your Schumann and your artworks and your books and all the other pretentious bullshit. And Dad was in his bubble too. Work, work, work. Money, money, money.'

All the while, Stephen tried to press past Garda Dempsey who looked as though he was tempted to hit him, except that there were too many witnesses. A man ought to be ashamed of talking to his mother like that, he was thinking. No matter what.

'That's enough guff out of you,' he said. 'Go down the stairs. Go down the stairs.'

'Get your hands off me, you fascist pig!'

'Stephen . . .' Anna Brennan said, her hands raised but not knowing where to go beyond waist height.

'Go down the stairs,' Dempsey repeated, and managed to shunt the young man down a few steps. 'Go down the stairs.'

The two uniforms took over from Dempsey and Stephen descended a willing step or two before glancing back. He wore an unexpectedly cynical leer. His voice had lost its adenoidal whine. He looked up at his big brother. The American's deliberate lack of expression spoke more eloquently of disgust than any words might have.

'Take her, Skip. She never wanted me. At least now I know why. But don't get too attached to her. You'll soon find out she doesn't do attachment.'

'Move along,' Helen said. 'Now, please. Everyone.'

The landing cleared and she was left standing there with a sense of déjà vu. How many times had she and her father seen Jamie explode like this, her father mutely appealing for calm, she herself silently contemptuous of her brother? These past few days, she'd been trying to get her head around Stephen Brennan's behaviour. Was it all an act, this whinging, put-upon pose? Was his self-obsession down to some Asperger's-like condition? Or had he, as even his mother appeared to believe, been irreparably damaged by her self-proclaimed inability to love?

She thought about Jamie. Always so needy, so demanding. For him, enough was never enough. And always there was someone else to blame when he got himself into trouble. Lying became a way of life for him, cheating, betrayal. Cruel intentions, devious means. To him, expressions of concern were character judgements. And the worst of it was that he hurt himself more than he hurt others. Instead of muddling through the confusions of childhood and adolescence as most more or less do, he became forever trapped in self-loathing and recrimination. 'He'll never stop beating himself up,' her despairing father had once said of him, 'not until he's finished himself off.'

In the end, Stephen Brennan's problem was much like Jamie's, Helen concluded. A problem that was at once similar and yet the polar opposite of Anna Brennan's. Despising herself, she was incapable of giving love. Despising himself, Stephen was incapable of receiving it. In that vast and unlit emotional space between them, Stephen had lost his moral compass. Which didn't, Helen knew, necessarily mean that he was a murderer. Made him a much more likely suspect than most, though.

Back at the Incident Room, she found Ben Murphy slumped forward at the long table, forehead resting on his folded arms. She felt tempted to let him alone, let him sleep and forget his troubles for a while. But he'd become aware of her presence and sat up sharply.

'Dozed off there,' he said, checking the time on his iPhone.

Just after ten. 'I'd better head. Traffic tell me it'll take at least two and a half hours to get to Crumlin.'

'Your mother can't stay with her?'

Ben Murphy stood up from the table. His stubbled cheeks were ready for their morning shave and the night hadn't even started yet. He looked older, at once more mature and more vulnerable.

'You know how it is with little girls,' he said. 'Sometimes it has to be Daddy.'

Helen felt utterly lost. She scrabbled among some papers on the conference table as though there might be something of importance among them.

'Yeah,' she said, and grief jammed itself into her throat and silenced her.

'You're not tackling that lot now, are you?' Murphy asked.

'Pointless going home. It'll take an age . . . and anyway . . .'

She wished he'd go but he hovered close by, putting on his coat, his scarf and gloves, watching her. He seemed to be about to approach her and she didn't know whether or not she wanted him to. Then he punched one soft-gloved fist into the other.

'Right then,' he said finally. 'I'd better be heading.'

'Yeah, safe journey,' she said.

44

While Leo waited in the office upstairs for Skip Sheridan to arrive, he recalled what he could of the North Carolina Cherokee mask back at Serpentine Crescent. The Booger Mask. Fashioned from a hornet's nest, it caricatured the bearded European enemies of the tribe. For the Booger Dance, the Indians donned the masks and dressed up in ragged European clothes. By satirizing the bumbling enemy, the Cherokee no longer feared them. That was the theory. The poor bastards, Leo reflected, had still lost everything and been dispatched along the infamous Trail of Tears to Oklahoma.

He returned to the paperwork at hand. The authorization of the reward payment to Laima Leipinš and her sister. Superintendent Heaphy would hit the roof. Leo had discussed the details of the payment with Sergeant Martha Corrigan earlier. The young Latvian girls had apparently been dubious, wondering what more was expected of them for such largesse from the police, but the ex-Rose of Tralee had assuaged their fears. Leo did the maths. Fifteen thousand for Laima and Sonia. Forty-four thousand seven hundred, he wrote, for the Garda Síochána Reward Fund.

At least Heaphy would like that bit, feel he had some control over the matter.

A light tapping on the door roused Leo from his reverie. He stood up and went to the window. Frosted patterns had begun to form on the outside of the glass. Must be minus four or five outside for that to happen. Inside the office, the same one from which Sean Doran had done a runner, the radiator was already beginning to lose its battle against the cold.

'Come in,' he called.

The door opened. Leo stayed put, watching the reflections. Garda Dempsey showing Skip Sheridan into the room.

'Mr Sheridan to see you, sir,' Dempsey said. 'Do you need me to stay?'

'No, you can go,' Leo said.

Sheridan stood by the chair at the other side of the desk, his head so bowed that Leo couldn't see his reflected face.

'Sit down, Mr Sheridan.'

He waited, keeping his back to the American, listened for shifting sounds or irritated sighs. None came. He threw in another thirty seconds or so of silence. Then he turned, giving Sheridan the full-on mask of collapse. The American dropped back involuntarily. Just as quickly, he straightened up. He met Leo's gaze with an unspoken apology.

'Why would you want to high-tail it over here to Ireland?' Leo asked gruffly, acting offended. 'It's not like Anna Brennan was in any mad rush to meet you. Are you running from something?'

'No, sir. I figured I was coming home. Guess I got that one wrong.'

'Because Mrs Brennan wants to keep you hidden from sight?'

'I wasn't referring to my mother,' Sheridan said, opening

the buttons of his lumber jacket. 'I was referring to most all of the people I've met since I came here.'

The American's gaze flitted around the room but returned again and again to Leo's face.

''Course, if you've something to hide,' Leo said, 'we can get you a solicitor – that'd be a lawyer in your lingo.'

'I don't need no lawyer,' Sheridan said. 'Look, I had no right to react to your . . . your misfortune like that. It's just . . . a couple of years before she died, Momma suffered a stroke and, well, one side of her body was paralysed and . . .'

Leo sat into his chair. He'd watched the American's performance closely. It seemed genuine enough.

'Apology accepted,' he said. 'But I didn't get a stroke. It's a condition called Bell's palsy.'

'Right,' Sheridan said and, to Leo's surprise, added, 'Like Sylvester Stallone?'

'Yeah. Stallone, George Clooney and me.'

'George Clooney?'

'Apparently so,' Leo said. 'Except he obviously ended up at the other end of the looks spectrum from me. I just happened to be stuck in the wrong place at the wrong time when it struck.'

Now Leo was playing another type of man who deserved honest answers. Not the offended type but the sad-clown type, the type who'd had the crap kicked out of him by life. Instinct told him that Skip Sheridan might empathize with the portrayal.

'I can see your difficulty, Skip,' he said. 'You risk losing your natural mother if you say anything that implicates Stephen in either or both murders. And who else have you got? You've lost both your adoptive parents, and I'm assuming you don't have any other brothers or sisters. And you've never married? Had kids of your own?'

Sheridan shook his head, an inner debate occupying him.

'So, there's no one,' Leo continued. 'No one else in your life. Believe me, son, I can understand how—'

'I had a brother,' Sheridan said abruptly, as though he hadn't been listening to Leo. 'He died when I was ten years old. He was seven. He drowned.'

'He was adopted too?' Leo asked.

'No. My folks were already late thirties when they adopted me. Last thing they figured was that they'd have a kid of their own but it happens. Happens pretty often, as a matter of fact.'

'And you were, how can I put it? You were relegated in their affections?'

'Not until the day he drowned.'

The young American's prematurely weathered features grew pained. The high colour on his cheeks was unhealthily blotched beneath the unforgiving fluorescent light. It occurred to Leo that the guy was or had been a heavy drinker. He followed a hunch.

'Were you in the water too?'

'Yeah.'

'They blamed you for your brother's death,' Leo said.

Sheridan looked him squarely in the eyes. Strange, Leo thought, how much colder the room felt when silence fell. Both men pulled the lapels of their jackets tighter.

'It was July, ninety Fahrenheit, humidity off the scale,' Sheridan began. 'We'd gone swimming, took a picnic, the full deal. Lake Bowen it was. So, we're there all day and come eight thirty, nine, me and my brother we're still diving in from this flatboard pier. But Momma's calling us back in.'

Leo had the sense that he was watching a young man grow old before him. The American's hardened hands clutched each other, the fingernails pressing into flesh as though he were hurting himself to see if he could still feel the pain.

'They told me that I jumped in the water,' he continued. 'That I started kidding around, pretending I was in trouble, flapping my arms about. They said my kid brother panicked and jumped in to rescue me. But what I remember is that he was the one kidding in the water and I jumped in to save him. And I can't remember the rest. Why can't I remember?'

'Memory has its tricks, Skip,' Leo said. 'Has to have. Otherwise, we'd remember so much, we wouldn't know who the hell we were.'

Leo imagined the young Sheridan shivering on that pier as his brother's body was taken from the water. Shivering all his youth long in the cold of his parents' aversion to him. An aversion doubled, Leo guessed, because they'd lost their natural son. What chance did a kid have of surviving a double chill like that? By finding a natural mother who loved him and finding a new brother to rescue from the water?

'Have you told Anna about all of this?' Leo asked.

'I guess so,' Sheridan said. He looked beyond Leo at the window with its decorative filigree of ice. 'I could've told her a hell of a lot more but she had her own problems and, besides, there's only so much pity you can take before it sickens you.'

There was an edge to his voice now, and Leo understood perfectly well why. Personally, he'd rather stare down the barrels of a sawn-off shotgun again than be the target of overweening pity.

'What else could you have told her, Skip?' Leo asked.

'Oh, the usual broken family deal,' Sheridan said with a shrug. 'Our lives fell apart. We moved from one town, one county, one state to the next. Pop couldn't hold a job down for drinking. My mother had to work two, sometimes three shifts in diners, bars, whatever, just to make ends meet. Me too. Never got to finish High School. Five years after the accident, Pop died. A heart attack. A broken heart, Momma said. Like we didn't all have broken hearts.'

'And your mother? Your adoptive mother.'

'She survived for two years after her stroke.'

'And you took care of her?'

'Yes, sir, I guess I did,' Sheridan said. 'It didn't mean a damn to her.'

'But you brought her ashes to Clogherhead like she asked,' Leo said.

'I did my duty. Just like she did hers.'

The encroaching cold in the office felt like it was coming all the way from Skip Sheridan's early years and from his final attempt to make amends for something he might or might not be guilty of.

'Maybe Anna ought to know the whole story,' Leo said. 'Not right now obviously.'

Skip Sheridan shook his head. It seemed to Leo that the young American had as little chance of finding some happy resolution in his life as he himself had. Sorry as he felt for Sheridan, he had to push on. Problem was, he knew neither where to start nor how to proceed without causing more unnecessary pain. Unintentionally, Sheridan gave him his cue.

'I'm leaving,' the young man said, his hands on his thighs as though to ready himself.

'Sorry, Skip, but we're not finished here yet.'

Sheridan smiled, almost chuckled, but without mirth.

'Leaving Ireland,' he explained. 'Heading back Stateside. Ain't nothing here for me, Inspector. I can just about get by earning one hundred euro a day but I been getting three, four days a week at best. Damn near cleared out my savings. Such as they were.'

'When do you plan to go?'

'Soon as I sort things. Sell the auto, some other bits and pieces. And I got a couple jobs to finish out. I don't like to disappoint people.'

An unspoken tagline hung in the air: *I leave that up to others.* Leo sensed that the young man was aware of the vague kinship that had arisen between them. He was sorry he had to break the ties.

'If Stephen turns out to be our man, you'll be charged at minimum with withholding of evidence. At max, it might even be an accomplice charge,' Leo said, and then gave the impression of relenting somewhat. 'Look, Skip, I need to rule the guy in or out.'

Sheridan looked cagily at him, ground his teeth over the problem of betrayal. Like many before him, Leo thought, present company included.

'So when you met Stephen last evening, how was he? Agitated? Hyped up?'

'You've done toxicology tests,' Sheridan said warily. 'You're gonna know he'd been sniffing some lines. So, yeah, he was hyped.'

'Cocaine?'

Sheridan nodded, glanced up at Leo from below his lowered brow. The eyes piercing in their almost other-worldly loneliness.

'Anything else he may have taken, I know nothing about. I swear.'

'There was more?'

'Later on, at the club, I was talking to a lady and . . . well . . . he was with a couple of shady-looking guys. I reckon he bought something, I don't know what-all, but he came down so fast I had to carry him out of the club.'

'And what about you? Did you do any lines?'

'No, sir. I'm done with all of that. Drank, sure enough. Guinness at the pub. Jack Daniel's at the club.'

Sheridan cracked a grim smile. Leo realized that the American had fast-forwarded the previous evening's proceedings. He couldn't tell if this was intentional.

'Stephen was agitated earlier,' Leo stated. 'How did that agitation express itself?' He let the question sink in for going on half a minute.

'He asked if he could stay overnight with me. Said he couldn't ever go back to the Sanctuary again after what he'd done.'

'Did he elaborate?'

Sheridan tucked his neck into his lumber jacket and thrust his hands deep into the pockets. The temperature in the room seemed to Leo to be plummeting.

'It sounds crazy. I can't say for sure if it's true, but he . . . he said he'd cut off a dog's head out there. Fed me some crazy shit about how the dog refused to die.'

'Did he talk about Gudrun Remer?'

'I asked him if she'd seen what he did. He said she had. And that was all. He didn't want to talk about it after that.'

'And he told you all of this while you were in the pub?'

'Yes, sir.'

371

'But you continued on to the club with him. That doesn't make a lot of sense given his state of mind, does it?'

Sheridan bristled. Anger did some interesting things to his weathered features. A tremor below his left eye spread downwards, pulling the corner of his mouth out of line. His eyes became opaque.

'Do you have a brother, Inspector?' he asked. 'No? Not even a half-brother?'

'No, I don't,' Leo said, and threw in a provocation. 'But if I had a half-brother like Stephen Brennan, I'd despise the little runt. Private schools, drops out of college, arses around a dog sanctuary, money in his pocket for all the booze and coke he wants. And still he spends his time whining over a cruel father who probably never lifted a finger to him. And crying because his mammy never really loved him. Aren't you pissed off with Anna Brennan protecting this little twerp at your expense? Pissed off enough to set him up for a murder charge, maybe?'

Sheridan stared at Leo like the ugly detective was the latest in a long line of turncoat friends.

'I've been straight with you, sir,' he said. 'I've told you all I know.'

'No one ever tells me all they know, Skip. It's one of the hazards of the job. What about his relationship with Gudrun Remer? What do you make of it?'

'He was just a kid getting laid for the first time on a regular basis is how I see it,' Sheridan said. 'He thought he'd go crazy if she went to jail. I mean, the guy seriously thought his folks were gonna pay her fine. Twenty thousand euro? Come on.'

Stephen Brennan's antipathy towards his father went back a long way. So, if he'd killed his father, something must have happened or some crisis come to a head late last Friday night. Was it, then, a final refusal on Dermot Brennan's part to pay the German woman's fine?

'Did Stephen talk to you about his father's death?'

'No, sir,' Sheridan answered too promptly.

'Doesn't that seem a little odd?' Leo said. 'You're with him for more or less the entire evening and Stephen never mentions his father? On the day of the funeral?'

Sheridan shifted some discomfort away.

'What d'you want me to tell you? That he admitted to killing his father? Which he did not. That he said he was glad his father was dead? Which he did not. The funeral came up, yeah. I told him he was an asshole not to go because of some dumb-assed argument over money. I told him I went to my momma's funeral even though she hated me.'

Sheridan pulled himself up short, got to his feet, his big fists hanging by his sides looking for something to do with themselves.

'I best be going home,' he said.

Leo stayed put, though the gardener looked like he might, at any moment, make a break for the door. One last harsh question, Leo thought.

'Did you tell him why your mother hated you?'

'No, sir,' Sheridan said. His face was an anguished stone mask unaware of the rain falling across it. 'Jeez, man. Haven't I given you enough already? Y'all know I've lost a second family telling you what I just told you.'

Leo followed the line of Sheridan's gaze and saw the snow drift thickly by the window. He stood up and looked out to see if it had begun to lodge. It had. In an hour or two, the road surface would be deadly. Maybe it already was.

'I'll have someone drive you home.' Leo gestured at the

snow-laden window. 'Might take a while to get to Clogherhead, though, on a night like this.'

Sheridan was buttoning up his jacket and didn't look up as he spoke.

'I may be staying at Attenboy House, sir,' he said. 'I think maybe she'll need some company tonight.'

'Why?'

'She's had to tell Stephen about me. That can't have been easy.'

One part of Leo couldn't decide if the fellow was a saint or a fool. The other part knew he trusted neither saints nor fools.

'How did you know that?'

'I met Stephen just now,' Sheridan said. 'They were taking him back down to his cell and I was on my way up here. He wanted to know why I never told him. What could I say?'

Sheridan had more dilemmas, Leo thought, than a reindeer had branches on its horns. He picked up the phone and told Garda Dempsey to bring the young American to Attenboy. A house that was never going to be home to this lost child. He wondered what kind of reception Sheridan would get from Anna. Would she cast him out into the cold? He texted Dempsey. *Stay & keep a watch on Attenboy 4 a few hrs. Keep me posted.*

A little after midnight, Leo fell asleep at his desk. He'd decided not to drive back to Serpentine Crescent. The snow fell unrelentingly and had hardened into packed ice. The journey home might have taken for ever. He dreamed that he was young again and had a perfect brother with a perfect face who could play the piano and the organ, the violin and the cello, the clarinet, the flute, everything. He had a father who smiled and a mother who sang and a bright, happy home. Then he realized he was a dog, their dog. He tried to speak to his brother but could only bark. And, besides, he didn't know his brother's name.

Saturday, 27 November

45

At Howth Garda Station, Detective Inspector Leo Woods emerged from a third or, perhaps, fourth sleep. He'd lost count. The station had come to life since he'd last woken around six. He sat at the desk, his mind empty but for a deep longing for a cigarette and a coffee, which he was too tired yet to satisfy. Beyond the office door, voices and footsteps echoed. He rubbed his chin and the sting of stubble stirred him. Then he saw the notebook on his desk. Ben Murphy's Miró notebook. He remembered someone bringing it to him during the night. Murphy had left without it. Leo hadn't opened it yet. He picked up the phone.

'Martha . . . Yeah, didn't bother going home. Can you send me up a coffee? . . . Great. And a razor . . . Yeah, a razor. Is Stephen Brennan's solicitor here yet? . . . Good. And Detective Sergeant Cooney? . . . Good. Tell him the interview with Stephen Brennan starts at half eight. I want to see him before we start. And, Martha, anything on the radio log from Garda Dempsey? . . . OK. And his last call? . . . Three thirty, right.'

He'd had a few texts from Dempsey too. Nothing to

report. The last one shortly after half three. He hoped the young fellow hadn't got a chill out of it.

His shoulder and neck muscles ached. He got up and walked the stiffness out of his bones. The snowlight at the window pierced his skull and blinded him for a few moments. He put the Miró notebook in his inside pocket and went downstairs to talk to a young man about a dog.

Alan Cobbe had the shakes. A combination, Detective Sergeant Helen Troy supposed, of the cold, the early hour, lack of alcohol and trepidation. The unshaven look didn't work on his middle-aged jowls, nor did the adolescent pout. Helen had just heard Ben Murphy deliver the news of Caroline Hunt's betrayal. Instead of the loud outburst they'd expected there was this sullen but wary withdrawal. His solicitor had tried to offer some muted advice but was rebuffed.

'I'll repeat the question, Mr Cobbe,' Helen said. 'On the same day she was murdered, you learned that Gudrun Remer had rung Enniscorthy Garda Station a few months ago to report your assault on Caroline Hunt. Your response was to suggest that – how did you put it? – "that German bitch will be sorry she ever came to Ireland". Would you care to elaborate?' She waited but no response came. She addressed the recording device on the table. 'Mr Cobbe refuses to answer the question.'

'On legal advice,' the solicitor insisted, looking up from the voluminous file he fiddled with. He looked like he hadn't slept for quite a while.

'Did you visit the Argos Sanctuary at any time during the past week?' Helen asked, and waited. 'Mr Cobbe refuses to answer the question.'

'She was lying,' Cobbe said.

'Who was lying?' Ben Murphy asked. 'Caroline Hunt or Gudrun Remer?'

'Both of them. Obviously.'

'Obviously?' Helen said. 'When Kitty Newman stated that you confronted Dermot Brennan, you told us she was lying too, didn't you? Until you had to admit she wasn't.'

Cobbe swept back the quiff of grey hair from his forehead.

'Stupid bloody women,' he said.

'Conspiring against you, are they, Mr Cobbe? The entire female species?' Murphy asked. 'Bit of a stretch, isn't it? Everyone's lying but you?'

'It's like this,' Cobbe said. 'You screw them a couple of times and they're already thinking eternal love. When you disabuse them, well, it's a case of hell hath no fury.'

'Seems to me the fury is all on your side, Mr Cobbe,' Murphy countered.

'Look,' he said, 'I've given you a list of everyone I met on Thursday. I've named every pub I visited. I was in the city all day and all evening and you know it. So there's no possible way I could've murdered Gudrun.'

'For a man who'd been drinking solidly all day as you claim, you have amazing recall of your movements on the day,' Murphy said.

'Check them out and you'll—'

'We've talked to everyone on your list, Mr Cobbe,' Murphy interrupted, 'and I'm afraid their recollections aren't quite as precise as yours, which means we have some possible gaps in the chronology. As much as two hours in one case. So, let's say, half an hour, thirty-five minutes to reach the Argos Sanctuary. Which leaves the best part of an hour for you to kill Ms Remer, tidy yourself up and get back into the city centre.'

'During which time I'm drunk as a bloody lord,' Cobbe sneered.

'During which time you *appear* to be drunk as a lord,' Helen corrected him. 'During which time also your predilection for beating up on women is—'

'My client has never been convicted on any such charge,' the solicitor objected tiredly.

'I've seen your client in action,' Helen said. 'I witnessed his attack on Kitty Newman and I'm pretty sure that if he hadn't realized he'd been rumbled, he'd have done a lot more damage. Isn't that so, Mr Cobbe?'

The sculptor lowered his head, his grey forelock falling over his eyes again.

They were getting nowhere fast, Helen knew. She turned to Ben Murphy, gestured with her eyes at the folder on the table before them. Murphy opened the folder and began to lay out a series of photographs.

The solicitor baulked at the images of the pulverized German woman, raised his gaze absurdly high.

'I have to object to the introduction of these . . . these . . .'

'Objection noted,' Murphy told him. 'But we have a reasonable suspicion that your client is responsible for the murder of Gudrun Remer. And because he's been less than cooperative we need to jog his memory. And his conscience.'

Cobbe skulked below his feathery grey hairline. His bulk seemed less muscled than flabby now.

'You're a hard man, Mr Cobbe,' Murphy continued. 'Surely you're not too squeamish to look?'

The sculptor managed a quick half glance at the photos before closing his eyes in pained disgust. Then he joined his solicitor in contemplating the mysteries of the wall behind the two detectives. He resisted the magnetic pull of the photos for all of a minute before appealing to Ben Murphy.

'For Christ's sake, put those damn things away,' he said, and when he raised his head it was as if he were trying to decide which of them to confide in. 'There are certain details I've withheld out of, let's call it, misplaced loyalty to someone I had great affection for.'

'Anna Brennan?' Helen cut in sharply.

Cobbe nodded.

'The interrogee confirms the suggestion,' Murphy said.

Next time you order the heating to be switched off in the interview room on the coldest day of the century thus far, Leo reminded himself, wear thermals. He felt colder than Stephen Brennan looked. In the circumstances, the slogan on the young man's black T-shirt – This Is The End – seemed less a cri de cœur than a prediction.

Beside Leo, Detective Sergeant Cooney sulked. He'd wanted to know where the tip-off about the Dorans had come from but Leo insisted it had been an anonymous call. He'd wanted to turn on the heating too but Leo told him it wasn't his call.

Stephen Brennan's solicitor was a stern, solid woman in her fifties. Dressed sensibly in an ankle-length coat and woollen scarf, she'd listened sceptically to Leo's excuses about the radiators. Her indifference to his facial shortcomings was refreshing. Ms Orla Prout handled her client with the authority of a schoolmistress and he was helplessly submissive. Clearly not having slept, Stephen inhabited a waking nightmare that wouldn't go away no matter how hard he pressed his fingers into his eyelids.

'We'll start with Rover,' Cooney began, as Leo had instructed earlier. 'You'd been involved in a dispute with Peter Prior over that dog. Is that the case?'

'You don't have to answer that,' Ms Prout told Stephen, 'if you feel it may incriminate you.'

'Ms Prout, your client has already incriminated himself with his lack of cooperation,' Leo pointed out. 'The longer he maintains this silence, the deeper the hole he's digging for himself. OK, then, Mr Brennan, let's try another angle. You say you can't remember what happened on the afternoon and evening of Gudrun Remer's murder. So, tell me this, what's your last memory from before this dreadful bout of amnesia?'

'I was spiked,' Stephen told the concrete floor. 'My drink was spiked. At the club probably.'

'Yeah, sure. Either that or you lost track of all the gear you were swallowing,' Leo said. 'So, your last memory from Thursday? You remember getting up? Washing? I'm presuming you do actually wash. Feeding the dogs?'

'Talking to you, actually, in the kitchen,' Stephen replied, catching Leo off guard. 'You were acting weird. You were speaking German. Weren't you?'

'Yeah,' Leo said, and moved swiftly on past the solicitor's quizzical look. 'And you weren't too happy about it. Threw a little jealous tantrum, didn't you? And tried to strike Gudrun. Remember that? And remember when I got out of the car earlier and we talked in the yard? You weren't convinced that the dog should die a natural death like Gudrun said he should, were you?'

Stephen Brennan muttered inaudibly. His solicitor leaned towards him and he re-enacted almost exactly his rejection of Gudrun's soothing approach on the morning Leo had visited the Sanctuary. He sank lower, his fingers crawling through his greasy hair.

'And after I leave,' Leo continued, 'you and Gudrun have a blazing row, right? And Rover is already a major bone of contention, pardon the pun.'

Ms Prout didn't. A dog-lover, Leo thought, just my luck.

'It wasn't like that,' Stephen said. 'Not exactly.'

'But we're getting closer to what happened to Gudrun, aren't we?' Leo said.

'Stop saying her name,' Stephen objected.

'Don't like to be reminded of what you did to her, is that it? To Gudrun?'

'You're intimidating my client,' Ms Prout said.

'I'm asking him a series of necessary questions and he's refusing to answer them,' Leo said. 'So, Stephen, you grab yourself an axe and lop the dog's head off. Only you don't stop there, do you? Because Gudrun's telling you that you can kiss your alibi for the night of your father's murder goodbye. And you can't have that, can you? You're thinking, I've murdered my father because he wouldn't pay her fine and now she's threatening to dump on me. So, you rape her first and then start the chopping. Or vice versa. Which was it, son?'

The young lank-haired man had begun to whimper.

'Speak up, would you?' Detective Sergeant Cooney snarled.

'I said, it wasn't fucking like that!' Stephen shouted at Cooney. 'We didn't argue. Actually, we ended up in bed. But the dog started howling. Not a sound out of it for hours on end and then this . . . awful . . . It was doing my head in and I couldn't take it any more. I got the axe, yeah, I got the axe.'

A brief spasm of tense silence passed through each of

them as though they somehow knew and did not know what was coming next. Then, with calm deliberation, Stephen Brennan pulled back, slammed his forehead down on to the desk, raised himself and slammed it down again. He tried a third shot but Ms Prout had got herself between him and the desk and she took the full force of his skull into the cheekbone, and when she hit the floor, Stephen got his third shot in on the timber of the desk. Cooney leapt to the fallen solicitor's side, moving more quickly than Leo had ever seen him move. Leo wasn't so quick to his feet but he got a hand across the table and grabbed a fistful of The End before the young fellow could finish the job on himself.

'You little play-acting bastard,' he said as Stephen's eyeballs did a few circuits of his eye sockets.

'I killed the dog,' the young man slurred. 'I killed Rover . . . He wouldn't die . . . he wouldn't stop looking at me like it was my fault Frankie killed himself . . .'

With that, he passed out, and his chin fell drooling on to Leo's fist.

46

'If this is another exercise in pointing the finger at Skip Sheridan, forget it, Mr Cobbe,' Detective Garda Ben Murphy said. 'We know that Anna Brennan was foolish enough to confide in you about the fact that she'd given a son up for adoption. And, what? You came to the conclusion that he was that long-lost son? So, to deflect attention from yourself, you told us Dermot Brennan was expecting to see Sheridan on the night of the murder. And, let me guess, you now have another nail for Skip's coffin. Am I right?'

'Sheridan's her son?' Cobbe said, his shock so profound that the catching and fluttering of his breath was almost audible.

'Why does that surprise you?' Helen asked. 'He's too young? He's not an artist? He doesn't possess your many attractions?'

She knew she was being facetious. The only explanation for his reaction that occurred to her was both too awful and too confusing to contemplate. She felt soiled for having entertained it for even a moment. Ben Murphy rescued her from the thought.

'You're not Sheridan's father, are you?' he asked of the sculptor.

'Don't be ridiculous,' Cobbe said. 'I didn't know Anna back then. I wish I bloody had. I might have disabused her of this self-flagellating Catholic guilt she indulges herself in.'

'Why so shocked to hear he's her son then?' Murphy asked.

Cobbe dismissed the question with a toss of his grey hair. He was trying for nonchalance. He didn't quite pull it off. He turned to his celebrity solicitor, whispered something they couldn't quite catch. The solicitor nodded his assent and Cobbe proceeded.

'What I have to tell you has nothing to do with Skip Sheridan,' he said. 'It concerns Stephen.'

The two detectives waited for Alan Cobbe to regain his equilibrium.

'The Brennans came back to Ireland in nineteen ninety-nine, as you probably know,' Cobbe began. 'What you don't know is that they came back because of Stephen's – how can I put it? – his behavioural problems.'

The sculptor struggled against some inner reluctance, battled wearily on.

'Stephen was having trouble with some other kid in his class. Who precisely was bullying whom remained a matter of dispute. What didn't was that Stephen added crushed glass to this kid's lunchtime drink. Luckily the kid didn't swallow the stuff. The case never reached the courts for one reason or another – some kind of pay-off no doubt. But Stephen admitted to his mother that he'd done it. And it wasn't the first of these vengeful pranks. Nor was it the last.'

Helen remembered the rats in the attic at Attenboy House, the trashing of Anna Brennan's charity shop.

'When they came back to Dublin, this peculiar carry-on continued,' Cobbe went on. 'He was expelled from two schools. Anna didn't tell me exactly why but, basically, it was more of the same. What she did tell me was that she refused to bring him to a psychiatrist or to submit him to any therapy because, to her, it would have been an admission of her own failure. I suppose she imagined he'd grow out of it, get some bloody sense eventually. Then came that dreadful business with Frankie Prior. It was unforgivable what Stephen did to that young fellow.'

Coming from a man capable of trouncing his lady friends, Helen thought, this last assertion seemed pretty rich.

'What did Stephen do?' Ben Murphy asked.

'The day Frankie dressed up in Anna's clothes,' the sculptor continued. 'That wasn't Frankie's idea, it was Stephen's. He was leading the poor kid on, playing on Frankie's confused sexuality, so to speak. Then he takes a photo of the kid on his mobile phone and – the little bastard – he texted the photo straight to some lecturer of theirs that Frankie had a crush on. So, the kid grabs the phone and smashes it and the fight starts. Dermot broke up the row. He washed his hands of Stephen after that and Anna was terrified that he'd take some revenge on his father.'

'She specifically mentioned that possibility?' Helen asked.

'Yes, she did,' Cobbe said. 'But the really bloody awful thing about all this is that Anna blames herself for the fact that Stephen's a sneaky little turd. She says she was never a good mother, that Stephen must have sensed from early on that there was some deficit there in their relationship. Which is utter bullshit. The boy's a bloody psychopath, full stop.'

Helen scribbled a note for Murphy and passed it to him. *We have to call a time-out and tell Leo immediately.* He read the note and nodded. Then he flicked worriedly down through a message on his iPhone.

'We'll take a break for, say, half an hour, OK?' Helen told the solicitor, whose eyes were popping at the revelations falling around him like frogs from the magnolia ceiling.

'And by the way,' Cobbe added petulantly, 'I wasn't lying about Dermot calling Sheridan's name that night.'

Detective Inspector Leo Woods dumped the tip of a Consulate cigarette in his pocket and lit up. He leaned halfway out of a top-floor window at Howth Garda Station. The chilly air tortured his torso. The radiator he sat side-saddle on roasted his rear end. A man of extremes, he mused, divided in his every conviction. Including the conviction that the young dog-botherer was guilty of the murder of Dermot Brennan and Gudrun Remer. Stephen had to be the killer. And yet . . .

Leo was blasted from his reverie by Superintendent Heaphy's thunderous entrance, an A4 sheet shivering in his hand.

'Jesus, Aonghus,' he complained as he stubbed the cigarette and aimed the butt at the ice-filled gutter. He missed. 'Don't barge in on a man like that.'

'You're smoking,' Heaphy said, stating the obvious. 'Is there any rule you haven't broken, Leo?'

'Don't know. Haven't read the rule book for years.'

For a moment, Leo thought the super had appreciated the joke. But it was just those teeth again, their default mode a gorilla grin.

'What in the name of God is going on downstairs?' Heaphy asked. 'Ms Prout's been ferried off in an ambulance with a fractured jaw. Don't you realize what this will do to my – to our reputation? And you can't refuse Stephen Brennan medical attention. It puts the entire case in jeopardy.'

'I haven't refused him medical attention,' Leo said. 'I've called a doctor in and he's been delayed with the icy roads. No way is that young fellow leaving the building. Not until I get the truth out of him.'

'He's our man then? You're sure of that?'

'I'll tell you when I get the truth out of him.'

Heaphy held up the sheet of paper and struggled to articulate its significance.

'And this . . . what were you thinking of when you . . . what gives you the right to . . . ?' he spluttered. 'You want me to sanction a reward of fifteen thousand euro to this Latvian girl? For what? She gave us little or no information.'

'She helped us move the case forward, Aonghus.'

'But this money – how much is it? – this fifty-nine thousand seven hundred euro, it's not ours to distribute willy-nilly. And another thing. That seems like a very suspicious amount to me. Why is it three hundred short of sixty thousand? Because if it turns out that one of ours has helped himself to a few bob . . .'

Leo's attention snapped towards the open window where a great fat ugly crow had landed on the snowy slates. So black against the white that you could see its true colour was blue. His stomach seemed to empty out. The vacuum hurt. He remembered his conversation with Sheridan from the night before. What was it the young man had said when he talked of returning to America? *I can just about get by earning one hundred euro a day.* And he'd done three days' work for the Brennans in the week prior to Dermot's murder before Kitty Newman had called a halt to the cutting down of the boundary trees. Had he been paid by Dermot with notes from the leather satchel when work was suspended? Or had he dropped by Attenboy House on Friday night for his money? Or been asked to drop by? And was that why Dermot called Sheridan's name as Cobbe had claimed?

'Leo?' Heaphy said with a note of concern. 'Are you all right? You've turned awful pale.'

'Aonghus,' Leo said. 'I may have perpetrated the greatest fuck-up of my career. And, given my record, that's saying something.'

'What have you done?'

'I'm not sure yet. And, even if I was, you wouldn't want to know.'

As he spoke, he was scrolling for Helen Troy's number. The superintendent sat in a chair by the door, defeated, his dreams of promotion fading by the second. In a final gesture of submission to his fate, he unfastened two buttons at his midriff and let his pot-belly find its true expanse.

Detective Sergeant Helen Troy's work mobile, unlike her personal phone, was still intact. She found Leo's number at the same moment as an inward call from him flashed up on her screen. It didn't feel like serendipity, it just felt like trouble.

'Leo, I was just about to ring you,' she said. 'Alan Cobbe has been feeding us some interesting background on—'

'Skip Sheridan?'

'No, on Stephen. He's got a history of pretty nasty tricks. Plus, Anna told Cobbe she was terrified he'd turn on his father. He sounds like a very disturbed guy.'

She wasn't quite sure how to take Leo's silence so she filled it in with more detail. The crushed glass, the school expulsions, the rats in the attic, the trashing of the charity shop.

'And he'd nothing to say about Sheridan?' Leo asked.

'Well, he was genuinely taken aback to hear that Skip was

Anna's son,' Helen said, then added hesitantly, 'I've had a thought on that but it's a bit off-the-wall.'

'Does he still claim to have heard Dermot Brennan call Sheridan's name that evening?'

'Yeah, he insists on it. I'm not sure why.'

'Because maybe it's true?'

'Have you spoken to Sheridan this morning?' Helen asked, knowing she was posing the right question but suspecting she wouldn't like the answer.

'No,' Leo said. 'I let him out last night. I'd nothing to hold him on.' His unease was infectious. 'He stayed overnight at Attenboy House. I had Dempsey keep a watch on the place.'

The silence at the other end of the phone bothered him. He threw Heaphy a get-lost glance but the super was lost in contemplation of what might have been.

'What?' he demanded of Helen.

'At the station last night, I dropped my phone,' she said. 'And Anna and Sheridan happened to be crossing paths on the landing just then. When they went about picking up the pieces of my phone, I got the impression that she was . . . not exactly afraid of him but wary. Of his physical closeness at least. It was like she didn't want to touch him, even accidentally. Just the other day at the church, he was the only one she reacted to with any affection. And we know what Laima saw. But now it's as if something has changed in their relationship, as if something has come between them.'

'Something like suspicion on her part?' Leo speculated aloud.

'Suspicion relating to the murder of Gudrun Remer?' Helen wondered.

'Possibly. But we know that Anna's been protecting

Stephen by keeping all that psycho stuff secret,' Leo said. 'And if we're to believe Sheridan, he'd do anything for Anna. He tried to persuade Stephen to go to the funeral on her behalf. According to him, he went out to Attenboy last night because he thought she might need the company. What if she persuaded him to cover for Stephen too and he'd begun to waver on that?'

'There's another possibility,' Helen said. 'Anna hadn't been getting on with her husband for quite a while. Their sex life was over. They seemed to live more or less separate lives. And he treated Stephen more harshly than she'd have wished. As for Gudrun Remer, she despised the woman. Maybe she couldn't tolerate the fact that Gudrun had replaced her in Stephen's affections.'

'You're suggesting that she manipulated Sheridan into carrying out the murders?' Leo said, and Superintendent Heaphy's attention returned to the present. 'You're right. We can't discount the possibility. You and Ben meet me at Attenboy House, pronto.'

'Ben can't come.'

Leo's reaction brought an outraged Superintendent Heaphy to his feet. His exposed teeth suggested he might have Leo for lunch.

'For Christ's sake, Helen, we've two corpses here and Murphy is so hung over again he can't do his job? Tell him from me, he's suspended as and from now.'

The superintendent made strange gurgling noises of protest. Helen's voice, when it came, was muted and fragile.

'Ben's got a kid with cystic fibrosis,' she said. 'She's been in Crumlin Children's Hospital for the last week with a serious chest infection. Her third time this year. He's been staying over there every night. And he's just been called to the hospital because there's been a deterioration in her condition. I'll see you at Attenboy.'

'Helen—' Leo said, but she'd cut the call. He rounded on Heaphy. 'Christ Jesus, did you know about this? Young Murphy having a child with cystic fibrosis?'

Heaphy refastened his midriff buttons, straightened himself and assumed the pretence of authority again.

'Listen, Leo, don't go blaming me for the fact that you treated him like dirt.'

'I treated him like I'd treat any new recruit,' Leo said.

Heaphy picked up the sheet containing Leo's request for approval of the reward to Laima. He scanned it with a shake of his head, an exasperated sigh. Leo felt sick to the stomach with himself.

'We'll need the Emergency Response Unit on standby at Attenboy,' he said.

A new gravity had entered the super's features. A gravity that, for once, wasn't undermined by his chimpanzee teeth. He picked up the office phone.

'I'll call them in,' he said as Leo went by him and headed for the door. 'You know, Leo, I've been wondering for months why you were so hard on Ben Murphy. But I see it now.'

Within a hand's reach of the door, Leo paused.

'You thought he was the Younger Leo Woods Mark Two,' Heaphy went on, his voice tight with old resentments. 'Snappy dresser, cock-of-the-walk arrogant, dismissive of everyone else's efforts. The kind of man who'd do anything to get ahead in the job. Anything to exact revenge. And anything to satisfy his lust.'

Leo turned to face his old comrade-in-arms. His gut ached.

'Ah, for Christ's sake, Aonghus,' he pleaded. 'That's ancient history.'

'I'm not referring to my wife,' Heaphy said. 'We came to terms with that a long time ago. We put our trust in God and hung in there.'

Someone tapped on the door. Leo wanted to defend himself, tell the story of his miserable past, his half-crazed present, his non-existent future. He wanted to tell the toothy one that his life comprised mistake after mistake and that another, perhaps fatal, mistake awaited him out at Attenboy.

'Yeah, well, next time you're talking to your God,' he said, 'thank Him from me for fucking my face over by way of punishment.'

A louder rap erupted at the door. Leo pulled it open.

'What?' he shouted.

The young Garda stepped back and proffered a sheaf of A4 pages. Leo snapped them from him.

'Print-outs of Dermot Brennan's emails, sir. Sergeant Corrigan said to read the first one. It's highlighted in yellow.'

'I spotted that,' Leo said, and read. 'Mother of Jesus.' He looked up at the messenger, the bringer of strange tidings.

'And, sir?' the young man added. 'Pacelli hasn't checked in this morning.'

'Who the fuck is Pacelli?'

'Garda Dempsey, sir.'

'Maybe he went straight home,' Leo said in desperation. 'I told him to stay at Attenboy for a few hours, not all night.'

'He might have done, sir. But he's not answering the car radio or his mobile.'

Leo punched the wall and launched himself down the stairs of Howth Garda Station and out into the blinding, baleful blizzard.

47

The snow had thickened, freezing almost as soon as it reached the ground along Howth Road. The siren and the flashing of blue light helped a little. Gaps opened up for the squad cars, inviting recklessness and speed. The hard-packed ice, however, reined them back. An overwhelming sense of constraint had Detective Sergeant Helen Troy rocking back and forth in the passenger seat of the lead car. The tension whipped up a storm inside her. And there was more than one house at the centre of the storm. Attenboy. And her father's house. She saw no choice now but to sell.

The squad car negotiated the snowy maelstrom of Sutton Cross. Here, their way was cleared by some uniformed Gardaí and she turned off the siren, passed the word back for the others to do likewise. They made quicker progress along the isthmus leading into Howth village and harbour. Helen readied her work mobile to type a text but the inner storm hadn't ended yet. Selling the house wasn't going to set Jamie on the straight and narrow. But nothing ever would, she realized. She had to wash her hands of him. She asked her father to forgive her.

Halfway up, the steep rise of Abbey Street defeated her driver. She packed her gun, called back for some of the uniforms to follow her, and got out of the car. The cold sliced into her as she zipped up her jacket. Already on the move, she typed two words into her phone and sent the message to her brother. *Sell. Helen.*

Breathless, his vision fizzing with white stars, Detective Inspector Leo Woods reached the virgin snow before the closed gates of Attenboy House. Further up the road stood the parked squad car. Four or five inches of snow lay upon the roof, window and bonnet. Garda Dempsey was nowhere to be seen. Leo posted two officers at the gates and took two more along with him. The greatcoat he'd found at the station had seemed a blessing when he'd set out. Now it was yet another burden. He wanted to throw it off but knew he probably shouldn't. He wanted to throw off the fear he felt too but knew he probably couldn't. The icy air numbed his face.

As he neared the car, he saw that there were no tracks in the snow around it either. If Dempsey wasn't inside, the absence of footprints in the snow suggested he must have left it at least an hour ago. And why would he leave the car? And, if he had, where was he now? From five yards off, he saw the young Garda slumped forward in the driver's seat. He tried to run but almost took a fall. He thought he'd never reach the car. He hoped he wouldn't. But he did.

At the car, Leo grabbed the handle of the passenger door. The burn of ice shot through from his fingertips to the muscles of his upper arm. He pulled the door back, whipped his hand away. The skin of his fingertips stayed on the door handle. His agonized groan was stifled by the sight of a startled Dempsey shooting bolt upright in his seat and spiriting his mobile away into a coat pocket.

'I fell asleep,' the young Garda cried as he fended off the punch Leo threw at him.

'I thought you were dead, you stupid bastard,' Leo said, and slammed the door in Dempsey's face.

The young fellow peered out at him with such embarrassed hurt that Leo didn't know whether to laugh or cry. He hated these moments of high absurdity that life threw at him. Here he was facing into Christ-only-knew-what kind of Greek tragedy behind the walls of Attenboy House – some perhaps shocking denouement for which he himself might be partly responsible – and what does he get to send him on his way? A reminder that it's all a bloody joke anyway; love, life, the whole damn thing.

Leo softened, gestured with a nod for Dempsey to follow him and turned back towards the house. Snow stung his good eye and fell into the well of the drooping one. He thought he felt a crystal form in there. Of their own accord, the bloodied fingers of his right hand formed a bared claw that the icy air began to anaesthetize.

From out of the blizzard back at the gates, Helen appeared, looking as young and innocent as a child in a snowy fairy tale. Too young to be a police officer and he too old. He took the sheet with Dermot Brennan's last email correspondence from among the tissues and the cigarette tips in his pocket and handed it to her. She scanned it. The sender was Jack Duggan, a private detective in the Bronx, New York.

'Jesus,' she said. 'He's not the son she gave up for adoption?'

'No. Anna's son drowned when he was a kid,' Leo said. 'Last night, Sheridan told me the whole story except he switched places with his half-brother. The family fell apart after the boy's death and Sheridan seems to have borne the brunt of his mother's grief. Maybe his father's too. My guess is he came over here looking for revenge.'

'He talked about making a new start,' Helen said. 'It might be as simple as that. It might be that he just got unlucky again and walked into a second screwed-up family.'

'It's possible,' Leo said. 'But he was a suspect in the murder of a fellow soldier at Fort Carson in Colorado before his discharge. And the discharge wasn't an honourable one.'

Helen continued to speed-read the email exchange as she listened. It was hard to tell which hurt her eyes more, the lash of snow or the scanned photo of Skip Sheridan – or, rather, Private Denis Anthony Sheridan in his Gulf War combats. Yellow-highlighted words flashed up at her. Iran, Afghanistan. Civilian deaths. Exonerated. Insubordination. AWOL.

'A pitbull terrier,' Leo said, and answered her quizzical glance. 'Trained to kill and blooded in war.'

'There's no mention of the adoption angle,' Helen said, flicking through the pages.

'I don't think Dermot Brennan knew about the adoption. But he was suspicious of the guy. Maybe he thought Sheridan was seeing Anna or just sniffing around her. So, he has him checked out. Then he gets this email from the private detective late Friday afternoon. Now he knows Sheridan has taken on a new identity.'

'But not why.'

'No, it seems not,' Leo said. 'He asks Sheridan to come over so he can pay him the three hundred euro he's owed for the gardening work. Brings him in for a drink maybe. The autopsy report on Dermot Brennan showed he'd been drinking brandy. Jesus Christ, why couldn't I see through his mask?'

Leo looked towards the house that was barely visible in the driving snow. Whatever it was that Sheridan had planned to do in there, he thought, had already been done. And done hours since, in all likelihood. Probably had his escape route sussed out long since too. Out by the walled garden door, along by the walking path behind the neighbouring houses further down and out of view of Dempsey's car. The sense of calamitous failure paralysed Leo.

'Do we go in?' Helen asked.

The high boundary wall to the left offered the cover they needed to skirt around to the back of the house. No. Not *they*. This was *his* cock-up. However slim the chances were that Sheridan was still inside, Leo wasn't going to put the young detective at risk.

'You stay here,' he said. 'The Emergency Response people should be here soon. Don't let them in until I call.'

'We should wait for them,' Helen objected. 'You can't go in alone.'

'I'll go with you,' Garda Dempsey said, aiming to impress Helen and pacify Leo but hoping his offer would be refused. It was.

Leo set off along the lane like a reluctant schoolboy, his shoulder brushing the wall. When he disappeared into the white void, Helen decided she was going after him.

'I've called Detective Sergeant Cooney,' she told Dempsey. 'Tell him the story when he gets here. And tell him to keep the Emergency Response Unit back. We'll call if we need them.'

'But Leo doesn't want you to go with him,' Dempsey pleaded, that worrisome infatuation in his gaze again, which she punctured guiltily. 'I should come with you.'

'Just do as I ask, right?' she said. 'I don't need a chaperone.'

She followed Leo into the void. She called his name once in a strained whisper but decided not to risk a second try. The snow in the lane was shin-deep. Her ankles twisted painfully on the rock-iced ruts beneath. Why would Sheridan kill Gudrun Remer? she asked herself. Wouldn't it make more sense for him to kill Stephen if revenge was his motive? No. The killing of Gudrun Remer was a more calculated move because it set up Stephen for both murders. Anna would be doubly punished. If so, the question now was whether he had reserved a third and final punishment for her.

She found Leo at the rear of the walled garden, shouldering the door without much success.

'Bloody door won't budge,' he said, twisted his sad-clown face into a smile. 'When was the last time you climbed a wall?'

'Climb the walls every night of the week.'

She measured the wall, adding her own height to Leo's in her mind's eye. Should just about make it, she thought.

'Lift me up here.'

He made a stirrup with his hands. When she stepped up, he wanted to cry out with the pain in his injured paw. She raised her left foot on to his shoulder, got hold of the top of the wall.

'Always thought I'd end up in a fucking circus,' Leo said as she lifted her other foot on to his left shoulder. 'Don't go over. Check the windows first.'

Helen took a peek over the wall cap. No lights shone in the house. The falling snow lace-curtained the windows.

'Can't see a bloody thing in there,' she whispered. 'And I doubt anyone can see me. Up and over.'

'Don't—' Leo warned, the weight of her feet vanishing from his shoulders.

He heard a soft thud from inside, a muttered curse, and then the drawing of the door bolt. Helen let him into the garden. An unspoken agreement was reached between them. They wouldn't speak from here on in to the house.

Along the garden pathway, the crunch of pebbles was replaced by the muted crunch of snow. Up ahead, the wrought-iron gate from the garden into the cobbled yard stood open. Their paths instinctively diverged so that they came to a halt at opposite sides of the gate.

Attenboy might have been any somnolent house on a gloomy, snowed-in morning. Not so much as a side light burned in the kitchen. Upstairs and to the right, the curtains on one long window remained closed. Helen tried to place the room in her mind's map of the upper floor. She felt certain it was Anna Brennan's bedroom. She reached inside her jacket for the Walther P99c.

Leo mimed a set of directions to her. Keep the gun hidden. While he walked in plain sight to the small window by the back door, she was to make her way in a stealthy crouch by the cover of some high evergreen shrubs to the kitchen window that overlooked the walled garden and whose blind was two-thirds lowered. He would test the back door if they both ascertained the kitchen was empty. If the door wasn't open, he wasn't sure what the hell they'd do. In any case, experience told him that plans were just the mind's way of fooling itself into thinking it had any real control over the future.

He stepped out on to the white-cushioned cobbles of the yard.

He reached the door, looked in through the small window

alongside. The kitchen might have been a slaughterhouse after they'd hauled the carcasses out but before they'd hosed the blood away. Pools of the stuff joined up by tributaries made of hand swipes and body slides. The walls splashed and streaked with blood too.

Leo heard Helen's gasp seconds after his own lungs forgot how to empty themselves. When she got to his side and grabbed his arm, he breathed again. He tried the door. It was open. Helen hadn't yet let go of his arm.

'No, Leo,' she whispered.

'Just cover me,' he said, and eased himself free of her. 'This wasn't done with a gun.'

He pointed at the knife block on the bloodied floor over by the sleek granite kitchen counter. Three of the carving knives had slipped forward from their grooves. The fourth was missing. He looked around the kitchen. No sign of it. Beneath a chair just by the back door, the coil of rope he'd seen in the outhouse where they'd found Dermot lay. Beside it, a thick roll of masking tape. The smell of blood was nauseating. More nauseating still was the stench of death that reached him now from beyond the door to the hallway where the trail of blood led. And it wasn't some imagined stench. It was the real thing. Someone had been dead here for hours.

The anger he felt towards himself branched out and entangled Skip Sheridan. He'd tear the bastard apart, Leo thought, limb from limb. No comfy cell with a TV and a wash-hand basin and Open University degrees in Floral fucking Arranging for Captain America.

He went around by the wall so as not to mess things up too much for the Technical Bureau gang. It felt like he was skirting some abyss. But he wasn't. He was in the abyss. The crackle of broken glass beneath his feet surprised him. Only now did the shards of a drinking glass and a broken brandy bottle embedded in the sticky blood suggest themselves.

Peering in by the tiled hallway, it became apparent that the blood tracks led to the foot of the stairway. Halfway along lay the fourth knife, a fearsomely curved and serrated instrument. He walked towards it, Helen in his wake. Maybe she'd get the shakes later, she thought, but the gun was steady in her hand and ready to fire. Leo made it out into the half light of the hallway and stopped dead. He raised a hand behind him to halt Helen's progress.

Sheridan had almost made it to the top. Three steps short of the first landing, his blood and his time had run out. His plaid shirt had been dragged up his torso in his efforts to climb, baring much of his spine. The wound, Leo guessed, had to be to the front. Or wounds. A wild thought crossed his mind. Was it possible that someone other than Anna Brennan had done this and was still in the house? Alan Cobbe and Stephen Brennan were down at the station holding rooms. Peter Prior, the Karate Kid? The heavies, Dumb and Dumber? Or that smarmy bastard Foley himself? Made no sense, Leo thought, none at all. It had to be Anna. But why? Had Sheridan planned to use the rope and masking tape on her?

Leo reached the body, checked for a pulse. There wasn't one. When he touched the flesh, it had the feel of packed ice, and he was suddenly aware of the burn in his fingertips again. He lifted Sheridan's left shoulder. Just then, Helen entered the hallway and looked up. Sheridan's eyes were still open. Unsurprised, waiting for the pain to end.

One wound, Leo noted. Sliced into the heart, it appeared. So, it's a defensive thrust rather than a surreptitious attack from behind. They're down in the kitchen. There's an argument. He comes at her. She lashes out with the knife. But she doesn't run outside or scream? Maybe he's blocking off the back door escape route. Or he's stabbed but still standing and she makes a break for the hallway and he's still moving so she legs it up the stairs and locks herself into her bedroom.

Leo counted ten doors along the upper landing. All of them closed.

'Mrs Brennan?' he called.

In the hard-edged acoustics of the freezing house, his voice rang sharply and so startled Helen that her finger almost slipped on the trigger of the Walther.

'Hers is the last room on the right,' she said, but he placed a finger to his lips.

He'd heard a whimper. Now he heard another.

'Mrs Brennan, it's me, Inspector Woods.'

Some answering words came but indecipherably.

Leo went by the upper landing doors. For all its subtle decoration and valuable artworks, the place was just another version of Heartbreak Hotel. A little more upmarket, a little less anonymous, but still a place for the broken-hearted.

'Mrs Brennan, you can come out now,' he said. 'It's over.'

At the other end of the landing, Helen covered him warily, half expecting one of the other doors to burst open. Leo tried the bedroom door. He got a two-inch gap and then a heavy item of furniture. Somewhere inside the room, Anna Brennan was crying quietly, but Leo couldn't see her.

'Everything's fine now,' he said. 'Everything will be fine.'

He put his shoulder to the door, easing the dead weight inwards. He could see her now, lying on the bed, her back to him. Her cream velvet dressing gown, torn and blood-stained. The pads of her feet, dark with clotted blood. Her russet hair, wild on the pillow into which she'd buried her face.

'Is he dead?' she asked between sobs.

'Yeah, he's dead,' Leo said.

He pushed some more and got himself into the room. His first instinct was to cover the bare exposed thigh that was mottled with cellulite but he couldn't bring himself to move any closer. He felt as though he was trespassing in the widow's room.

'It's my fault,' she said. 'I killed all of them.'

Helen entered the room behind Leo and went straight to the bed. She took the bedspread that had fallen on the floor and placed it over Anna Brennan.

'We'll call a doctor,' Helen said. She stroked the woman's hair, pulled it back from the face. 'You'll be— Oh my God.'

Leo approached the bed. It wasn't Anna Brennan's face. Rather, it was a bruised and bloated thing; shapeless, incapable of expression. The pout of her grossly swollen lips revealed the bloodied cave of her mouth and a set of miniature stalagmites and stalactites where her teeth used to be.

'I told him it had to stop,' she moaned.

'The killing?' Leo asked.

'I told him weeks ago we'd have to stop . . . to stop meeting,' the widow said, oblivious of the ugly detective's question, oblivious perhaps of his presence. 'I thought he'd accepted it. I thought he'd come to realize that we couldn't be lovers . . . that it was unnatural. I should never have let it happen. And now I've killed him . . . my own son . . . my own flesh and . . .'

The two detectives shared an unspoken and shocking conclusion. Neither one was sure how to continue. Her days working on the Register of Sex Offenders had given Helen a keen insight not only into the murkier depths of sexuality but the sadder ones. Genetic Sexual Attraction was about as sad and confusing and shaming as sex could get. Telling Anna that Sheridan wasn't her son might reverse the sin of incest in her mind but, Helen suspected, the stain could never be removed. The widow would always know that she was capable of this elemental transgression. One stain, however, could be wholly removed: the misguided conviction that she'd killed her own son.

Helen knelt down on the floor by the bed, laid a protecting arm across the broken woman.

'Look at me, Mrs Brennan,' she said. The swelling around Anna's eyes allowed only the barest parting of the lids. 'You've no cause for shame. Skip Sheridan wasn't your son. He was the natural son of the couple who adopted your little boy.'

The widow tried to raise herself but gained a few mere inches before falling back on the pillow.

'The boy who drowned?' she said. 'He told me his brother had drowned. Was that my son?'

'I'm afraid so,' Helen said.

'But last night he told me I'd condemned him to a life of misery when I gave him up,' Anna said. 'He told me he'd come to Ireland to destroy ours but he'd . . . he'd fallen in love with me and I . . . I let it happen because when I met him I felt nothing. Nothing. I had to give him . . . something.'

Leo sat heavily into a chair at the end of the bed, thinking about the monster he'd unleashed on this woman when he'd let Sheridan go, thinking that maybe he wasn't up to this any more, that he should retire to his mask room and count the minutes that passed between the trains going by Serpentine

Crescent. He watched Helen hold the widow's hand, stroke it. Why hadn't Sheridan told her last night that he wasn't her son? he wondered. So that she would believe with her dying breath that it was her own child who'd come back to kill her? As acts of revenge went, it was the most insidious Leo had ever come across.

'I've lost everything now,' Anna said.

'There's Stephen,' Helen said.

'He'll never forgive me. He knows I doubted him. But Skip had convinced me. Until last night.'

'This can wait,' the young detective assured her.

Some poisons, Leo thought, had to be sucked and spat out as soon as possible no matter how much you ached, no matter how much you wanted to close your eyes and die.

'I asked him not to come here any more,' Anna said. 'And when he did, I knew right away that he'd changed towards me. He was wired up, impatient with me, drinking. He wanted me to sleep with him again. And he's got this glass of brandy poured for me and keeps insisting I drink it and I tell him no. But he keeps on insisting and I know then . . . I can't say how but I know there's something in the drink and I tell him so and he flips.'

Helen remembered Stephen's insistence that his drink had been spiked at the night club. Leo remembered the brandy bottle on the kitchen counter at Attenboy. What better way to bring a big man to his knees, prepare him for execution, than to slip some hypnotic or other into his drink?

'I couldn't believe what I was hearing,' the widow continued. 'That he'd done those terrible things so there'd be just the two of us left. When I told him he was crazy, he started to punch and kick me and tried to pull off my nightdress.'

'But did you not scream?' Leo heard himself ask. 'Surely you screamed?'

Both women looked at him. The young, pretty one and the one made ugly by Sheridan's fists.

'What's the worst thing that's ever happened to you, Inspector?' Anna Brennan asked.

'Bell's palsy. The day they told me it was irreversible.'

'Did you scream?'

'No. Not so's you could hear anyway,' Leo answered. He stood up. 'I'll call an ambulance, Mrs Brennan. You'll be fine. You'll be beautiful again.'

'Do you really think that matters to us now, Inspector?' the widow said.

'Us?'

'Me,' she said. 'You.'

48

The half-hour drive from Howth to Ballsbridge took two hours to complete. Leo wouldn't have minded if the journey had lasted another two hours. The endlessly crawling lines of traffic, their headlights brightening the snow's descent, invoked an oddly celebratory mood in spite of the Big Freeze. But that instinct for premonition that Charlie Llunga had once spoken of had kicked in again. Fate, Leo knew, hadn't finished working him over yet. He wasn't wrong.

At the junction of Merrion and Anglesea Roads, a couple of cars had slammed into each other. It wasn't traffic any more. It was one great parking lot. Leo bailed out.

The footpath on Merrion was well-trodden and manageable. On Serpentine Avenue, however, he negotiated the slippery surface, holding himself up by the rails with his bandaged hand, along by the AIB Bank Centre towards home. He might as well have been drunk. He soon would be. And high as a kite if he could get hold of Dripsy.

At the corner of Serpentine Crescent, he tried to fish the keys out of his right-hand trouser pocket. His bandaged fist wouldn't fit. He twisted awkwardly, about to get his left hand in. And fell. Hard. The back of his head hit the pavement. And he woke up dead. Or in a dream. Or in some dimension that seemed utterly unreal. One way or the other, he found his feet again. The keys were in his left hand and he was standing at his own front door.

Under the jaundiced street light, the frozen pool that had spread outwards from under the front door might have been blood. He turned the key in the lock. He had to kick the door in because it was cemented at the base with ice. He switched on the hall light. It flickered and sizzled for a while before it decided to stay with him. The patterns on the hallway tiles seemed oddly magnified by the hard, transparent crust of ice that covered them. The muted hiss of water still escaping reached Leo. The attic, he guessed, where the water tank stood directly above the mask room.

He negotiated the hallway and began the climb upstairs. The carpet squelched here, crackled there as he ascended. The further up he went, the less ice there was, the more water. The timbers of the first-floor landing had warped under the weight of water. He stepped across the little pool. The mask room door was drooling. The thicker lock and key here proved more difficult to manage with his left hand than those on the front door. Yet, his calm and patience surprised him.

Better not flick the switch here, Leo thought, as the door swung inwards. There was enough light from the landing anyway. Too much. Things floated on the floor. A half-full ashtray, a couple of DVD covers, some masks. The water, it appeared, had cascaded down along the wall of masks, loosening some, knocking others awry. Those made of papier-mâché had begun to swell and distort like Anna

Brennan's face. Some colours had begun to leach from a few. Red mostly.

He went inside and sat on his low-slung swivel chair. His father's chair. He reached for the whiskey bottle that stood on the sideboard and took a long swig.

His throat burned but the rest of him shivered. He felt dizzy enough to be drunk but he knew it wasn't the whiskey. He popped the filter from a cigarette and lit up. The room was spinning slowly round his head. The masks laughing and scowling and grieving and cursing at him.

He wondered how or where he was going to sleep tonight. He could always try some Rohypnol tabs, like the ones they'd found in Skip Sheridan's jacket, a drug almost impossible to detect in a post-mortem or a toxicology test. If anyone could source it, Dripsy Scullion could. But no, the whiskey would do the job. Along with some weed and a downer or three.

He fumbled left-handed through his pockets for his personal mobile. The work mobile came first to hand and he chucked it across the wet floor. Then, Ben Murphy's Miró notebook. He flicked through the pages. Some had interview notes and observations on them but mostly they contained a child's efforts to copy out her father's ABCs and his drawings of boxy houses, bushy trees, matchstick people. Leo cried his first real tears in living memory. Then he got Dripsy Scullion's number up on his mobile and rang him.

'Hey, Eric, how's the goin'?'

'Dripsy, son, I need a five spot and few downers, pronto.'

'Jesus, man, I'm in Phibsboro. The roads are like ice. How'm I supposed to deliver to Ballsbridge?'

'You'll find a way.'

'You think I'm Santa Claus with a bleedin' sleigh or what?'

'I'll have to reopen the file on that handbag snatch on

Westmoreland Street last year then, won't I? Remember the one? Suspect had a limp until he broke into a run?'

'You're a bastard, Leo.'

'Call me Eric. Which reminds me. It's not E-r-i-k. It's E-r-i-c as in Eric Cantona.'

'I wasn't thinking of Eric Cantona when I gave you the name. You know I hate Man U.'

'Who were you thinking of then?'

'Forget it, man.'

'Dripsy. Remember Westmoreland Street.'

'Jesus, you'll skin me alive if I tell you.'

'Out with it, Dripsy.'

'The guy with the mask in *The Phantom of the Opera*. His name is Erik. With a "k". Sorry, man.'

But Leo could only laugh. What else could you do when you were an ugly detective?

Mark O'Sullivan has published nine novels. His work has won several awards in Ireland and France and been translated into six languages. He has also published short stories and poetry in various magazines and journals. His first crime novel featuring Detective Inspector Leo Woods, *Crocodile Tears*, was published to critical acclaim. Mark is married with two daughters and lives in Thurles, County Tipperary.